THE REBELLIOUS RANI OF BELAVADI AND OTHER STORIES

THE REBELLIOUS RANI OF BELAVADI AND OTHER STORIES

BASAVARAJ NAIKAR

ATLANTIC PUBLISHERS AND DISTRIBUTORS

Published by
ATLANTIC PUBLISHERS AND DISTRIBUTORS
B-2, Vishal Enclave, Opp. Rajouri Garden, New Delhi-27
Phones : 5413460, 5429987

Sales Office
4215/1, Ansari Road, Darya Ganj, New Delhi-110 002
Phones : 3273880, 3285873, 3280451
Fax : 91-11-3285873
e-mail : info@atlanticbooks.com
web : www.atlanticbooks.com

ISBN 81-269-0127-6

Typeset at
APD Computer Graphics, Delhi

Printed in India at
Mehra Offset Press, Delhi

Unto

The Holy-Feet of

My Father

Sri Sivasankarappa

PREFACE

The Rebellious Rani of Belavadi and Other Stories happens to be my second collection of short stories written over the past twenty-five years, dealing with various aspects of Indian life. The themes range from the historical to the contemporary, from the religious to the secular, and from the elemental to the academic. These stories, I believe, will capture the attention of the reader on account of the Indian sensibility operating in them and add up to the image of Indian life in some way or the other. I leave it to the discerning reader to enjoy the aesthetic pleasure according to the quality of his response.

BASAVARAJ NAIKAR

CONTENTS

1

The Rebellious Rani of Belavadi

THE KINGS of Swadi Kingdom were formerly Lingayats and later became Jains. During the last phase of Vijayanagara Empire they become Ksatriyas. When the great Emperor Sri Krisnadevarya of Vijayanagara established blood relationship with the family of Swadi Kings, the latter were at the zenith of their glory. Arasappa Nayaka was happy to have a son called Madhulinga Nayaka born from the grace of Lord Madhukeswara of Banavasi temple. When Madhulinga Nayaka attained puberty, he embraced Lingayat faith. His wife Viramma was a very pious lady devoted to her husband. Thus their kingdom was known for peace, prosperity and happiness. Madhulinga Nayaka's maternal aunt Nilammaji was the Maharani of Belavadi Kingdom.

Although Madhulinga Nayaka had everything in his kingdom, God had created a scarcity in his life *i.e.* lack of progeny. His Rani Virammaji was deeply worried about it. She, therefore, distributed many gifts to priests and holy men. Madhulinga Nayaka even conducted a *Putrakamesthi Yaga* with the hope of getting issues. But unfortunately their hopes were not fulfilled for many years.

Once a great yogi called Soppi Siddhabasava came to Swadi Kingdom. On hearing the news of the yogi's arrival, the royal couple invited him to their palace and treated him with great care and reverence. Consequently the yogi was immensely pleased and blessed them whole-heartedly. One day when Rani Viramma completed the worship of the yogi's feet, she gently broached the subject of her anxiety, "Maharaj, although we have everything for our happiness in our palace and kingdom, God has created a big lacuna in our life." "What is that lacuna, tell me daughter," said His Holiness Siddhabasava. "Maharaj, my husband and I are deeply worried about our childlessness. We conducted even the *Putrakamesthi Yaga*, practiced ample charity, fed many holy men and distributed countless gifts to the poor. Yet we have not been able to have any progeny." His Holiness Siddhabasava looked at Viramma's face and understood her deep-seated anxiety hidden behind her beautiful face. Rani Virammaji looked imploringly at the holy man and saw his compassionate eyes. She knew that His Holiness Siddhabasava was a man of many spiritual powers. He thought for a while and said, "Daughter, I understand the nature of your anxiety and the far-reaching consequences of your childlessness. I, therefore, would like to suggest to you that you may undertake a vow to Lord Kartika and render five worships during the night so that your dream may come true." Rani Viramma felt happy to hear the solution from the holy man. "Maharaj, I shall definitely do as suggested by you," said Viramma and bowed down to his feet once again. After a couple of days, His Holiness Siddhabasava took leave of the royal couple and returned to his monastery at Soppi.

After the departure of the holy man, the royal couple immersed themselves in the routine life. But Rani Viramma remembered when to observe the rite suggested by the holy man. She also confided her wish to Madhulinga Nayaka who readily gave his consent. Accordingly, Rani Viramma had her ritual bath on the solar Sankramana day in Scorpio division of Zodiac and established the icon of Lord Kartika with a holy attitude. She started the worship of the deity in the evening and conducted a total of five worships at regular intervals of time before the next dawn. Then she fed several citizens, priests and religious men with a variety of delicious dishes. All of them who partook of the meal blessed her with the fulfilment of all her wishes. Lord Kartika seemed to be pleased with the vow observed by Rani Viramma. He, therefore, appeared to her in her dream, granted her two boons *i.e.* a son and a daughter and disappeared.

When Rani Viramma woke up in the morning and narrated the dream to her husband, he felt extremely happy and began to wait for the birth of a child. As months went by, Rani Viramma noticed that she did not have her monthly periods for two months consequently and felt very happy. She confided the secret to Raja Madhulinga Nayaka, who felt very happy about it. After another month or so, Rani Viramma developed a slight bulge in her belly and felt proud of the prospects of motherhood. She completed the gestation of nine lunar months and nine days and was delivered of a male child on the astami tithi of Kartika Paksa, of Sravana month of Salivahana Saka 1580. Raja Madhulinga Nayaka was simply ecstatic about the event and therefore celebrated it with distribution of feast and alms to brahmins, jangamas and the poor people of the capital. In memory of the happy event, he made a generous land-grant to Madhukeswara Temple and got a Dining Hall constructed on the precincts of the temple. He baptized his son as Sadasivanayaka.

Rani Viramma continued her vow to Lord Kartika during the month of every Kartika. Consequently, she gave birth to a female child on the astami tithi, Krisna Paksa of Sravana month of Salivahana Saka 1582. Raja Madhulinga Nayaka was extremely happy about the birth of a daughter to him. He celebrated the naming ceremony of the daughter with great pomp and distributed gold, silver and alms to countless jangamas, brahmins and poor people. He named his daughter as 'Mallamma' which meant 'Jasmine'.

Baby Mallamma was very bewitching to look at. Her face was radiant like the full moon. Her eyes were like the petals of a lotus. She was a bonny child with great lustre. Everybody who saw her felt like cuddling her. Rani Viramma lavished her love and affection on the baby. As years went by, baby Mallamma grew into a very beautiful girl of five years. Then Raja Madhulinga Nayaka arranged for her education along with her brother's. Both Sadasivanayaka and Mallamma were taught by experienced teachers. They learnt Kannada, Marathi, Urdu and Sanskrit languages and attained proficiency in them over a period of ten years. In the *pathasala* there were ten famous *Sastris* to teach various subjects. Among them Sankarabhatta was a great Sanskrit scholar who was an expert in literature, grammar and logic. There were about two hundred girls and two hundred boys who were the classmates of Sadasivanayaka and Mallamma. The school had a secular atmosphere about it. Among the students of the school, there happened to be a hundred Havyakas, a hundred Gauda Saraswata Brahmins, a hundred Nadavas, a hundred Okkaligas, fifty Lingayats, two Madhvas and twenty Desasthas.

Sadasivanayaka and Mallamma were very serious students of the royal school and acquired great expertise in the subjects of their liking. They easily outshone the other students of the school. By the time Mallamma attained twelve years, she could compose poems in Kannada as well as Sanskrit. Likewise, Sadasivanayaka evinced signs of becoming a great scholar in Kannada. Raja Madhulinga Nayaka and Rani Viramma felt happy to watch the steady progress of their son and daughter.

Now Raja Madhulinga Nayaka arranged for the military education for all the students of the royal school. He appointed a famous soldier called Ranavir Singh to teach the military discipline. Initially Sadasivanayaka learnt the art of swordplay and became an expert in it. Mallamma felt inspired by her brother and therefore she also began to wield the sword successfully. She became an expert in shooting the arrows, throwing the spears and riding the horses. She was not only equal to boys but even surpassed them in the military heroism. Thus at a very young age she attained the fame of being a very heroic girl in the Kingdom.

Although Mallamma could easily outshine the boys in military heroism, she never neglected the traditional family discipline. She had great reverence for her parents. Everyday, she used to get up early in the morning along with her elder brother, complete the morning ablutions and have bath and render holy service to Lord Siva and the *bhel*-tree. She would go round the tree for five times and prostrate to it. After the holy service, she used to go to the kitchen, cook two dishes, serve food to her father and brother and finally have her own lunch with her mother. This was her daily timetable.

One day Sri Siddhavirayogi Maharaj, Pontiff of Huli Monastery went to Gokarna and had his *darsan* of Lord Mahabaleswara. Then His Holiness was invited by Raja Madhulinga Nayaka to be the royal guest. The Raja treated the holy man with great reverence and attention. He assigned the task of treating the holy guest to the young Sadasivanayaka and Mallamma. Both brother and sister treated His Holiness with great care and reverence.

One evening, Raja Madhulinga Nayaka and Rani Viramma sat conversing with His Holiness Sri Siddhavirayogi Maharaj in the guestroom. "Hope everything is all right, Your Holiness. I believe that your holy service and meditation are not hindered in any way in our palace," said Raja Madhulinga Nayaka. His Holiness said, "No hindrance at all, royal sir. I am extremely pleased by the nice treatment extended to me here. Your son and daughter have been lavishing their care and attention on me. They are going to be very heroic and glorious in future, as they are born from the grace of Lord Kartika. They will definitely bring great reputation to your family and kingdom." Rani Viramma and Raja Madhulinga Nayaka were very happy to hear the words of the holy man. His Holiness continued, "But Mallamma has to pass through a dangerous period during her sixteenth year." Raja Madhulinga Nayaka was rather disconcerted to hear the ominous words uttered by the holy man. Rani Viramma also felt deflated as it were. Raja Madhulinga Nayaka made bold to ask the holy guest, "Your Holiness, could you kindly tell us as to what sort of danger it will be and if it is possible to ward it off." The Raja appeared to be very anxious. His Holiness waved his palms and assured the royal couple, "Don't you have any anxiety about it. Your daughter will have to face the danger from a wild animal. If she survives that crisis, she will shine like a great Rani in future." The royal couple felt scared further. The Raja asked the holy man for clarification, "Your Holiness, would you kindly explain in a little more detail? Also kindly guide us as to how to ward it off." "Don't you worry, Maharaj. Wild animal means a tiger. You can avoid the danger with some effort. God will be there to protect her." The Raja and the Rani felt a bit relieved. His Holiness blessed the members of the royal family and returned to his monastery.

Although the holy man assured Raja Madhulinga Nayaka that his daughter would survive the danger, he began to worry about it deep in his heart. He invited many astrologers and consulted them about the problem and sought their advice to avoid the possible danger, but nobody could offer him a concrete solution.

One day, Raja Madhulinga Nayaka sat in the royal garden secretly worrying about his daughter's future. Princess Mallamma happened to go there with her bosom friend Gouramma. She saw her father seemed to be rather worried about something. She, therefore, made bold to ask him directly, "Father, you seem to be worried about something. Please tell me what the problem is. I shall solve it for you." Raja Madhulinga Nayaka was confounded by her question and did not know how to answer it. Princess Mallamma pressed him further, "Please tell me the problem. Don't conceal anything from me." "What shall I tell you, my daughter," said Raja Madhulinga Nayaka, "I'm worried about your future and about how to ward off the tigerish danger." Princess Mallamma understood the reason for her father's deep anxiety and assured him, "Father, why do you worry about it unnecessarily? I shall kill any number of tigers. I am very confident of that. You don't worry about it at all." Raja Madhulinga Nayaka said, "My dear daughter, I really feel enheartened by your heroic words. But how can a girl like you accomplish the task?" Princess Mallamma understood the anxiety of the father and knew that he was still doubtful about the solution. She, therefore, said to him, "Father, if you are still doubtful about my safety, you better marry me off to a prince who is an expert in tiger-hunt. In that case, I can easily overcome any number of dangers." The Maharaja listened to her and counter-questioned her, "Daughter, how to ascertain who is an expert hero in tiger-hunting?" Then Princes Mallamma said, "Father, please listen to me. I shall tell you a plan. You marry me off to a prince who will bring within a month as many tigers killed by him as the years of his age. Then there'll be no problem at all." On hearing these words of solution from his daughter, Raja Madhulinga Nayaka felt a bit relieved of his tension.

Accordingly, he sent a message of *swayamvara* to all the neighbouring princes in different directions. The royal messengers carried the scrolls of message with them and rode to different kingdoms and conveyed the message of the *swayamvara*. The princes who learnt the message took it as a challenge to their manhood and heroism and instantly started hunting the tigers in the woods of vicinity. As there was not much time, they began to frequent the woods and tried to hunt and kill as many tigers as they could and collected the heads and hides of the kill.

On the scheduled date after a month, many young princes collected their hunted tigers and brought them to Banavasi along with their attendants and stayed in the guesthouses allotted to them. At the scheduled time of *swayamvara,* all of them gathered in the wedding parlour and exhibited the tiger heads and hides on an elevated platform. Raja Madhulinga Nayaka, Princess Mallamma and their courtiers walked to the parlour and examined the exhibition of killed tigers brought in by the princes. The Prince of Keladi had brought tigers half the number of his years of age; the Prince of Kodagu had brought tigers three-fourth in number of his age; the Prince of Mysore had brought tigers four-fifth in number of his age; the Prince of Anegundi had brought tigers one-fourth in number of his age; the Prince of Bundelkhand had brought tigers three-fourth in number of his age; Prince Vardhamana had brought tigers three less than his age; the two sons of Chhatrapati Sivaji had brought tigers three-fourth in number of their age; the Prince of Jaipur had brought tigers two-third in number of his age; the Rana of Udaipur had brought tigers one less than his age; the Prince of Kashmir had brought tigers five-sixth in number of his age and Prince Iswaraprabhu of Belavadi had brought tigers one more in number than his age. Prince Iswaraprabhu was twenty years old and had brought twenty-one tigers, which he had hunted and killed within the stipulated time of a month.

The hearts of the princes were palpitating with hope and anxiety when Raja Madhulinga Nayaka, Princess Mallamma and the courtiers of Swadi Kingdom examined the exhibition of tigers and tallied the number of tigers with the years of their age. The clerks of the Kingdom examined the documents and horoscopes indicating their dates of birth. The heaps of yellow and black stripped hides and the ferocious heads of dead tigers were thrilling and frightening at the same time. The courtiers feasted their eyes on the unprecedented sight. After the elaborate verification it was found that Prince Iswaraprabhu from Belavadi had killed the highest number of tigers and that too one tiger more in number than the years of his age. When Prince Iswaraprabhu was declared as the winner, all other princes felt humiliated inwardly but congratulated the winner in keeping with the royal decorum and dignity.

Then all the princes were invited into the wedding hall where drummers and pipers were playing upon their instruments. The hall was decorated with festoons of various flowers and mango leaves. At the auspicious moment, Prince Iswaraprabhu was requested by the courtiers to go to the centre stage of the hall. Then Princess Mallamma also walked to the stage accompanied by her mother and other royal ladies. She was decked with a variety of flashy golden ornaments studded with rubies, diamonds and jewels and looked like a veritable goddess called Rati. Prince Iswaraprabhu looked like the veritable god Kama. At the suggestion of the priest, they garlanded each other and drank in each other's beauty with their eyes. Everybody sprinkled flowers and turmeric coloured rice grains upon the bride and the groom. All the princes offered valuable gifts of golden ornaments and silken garments to the couple. It was followed by a grand feast of a variety of delicious dishes. The marriage ritual continued for ten days. Raja Madhulinga Nayaka and Rani Viramma's happiness knew no bounds. The Raja spent nearly a lakh of *niskas* on the marriage. All through the ten days, brahmins, jangamas, and the poor people were fed in the *dasoha* banquet. The Ingreji merchants, the ministers of the Badshah of Golkonda and of the Badshah of Bijapur attended the marriage and offered valuable gifts to the young couple. The *Panchacharya* swamis blessed the young couple whole-heartedly. In return they were offered generous gifts of gold and garments. The Jagadgurus of Huli Monastery and Keladi Monastery, Sankeswara Monastery and Uttaradi Monastery graced the occasion with their holy presence. Thousands of lamps were lit in multiple rows to mark the auspicious occasion. The ten thousand soldiers of the Swadi Kingdom were offered valuable gifts of gold and garments. On the whole the wedding ceremony was so grand and beautiful that all the participants exclaimed that it was an unprecedented event in their lifetime. After the wedding ceremony was over, Raja Madhulinga Nayaka and Rani Virammaji sent the young couple to Belavadi with great pomp and accompanied by a number of beautiful stallions, camels and elephants.

Raja Isaprahu and Rani Mallamma were very able administrators. As directed by Raja Madhulinga Nayaka of Swadi Kingdom, the Raja and the Rani of Belavadi maintained an army of ten thousand soldiers for the protection of their kingdom. They had all the rowdies and rebels who were potential threats to the peace and security of the kingdom arrested and imprisoned. They appointed able and morally inclined people as the courtiers and treated the farmers with care and affection. They provided a number of facilities to merchants in order to facilitate mutual transaction between Belavadi Kingdom and Swadi Kingdom. They arranged for the import and export of merchandise from the ports of Karwar, Kumata and Gokarna cities. The total income of Belavadi Kingdom was about ten lakh *niskas*, whereas that of Swadi Kingdom was about fifty lakh *niskas*. Whereas pepper, cummin, cardamom, jajikai and other spices were produced abundantly in Swadi Kingdom, rice, wheat, jowar, pulse, jaggery and sugar were produced amply in Belavadi Kingdom.

The Belavadi Kingdom had three hundred and sixty villages in its possession. Out of these, five villages like Lingadalli, Bisanalli, Hulikatti, Gudikatti and Nadagondikoppa were granted to the temple of Lord Virabhadra of Belavadi city, to cover the expenses of the upkeep, regular *puja* and fairs of the temple. A village called Siddhasamudra was granted as a gift to the Guru Maharaja of Huli Monastery, for the maintenance of the religious institute and arrangement of religious activities like *puja* and discourses. The Kingdom of Belavadi extended from Yakkundi to Devarahubballi and from Gokak to Halyal. The subjects of the Kingdom lived in peace and were happy in all respects.

Prince Sadasivanayaka took the reigns of administration of Swadi Kingdom when Raja Madhulinga Nayaka was still alive. He was a very efficient administrator. The British merchants sought permission from Raja Sadasivanayaka and started their trade in Karwar port. The Swadi Kingdom was situated to the south of Belavadi Kingdom. The Keladi Kingdom was situated to the south of Swadi Kingdom. The Kodagu Kingdom was situated to the south of Keladi Kingdom. All these four Kingdoms belonged to Lingayat faith. They stuck to the Lingayat faith even when the Kings of Mysore renounced Lingayat faith and accepted Vaisnava faith.

The Swadi Kingdom made enormous progress after establishing harmonious relationship with Belavadi Kingdom. Raja Isaprabhu and Rani Mallamma commanded great respect from their subjects. Religiously inclined as they were, they used to visit the holy shrines of Huli, Pampaksetra and Sondur as well as holy rivers like Malapaharini and Tungabhadra regularly. Once they visited all these holy places and went to Swadi

Kingdom and stayed there for about a week. Then they sent all their bodyguards and companions away to Belavadi and only two of them went to Gokarna to have the *darsan* of Lord Mahabaleswara.

Ever since the young Princess Mallamma had married Prince Isaprabhu, she had felt a sense of fulfilment in her life and never lacked anything for her happiness. Whereas she had a bewitching figure of Goddess Rati, Isaprabhu was handsome like the mythical Lord Kama himself. Both husband and wife were the pious followers of Virasaiva faith. They visited the temple of their family deity Lord Virabhadra every day and offered worship to him. All the members of the royal household and her courtiers revered her as a mother figure, though she was quite young in age. The whole family used to be guided by the Pontiff of Brihanmatha of Huli in spiritual as well as secular matters. They lived in a strong fortress and their city of Belavadi was protected by a sturdy circular wall of brown stone.

Before marrying Iswaraprabhu, the young Mallamma had seen her parents' encounter with the Portuguese, the Dutch and the English on the one hand and with Mughals and Marathas on the other. The fire of patriotism was kept alive in her right from her childhood. Ever since she had married Iswaraprabhu, she had identified herself completely with the Ratta or Rastrakuta dynasty from which her husband descended.

On a Monday morning, both Raja Isaprabhu and Rani Mallamma went on a palanquin to the temple of Lord Virabhadra and attended the special worship of the deity. The pipe and drum players were playing upon their instruments as the *puja* began inside the temple. The priest washed the idol of Lord Virabhadra in cold water and smeared the marks of *vibhuti* and vermillion on the forehead, arms, belly and feet of the idol. Then he decked it with jasmines and other flowers. He lit the incense on the thurible and waved it around the deity. The thick spirals of smoke rose and filled the temple with its sweet aroma. Then he cracked two coconuts and offered the *prasada* of consecrated dishes to the deity. When he brought the *arati* plate to Isaprabhu and Mallamma, they dropped a few silver coins on it and joined their palms in reverence to the deity. Both the king and the queen felt a spiritual calm in their hearts. Then they sat on their palanquin which was carried by bearers back to the palace.

That afternoon, a special lunch was prepared in honour of the family deity Lord Virabhadra. The royal cooks prepared *holige, kadabu, sendige, rice, rottis and chutneys* of various kinds. Rani Mallamma sent word to Raja Isaprabhu to come to the dining hall and partake of the meal. The maid-servant went to the chamber and said, "Sarkar, Rani Sarkar says that the lunch is ready and requests you to partake of the same," and bowed herself out. Raja Isaprabhu said, "All right, I'll come there instantly." He closed the bundle of palm leaves containing the *vacana* literature. He was habituated to reading the sacred text everyday in his leisure hours. He walked upto the dining hall, washed his hands, face and feet. A maid-servant offered him a towel with which he rubbed his limbs clean and squatted on the wooden seat. Rani Mallamma placed a number of plates and bowls of various sweet and delicious dishes before him. The sweet aroma flooded Raja Isaprabhu's nostrils and made his mouth water. "Why all this special preparation, Malla?" asked he. "Don't remember *Sarkar* that today happens to be the first holy Monday of *Sravan* month? Hence the special feast," replied Rani Mallamma. "Then why not you join me?" asked Raja Isaprabhu. "No, *Sarkar,* you have your lunch first. I shall have it only after you have it. I'll have it with other ladies and children of the household," replied Rani Mallamma. "All right, do as you please," said Raja Isaprabhu and began to savour the dishes. Rani Mallamma served him the various dishes with love and watched him eat happily. After he was through with his lunch, she offered him a roll of edible leaf, betel, lime, cloves and cardamoms. Isaprabhu munched the combination leisurely and incarnadined his lips. After a few minutes he began to feel sleepy. The afternoon was very hot. So he retired to his bedroom and fell asleep on the royal cushion. Soon he began to snore deeply.

Raja Isaprabhu was a very religious minded King. He had great respect for the holy shrines like Huli, Pampaksetra, Sondur and rivers like Malapaharini and Tungabhadra etc. He, therefore, undertook a holy pilgrimage to those shrines along with the members of his family.

Once Raja Isaprabhu and Rani Mallamma went to Swadi Kingdom and spent a week there peacefully. Then they rode their horses to Gokarna for a *darsan* of Lord Mahabaleswara. They were not accompanied by any of their usual retinue or bodyguards. Rani Mallamma was only sixteen years old then. On the saptami day of Krisna Paksa of Kartika month of Saka 1598, they reached Gokarna and arranged for the *abhiseka* and worship of Lord Mahabaleswara and distributed alms to brahmin priests generously. Then they rested in a guesthouse for the day.

Next morning, they again had their *darsan* of the deity. After lunch they started riding their horses towards the Swadi Kingdom. They were not accompanied by any bodyguards. The horses started slowly for a little distance and later picked up speed. Raja Isaprabhu and Rani Mallamma were drinking in the beauty of undulating landscape, the greenery and the hills. As they descended a hillock, they saw a beautiful lake in front of them. Isaprabhu felt thrilled by the sight of the lake when he was scorched by the hot sun of the afternoon. "Darling," said Isaprabhu, "we shall halt near this lake for a short while and have our snacks." "As you please, Sarkar," said Rani Mallamma. Both of them therefore alighted from their horses and tethered them to the nearby trees. Then they washed their hands, faces and feet in the water of the lake. They sat on the green grass beneath the shade of a big banyan tree. Rani Mallamma opened the packet of snacks like sweet balls, fried parched-rice and fruits brought from Gokarna and offered them to her husband. Both of them savoured the eatables and quaffed the cool water from the lake. The cool breeze was blowing gently. Raja Isaprabhu began to doze and fell into a nap. Rani Mallamma also lay down on the grass to relax for a while. Both of them slept very peacefully. The whinnying of the horses suddenly awakened Rani

Mallamma. She sat up and saw that Isaprabhu was snoring. She sat up silently watching the trees and birds around her. She did not want to disturb her husband. When she was immersed in the beauty of Nature, she was taken aback by an unexpected sight. Lo! There were two tigers springing towards them. One tiger rushed at the horse and the other one rushed towards her. Rani Mallamma did not want to wake up her husband. Instantly she sprang to her feet and stood ready to attack it. Before the numerous claws of the tiger could pierce her, she lifted her sword and struck it forcefully on the face of the wild animal. Suddenly the roar of the tiger subsided. Its head split into two halves and blood spurted out in a jet. The tiger sagged to the earth in a pathetic posture. Rani Mallamma then rushed towards the other tiger, which was about to pounce upon the horse. She took her lance and darted it forcefully at that tiger which was thundering. Lo! The lance pierced the flanks of the tiger, which fell to the ground. Then she struck it repeatedly with her sword until it fell dead.

Raja Isaprabhu was suddenly awakened by the noise around him. He was shocked and surprised by what he saw there. The two tigers had fallen piteously on the ground. The blood was oozing out of the gashes. He stood up, walked to the spot where the tigers lay. Rani Mallamma stood there with the blood stained sword in her hand and looked like Goddess Chamundi herself. He asked her, "Darling, what happened when I was asleep? Why did you not wake me up?" Rani Mallamma was still panting for breath and excited. She took a few seconds to compose herself. Then she replied, "Dear Sarkar, I saw these two tigers rushing towards us. But I did not want to disturb your sleep. Nor did I want to lose time. So I killed the two tigers one after another single-handed." Raja Isaprabhu was overwhelmed with admiration for his heroic wife. He exclaimed, "Bravo, my darling Rani. I am really proud of you. You have put the menfolk to shame. You have proved that woman is never weak or helpless. Our Kingdom is really proud of a heroic Rani like you." Rani Mallamma felt shy and blushed when she heard the words of appreciation by her husband. Raja Isaprabhu continued, "My darling, your heroism has warded off the danger. I am really sorry that I could not ward off the danger for which you married me." Rani Mallamma was touched by the apologetic words of her husband. She said, "Dear Sarkar, everything in this world happens according to Lord God's will. I also escaped from the calamity as per God's will." Raja Isaprabhu was speechless with admiration for his wife's heroism and piety.

Then both of them examined the horse, which was clawed by the tiger. There were some bruises on the body of the horse. Blood was oozing out of them. They tore a few medicinal leaves from the trees, pounded them with stones and applied the juice to the bruises on the body of the horse. The horse whinnied with pain. Then they washed the swords and the lances in the lake. By that time the sun had descended to the western horizon. They mounted the horse and rode back to Swadi. Raja Madhulinga Nayaka felt happy when he learnt that his daughter had killed two tigers single-handed. He felicitated his daughter and son-in-law and sent them back to Belavadi Kingdom with bodyguards and soldiers.

Raja Isaprabhu and Rani Mallamma spent their days in peace and plenty. They were always concerned with the welfare of their kingdom. On all religious occasions, they used to invite the Mahaswami of Brihanmath situated at Huli. The vassals of Belavadi used to pay their annuity and maintain a cordial relation with Raja Isaprabhu.

*****

Chhatrapati Sivaji who was a staunch supporter of Hinduism had fought vehemently with Aurangzeb, the great Mughal Emperor. He was popularly known as the protector of Hindu faith. During the last part of his life, Sivaji undertook his imperialistic journey in south India. Around 1676-78 AD he attacked Tanjavuru and conquered it. On his return journey, he attacked the cities of Karnataka also. He and his soldiers robbed and looted the city of Hubballi. Then they left Hubballi and camped at Yadavada village near Belavadi city.

Raja Isaprabhu heard the news that Chhatrapati Sivaji had camped at Yadavada. Raja Isaprabhu felt very happy to know that the protector of Hindu faith had come and camped near his own Kingdom. He, therefore, consulted his wife confidentially. The next day, he called a meeting of his Sardars and Desais in the Durbar Hall of the Palace. When all the invitees had gathered in the Hall, Raja Isaprabhu sat upright on his throne and addressed them, "Dear friends and well-wishers of the Belavadi Kingdom, we have called this meeting specially to discuss something urgent." The listeners cocked their ears and sat attentive to hear what their beloved king had to say. Raja Isaprabhu continued, "We have heard the news from our messengers that Chhatrapati Sivaji Maharaj, the spirited protector of Hindu faith has arrived in our area and been camping at Yadavada village nearby. I, therefore, feel that we should invite him to our palace, extend our hospitality and honour him. I would like to know your opinion about this." Then the Sardars and Desais whispered among themselves. After a little bit of murmuring and whispering, a senior Sardar adjusted his shiny turban on his head, stood up and said, "Sarkar, you have taken a very agreeable decision. We all support it whole-heartedly. We think that it is our moral duty to invite and honour Chhatrapati Sivaji Maharaj, who is the great protector of Hindu religion." Then a few other Sardars stood up and repeated their consent. Raja Isaprabhu beamed with a sense of satisfaction. He said, "My dear friends, I am really very happy to have your whole-hearted consent for the programme. I request you, all the officers to make arrangements for the said function within three days. Then we shall send our Diwan to formally extend our invitation to Chhatrapati Sivaji Maharaj." Then all the members of the court discussed their respective duties. After the meeting was over, everybody dispersed to his respective abode.

*****

When Chhatrapati Sivaji's army was camping at Yadavada, they fell short of provision. A detachment of their army, therefore, began to loot the houses and shops of surrounding villages and collect cereals, flour and provisional items necessary for their food. After they had collected enough of provision, they remembered that they were running short of milk and curd. They, therefore, marched to Belavadi and stood near the cottages of milkmen belonging to the community of *Gollas*. One of the leading soldiers sat upright on his horse and accosted a milkman, "Dear friend, who is the leader of the milkmen here? I would like to buy some milk from you." Then the milkman went into the lane of milkmen and brought an elderly person with big mustaches. The elderly man greeted the soldier by joining his palms in reverence and asked him gently, "What's the matter sir?" The leading soldier asked him, "See man, we require some milk for our fellow soldiers. How much milk can you sell us everyday? The milkman mentally calculated the quantity of milk that he could spare for the soldiers and replied, "We, the whole community of *Gollas* can give you twenty seers of milk." The leader was rather disappointed by the reply of the milkman. He said, "No man, that will be too little for us. We require at least eighty to hundred seers of milk." Then the elderly milkman said, "Sorry sir, we cannot spare that much of milk. We have our regular customers at Belavadi whom we don't want to lose." Then the leader felt angry and said, "No, you must give us as much milk as we want. We don't bother about your regular customers." The elderly milkman was also exasperated and therefore raised his voice and replied, "How is that possible? You can take as much milk as we give you. More than that, we cannot spare." The leader grew terribly angry but controlled it. He said, "All right, man. We know how to take the required quantity of milk from you." He whipped his horse sharply. The horse began to walk slowly. The other soldiers on horseback followed him. After their departure, the elderly milkman looked at the younger ones who had gathered there by now and laughed at the soldiers. In the evening they milked their cows and distributed the milk to the regular customers. At night they had their dinner and slept peacefully as usual.

*****

The soldiers of the detachment of Sivaji's army were really angered by the milkman's frank refusal to spare all the milk that they could get from their cows. So they were planning something secretly. The leader told his soldiers the plan of action that they had to follow that night. They finished their dinner in their tents and slept like logs. About seven to eight hours after sunset, the leader was awakened by the urgent desire to urinate. So he got up quickly, went out and urinated on a nearby stone. He felt relieved. He looked up and saw the countless stars twinkling beautifully in the sky. Then he gave a whistle sound twice. Instantly the soldiers of his detachment woke up and dressed themselves in their uniforms. Within a few minutes they were all ready and mounted their horses. The leader led them towards the huts of the milkmen of Belavadi. Two soldiers held torches in their hands and the rest of them rode ahead in the dim light of the torch. The horses neighed occasionally. The poor animals did not know what was happening in the human world. They just responded to the lashes of whips and digging of spurs into their flanks. The soldiers rode silently for about an hour or so.

As they went near Belavadi, the leader gave a whistle and all the soldiers stopped. "You tether the horses to the nearby trees. Two of you may stand guard here, while we will go into the lane of milkmen." Accordingly all the soldiers tethered their horses to the nearby trees. Two soldiers stood guard there. Then the leader walked ahead followed by others. They could see the profile of the milkmen's lane in the dim starlight. But they could see things quite clearly in the torchlight they carried. The leader stood for a few moments and whispered to his followers, "Dear friends, all of you go into the lane silently and cut the ropes securing the cows. Then you whip all the cows out of the lane. Then we shall drive them towards our camp." All the followers agreed to carry out the plan.

The soldiers held the naked daggers ready for the purpose. As they walked ahead into the milkmen's lane, each one of them entered the open cattlesheds and cut loose the ropes and whipped the cows out. The milkmen who were sleeping soundly at the advanced hours of night could not know what was happening to their cows outside their cottages. Within half an hour's time all the cows of the *Gollas'* lane were driven out. They drove the cows with sticks and tree branches and chuckled among themselves. As they reached the spot where they had tethered their horses, they untethered them, and began to whip them. The cows were scared of the whinnying of horses ridden by the soldiers. First the cows began to run fast, as they seemed to be scared of the soldiers. Then they got used to them and slowed down their speed. After crossing the borders of Belavadi, the soldiers began to sing love songs merrily. The cows did not understand where they were being driven. They bellowed in confusion. The soldiers reached their camp and secured all the cows to the trees near their tents and slept once again to have their early morning sleep.

*****

When the milkmen of the *Gollas'* lane got up in the morning and went to the cowsheds for milking, they were shocked to discover that their cows were missing mysteriously. They consulted one another and searched all the cowsheds in their lane. All of them gathered in front of their huts and began to discuss the matter. "Who must have taken our cows and where?" asked a younger milkman. The elderly man of the lane replied, "I suspect that the soldiers of Sivaji's army must have done this mean thing." Then another youngman said, "Had we agreed to sell all the milk that we could produce, this unpleasant event would not have happened." "But how could we do that? Isn't it not against our business ethics?" quipped the elderly man. "Are you sure that it is the soldiers of Sivaji who have stolen our cows?" asked a young milkman. "I suspect that it must be they," said the elderly man, "but I am not sure. One of you can walk up to the soldier's camp at Yadavada and confirm." Immediately a hale and healthy youngman was sent to Yadavada. He tied a towel around his head, held a staff in his hand and walked towards Yadavada crooning a song all along the way. After an hour or so, he reached the area where Sivaji's large army was camping. He could hear the horses neighing occasionally. He could not dare go near the camp, but watched the different sections of the camp from a safe distance. Finally he could cast his eyes on a group of cows whose shape, colour and horns he could make out even from the distance. "Lo! Our cows are here. The poor animals! What if the soldiers butcher them for their food?" thought he and a shudder of pity went through his veins. He turned back and walked briskly to his lane at Belavadi and reported the whole thing to his professional friends and relatives, who felt shocked by the news. The whole day, they spent in idling and explaining the strange experience to the regular customers. They felt so sad for their cows that they spent the whole day as if in mourning. They kept themselves away from food and water.

In the evening, they gathered again and discussed among themselves their own plight as well as that of their cows. "What shall we do now?" asked the elderly man. "We cannot go and fight with the soldiers. Instead of regaining our cows, we may lose our lives," said a youngman. "I suspect that the soldiers might butcher the cows for their meal. I just cannot stand that idea," said another youngman. "So there is no way out. O God, what a fate has befallen us!" exclaimed another man. When they were worrying about their plight, an idea flashed across the mind of the elderly man who said, "Dear friends, why not bring this news to His Highness Isaprabhu's notice?" Everybody seemed to like the idea. "Yes, that's a very good idea. Let's go and report the matter to the *karbhari* of the palace," said a middle aged man. Accordingly some of them went to the palace office, met the *karbhari* and reported the matter pathetically.

When the news reached Raja Isaprabhu, he felt rather disconcerted. He called a meeting of his courtiers in the Durbar

Hall and expressed his sense of surprise, "I am really puzzled by the irony of the present situation. We have actually made arrangements for honouring Chhatrapati Sivaji Maharaj. But the news of his soldiers' abduction of cows from our kingdom is very disturbing. We must get ready for the fight with Sivaji's soldiers. Commander sir, please keep the army ready. We shall go there today itself." All the courtiers and officers approved of Raja Isaprabhu's decision. But before they could execute their plan, Rani Mallamma entered the Durbar Hall and said to Raja Isaprabhu, "My dear sarkar, I request you not to proceed in this matter." Everybody including Raja Isaprabhu felt puzzled. Raja Isaprabhu asked her, "But why, my darling? Why should I not go and regain the cows of our milkmen? Who else can go there if we cannot go?" Rani Mallamma said in her firm voice, "Sarkar, instead of yourself, I shall go there along with the women soldiers of Belavadi and regain the cows." Raja Isaprabhu and his courtiers, who knew the inborn heroism of Rani Mallamma, could not doubt her capacity. They simply stared at one another meaningfully. Finally Raja Isaprabhu said, "All right, my dear Rani, I have no doubt about your heroism. You do as you wish. Our Commander will help you to get whatever weapons you want." The courtiers stood silently wondering at the extraordinary courage of a woman and even felt ashamed of themselves inwardly.

Rani Mallamma sent for all the women soldiers of Belavadi. She dressed herself in the military fashion. She tucked the knot of her sari behind her. She tied her hair into a bun. She hung the sheath and the sword by her left side and held a shield in her left hand. The other women soldiers who came to the palace ground also dressed themselves in a similar manner. When all of them were ready, they mounted their horses and rode towards the camp at Yadavada. First they took a round around the camp of soldiers who had held their cows. The male soldiers of the detachment of Chhatrapati Sivaji's army were relaxing in their tents in the afternoon. When Rani Mallamma gave a signal, her assistant gave a bugle cry. Thus all of them rode to the tents and began to fight with the male soldiers. The soldiers who were in a relaxing mood were taken aback by the sight of the female soldiers ready to charge at them. Many of them were not properly dressed in their uniform. They searched for their swords and tried to put up a good show. But before they could mentally prepare themselves to face the unexpected situation, Rani Mallamma and her female companions hacked and mangled many Maratha soldiers to death. Their swords clanked fiercely and produced sparks of fire. The female soldiers uttered the heroic slogans, "Jai Virabhadra," repeatedly and continued to hack and pierce the enemies. The blades of their swords were smeared with the blood of lurid red colour. Within a couple of hours, more than half of the Maratha soldiers had lost their lives. And the rest of them began to run for life. The female soldiers burst into the slogan, "Victory to Rani Mallamma of Belavadi." They were all enthused by their success in the fight with Sivaji's soldiers. They cut the ropes of the cows and drove them back to Belavadi. The cows bellowed excitedly and walked back to their familiar village. The milkmen of the lane of *Gollas* were overjoyed to see their cows brought back by Rani Mallamma and her female soldiers. They burst into slogans, "Victory to Rani Mallamma, Victory to Mother Mallamma." They got tears of joy in their eyes. "My dear milkmen brothers, you don't worry about your cows now onwards. Be happy and free from anxiety," said Rani Mallamma and went back to the palace. Raja Isaprabhu heard from her and her companions what they had accomplished. "Bravo, my dear Rani. I am really proud of you. You have disproved the traditional notion that woman is weak and helpless. You have indeed become Goddess Chandi in your military achievement," exclaimed Raja Isaprabhu and appreciated her heroism whole-heartedly. The courtiers and the citizens of Belavadi wondered at the valiance of their Rani and felt proud of her.

*****

When Chhatrapati Sivaji was resting in his camp, a messenger came and saluted him formally and said, "Maharaj, the soldiers of one of our detachments had kidnapped the cows belonging to Belavadi Kingdom. But yesterday, Rani Mallamma came to our camping area with her female soldiers, killed many of our soldiers and took back all the cows." Chhatrapati Sivaji was rather puzzled by the news. He sat upright, caressed his beard, cocked his ears and listened to many other details. Then he burst out, "*Vah vah*! Our soldiers are destroyed by the Rani and her female army of Belavadi. I must admire the heroism of the wonderful lady. But why did our foolish soldiers kidnap their cows? Who permitted them to indulge in this immoral act? These fools are rewarded properly for their foolishness." His Ministers, Commander and other military officers were listening to the angry words of Chhatrapati Sivaji. A few moments went by in embarrassing silence. He then continued his wrathful talk, "These fools not only lost their lives, but have tarnished our image as well. We have achieved a memorable success in conquering the Kingdom of Tanjavuru in the south. But I cannot relish this insulting defeat by a Rani of a small Kingdom of Belavadi. This is a black spot on my immaculate image. I must avenge it." Chhatrapati Sivaji gnashed his teeth and struck his left palm with his right fist. He looked at all the military officers gathered there. He said, "Commander-in-Chief Dadaji, tomorrow you take the army to Belavadi and see that the small Kingdom is defeated in the shortest period." "Yes, Maharaj," said Commander Dhanaji, "I shall do it tomorrow itself." Then all the officers bowed themselves out of the large tent of Chhatrapati Sivaji.

*****

The next morning Commander Dadaji took a big army and marched towards Belavadi. They camped at some distance from Belavadi and had their rest. Commander Dadaji sent half a dozen soldiers to go near Belavadi and study the details of the fortress and the compound and the gates etc., of the Kingdom. Accordingly the soldiers went there in civil dress and studied the details.

Meanwhile, Raja Isaprabhu's messengers supplied intelligence to him about Chhatrapati Sivaji's army headed by Commander Dadaji camping a couple of miles away from Belavadi. Raja Isaprabhu was deeply disturbed by the news. He called an emergency meeting of his officers, ministers and the Commander and asked them to be prepared for the war. Soon there was a flurry of activities inside the kingdom. The soldiers were urgently summoned and asked to rehearse the martial art. The other civilians in the kingdom began to make preparations for the supply of food items for the soldiers. Raja Isaprabhu sent messages to His Holiness of the Brihanmatha of Huli requesting him to send Gaviyappa Nayaka along with his army within a couple of days. Likewise he sent a message to Virappagouda of Sigehalli and asked him to help with his army to fight the war with Chhatrapati Sivaji's army. Raja Isaprabhu hoped that he would certainly get some help from them.

Raja Isaprabhu's spies went around Belavadi to inspect the movements of Sivaji's soldiers. They came back and reported to him that the enemies were ready to attack the fort of Belavadi. Raja Isaprabhu, therefore, ordered that all the gates of the city compound should be locked from inside. Inside the fort everybody busied himself with his respective duty of contributing to the fight. The Commander of Raja Isaprabhu's army ordered his soldiers to occupy their place behind the parapets and turrets of the fortification and be ready with cannons. Accordingly the soldiers occupied the strategic places on the terrace of the palace and waited for the signal from the enemy.

One day, the expected fight started. Commander Dadaji ordered his soldiers to attack the fort. The Maratha soldiers rode towards the fort of Belavadi and discovered that the wall of the fort was impregnable. It was built with big boulders of brown granite stone. Besides, they could not go near the wall, as they used to be attacked with arrows and cannon fire by the soldiers of Belavadi from the parapets and turrets. Soon the mood of war caught hold of both the parties. Isaprabhu decided to fight with the army of Sivaji from the top of his fortress as long as he could. Meanwhile he eagerly waited for their military help from Gaviappa Nayaka of Huli and Virappagouda of Sigehalli. Day in and day out, the fight continued. The soldiers of Sivaji used to try to break the wall of the fort as and when they could. But in spite of their efforts they found that the wall was very strong and built with very big boulders. It, therefore, could not be broken easily. They despaired of breaking it, but yet continued their effort rather half-heartedly. At night, they used to make vain efforts to break open the main gate. Thus the fight continued for about a week.

Raja Isaprabhu waited for the help from his neighbouring friends, though he continued his fight with Sivaji's army. The second week passed in the usual fight. The soldiers of Sivaji's army had continued their efforts to break the strong wall of the fort of Belavadi. They felt both angry and helpless at the same time. The third week also went by. When the fight reached the twenty-sixth day, the soldiers of Belavadi began to feel the acute shortage of food and water inside the fort. The soldiers felt famished and enervated. Raja Isaprabhu consulted his wife Rani Mallamma about what to do next. As a young girl, Mallamma had been familiar with such political emergencies in her parents' palace at Swadi. She enheartened him, "My dear lord, why do you worry? We are the heroes of Kannada land. We must fight bravely in the battle. We shall achieve either victory in the war or attain heroic death on the battlefield. Let our heroism be tested finally. You better open the main gate of the fort and take out the limited army and fight with the enemy." Raja Isaprabhu felt enthused by her words and prepared himself mentally to face the situation heroically. He called a meeting of his Minister, military officers and the Commander and instructed them the strategy of war to be followed after the opening of the main gate. In the meanwhile, the soldiers of Belavadi continued to fight from the rooftop of the fort.

One day, a fiery arrow was shot by a Maratha soldier across the fort wall of Belavadi. The arrow darted speedily and fell on a big haystack within the compound. Lo! The haystack began to burn slowly. The flames began to spread to the neighbouring houses. There was a big hullabaloo in the city. The civilians rushed out of their houses and watched the flames helplessly. Some of them tried to extinguish the fire by throwing loose earth on it. Some others tried to throw some water on it. The news reached Raja Isaprabhu who was now at the end of his patience. He, therefore, ordered his Commander-in-Chief, "Commander sir, please arrange to open the main gate and let us reach out of the city and face the enemy." The Commander nodded his assent with a salute and rode to his soldiers who were ready to face the emergency. When the gate was opened, the Maratha soldiers entered the city. Thus there was a fierce fight between the two armies. Raja Isaprabhu wielded his sword dexterously and heroically and killed a number of Maratha soldiers. The soldiers of Belavadi who noticed their Raja fighting heroically felt enthused and followed his example.

But Fate had something else in store for them. When Raja Isaprabhu was fighting with the Maratha soldiers, one of the latter sneaked silently behind him and stabbed him in the back. Blood gushed out of the gashes. Lo! Raja Isaprabhu sagged down from the horseback and fell on the earth. A sense of satisfaction was writ large on his face. His fingers had clutched the sword so tightly that it could not be easily removed from his grip. Raja Isaprabhu had attained heroic heaven on the battlefield in keeping with his magnetic personality. His death caused consternation in the minds of his soldiers. Soon a messenger rushed to the palace and stood silently crying in front of Rani Mallamma on the rooftop of the palace. "What's the matter? Why are you crying? Tell me quickly," asked the Rani. The messenger managed to say in-between his sobs, "Rani Sarkar, Our Isaprabhu Maharaj is mortally wounded in the battle." Rani Mallamma was shocked out of her wits. Another messenger narrated how Raja Isaprabhu was stabbed in the back by a Maratha soldier. Rani Mallamma felt as if the whole sky was falling down on her head. For a few seconds, she sat silent and confused. Tears trickled down her cheeks without her being conscious of them. A few seconds passed before she consolidated her will. Then she articulated, "My dear brothers, the kingdom does not belong to Raja Isaprabhu alone. It belongs to all of us. Nobody can take it away from us. Let's fight as long as we are alive. Come on, let's rush ahead." She forgot the sorrow caused by her husband's death. She jumped on to the horseback, held a sword in her right hand and led the soldiers. She cheered them with the hortatory slogan, "Hara, Hara, Mahadev." When the soldiers of Belavadi heard the heroic voice of a female fighter, they felt doubly enthused and began to fight with the Maratha soldiers with renewed vigour. Rani Mallamma fought with the enemy like the terrific Goddess Chandi. Consequently, the Maratha army was defeated within no time. Many of them lost their lives in the fight and a few who survived ran for life. The battlefield was cluttered with dead bodies of soldiers lying in a variety of picturesque poses. The ground was bespattered with blood turning darkish. The eagles were circling in the sky and eagerly waiting for their dinner of carcasses. As the Maratha army turned back, the soldiers of Belavadi cheered at the top of their voices, "Victory to Rani Mallamma, Victory to Raja Isaprabhu of Belavadi Kingdom." They returned to the fort and locked all the gates. By that time Virappagouda of Sigehalli and Gaviyappa Nayaka of Huli came with sufficient provision of food items and ammunition. When the news reached Rani Mallamma, she ordered the gates to be opened and the army of the well-wishers be admitted into the fort. The soldiers of Belavadi who were running short of provision felt relieved by the provision brought by Virappagouda and Gaviyappa Nayaka. With the new soldiers added to the native ones, the strength of the army was doubled. Temporarily at least Rani Mallamma heaved a sight of relief.

Now that the strength of Rani Mallamma's army was about six hundred, she resumed the battle with a renewed enthusiasm. She ordered the cannons to be fired at the Maratha soldiers. As the cannons rumbled repeatedly, several Maratha soldiers lost their lives and sagged down on the battlefield. The senapati who saw many of his soldiers dying, felt deeply disheartened. He noticed that their ammunition was exhausted. He felt disheartened and took to his heels. The soldiers of Belavadi felt ecstatic at the sight of the enemy running away from the battlefield. Everybody cheered, "Victory to Rani Mallamma, Victory to Belavadi Kingdom." Rani Mallamma felt a sense of satisfaction. She further wanted to chase the enemies. But many of her sardars advised her, "Rani Sarkar, the enemies have had a memorable experience about your heroism. But we do not know when they will return to attack us. Let's return to the fort and make the necessary arrangements." So Rani Mallamma yielded to the advice of the well-wishing sardars and returned to the fort with her army.

*****

Meanwhile Sri Siddhavira Yogiraj had gone to the spot where Raja Isaprabhu had been wounded and transported him in a palanquin to the palace. He had arranged for the nursing of Raja Isaprabhu Maharaj. Servants were busy dressing and bandaging the wounds of the beloved king. When Rani Mallamma returned to the palace, she rushed to the chamber to break the news of victory to her husband. But she was shocked to notice that Raja Isaprabhu was moaning with pain. She tried her best to medicate his wounds, but alas, it was all in vein! Finally Raja Isaprabhu said, "My dear Rani, I know your heroism from the beginning. I'll be happy only when you defeat Sivaji and achieve the crown of glory. You promise me like that." Rani Mallamma looked at her husband and said, "My dear lord, you rest assured that I shall defeat Sivaji or die on the battlefield." Raja Isaprabhu felt satisfied with the heroic words of his Rani. He then said, "My dear Rani, I am not going to live for long. You better stop worrying about me and continue the battle. Meanwhile you bathe me in the hot water consecrated by Gurumaharaj and pour a little of it into my mouth." When the sardars and the relatives heard these words, they began to sob with sorrow. The womenfolk began to weep in muffled voices.

Rani Mallamma tried to control her tears gushing out of her eyes. She beckoned to the royal servants to arrange for the bath. Accordingly a cauldron of water was consecrated by the holy touch of Sri Siddhavira Yogi Maharaj and warmed on a large size oven in the kitchen. Then they gently lifted him to the bathroom, washed his limbs and covered him with fresh garments. Then they gently lifted him and carried him back to the chamber. Then they placed all the items of *puja* like water, vermilion powder, holy ash, flowers, *bhel* leaves, incense and bells etc., in front of him. Rani Mallamma placed the icon of *istalinga* on his left palm and helped him do the *puja*. Accordingly Raja Isaprabhu completed his brief *puja*. Then the Rani poured into his mouth a little water consecrated by the feet of Sri Siddhavira Yogi Maharaj. The whole gathering of relatives and courtiers were watching the scene with pindrop silence. Raja Isaprabhu gulped down the holy water and invoked the name of the Lord, 'Siva, Siva, Siva.' Then he bowed down and kept his head on the lotus feet of His Holiness Sri Siddhavira Yogiraj. His Holiness bent down a little and blessed Raja Isaprabhu by placing his palms on the latter's head. When he lifted up Raja Isaprabhu's head, he noticed that the bird of his breath had flown away. When people learnt that their lord Isaprabhu was no more, they began to wail and cry at the highest pitch of their voices. Rani Mallamma began to cry in an uncontrollable manner. Nobody was in a position to console one another. Even His Holiness Siddhavira Yogiraj began to get tears in his eyes in spite of his spiritual detachment from the mundane life. Then the funeral ceremony was arranged with all the royal pomp and glory. All the relatives and followers of Raja Isaprabhu buried him according to the Virasaiva ritual rules.

The next morning Rani Mallamma was very disconsolate. As she had removed the vermilion dot from her forehead, nose-stud from her nose, sacramental *tali* from her neck, bangles from her wrists and toe-rings from her toes, she appeared rather fierce to the eyes of Sri Siddhavira Yogiraj who visited her in the palace and tried his best to console her. The other courtiers also came there to offer their condolences to the widowed Rani.

After a few days had gone by, Rani Mallamma began to think of facing the army of Sivaji, which might attack Belavadi any time. She had to satisfy the spirit of her husband by defeating Sivaji. She, therefore, kept herself busy instructing and inspiring her soldiers and kept them ready for any emergency.

Meanwhile Sri Siddhavira Yogiraja thought of some plan of helping the Rani in some way or the other. He, therefore, called Santayya who was an expert in disguising himself in different ways and spying upon the enemy and instructed him something in secret. Accordingly Santayya assumed the guise of a sanyasi, wore a rosary of *rudraksi* around his neck, held a staff in one hand and a begging bowl in the other. He walked towards the camp of Sivaji's army and his officers. He stood before the tent of the captain and begged, *Bhavati bhiksandehi.* He noticed that the captain was deeply worried and therefore consulting four of his sardars. Suddenly they turned towards him and looked askance. The sanyasi made bold to speak to them in a polite manner, "Sardar saheb, what are you thinking about? All your plans are going to be a waste. There is a big hindrance in your way of capturing Belavadi kingdom." Then the captain cocked his ears and thought that the sanyasi might be a diviner. He, therefore, came out of his tent and said, "Swami Maharaj, please tell us quickly what the hindrance is. We'll give you ample gifts." The sanyasi assumed a confidential tone and said, "Custom demands that I must not divulge the secret to anyone except your king. Then everything will be all right." The captain was silenced by the sanyasi's answer. He then conducted him to Sivaji's tent and introduced him to the king. There was nobody in the tent except Chhatrapati Sivaji and the sanyasi. They discussed many details of the attack on Belavadi. Chhatrapati Sivaji asked him about the hindrance and the way of overcoming it. Then the sanyasi said, "Sarkar, there is a holy shrine of Goddess Jagadamba locally known as Goddess Dyamavva in

Lokur village. Everybody has to seek her blessings before launching upon any work. Your Majesty does not seem to have had even her *darsan.* Then how is it possible for the battle to be over? Tomorrow happens to be Friday. Sarkar, you may have her *darsan* and blessing tomorrow and then see the change in the course of the battle." Chhatrapati Sivaji felt convinced by the words of the sanyasi. He was a staunch devotee of Goddess Jagadamba and a firm believer in the practice of devotion. By that time Dhanaji, the Captain of the army entered the tent and sat listening to their conversation. Then Chhattrapati Sivaji turned to the Captain and ordered, "Dhanaji, there is some truth in what the sanyasi says. You offer him abundant alms. You attack the fort of Belavadi and tomorrow morning, we shall go to the holy shrine of Jagadamba for *darsan*." Then the Captain took the sanyasi to another tent and ordered his assistant to offer a purse full of gold coins. The sanyasi collected his alms, saluted the Captain and took his leave from there.

Santayya returned to Siddhasamudra in the evening and narrated the whole thing to Sri Siddhavira Yogiraja who felt very happy to note that his plan had turned out to be auspicious for the Rani of Belavadi. Then he ordered Santayya, "You rush to Belavadi quickly and inform everything to Rani Mallamma. Then ask her to bring a platoon of two hundred female cavalry and her son Nagabhusana here before this midnight." Santayya saluted His Holiness and left his chamber. He went to the kitchen of the monastery and had his meal of *rotti*, vegetables and wheat porridge. Then he rode on horseback to Belavadi and narrated everything that had happened and conveyed His Holiness's message. Accordingly Rani Mallamma lost no time in organizing her female cavalry of two hundred. She sent word to all the women soldiers who were ever ready to obey their beloved leader. They went to the palace and met the Rani who enheartened them to meet the emergency and asked them to come prepared for the battle with Sivaji. She distributed ample gifts of gold and silver to all her women soldiers, who were overjoyed to be honoured by her. They went home, had their hurried meal and wore their military outfit and went riding their horses to the palace. Meanwhile the Rani felt a lump in her throat. She addressed the important people gathered there in a very feelingful way, "My dear brothers and sisters, this is our last meeting for the day. I shall return tomorrow and see you. Until then you obey our Gaviyappa Nayaka." When the people listened to her words, they were surprised beyond measure. Then Rani Mallamma put on her military outfit. She secured the end of her sari by tying it to her waist. Then she wore the steel shirt over which she put on a filigreed blouse. She fitted a girdle around her waist. She wore the helmet on her head and put on her husband's crest on the helmet. When the sardars saw her in the military dress, they burst out, "Bravo, Rani Sarkar. Your heroism becomes the battlefield. If some evil happens to you, we shall not allow the Maratha soldiers to touch your royal person." Rani Mallamma felt proud of her sardars who were so concerned about her well-being and honour. The ostler brought the stallion, which belonged to her late husband. First she made her little son Nagabhusana sit on horseback. Then she jumped on to it behind her son. The female cavalry stood in order behind her. The natives of Belavadi stood on both the sides of the palace compound. As Rani Mallamma whipped her horse, the natives raised their hands in salutation to her. The Rani received their salute and rode ahead. The female cavalry followed her. She followed the secret path in the growing darkness of night. After a little time, she reached Siddhasamudra. Sri Siddhavira Yogiraja felt happy to welcome the Rani and her female soldiers. He made arrangements for their supper and rest in the monastery. When all the soldiers had their food and rested for the night, His Holiness sat immersed in the *istalinga puja*.

In the early morning when His Holiness concluded his puja, Rani Mallamma and her female soldiers were ready to go to the battlefield. She went to his chamber. Sri Siddhavira Yogiraja sat on the tiger-skin cushion. The triple marks of immaculate white *vibhuti* shone beautifully on his forehead. Rani Mallamma bowed down to his feet and prayed to him, "Your Holiness, kindly bless me and help me fulfil my late husband's wish. Kindly forgive me if I have committed any mistake." Then Sri Siddhavira Yogiraja said, "My dear daughter, you please don't have any doubt at all. You are going to achieve victory in the battle today. But don't harm Sivaji." Rani Mallamma was enthused by His Holiness's blessings, but she was enraged by his last sentence. She, therefore, burst out, "Your Holiness, today I am going to end Sivaji's life. He will follow the path that my husband has followed." Sri Siddhavira Yogiraja grew apprehensive. He, therefore, said, "Daughter, though it is possible for you to kill him, it is not permitted by Goddess Jagadamba. Sivaji is a great devotee of the goddess. You think that you are victorious if he just apologizes to you." Rani Mallamma felt convinced by His Holiness's words. She said, "All right, Your Holiness, I shall abide by your order. Kindly bless me." She bowed down once again to his feet. Sri Siddhavira Yogiraja raised his palms, muttered some *mantras* and blessed her whole-heartedly, "May God grant you victory in the battle." The Rani felt as if a new energy filled her veins. She walked back to the front yard of the monastery where her female soldiers sat ready on their horses. Rani Mallamma beckoned to them and rode ahead of them. The horses ran ahead with the clop-clop of hooves and raising cloud lets of dust. After a few minutes of slow walking, the horses began to canter. After an hour's high speed riding, they reached Lokur village.

Meanwhile, Chhatrapati Sivaji had gone to the shrine of Goddess Jagadamba. He was accompanied by eight sardars. He offered a special worship to the goddess. The priest decked the idol with flowers and offered it the consecrated *prasada*. When Chhatrapati Sivaji sat in front of the deity, the priest offered him *prasada*, which he thought was not an auspicious sign. But anyway, he consoled himself of having offered his homage to the goddess. Then he mounted his stallion and began to ride back to his tent with his sardars. But on the way he and his small group of sardars were unexpectedly attacked by a big female army led by Rani Mallamma. Chhatrapati was utterly surprised by the unforeseen event. He could not identify the Rani and her female soldiers. Each of them were surrounded by about twenty-five female soldiers and they simply did not know how to face the situation. But they fought desperately with the women soldiers. A few Maratha soldiers rushed towards Rani Mallamma and tried to attack her. But she swung her sword so fiercely that they fell on the ground from the horse backs with a thud. The confused horses whinnied helplessly and ran helter-skelter. Chhatrapati watched the situation and felt rather helpless. Rani Mallamma now directed her attention on Sivaji and rushed towards him with a raised sword ready to strike him dead. Chhatrapati felt really nervous for the first time in his life. He thought that they were not mere women but incarnations of Goddess Jagadamba who must have been angry with him. He, therefore, dismounted from his horse, stood in front of the Rani with joined palms. He requested her in Sanskrit prayer, "O Jagadama, Goddess Great, kindly protect me. O Goddess with lotus-eyes, kindly grant me great happiness in life." Then he requested her in Marathi, "O Goddess, kindly forgive me my sin. I am an ignorant fellow. I cannot understand the greatness of your sacred shrine here. If I have committed any sin, kindly forgive me. I am your son. Kindly protect me." When Rani Mallamma heard his pathetic prayer, she said, "You scoundrel, you have taken away the life of my lord and now you are asking for pardon so shamelessly. Let us test your heroism today. Today I am sure to rob you of your life and fulfil my husband's wish. Come on, you show me your worth today." After listening to these words, Chhatrapati Sivaji realized the whole thing and learnt that she was none other than the Rani of Belavadi whose husband had been killed in the battle by his own soldiers. He thought inwardly that he was very lonely and helpless in that situation and that the Rani had come to attack him with all the preparation. He thought it to be a folly to fight with her and lose his life. He wanted to use the better part of his discretion and wriggle out of the situation in a very realistic manner. He, therefore, saluted Rani Mallamma with joined palms and said, "Dear Mother, it is true that I had ordered my sardar to capture your lord and bring him to me. But the wicked sardar killed him instead of capturing him. For this disobedience, I had that sardar's eyes extracted. After the battle is over, I shall leave him in the nearby fort of Munavalli. You may punish him as you like. Really speaking, I am not guilty of anything. Mother, your heroism is really great. You look like Goddess Jagadamba herself to me. Your candid words sound like those of my own mother Jijabayi and touch me deeply. Dear mother, kindly forgive me. I have been struggling only to destroy the Mussalmans. But here I made a mistake. You may sever my head for this sin, if you like." With these words Chhatrapati Sivaji bent and touched the feet of Rani Mallamma. The female soldiers observed the pathetic situation silently. Both the warriors felt pity for each other and realized that the evil situation was brought about by mutual misunderstanding and bad luck. Rani Mallamma was touched by Chhatrapati Sivaji's words, which had a ring of truth about them. She wished to forgive him and therefore, said to him, "Maharaj, now I understand everything. I forgive you whole-heartedly. But kindly note that we are put to great loss. I, therefore, request you to withdraw your army from Belavadi fort and sign an agreement according to our wish." Chhatrapati Sivaji happily gave his assent to her suggestions. He, then, arranged for the proper funeral for his dead soldiers and returned to Yadavada. Rani Mallamma returned with her female army to Siddhasamudra and reported everything to H.H. Siddhavira Yogiraja who felt extremely happy. Then he arranged for the lunch for all the soldiers of the Rani and sent them back to Belavadi.

*****

After Rani Mallamma and her female soldiers left Siddhasamudra for Belavadi, Sri Siddhavira Yogiraja mounted the *sarot* and sat in it. The driver whipped the horses gently. The horses began to gain speed gradually thereby raising cloudlets of dust behind them. When he reached Chhatrapati Sivaji's camp, he sent word to the Maratha King. The servants of the King conducted Sri Siddhavira Yogiraja into the big tent of Chhatrapati Sivaji who welcomed him with great respect and bowed down to his feet. Then Sri Siddhavira Yogiraja explained to Chhatrapati Sivaji how Rani Mallamma was a spirited and heroic queen, how he dissuaded her from pursuing war against Sivaji Maharaj who was a great champion of Hindu religion and how she obeyed his order etc. Chhatrapati Sivaji felt very happy to learn that the Rani and the Yogiraja understood his great concern for Hindu religion and felt very sorry for having attacked such a spirited Hindu queen as Mallamma. He said to Sri Siddhavira Yogiraja, "Your Holiness, I apologize for my mistake in attacking the king and queen of Belavadi without any discrimination. I feel extremely sorry to know that my soldiers attacked Belavadi when King Isaprabhu was said to be making preparations for my reception and felicitation in his palace. Everything has unfortunately misfired. But it is never too late to mend this mistake. Right now I shall send the palanquin *saranjam* to Belavadi to bring the Rani with honour here and make peace with her." Sri Siddhavira Yogiraja felt extremely happy to note the great transformation in Chhatrapati Sivaji's attitude and thanked God inwardly. Then the Yogiraja blessed Sivaji whole-heartedly and returned to Siddhasamudra with a lightened heart.

*****

When Rani Mallamma returned to Belavadi along with her female soldiers she was desirous of putting an end to the war as Chhatrapati had sought her forgiveness. But when she reached her palace, she was surprised by the vehement attack of her fort by the Maratha soldiers. Her Commander had been fighting very boldly. She thought it was her duty to protect her Kingdom to the last breath of her life. She, therefore, gave her final order to her soldiers, "My dear brother-soldiers, this is our final war. We must either achieve victory or court heroic death on the battlefield. First, let us face these Maratha soldiers and then tackle Sivaji." All the soldiers felt enthused by her words and began to fight heroically with the enemies. Rani Mallamma rode her stallion right into the midst of the Maratha soldiers and began to gladiate her sword dexterously. She used to strike and kill the Maratha soldiers and sardars with a remarkable speed even before they could attack her properly. Many of her female soldiers were in the male guise and fighting with the Marathas. While the fighting was in its full swing, a Maratha soldier struck a soldier of Belavadi who happened to be a lady called Gauramma in the male guise. Gouramma shrieked piteously as blood began to gush out of her wound. Rani Mallamma felt a great sympathy for her companion Gauramma and a terrible exasperation towards the merciless Maratha soldier who had struck her. Anger surged through her veins. Rani Mallamma, therefore, lost no time in attacking that soldier. She raised her sword high in the air and brought it down with all her force on the chest of the Maratha soldier who sagged to the earth with a pitiable cry and moan. Rani Mallamma then rode her horse forward. But Dhanaji, the Sardar of the Maratha army was following her very closely. As he went near her horse, he struck the hind legs of her horse treacherously. Lo, the horse sagged to the earth helplessly. Rani Mallamma lost her balance and fell on the ground. But she instantly jumped up and pierced Dhanaji's belly with her lance ferociously and lo! Dhanaji gave a pathetic shriek and fell on the ground. Hearing his shriek, five Maratha soldiers rushed their horses towards the Rani and tried to attack her. But Rani Mallamma showed her superhuman strength and heroism in dealing with them. She swished her sword in many directions and killed all the five soldiers within no time. Dhanaji who was lying wounded and helpless on the battleground was witnessing her heroic feat. Though he was sorry to see his own Maratha soldiers being killed by the Rani, he could not help admiring her. He burst out, "Bravo, Rani Sarkar!"

By that time, there came a few sardars from Sivaji waving the white flag of peace and carrying an empty palanquin. They approached the Commander of Belavadi and explained the details of Chhatrapati Sivaji's order. The Commander of Belavadi army gave his assent to the peace agreement. The sardars of Sivaji hoisted the flag of peace on a tall post. The soldiers from both the sides understood the symbolic meaning of the white flag and stopped the war. Dhanaji was wounded severely on different parts of his person. He managed to stand up before Rani Mallamma and requested her, "Rani Sarkar, you please sit on the palanquin. Our Chhatrapati has ordered us to stop the war. Kindly permit us to return to our camp." Rani Mallamma was glad to hear the supplication of Dhanaji. She, therefore, began to search for her own sardars. But by that time Gaviyappa Nayaka was mortally wounded and was about to die. The soldiers placed him gently on the palanquin and transported him towards Chhatrapati Maharaj. Chhatrapati Maharaj and Guru Maharaj were both waiting for them in their tents. As soon as Rani Mallamma alighted from the palanquin, Sivaji Maharaj requested her to be seated on the throne and bowed down to her by kneeling on his right knee and folding his palms in reverence. Sri Siddhavira Yogiraja who watched the unprecedented scene felt simply ecstatic. Chhatrapati Maharaj exclaimed, "O my dear Mother, it is not possible to see a heroic soldier like you even among men-soldiers, let alone among women-soldiers. I had a mother called Jijabayi. But from today onwards, you have become my mother. You have saved not only my own life, but of many of my soldiers. Kindly forgive us all. Mother, kindly bless us so that we may succeed in our future ventures elsewhere." Rani Mallamma listened to him carefully although she was smarting with pain of a couple of severe wounds. She was not in a position to talk properly. Even then she mustered up her strength and managed to reply, "Chhatrapati Maharaj, everything that happened today was as per the order of our Guru Maharaj. Otherwise, both you and I and many soldiers would have lost our lives." She heaved a deep exclamation. Then Guru Maharaj said, "Dear daughter, that ill time is over now. Please look around here. All these people are like your children. Calm yourself and bless everybody." Then Rani Mallamma prostrated at the feet of Sri Siddhavira Yogiraja, remembered her late husband and wailed piteously, "Dear father, everything is over and everything is all right now. But where did the lord of my heart go? How can I be happy without him? How can I live without him?" She cried loudly and piteously. When the soldiers, Chhatrapati Maharaj and Guru Maharaj heard her wail, tears trickled in their eyes also. Guru Maharaj held her hands tightly and tried to console her with enheartening words. For a moment, anger surged in her veins and she wished to swish the sword. But by that time Chhatrapati Sivaji touched her feet and requested her, "Dear Mother, please calm down. Otherwise you sever our heads. We are seated here silently." On hearing these words from Chhatrapati Maharaj, Rani Mallamma was confounded. But she did not know what to do or talk. She, therefore, remained silent for a long time. Time seemed to hang heavily on all the dignitaries gathered there. Then Guru Maharaj gently broached the subject, "Dear daughter, why do you worry unnecessarily? Both of you rule over your territories by helping each other mutually. From both sides *i.e.* your side as well as Chhatrapati Maharaj's side, you give forty villages to Sri Virappagouda of Sigehalli thereby making him your *Subhedar*. You run your administration through the *Subhedar*. Your son is only one year old. Until he attains puberty, you be the regent Rani." Chhatrapati Sivaji listened to these words carefully and readily gave his consent. He further presented her with valuable garments and ornaments and honoured her profusely. Rani Mallamma was quietened at least temporarily. After a while, she said to Chhatrapati Sivaji, "Maharaj, you have committed a terrific sin by murdering my husband. As a result of your sin, your son will die a similar death as my husband did. In fact my husband's death was caused by a soldier instigated by your son." Chhatrapati Sivaji was really frightened by Rani Mallamma's curse. In order to ward it off, he did his best to placate her. He gave his assent to all that she demanded. He readily made an agreement with her.

By that time Rani Mallamma's brother Raja Sadasivanayaka of Swadi Kingdom brought an army of about ten thousand soldiers and camped in the vicinity. Raja Sadasivanayaka walked forward and consoled his younger sister. Rani Mallamma narrated everything to him in detail and chalked out the future plans for her kingdom. Raja Sadasivanayaka was happy to learn that Chhatrapati Sivaji had treated his sister with due respect and consideration. As per Rani Mallamma's suggestion, Raja Sadasivanayaka escorted Chhatrapati Sivaji up to Toragallu. Sivaji Maharaj took rest at Toragallu for a couple of days. Then he wended his way to his capital via Panhale. After a few months, Sivaji Maharaj breathed his last in Rudranama year of Saka 1602.

Rani Mallamma returned to Belavadi Kingdom and immersed herself in the routine life. She grew reconciled to her widowhood and tried to bring up her son with utmost care and affection. But the memory of her late husband was kept alive in her mind and acted as a guiding principle in all her day-to-day activities. Her elder brother Raja Sadasivanayaka gave her moral support in all the matters of her kingdom.

After the death of Chhatrapati Sivaji, his son Sambhaji occupied the throne. Then slowly he began to think of conquering the Belavadi Kingdom. Not only that. His evil thoughts began to advance further. He knew that Rani Mallamma was a widow. He also knew that she was not only young but extraordinarily beautiful. His carnal imagination began to paint her in different contours and postures. He secretly wished to recruit her as one of his mistresses or wives and keep her in his gynaceum. He even shared these thoughts with his confidants and officers. The secret news circulated far and wide with extraordinary speed. When Rani Tarabayi heard the news, she was simply shocked and disconcerted. She did not like a widow like Rani Mallamma to be exploited by a powerful but evil king. She, therefore, went secretly to Belavadi Kingdom and alerted Rani Mallamma about it. Rani Mallamma was very careful about her purity of mind and body. She worshipped her late husband in heart and devoted her attention to looking after her young son.

After a few years, Sambhaji was killed in the battle by Aurangzeb and Rani Tarabayi, therefore, invited Rani Mallamma to her kingdom and honoured her profusely. In honour of Rani Mallamma's heroism, Rani Tarabayi arranged many memorial stones on the borders of her kingdom and intimated the same to Rani Mallamma who felt a sense of satisfaction. Rani Mallamma returned to the Kingdom of Belavadi and lived peacefully. She achieved liberation from the mortal world in Saka 1639.

2

Change of Heart

SIVALILA WAS chatting with her friends in the verandah of her house. As dusk descended upon the earth, darkness thickened everywhere. She remembered that it was a New Moon Day and went into the kitchen to light the wick-lamps. She lit two joss sticks also and waved them before the idols of family deities of Goddess Yallamma and Lord Virabhadra. She prayed to them mentally for the advancement of the family in general. She came out of the kitchen with a tiny silver box of saffron powder. She called her friends into the central hall and dotted the saffron powder on their foreheads and they in turn dotted her forehead with the same powder. Now they sat on the wooden chairs to chat further. The fragrance of the joss sticks was filling the hall with curly spirals. In the glittering light of the electric lamp in the hall, the golden bangles of Sivalila's wrists were shining brightly. Annapurna who noticed them asked her, "O Sivalila, when did you get these bangles? They are so beautiful." Sivalila became a bit self-conscious. "Oh, don't be surprised, Anu. These are old bangles only. Recently I got them recast. That's all." "Even then," said Annapurna, "they look like brand new bangles. How I wish I also had such bangles!" and sighed. Sivalila told her teasingly, "Don't you worry, Annapurna. When you get married, your husband will deck you with ample gold." Annapurna blushed and said, "Go, madam, go," and sat with her head tilted down. Girija changed the topic and asked Sivalila, "How much did you pay for this new sari, friend? It fits you so well." "Do you really like it?" asked Sivalila and continued, "my husband brought it from Kanjivaram when he went there for business. He has paid three thousand and odd rupees for this." Annapurna and Girija stretched the filigree border of Sivalila's sari and examined its beauty and quality with the concentration of a scientist examining the bacteria under a microscope. Girija said in a regretting tone, "Nowadays the cost of saris has gone up so much that one cannot buy them as easily as in the past. These saris used to cost only a thousand rupees, but now they cost thrice as much or even more." There was a brief silence for a moment. Annapurna who had overcome her shyness by now asked them, "Have you seen the latest film, madam? I liked it immensely. Rajakumar and Kalpana have acted so well in it!" "Is that so?" asked Sivalila, "In that case I must see it. Will you join me tomorrow? We can go for the matinee." "Yes, yes, why not? I feel so bored in the afternoons. I don't want to miss such a good movie," said Girija. "In that case," said Annapurna, "I shall come to you at 2 o'clock in the afternoon. You be ready by then." "Oh yes. Without fail," replied Sivalila.

As the sound of footsteps was heard outside, Sivalila's friends got up, bid farewell to her and went away from there adjusting the hems of their saris upon their buxom breasts. Siddhalinga entered the house with a wan smile and appeared to be very tired. He went straight to the bedroom and doffed his yellow silk shirt and white terycot pyjama. "Why are you so late today?" asked Sivalila. "Oh, there was such a heavy rush today. So many customers were there to buy gold and silver, because of the marriage season," said Siddhalinga and walked to the bathroom. "First, let me have some good tea. I shall have the meal later," said he while washing his hands, face and legs with the fragrant Lyril soap. Sivalila went to the kitchen and prepared the mixture of sugar, tea-powder and milk in a bowl and kept it on the oven, which she lit with an electronic lighter. Siddhalinga rubbed his limbs with a green towel. He went to the niche of deities, smeared his forehead with triple marks of *vibhuti* with his right fingers and joined his palms in reverence to Lord Virabhadra and Goddess Yallamma. He went to the dining hall and slumped on the sofa and switched on the radio. The sweet notes of santur seemed to soothe his tired self. Sivalila brought the tray with a cup of tea on it and said with a smile on her face, "Take this hot tea." Siddhalinga began to sip the hot tea with real gusto. Sivalila also sat before him on the chair with her face beaming with satisfaction. "Why darling, you are looking so jovial today. What's the matter?" asked he. "Nothing special. Today my friends appreciated the shape and glitter of my golden bangles." "Oh, I see. That explains why your face is beaming so bright today. But darling, you are better than any gold or gem for me. Because you are my golden girl. Come on, give me a kiss," said Siddhalinga in a poetic vein. Sivalila blushed and said, "Go, go. Don't you know that the door is still open? You are talking like an actor in a play." She got up, collected the cup and saucer and walked into the kitchen. Siddhalinga sat beating the rhythm with his fingers on the arms of the sofa in tune with the music of the radio.

As Siddhalinga went to the kitchen, he saw his wife kneading the dough of wheat flour. 'What are you doing, darling?" asked he. "Don't you know today is the new Moon Day?" said she, "I am going to prepare *holige*." "All right. Shall I relax until then?" said Siddhalinga, went to the bedroom and switched on the lamp. He leant against the sponge pillow and began to read the novel, *The Maker's Mint* written by the popular novelist, Tipperudraswamy. He was very fond of reading religious fiction and poetry.

Siddhalinga was jerked out of his literary rapture when Sivalila came to the room and shook his shoulders and announced, "Dinner is ready, please come on into the dining hall." "Darling, I had forgotten my hunger while I was absorbed in reading. But now I am feeling all the more hungry simply because you reminded me of it." He closed the book, switched off the lamp and rushed to the dining hall. Both of them tasted the variety of delicacies. He savored the *holige,* rice chips and lemon pickles with gusto. After the feast, Sivalila opened the silver box from which she took the edible leaves, slivers of betel, lime, cardamom and cloves and prepared the roll and gave it to her husband. She prepared one more roll for herself and began to chew it.

Both of them were feeling sleepy on account of the heavy feast that they had. They went to the bedroom and lay on the foam bed. Siddhalinga stretched out his left hand and switched off the bedlamp. They were chatting about this and that until slowly they fell into sound sleep. Supreme silence reigned everywhere in the city. A dog here and a dog there were barking occasionally. Siddhalinga was awakened by a sudden thumping sound in the hall. For a moment, he thought, "It must be the cat which prowls around in the night," and closed his eyes. Before another couple of minutes had gone by, he heard the creaking of doors and rattle of plates. He was surprised at the strange sounds coming from the hall of his house. He groped for the electric button and switched on the bedlamp and walked towards the hall. There also he groped for the switchboard and put the light on. Lo! He was shocked out of his wits for a moment by what he saw there. Three hefty men with faces covered in black cloth except for the holes for the eyes stood there menacingly. Siddhalinga looked up at the ceiling and saw a big gap of the size of four tiles. He realized how the thieves had managed to enter his house. He wanted to open the front door and call in the neighbours to help him. But one of the three thieves stood exactly near the door leading to the main door. Siddhalinga's heart began to thump ceaselessly and a cold shiver ran through his entire body. Yet he could not back out. He mustered up his courage and shouted at the top of his tremulous voice, "Who are you? Why have you come here at this time? What is it you want?" The tallest and heftiest of the three giggled behind his dark muffler and said in a regally indifferent style, "You'll soon realize who we all are. We've no time to answer all your questions. You give us the key of your almirah. Otherwise you'll have to leave this mortal world for good. Can you see the shining blade of these daggers?" Siddhalinga shuddered for a moment. Sivalila, who was also awakened by the shouts, had came and stood near the door of the hall. Siddhalinga asked his wife to ring up to the Police Station. The chief of the thieves who overheard his words said in a stylish way, "We have taken care to cut the telephone wire in order to spare you that botheration." Siddhalinga was nonplussed. He did not know what to do. He looked at his wife askance. The chief of the thieves thundered again, "Don't waste our precious time. We have other places to visit." He beckoned to his two companions who stretched their right hands with daggers and slowly walked towards Siddhalinga. Sivalila's heart began to beat wildly and her legs started shivering. "What if they stab my husband? What about my *mangalya*?" She worried inwardly. She rushed to the bedroom and brought out the key of the almirah. She gave it to her husband and whispered into his ears. Siddhalinga understood the point of view of his wife. They had no time to shilly shally now. He, therefore, tossed the key towards the chief of the thieves who caught it without letting it fall down. One of the thieves stood near the hall door leading to the main door. Another thief followed his chief towards the steel almirah. The chief opened the almirah with the key and rummaged through it by throwing out the precious clothes and things. Siddhalinga whispered into his wife's ears, "What if they knock out all the gold?" Sivalila whispered back, "Don't worry. Our lives are more precious than any gold or silver." They stood dumbly watching the thieves inspecting all the compartments of the cupboard. Nearly ten minutes elapsed like this. The chief of the thieves returned from the almirah followed by his companion. He was fuming with anger. "Oh, mister, don't play this dirty trick upon me. Except some clothes and silver, there is nothing in there. Now don't irritate me. Go and bring all the golden ornaments in your possession. Otherwise I'll send you to Heaven with a gash of this." He held the dagger near Siddhalinga's chest menacingly. Siddhalinga's mouth was dehydrated of saliva and he did not know what to say. Sivalila was trembling incessantly. But yet she mustered up her courage. She drew her husband back and walked forward and stood before the chief of the thieves. "See man, you're not satisfied even if we gave you the key of the almirah. As you are bent upon having gold and nothing else, I shall give you all that I have." She then slipped her golden bangles off her wrists and gave them to the chief of thieves. Not satisfied even with that, he ordered her, "Let me have your necklace also." Sivalila looked at her husband for a moment and took off her *mangalya sutra* and offered it to the chief who smiled with a sense of satisfaction. Tears had already gathered in Sivalila's eyes. The chief asked them further, "Give us other ornaments of yours." Now Sivalila's anger shot up. She shouted, "We've given you everything we have. I have given you even the sacred *tali*. We have nothing else to give you. If you are not satisfied, you may kill me first and then my husband." The thieves did not know how to react. They looked at one another with a sense of embarrassment. "All right," said the chief, "We go away now. But be careful. If you inform the police about this, we shall come again and gag you both." All of them made towards the main door. But before they could unbolt it, they heard Sivalila call them. They walked back towards her and asked, "Why did you call us back?" "Nothing man. If you don't misunderstand me, I have a request." "Come on, tell me what it is," asked the chief. Sivalila cleared her throat and said, "See man, please don't waste this gold by drinking or playing cards. You are like my brothers. You start some shop or some other business with that money and settle down to a respectable life instead of leading such an irregular life. That's all I wanted to say." The chief of the thieves said rather arrogantly, "We know what to do with it. You need not advise us about that." Then he walked straight to the main door, unbolted it and disappeared in the darkness, along with his companions. Siddhalinga and Sivalila were scared so much by the unexpected event that they could not sleep even a wink for the rest of the night. They closed the main door and sat listening to some Kannada devotional songs on the tape-recorder until the break of dawn.

In the morning, the neighbours gathered in Sivalila's house in order to console her. Gangamma exclaimed, "Thank God. The thieves have not stabbed either of you. You may earn any amount of gold. But you could not have regained your life."

They walked to the big hall and stared at the gap in the ceiling caused by the removal of four tiles. The sight of it sent a tremor through their spines. What if it had happened in their houses! They shuddered at the very thought of it. Annapurna suggested to Sivalila, "Why not lodge a police complaint at the Police Station?" Lingaraj said, "What can the police fellows do nowadays? Many times they are in league with such thieves. That's why thieves get scot free." The shriveled old Tungabai asked Sivalila, "Why not consult that astrologer Dixit and ask him whether you will get back your gold or not?" Siddhalinga was listening to their words silently. He said, "I have never cheated or hurt even a fly, let alone human beings. I really do not understand why such a thing should have happened to me." Sivasankar turned to Siddhalinga and said, "Why not lodge a complaint to the Police? They will try to hunt those fellows." "No, Mr. Sivasankar," said Siddhalinga, "Perhaps you do not know these fellows. They not only do not hunt for the thieves, but also on the contrary, extract money from us. I am not the sort of person who would visit the Police Station. As far as possible, I would like to be away from the Police fellows, lawyers and even doctors." The neighbours appeared to be disarmed by his answer. They went away to their homes one after another.

Siddhalinga went out and brought a mason who climbed the roof and began to refix the red tiles. He had his lunch of *rotti*, brinjal, rice and curry and went to his shop. Sivalila cancelled her visit to the theatre, as she was not in the right mood. Throughout the afternoon she sat playing carrum with her friends who tried their best to humour her with jokes and anecdotes.

About fifteen days went by. Sivalila and Siddhalinga were reconciled to their lot and forgot all about the event of theft in the house.

That evening, Siddhalinga returned home quite early and took his wife for a walk in the Kittur Chennamma Park. They sat on the beautiful lawn near the kiosque. Everywhere they saw flowers of different sizes and colours. The crows and sparrows were flying over and perching on the Thackeray Memorial tomb in the park. The military band players clad in khaki uniforms stood in a semi-circle. As the leader gave a signal by the downward wave of his cane, they began to play the beautiful tunes of film music. Siddhalinga bought two cones of salted groundnuts. They began too munch them slowly and casually. The band set played nine different songs. At last they started playing the national anthem *Jana Gana Mana*...when everybody in the park stood up by way of respect to their country. Siddhalinga and Sivalila also did the same. As the band players went out of the park through the narrow gate and sat in the dark coloured van, Siddhalinga left the park with his wife and returned home.

After dinner, the couple sat in the verandah, chatting. The full moon was exuding serene light all around. They were thrilled by the pleasant moonlight. As the clock in the hall chimed nine, Sivalila went to the bedroom and lay down on the foam bed. Siddhalinga followed her and began to read *Chelva Kogile*, a religious novel by Devendrakumar Hakari. He began to feel sleepy after reading a few chapters. He switched off the lamp and lay beside his wife. A couple of hours went by. The couple was oblivious of everything as they were in a state of sound sleep. But they were suddenly awakened by the knock on the door. Siddhalinga asked his wife, "Who must be knocking at this time of the night?" Sivalila said, "It must be my maternal uncle. Usually he comes late in the night as the train comes here at the odd hour." Siddhalinga switched on the lamp and went to the main door. However, before opening the door, he asked, "Who's that?" "It is we," came the answer from outside the door. Sivalila also got up and stood near the hall door. Siddhalinga opened the door and lo he was surprised to know that all the three were perfect strangers. Siddhalinga asked them, "Gentlemen, who are you and what do you want?" The tallest of the three strangers said with a courteous smile, "We have something to discuss with you and your missus." "In that case," said Siddhalinga, "please come inside and take your seats." Sivalila had stood in the hall. Her husband led the strangers to the hall and showed them the chairs. The tallest of the three walked towards Sivalila and knelt down and bowed his head to her feet. Sivalila felt rather embarrassed by the stranger's salute. Siddhalinga also did not understand the logic of it all. Then the other two strangers also touched their foreheads to Sivalila's feet reverentially. Unable to control her curiosity, Sivalila asked them, "Gentlemen, who are you and why are you bowing down to me? I have not seen you before." The tallest of the three said in a penitential tone, "Dear madam, you are not an ordinary lady, but a veritable goddess. You are like my eldest sister. That day when we robbed you of your gold, you advised me like a sister to make use of that money for some useful investment. I have burgled many houses, but never did I receive such a heart-felt advice. From that day your words have been ringing in my ears. Without my knowing, my heart had accepted you as my sister. I have now decided to stop thieving and start leading a respectable life. My dear sister, please take back this gold and bless me to lead a pious life." He took out the golden ornaments from the pocket of his nehru-shirt and placed them near Sivalila's feet. Tears gushed out of her eyes. She said in-between her tears, "Dear brother, I am glad that God has blessed you with a new wisdom. I am really proud of having you as my brother." Siddhalinga's eyes were also brimmed with tears. The tallest of the three said, "We'll take leave of you now. We're very sorry to have disturbed you at this odd hour." "Please have some tea at least, before going," said Siddhalinga. "No sir, thank you very much for your good will," said the tallest man. They saluted Sivalila once again by joining their palms and said, "We'll take leave of you, sister." They walked out of the main door briskly. Siddhalinga exclaimed, "What a wonder is this, dear?" "I could never imagine such a thing to happen in life," said Sivalila. As the night was advancing, they closed the main door and retired to their bedroom.

The next morning when Sivalila narrated the whole episode to her neighbours, Annapurna exclaimed, "I had heard such things happened only in fairy tales. I could never imagine that there could be such good people even in the *Kaliyuga*." Girija said, "I had read somewhere that truth is stranger than fiction. Today I have realized the truth of this statement." Then all of them dispersed wondering about the unexpected goodness of man in this world.

3

Blood for Blood

THE SUN was very hot. That was the reason why I was fanning myself with the little red fan of coconut frond. My bunyan had stuck to my back because of heavy sweating. In the kitchen and the middle room my wife and three daughters were busy making cooking arrangements. From my room I could hear my wife scraping the coconut and my first daughter Sarada cutting onions and coriander on the wooden board. My nostrils began to dilate at the sweet smell of the boiling oil wafting out of the kitchen. I could not resist the temptation and therefore, went into the kitchen to see what was going on there. As I entered the kitchen, all the four of them looked at me and smiled. I cracked a joke to my second daughter Girija, "See, our Girija is so active today. Have you seen her so busy any other day?" Girija said, "You papa" and bent her blushing face. In order to tease her I asked her to scan the groom carefully so that she may have no reason to complain against him later. Girija blushed rosier than ever. I went to the bath-room, washed my face and feet and returned to my room. Then I put on a neatly ironed khadi *dhoti* and arranged the pleats carefully and slipped on a khadi shirt and a gandhi-cap on my head and sat expecting the bridegroom and his parents and relatives.

As the wall-clock struck four, I got up and asked my two sons to arrange the seats and pillows properly in the middle room. They stopped playing 'the tiger-house' and attended to the work I had assigned to them. Hardly had ten minutes passed when I heard the honking of a horn outside our house. My wife and daughters grew alert. They prinked themselves hurriedly. I went to the door and welcomed the guests. The groom's father

Viranagouda got off the car first and was followed by others. Viranagouda joined his palms and wished me. Then he arranged his immaculate gandhi-cap neatly on his head. My sons offered water to the guests in small tumblers. Each one of them sprinkled water on their feet, washed their faces and rubbed them clean with towels offered to them. Then they entered our house and were conducted into the middle room. The men and women sat separately into two groups in the middle room. The bridegroom sat in the centre flanked by his father and mother.

I sat among them and beckoned to my wife who understood the meaning and attended to the preparation of tiffin in the kitchen. I was chatting with Viranagouda about rains, crops and current politics including Nehru's foreign policy. Viranagouda spoke very jovially about his village and rural politics. He seemed to have great admiration for Nehru and Gandhi. I inwardly felt proud of having alliance with his family. Viranagouda was known in the neighbouring villages and even towns as a dynamic leader and social reformer. I was, therefore, eager to have blood relationship with his family. I called my eldest son and asked him, "Please get the tiffin for the guests." He immediately rushed into the kitchen. After a couple of minutes my two sons brought big trays and served the guests with sweet balls, bananas, parched rice and tea. Everybody was eating silently and looked serious. After they had their tea, my youngest son offered them edible leaves, betel, lime, cardamom and cloves. I offered a filter-tipped cigarette to Viranagouda who took it and began to puff it with style. His relatives and followers could not dare smoke in his presence. Then Panchayya, the priest suggested that the bride may be shown. I deliberately looked at the bridegroom clad in *dhoti* and nehru-shirt. He smiled a bit and consciously tightened his lips. My second daughter Girija came out of the kitchen shyly but gracefully. She was clad in a green silk sari and a green blouse with a big rosy border decorated with thick embroidery. As she walked gently, her silver anklets tinkled musically. Her ear-rings, nose-rings, armlets, waistbands and necklaces glistened and glittered alternately. My daughter looked as pretty as Goddess Rati herself and I was, therefore, very proud of her. I was sure that she would win the bridegroom's heart. The priest Panchayya asked her to be seated on the wooden seat with her face to the east. She touched the floor with her palms and symbolically saluted all those seated there and sat on the wooden seat in a lotus posture. Then Panchayya went and sat facing the bride, took her left palm and examined the lines on it meticulously like a scientist examining the bacteria through a microscope. While doing this priestly job he nodded his head by way of approval. Then he asked her to stand up. She lifted up her sari six inches from her feet so that everybody could see the symmetry of her toes and ankles. Then she lowered her sari and covered her feet. Panchayya took out a *Siva*-string of silk and measured her ten fingers and two palms and compared it with her height *i.e.* from feet to the vermilion dot on her forehead. Panchayya then sat away from her and asked her for her name. My daughter bent her head slightly and spelled her name as Girija. Then the priest gave her a Kannada book to read. She read a para from it in a very clear and melodious voice. By this time she seemed to have completed her ordeal. Beads of perspiration had decked her forehead and nose. The bridegroom was stealing a look or two at the bride occasionally. Panchayya's job was over. He, therefore, asked the bridegroom's mother to complete the ritual. Daksayani offered a bunch of eleven bananas, sugercandy, vermilion and jasmine garland to the bride who collected them in the hem of her sari and symbolically saluted everyone there and walked back into the kitchen jingling her anklets rhythmically. The bridegroom seemed to be beaming with joy though he never opened his mouth throughout the bride-examination.

A second round of tea and biscuits was served to everyone. The wall-clock chimed five. Viranagouda got up as he said he had to attend a meeting at the Panchayat Hall. He said, "I will send word about our approval through our servant within a couple of days." He joined his palms at me and went towards his Ambassador car. His relatives and followers went behind him and sat in the car. The driver revved the machine and the car zoomed along the road. The smell of the petrol made my nostrils dilate.

After the guests left, I went to the middle room where the entire family had gathered and were giggling and gossiping at the top of their voices. Girija was still seated in a shy and shrunken position. Everybody was teasing her. I too asked her, "Girija, what do you think of the groom? Do you like him?" She did not answer but sat silently suppressing her smile.

Three days had passed when an ordinary man came and saluted me. I asked him, "Who are you and where do you come from?" He introduced himself as the servant of Viranagouda and had come to deliver his master's message. "Tell me the message," said I gently. He sat on his haunches and said very courteously, "Our Gowdru has conveyed the message that he and the members of his family including the bridegroom have liked the bride immensely and are eager to have this alliance. If the same is agreeable to your family also, Gowdru has suggested that you should go to their village for the engagement ceremony." I felt very happy about the positive sign of the course of events. I felt really proud of my daughter's prettiness, which would capture the heart of any sensible youngman. Then I asked my wife to feed the servant properly. My wife brought a large plate with *rottis,* brinjal curry, rice and curds and offered it to the servant. The servant sat on the bare floor and ate his lunch and belched with satisfaction. I told him, "Durgappa, please tell your Gowdru that I shall send my opinion with a servant within a week's time." The servant took his staff, saluted me and took his leave in the hot sun.

Nearly a week had passed when I remembered that I had to transport half a dozen cotton bales to the Co-operative Society of Naragund. I took three carts including two hired ones and transported the cotton bales to the Society and spoke to the clerk about the business. Immediately the cotton bales were weighed in the large iron scales and I was given a receipt of acknowledgement by the clerk. By this time afternoon had advanced into early evening. My three cartmen wanted to meet their friends and relax for the evening. I gave them some money and allowed them four hour's time. They parked the carts in the compound of the Society. The oxen were tethered to the Portia tree nearby.

All the three of us dispersed. I too felt like entertaining myself. But I could not go to a movie, as I had no patience to sit through the lengthy show. I, therefore, decided to meet an old friend of mine called Channappa who worked as a clerk in the Tahasildar office there. As soon as he passed his mulki-examination, Channappa had left our village and finally succeeded in getting a job as clerk in the revenue department. I crossed all the familiar streets of Naragund and knocked on his door. Luckily Channappa was there at home and was overjoyed to see me after such a long interval. We exchanged amicabilities. Then we discussed rains, crops and harvest of the year. Channappa's wife served us with the tiffin of parched rice and tea. We ate our tiffin and drank our tea silently. Then we chewed edible leaves, betel and lime. Channappa asked me casually if I had been searching for a bridegroom for my daughter. I said very proudly, "Yes, friend. Recently Viranagouda had come to see my daughter for his son." "That's very good. Did you like the groom? Did the groom like the bride?" asked Channappa. I said again, "Yes, yes. Viranagouda had sent word that they had all liked my daughter and that we could arrange the engagement." Channappa kept quiet for a few seconds. Then I asked him if the alliance was ok. Channappa burst into a mild guffaw and said, "The alliance is perfectly all right if both the parties have liked each other." But I was not satisfied by his straight answer. I sensed something ironical about it. I wanted to elicit his real opinion and therefore, requested him, "Dear friend, do you know anything about the background of Viranagouda's family?" Channappa replied rather nonchalantly, "Once you have liked the family, there is no reason why you should bother about such problems. You can go ahead with it." I felt that he was trying to reserve his opinion. "Dear friend," said I, "you should not keep me in the dark. Please tell me whatever you know about their family. After all, you are my close friend and well-wisher too. I rely upon your honest opinion." Channappa seemed to hesitate for a moment. When I urged him further he said, "Dear friend, the elders say that we must speak ten lies to arrange an alliance. That's why I don't want to speak the bitter truth." Then I insisted, "Friend, you are almost like one of the members of my own family. You don't have any hesitation at all in telling me the truth. I care for my daughter's future. I must take a wise decision. So you please tell me whatever you know about Viranagouda's family." My appeal seemed to have touched him deeply. He, therefore, cleared his throat and said, "Dear friend, if you are so keen on knowing it, please listen to me." I cocked my ears and began to listen to his narration.

There was a great rivalry between Viranagouda of Yamanur and Kalappa of Kalwad. The ordinary difference of opinion between the two had grown over the years into bitter enmity. Kalappa of Kalwad was known for his heroism, nay, rowdyism. He had become a terror for the people of the nearby villages. Kalappa was so bold that he had murdered even a Police Sub-Inspector called Rangappa. Ever since he had done that feat, his glory had spread far and wide. Viranagouda who had married the daughter of Parvatagouda naturally came to belong to the group of Kalappa's enemies. Viranagouda had lost his father early in life and been leading a forlorn life. He had to struggle hard for his livelihood. Everyday he had to go to field for ploughing or for mowing the crops. In his spare time he used to take part in the village politics. Because of his desperate condition he was boiling with rage at his uncle who had been torturing him at every stage of his life. The uncle had thus become the veritable Lord Sani for Viranagouda. At this juncture Viranagouda's close friends gave him moral support and advised him to marry into a big family so that he could have some help from his father-in-law and other relatives. That is why he had approached Parvatagouda for his daughter's hand. Parvatagouda had deemed it to be a good opportunity for taking revenge upon Kalappa by supporting the latter's enemies. That is why Parvatagouda had come forward to give his daughter Daksayini in marriage to Viranagouda and humiliate his enemy through his son-in-law. He arranged the marriage in his own village and celebrated it in a very grand fashion. The friends and relatives from seven villages had gathered there to bless the couple. The villagers had not kindled their ovens for three complete days, because they were all fed by Parvatagouda. Thus Viranagouda had come to have a modicum of emotional and social security.

Ever since Viranagouda had become the son-in-law of Parvatagouda, Kalappa of Kalwad had grown into an exasperated serpent. So he was secretly sharpening his dagger against the enemy. One day in summer, Parvatagouda was returning to his village after spending a few days at the son-in-law's house on account of Ugadi festival. He had boarded the bus about 7 o'clock in the morning and had been travelling towards his village. Kalappa who was moving about in his village came to know this. He immediately took a car and rushed to the spot where the bus from Yamanur was to come. The spot was half way between Yamanur and Kalwad. Kalappa stood there along with his gang. The blue coloured bus was jigging up and down along the road from Yamanur. Kalappa's followers had piled big and small stones across the road. Parvatagouda never suspected that it was his enemy's work. He thought it must be the result of children's mischief. Kalappa and his followers had hidden themselves behind the wayside bushes. As the bus came near the barricade, the driver had to stop the bus inevitably. The passengers were curious and were peeping out of the window. Hardly had the khaki-clad bus-conductor jumped off the bus to examine the barricade when Kalappa and his followers rushed into the bus. Now Parvatagouda was in trouble. He knew that his last day had come. No sooner had he sensed danger than he jumped out of the bus and began to run desperately into the open fields. Being alone and helpless, he could not dare to put up a heroic fight with the enemy. But his enemy and his followers chased him. Parvatagouda went on cantering like a stag to save his life. He thus ran continuously for nearly half a mile. Kalappa and his followers ran close behind him. Parvatagouda was gasping for breath. He felt enervated. His legs began to ache severely. His head was reeling and his eyesight grew dim for a while. At last Parvatagouda fell to the earth out of sheer exhaustion. Kalappa and his followers surrounded him. Parvatagouda's throat was parched. He requested his enemy in a faint voice, "Please save me friend. I shall give you anything you want." But Kalappa's anger knew no bounds. He was not in a position to listen. He hacked Parvatagouda with his big and sharp axe. His followers also hacked the enemy indiscriminately. Blood spurted out of the inert body of Parvatagouda. They had mangled his body as if it was a vegetable. Kalappa and his followers heaved a sigh of relief. They turned back and looked at the road but the bus was not there. The sun was blazing in the sky. Kalappa and his gang went to the nearby brook and bathed in the cool water.

When the news of her father's death reached her, Daksayini began to wail and cry and beat her chest. Her co-sisters and other neighbouring ladies came to her house and began to console her. Viranagouda heard the news and grew pale with fear and anger. He felt insecure for a moment. His imagination grew alert and started planning the future. He thought his survival itself was threatened by the presence of Kalappa. He feared that Kalappa would take his life also in future. Viranagouda's logic goaded him to take his enemy's life. In the past he had been harassed by his uncle and had to think of his wife and children. And more than that it was a question of prestige for him. His prestige demanded that he should not take the insult lying down. He thought it becoming his dignity to fight the enemy and take his life if possible. Only then will he have the moral satisfaction of avenging his father-in-law's death. Only then will he be known as a hero who has maintained the law of justice *i.e.* tit for tat. Thus in contemplating 'revenge,' Viranagouda forgot his sorrow about the loss of his father-in-law and began to think of various plans. Whereas Viranagouda was sad about the murder of his father-in-law, his wife was sadder still. Kalappa became the theme of their plans, discussions and obsessions. Viranagouda was constantly waiting for an opportunity to avenge the murder of his father-in-law. He, therefore, strengthened his own group by including new followers. Since it was a matter of prestige, Viranagouda had to maintain them at the cost of enormous money. He used to reserve half of the harvest-income for them. It became part of his duty to feed them with tiffin and food, offer them country liquors regularly at night and take care of their basic needs of life. Sometimes, he even had to offer them cotton *dhotis* and black woolen blankets. As a result of this huge expenditure on the part of Viranagouda, the loyalty of his followers for him grew deeper and deeper. Consequently Viranagouda gained a little confidence and courage. He came to be addressed as 'master' by the followers.

One day Viranagouda called a confidential meeting in his farm-house and asked them, "Dear friends, you are all my loyal friends. You must help me to remove my arch-enemy Kalappa from the face of the earth." His followers looked at him meaningfully. The leader among them replied, "Master, we have eaten your salt. We'll do anything and everything that you order us to. We have asked our wives to be prepared for widowhood if need be." Viranagouda felt elated to be the master of so many followers. His voice grew tremulous with joy. He said, "Dear friends, from now on our sole purpose will be to remove that cobra from the world and that at the earliest opportunity." Then the entire group of followers answered in an affirmative chorus. They celebrated their murderous decision with drinks and non-vegetarian dishes.

A couple of months elapsed like this in expectation and planning. One day a few of Viranagouda's confidants came and told him that his arch enemy was put behind bars at Dharwad on account of his crime. Viranagouda felt ecstatic about the news. But that joy did not last long. He thought an enemy is always an enemy. Viranagouda became helpless because he could not lay hands on the enemy even if he wanted to. He had even been advised by some elders to forgive the enemy. But his followers had raised a new fear in his mind. "Kalappa may not keep quiet, master. He may harm your son, if not you," said one of the followers. The idea of the likelihood of his son's murder by the enemy made him acutely apprehensive. What if he lost his only son? Who then will continue the light of his family? There cannot be anything more insulting than that his family should come to an end for the lack of a heir? What about his prestige? Should he not have a son of his to avenge his possible death in the game of revenge? More than his own self, Viranagouda had to save his son from the enemy. He, therefore, decided to remove the enemy from the earth itself. He meditated various plans for days together and ultimately hitched upon a particular one.

On a Thursday morning, Viranagouda went to Dharwad along with four confidants of his. He left his followers at a relative's house and went to the residence of the Police Inspector situated on the hill to the west of the city. The Inspector received Viranagouda in his chamber with a reserved look on his face. The Inspector had a look of a wild animal. His eyes blinked in a blank manner. Viranagouda was not at all embarrassed by the blank look, as he was quite used to it. The Inspector had heard much about Viranagouda's reputation in the villages around there. He was both curious and nervous to know as to why the Gouda must have come to his door. After the exchange of formalities, Viranagouda beckoned to the Inspector to close the door so that he could have a confidential discussion with him. The Inspector sent his servant away on some errand and closed the door. Both of them settled in their chairs. Viranagouda lent forward in his chair and began to speak in a hushed voice. The Inspector also leant forward, reclined his face on his palms and listened to the Gouda's confidential words. "Inspector saheb, I have come for some private work," said the Gouda. "What's it, please tell me sir," said the Inspector. "I need your cooperation for this task." Please don't think that I am asking for any favour gratis. I shall give you Rs. 2000/- if you oblige me," said Viranagouda. "What's the nature of the work? Goudre, I shall do it only if I can *i.e.* without risking my job." Then Viranagouda leant forward and whispered something in his ear. The Inspector understood the risk involved in the task but thought that he could manage it intelligently. The very idea of a big sum made the Inspector salivate. He thought he could easily buy ten acres of land for his children. He thought he could become a man with a little of daring. He even thought of negative possibilities. In case he is detected by the higher authorities, he decided to resign from his post and take to the management of agriculture. Thus ultimately he made up his mind to hit the iron when it was hot. The Gouda was keenly observing the Inspector's face. He saw that the Inspector's face which was rather contorted in the beginning began to grow relaxed though slowly. The blank eyes gleamed. The voice grew more familiar and informal. The Inspector stretched his hand and placed his palm on that of Viranagouda. "All right, Goudre, I shall do your work, provided you give the money in advance," said the Inspector. "Don't you worry about it, Inspector saheb. I shall arrange for it immediately," said the Gouda. The covenant being agreed upon, they had some sweet-balls and parched rice and tea. Viranagouda had begun to feel a new confidence because he had already booked the Inspector for the task. He joined his palms once again to the Inspector and took his leave.

Viranagouda had come back to his village and eagerly waited for the day when his enemy would depart from the mortal world. When the term of Kalappa's imprisonment was about to expire, Viranagouda sent his confidant to know when the important task would be accomplished. The confidant servant returned with the happy news that the deed would be done within a week's time. Viranagouda had become so impatient that minutes had become almost elongated years, for him.

On the scheduled day *i.e.* Saturday, the Inspector got up early in the morning and put on his khaki uniform and went to the Police Station. The loyal police constable also had come there already. It was still dark. The entire Police Station was silent and looking deserted. The constable who was guarding the jail throughout the night was relieved of his duty at the Inspector's suggestion. The Inspector went to the prison and saw that Kalappa was lying sound asleep and snoring loudly. His blue shorts and shirt were completely soiled. The Inspector thought it to be the golden opportunity to carry out his plan. He had already briefed his confidant constable about it and promised him a share in the profit. He, therefore, beckoned to him. The constable loaded the gun with new cartridges. His conscience woke up and began to cry. But the constable silenced his conscience by mentally declaring the economic gain he was going to have. The Inspector could not stand the sight of the murder of the prisoner and therefore, went back to his chamber and sat eagerly waiting there. The constable took his position by the side of the prison window, tightened his grip around the gun. He aimed at the sleeping prisoner and shot three times continuously. The three bullets pierced Kalappa's body. Blood began to spurt from the holes. Kalappa gave a shrill cry and his convoluted body lay inert on the floor. The police constable ran to the Inspector's chamber and informed him what he had accomplished. He was feeling very nervous and guilty and shivering in his shoes. The Inspector controlled his own inner excitement and consoled and cheered up the constable. Immediately both of them dragged the corpse out of the prison up to a few yards outside the compound and left it there. The Inspector came back to the prison and saw to it that the blood stains were wiped from the floor. When the crows began to caw at the break of the day, the other constables came to the Police Station for the morning duty. The Inspector instantly created a myth and circulated it. The constables spread the myth in the city before the public. Soon there was a big crowd gathered around the dead body. A constable was guarding it. One of the spectators made bold to ask the constable, "Police saheb, how did this man die?" The constable said in an indifferent manner, "This prisoner tried to escape from the jail in the early morning. Therefore, he was shot dead by the constable on duty." "Poor fellow. He should not have done that foolish attempt. He has lost his life unnecessarily," said one of the spectators. As the news circulated among the people, they whispered and murmured among themselves and felt pity for the dead man.

The crowd of people could not dare to doubt the words of the constables as they thought them to be the veritable incarnations of legal truth. The people went on talking about it among themselves. Within half an hour's time the myth had become a reality. The Inspector called another constable and instructed him to prepare the paper for *panchanama.* The constable filled in the blanks with the details supplied by the Inspector. The constable wrote in the column of the ledger as follows : "The culprit Mr. Kalappa was trying to escape from the prison in the early hours of morning on 13-7-1949. He was therefore shot dead by the constable on duty." Then the constable, the Inspector and three others signed at the appropriate places. Then they sent the information in a sealed cover to the Divisional Inspector General. By midday the police department arranged the funeral of the deadbody and buried him in the cemetery near the hill to the east of the town.

Viranagouda felt ecstatic when the Inspector's confidential servant came and told him that the task had been accomplished most superbly. Viranagouda got sweet balls and milk for himself and the servant. A great sense of satisfaction pervaded his soul. The sense of fear had been replaced by that of repose. He sent back the servant with a purse full of two hundred silver coins. One of the great enemies being destroyed now, Viranagouda felt relieved of great tension. He thought he could move about more freely now than in the past. He also felt confident that his son who was studying in the sixth standard was free from danger. Otherwise Viranagouda and his wife used to feel anxious until their son returned home in the evening every day. Now there was no likelihood of his son being drowned in the well or stabbed in the jowar field by the members of Kalappa's gang. But Viranagouda's wife, woman as she was after all, felt pity for the widow of Kalappa. She was sympathetic towards Kalappa's wife Halavva and shed tears incessantly about her. When Viranagouda asked his wife, "Why are you still crying? That is even after the enemy is got rid off?" She replied in a muffled voice, "Of course, the enemy is got rid off. But my heart cries for the plight of his widow. Poor woman! I don't know how she would live without her husband, the bread winner of the family!" She sobbed again and said, "Only a woman can understand another woman." Viranagouda was touched by his wife's words, which awakened a new awareness in him. He closed his eyes for a few seconds and assured his wife, "Don't you worry about her, dear. I shall make arrangements for her livelihood. It is my responsibility." "Do you really mean what you say?" asked his wife. "Why, dear? Do you doubt my words? Think that it is done within a month's time." Viranagouda felt a bit relieved and relatively free from the burden of sorrow.

After fifteen days had elapsed, Viranagouda sent his messenger to Halavva who had been doing nothing but wailing and mourning her husband's death. The messenger sat on his own woolen blanket and talked tender words to Halavva. When Halavva was tired of wailing and grew silent, the messenger took out an envelope from his pocket, spread it wide before him and asked Halavva to listen to him. He read out the contents of the letter. Then he said to her, "See, mother, it is true that Viranagoudru has got your husband murdered. The reason for this murder is known to you better than to anyone else. But he has no enmity against you at all." Halavva moaned and burst out, "How shall I live without him? Where shall I go? How should I bring up my children who are furlorned at such an early age?" Then she continued her sobbing.

The messenger watched her and felt pity for her. Tears welled up in his eyes too. He rubbed them with the end of his towel and waited for Halavva to stop crying. After a few moments he cleared his throat and said, "See mother, our Viranagoudru is a big hearted man. That's why he has sent this letter and promised to gift two acres of land for your livelihood. Mother, whatever was destined to happen has happened. And the past cannot be revoked now. Please accept the gift of land and live for your children henceforward." Halavva was too helpless to say anything. Since she had removed her nose-rings, vermilion dot on the forehead and the sacramental *tali* around her neck, her face appeared to be rather ghastly. The messenger placed the document before her, saluted her with joined palms and took his departure. Halavva was still looking at him blankly.

Viranagouda could breathe freely now. He could enjoy his food and sleep nowadays. He felt relaxed as though he had an oil-bath. But this condition of carefreeness did not last long. One day two of his followers came to his house and saluted to him rather seriously. "What's the matter, friends? You look rather grim today?" asked Viranagouda. One of them replied, "Goudre, we have heard the news that the Setty of Savadatti has taken the murder of Kalappa very seriously and been thinking of vengeance." Another follower added, "that's why we came to alert you, Goudre. Please be careful. That's all." The news touched Viranagouda deeply and made him a bit uneasy. He had no choice but to accept him as his enemy on many counts. In fact the Setty was his double enemy. Setty was the short from of Nagasetty who belonged to the party of Viranagouda's uncle. On the other hand, the Setty had identified himself with Kalappa's gang. In fact, he viewed himself as the veritable heir to the late hero Kalappa. He was planning to avenge the murder of his master. The Setty's name was proverbially associated with murderous deeds. He had no scruples whatever in his thoughts and actions. Once he had stopped a marriage party coming from Alagawadi and looted all their gold, silver and food. He could not tolerate the tyranny of morals. He would never hesitate to seduce the woman he saw no matter whether she was a virgin, or a married one or a widow. Once he had his enemy's leg cut off by his followers. Viranagouda remembered all these details about the Setty. He felt that a man of Setty's notoriety should not be ignored at all. He had learnt that the Setty had been challenging his followers with taunts and threats. Viranagouda felt secretly unnerved and exasperated simultaneously. He, therefore, began to take the enemy seriously and to collect intelligence about his movements and opinions. "I must remove this cobra from the face of the earth, if the members of my family are to be safe," thought Viranagouda.

Viranagouda called a secret meeting of only four confidential followers out of about thirty-five in his farmhouse at night. The meeting was strictly guarded by his servants. It was past midnight when the entire village had slept soundly. Viranagouda asked his followers, "Dear friends, what do you think we should do about the Setty?" One of the followers who squatted below the Gouda's chair said, "Goudre, you should not hesitate to go ahead when we, your followers, are alive." "What are we here for? Can't we do this little work?" said another follower. "It's our duty to see that even a single hair of yours is not hurt by the enemy," said the third one. Viranagouda listened to their words carefully and understood their unswerving loyalty. He felt quite confident after listening to their enheartening words. His followers required a couple of months' time for the accomplishment of the task. They were all sharpening their axes secretly.

Nagasetty had been growing rather overconfident. It had been his regular habit to taunt and insult his enemy Viranagouda before the people he met in the streets or shops or Panchayat Houses. Viranagouda used to receive regular reports about his enemy's challenges and insults. Recently Nagasetty was said to have raped a girl of flower-vendor caste near the village tank. The relatives of the girl had come and complained to Viranagouda and requested him to punish the public enemy. Now Viranagouda found sufficient justification to expedite his action. This time his personal revenge was morally supported by the public revenge.

The Ugadi Festival was over. The people in the villages were relaxing after the hard work of busy harvesting. Now the fields were all ploughed neatly and the ridges of mud in the field looked like the folds of a black Ilkal sari. Viranagouda fixed a day and ordered his followers for the task for which they were mentally ready. They had worked out the details of their plan. Accordingly on a Saturday Viranagouda and his followers parked their car near the temple of Goddess Marikamba at the outskirts of the village. The car had been brought on hire from Hubballi. They sat there watching the movements of Nagasetty. A few others of his group were spying around Nagasetty's house near the temple of Lord Basavanna. The roseate hue of the eastern sky slowly turned to silver brightness as the sun rose to an elbow's length from the horizon. They heard the loud rattling and whizzing sound of a truck come out of the village and go to the west. The truck had been transporting manure from Amaragol and Kalakeri to Yamanur. A follower of Viranagouda came running to him and told him that Nagasetty went in the truck. Viranagouda lost no time in getting into the car. His three followers also sat in the car. Viranagouda asked the driver to follow the truck. Allabaksh was seated beside the driver and directing him. He was one of the loyal servants of Viranagouda for nearly twenty years. He used to depend upon his master for food grains and clothes. Nagasetty seated in the truck must have sensed danger when he saw the car following the vehicle. Viranagouda and his gang were extremely alert.

The big axes they had kept below the seats were clinking. They followed the enemy for nearly half an hour. Viranagouda asked the driver to overtake the truck and obstruct their way. The driver changed the gear and within a minute the car zoomed along and overtook the truck. The driver immediately took a sharp curve and parked the car across the truck right in the middle of the road. Nagasetty had already sensed the danger. He instantly jumped out of the cabin and began to run for life in the open fields. He thought his enemies could not bring the car into the fields. But lo, his expectations were wrong. He wanted to hide himself somewhere, but unfortunately for him there was neither a tree, nor a bush nor a hut. He looked back and lo the car was chasing him. He seemed to see Lord Yama laughing at him as it were. He made a vain attempt to run further. He was panting for breath and sagged on the soil of the field. Viranagouda and his three followers rushed out of the car with big axes in their hands. Nagasetty's heart began to palpitate wildly at the sight of axes. All the four enemics stood in a circle around him with their deadly weapons. Nagasetty had lost his voice and began to beckon to them not to kill him. He helplessly joined his palms in supplication. He turned to Viranagouda and implored him in a faint voice, "Save me friend, save me. I shall be your follower." Seeing the helpless condition in which the enemy was writhing and hearing the plaintive request, Viranagouda felt pity for him. His heart melted at the pitiable sight. He instantly revised his plan and asked his followers to spare the enemy's life. But the short-tempered Allabaksh said, "How can you forgive an enemy? An enemy is an enemy. Master, you don't understand his trick." With these words Allabaksh lifted his axe high up in the air and struck the chest of the enemy. Lo, Nagasetty gave out a piteous and heart-rending growl. Another follower also struck a blow on the enemy's head. The blood spurted out and sprinkled on their bodies. Nagasetty's dead body lay there mangled picturesequely. Now that the sense of vengeance was satisfied, Viranagouda and his followers boarded their car and drove it to Bennihalla and bathed themselves clean. Viranagouda's imagination had already grown alert and planning an escape from the clutches of legality. He, therefore, asked the driver to take the car to Ron. He told the driver to manage to create an accident by running the car over an animal. The driver knew that obedience to the gouda would never go unrewarded. They took an hour to reach Ron. They went past the Tahasildar Office and ran the car near a hillock where they could find some animal. Hardly had they gone for a furlong when they set eyes on a herd of asses grazing by the roadside. Besides, the spot was deserted. The driver deliberately drove the car to the left side and ran it on the herd of asses. The frightened asses began to bray and scatter. One of them was struck and crushed beneath the front wheel. Viranagouda and others came out of the car to inspect whether their task was successful. They saw that the entrails of the poor ass had come out of the body and blood was oozing out of them. The left side of the car was stained with the drops of blood, which was exactly what they wanted. Viranagouda and his murderous gang took the car to the Police Station and reported the accident to the Police Sub-Inspector who took the application from the Gouda and registered it in his casebook. Then heaving a sigh of relief, Viranagouda and his gang went to a local lodge where they bathed, washed and fed themselves sumptuously. After a few hours' rest they drove back to Yamanur.

Viranagouda felt calm and reposed. He used to enjoy his meals with gusto and sleep carefully. He used to play his cards or 'tiger-house' at his leisure hours. Because of his inner peace, he began to treat his wife as a human being. His wife had lately developed a new luster on her face because of the 'bed-pleasure' she had been receiving from her husband. Outside the Gouda's house, the villagers used to talk in hushed voices about the murder of Kalappa by the Police authorities. Though they suspected that Viranagouda had a hand in that, they could not discuss it in public with courage and confidence. Since Viranagouda had warmed the palms of the Police authorities quite sumptuously, he had escaped from all the troubles of legality. Thus the Gouda had no problem whatever. He led a very carefree life for about six months.

The womenfolk of the village had been discussing secretly the murder of Nagasetty and attributed it to Viranagouda. When men heard this news they also began to think along the same line. One day when Allabaksh heard this news from the villagers, he felt deeply hurt and irritated. He knew that it was he and not the Gouda who had killed the Setty with his axe. He felt envious of the Gouda who became a hero in the eyes of the villagers. Allabaksh thought that the credit of the murder should go to him instead of to the Gouda. The feeling of irritation was simmering in his soul. Once when he sat in the village canteen sipping his tea, he heard the villagers discussing the heroism of Viranagouda. Allabaksh heard it patiently but could not control himself. He therefore took one of the villagers and whispered into his ears, "Friend, people do not know the truth. It was I and not Viranagouda who hacked Nagasetty to death. But the Gouda took the credit for it. Please keep this to yourself." The villager who heard the news was flabbergasted so much that he remained speechless for a few seconds. Later Allabaksh circulated the news of self-glorification among the villagers until it became widely known to the people.

One day when Viranagouda went to the field to supervise the mowing of crops, he was relaxing under the shade of a mango tree. His loyal farmer came to him and sat near him. "How are you Rudrappa?" asked Viranagouda. "I'm all right, Goudre," said Rudrappa and scratched his head. Then he continued, "Goudre, I have heard some news which I could not believe." "What's that Rudrappa?" asked Viranagouda. "People in the village have been discussing the murder of Nagasetty and associate your name with it." Viranagouda felt deeply disturbed but pretended to be calm and said, "How am I connected with that murder? It must be just loose talk." "But Goudre, I have heard that your own driver Allabaksh has been boasting of having murdered Nagasetty." When Viranagouda heard this, he felt terribly disturbed. But still he pretended to be calm about it and denied the charge, 'No, Rudrappa. That Allabaksh must be a fool. He may not know what he babbles." "Please do not misunderstand me, Goudre. I just wanted to bring it to your notice. I do not believe in the truth of the news at all." Viranagouda liked Rudrappa for his gullible loyalty, but began to think of taking some action against his driver. He went home and called his followers and ordered them to collect intelligence about Allabaksh's boasting and the circulation of the news among the villagers. Within a week's time Viranagouda came to confirm the fact that Allabaksh had been spreading the news, which might land the former in trouble one day in future. He grew obsessed with it so much that he could not enjoy his sleep at all. He feared that the brainless Allabaksh might go on babbling in public and leak out all the confidential information to the villagers. Viranagouda was thus obsessed with a new fear. Far-sighted as he was, he visualized the worst possible danger if Allabaksh were, by some chance, to turn against himself. At night when Viranagouda lay on his bed he thought of the worst possibilities. "Allabaksh may leak out the truth to the public or even join hands with my enemies and get me involved in criminal cases. Or he may harm me unexpectedly. Or he may even go to the extent of conspiring against me or my only son." He thought of the various possibilities of solving the problem. Finally he came to the conclusion that the only way of punishing Allabaksh was to remove him from the mortal world itself. That night Viranagouda confided all his doubts and fears to his wife who lay beside him in the bed. She listened to him with surprise and felt concerned about her own son who was still a boy. Viranagouda gave some plans for his wife to execute.

The next day Parvatamma collected intelligence about Allabaksh through other maidservants and confirmed her doubts about him and felt that her husband was right in his apprehension. She knew that Allabaksh knew all the ins and outs of their family because he had served them for more than ten years. She suspected that he might betray the family any time in future and be the cause of ruin of their family. With this new alertness about their own driver, the members of Viranagouda's family stopped discussing confidential matters in the presence of Allabaksh.

On a Saturday, Viranagouda instructed his wife to do the preliminary work for the secret task. He instructed three of his followers also about it. About 3 o'clock in the afternoon, Allabaksh came to the Gouda's house as usual. Parvatamma got up from the bed and washed her face. Others were still having their siesta in the afternoon. Parvatamma called Allabaksh to the middle room and talked sweetly with him. Then she asked him very gently and persuasively, "My son, tonight I am going to prepare some special delicacies like sweet *chapatis* and *bhajis*. Please come home in the evening for dinner. Do not miss it." Allabaksh's mouth began to salivate at the mention of sweets. More than that he felt elated to be invited by the wife of the master himself. He did not want to insult them by disobeying them. His face relaxed in a smile and he replied, "Mother, I shall come at the right time." He then went home and told his wife about the invitation with great enthusiasm. His wife teased him about it. She said, "You are indeed very lucky to be the guest in your own master's house." Parvatamma was very happy to play her role in the game. Viranagouda made every arrangement for the task. That was not at all new to his followers as they were sufficiently experienced in it. About twilight the three followers came to the Gouda's house and sat in the middle room, which was deliberately kept dark. The Gouda was waiting in his bedroom. Allabaksh came to the Gouda's house and found nobody in the front room. He was clad in black soiled trousers and a bluish cotton shirt. So he called the mistress of the house, "Avva, I have come at the right time." Parvatamma heard these words but did not come out. Instead, she raised her voice and asked him to be seated in the middle room. Allabaksh was so innocent that he did not suspect anything or anybody. He left his *chappals* at the threshold of the front room and slowly entered the middle room. And lo! Before he could feel his way through the dark passage, he felt a jerk. He felt somebody dragged him. Within a wink of an eye he was knocked down to the floor and choked to death. Allabaksh felt a sudden blackout of consciousness and his body lay inert but for the convolutions. The Gouda was there at the door twirling his mustaches. His wife brought a lantern and kept it there. She went back and brought a jute bag and gave it to the loyal murderers. They thrust Allabaksh's body into the bag and tied it tightly. Then they carried the bag to the car waiting outside and kept it in the dickey. The car zoomed along the road. There was pitch darkness everywhere. Nobody talked anything..As they reached the local brook called Bennihalla, they got off the car. They took out the bag from the dickey and threaded their way through the thorny hedges and finally hauled the bag into the water. They heard the splashing sound and the murmur of ripples. The Gouda heaved a deep sigh of relief, "At last the thorn is gone." His followers cheered him and took their leave from him.

*****

When Channappa finished the story, I was still in my trance of listening. I was so much absorbed in the story that I felt shocked by the silence. It was already 8:30 P.M. I remembered that my servants were waiting for me at the Society building. I stood up, joined my palms to Channappa and took my departure. I trod my way through the narrow lanes of the town. My servants were waiting for me rather impatiently. I jumped into the cart and reached my village late into the night.

The next morning I had my breakfast and narrated the whole story to my wife and children. As they listened to the story of Viranagouda, they grew rather pale and serious. I asked my second daughter, "My daughter, are you willing to marry Viranagouda's son?" She flatly refused, "I'm not willing, father." She then went to the middle room and slept there throughout the day. I wanted to test my wife's interest. I said, "It would be a matter of prestige for us to have an alliance with Viranagouda's family." My wife grew extremely angry and retorted, "Do you want to give your daughter in marriage to a murderer's son? Do you think she is a burden to the family? I'll never allow this alliance. Who the hell wants it?" With these words she went into the backyard and began to water the plants. I laughed at their reactions.

A week later Viranagouda's messenger came to our house and asked for our opinion about the alliance. We fed him with sweet balls, parched rice and tea. Then I diplomatically told him, "You tell your Gouda that my daughter is not willing to get married for another two years as she wants to study for her B.A. degree and ask your Gouda to see the brides elsewhere." The messenger grew pale with disappointment and took his leave. After his departure all the members of the family felt a great relief as though a great burden had been lifted off our chest.

4

Cross-Roads

AS THE motorbike was covering the distance, the road was receding stage by stage. The battering sound of the vehicle was deafening my ears and exciting me. I would accelerate the speed and there would be a competition as it were between the noise and the speed of the motorbike. I felt as though I was riding the speed itself. The trees along the road, the oxen, the buffaloes, men and women would come before me and disappear within no time. Similarly, Kalpana also disappeared from the road of my life! I can touch all the things that fly away from me as it were as I ride along the road. But Kalpana! How I wish I would be able to reach her, and recognize her! My sister advises me to forget Kalpana. 'When,' says Mother, 'are you going to marry, my son? Probably after my death, isn't it?' Father showed me many a bride, grew tired of repeating it; become indifferent and at last kept silent about it. But how to forget her! Both of us had sworn to marry or remain unmarried forever in case of any hindrance. The rebellion of the Rajakars in our state had brought a great disaster in our life.

The horn sound of the Leyland coming before me pierced my ears. O God! I realized that I had come right into the middle of the road and turned the motorbike to the left, decreased the speed and continued the ride. All of a sudden I felt the vehicle stopped with a jerk as though somebody had pressed the brakes. I tried to change the gear and decrease the speed but somehow the vehicle didn't move an inch. Before I could brake it completely, I felt something was winding around my rainy shoes! I bent my head a little, and saw a snake there! The bike pushed me away. The bike slid and lay on the road and I fell beside it. The snake was hurriedly sliding its way through the spokes of the wheel! My entire body was shivering and sweating. The rear wheel was still rotating. A few passersby rushed to the spot. "What a ferocious snake it is,' said somebody and lifted me up by extending his hands, 'it's a miracle that you were saved from the danger.' The other two lifted the motorbike and erected it and said, 'No damage to the vehicle. Nothing to bother."

"See Sir," said another, "Now you cannot go ahead. The entire day's work will be cancelled if you come across a snake on the road." Helpless in this unexpected condition I made up my mind to take rest for an hour or two. Kneading my squirted ankle, I started laming for the nearby Sanat Nagar Guest House. I gave a rupee to the boys who pushed the motorbike up to the building and asked the watchman there to keep an eye on it. I booked a room in the Guest House, and as it was already two hours since I left Hyderabad and now it was 6 o'clock in the evening, I decided to stay over the night there. I asked the bearer about the bathroom, went in, bathed and came out. Then I put on my *lungi* and Nehru shirt. I opened the window shutters and saw the cotton-like clouds in the sky dipped into the rosy tint of the shining sun. The regaling wind rushed into the room and awoke the silence therein. I felt relieved and lay on the Dunlop bed and closed my eyes. As the rotation of the fan was weaving the thread of the rosy sunlight peeping through the window, I felt as though I was sliding into the bed and sinking deeper and deeper. The bike-wheel wound with the snake grew rotating more and more speedily in my mind, and the scroll of memories began to unwind itself. The memories of innumerable experiences of the past began to rush into my mind. I heaved a deep sigh. I took out the photo of Kalpana from the purse in my pocket and stared at it for a while. The same look, the sparkling wide eyes, clear cut features and wreathe of smile. The same beauty which I had seen in her in my first meeting. That day.... Already ten years have elapsed since that meeting. Time is a strange thing indeed. Time, they say, has stood still. It moves neither backward nor forward.

It has no limits to this side or that. Is it then infinite? I remember the poem of Kanavi who says he would like to thrash the animal called Time if he could come across it. I think for myself and decide not to leave this animal unthrashed. Time is travelling eternally far and far ahead with me on the road. We breathe but an infinitesimal moment of this eternity and thread our sensations and disappear into oblivion. What remains there is only the aura of existence. Kalpana saw me at such a moment or rather I saw her. O, she disappeared from my life unexpectedly without allowing me to have that moment again! This happened ten years ago. I had been to the 'Baage-Aam' Public Garden at Hyderabad. That evening, like today the trees and creepers of the garden were covered with the *shalwar* of the rosy sunlight. I bought some eatables and threw them to the herd of peacocks in the corner and when I came near the Banyan tree with its pendant and twining roots, I saw a girl standing there with a tired face and frightened eyes, searching for somebody! The people who had come to see the Zoo in the garden were going in groups without noticing this girl.

"You are looking for somebody, aren't you?" I asked her. "See," said she in a shivering voice, "My little sister and I came together here. When we were looking at that herd of peacocks, my little sister saw other children eating *pakodas* and asked for the same. I asked her to wait here and went to the canteen. When I returned she was not here. I searched for her everywhere. I enquired everybody. Already half an hour has gone by. She was my only sister Pratibha...I don't know what to do and where to search for her."

"Don't you worry," said I, "Let's lodge a complaint to the police and let us also search for her." She began to sob. I consoled her and made her stand near the pigeon quarter. Instantly I rushed to the main gate and told the news to the officers who sent four police constables immediately. All of us inspected the divisions of water-elephants, deer, slides, and swings etc., with a lightning speed and returned disappointed. On the way, I went along the footpath leading us beyond the bamboo clusters in the corner of the lake, and saw the raindrops pouring on the petals of roses and the six years old skirt-queen shedding tears.

"Pratibha," I shouted.

"Didi…Didi…." She lifted her voice and began to cry, "Kalpana Didi…Didi…."

"You are Pratibha, aren't you? You are a good girl. Your Didi is here only. Don't cry," I wiped out the tears running on her milky cheeks and lifting her in my arms I came to the pigeon quarter. At the sight of Pratibha, Kalpana jumped at her like a deer and hugged her. I said, "please stop crying." By this time the police constables came there from different corners and said, "see sir, a child-lifting gang has entered the city. That's why we were really frightened. Please be careful about children sir." Then they took leave of us.

The evening was growing darker and darker gradually.

"Come on, I'll leave you at your home…. By the way, where's your house?"

"In the Gagan Mahal Road. We can go ourselves. Why do you take so much trouble….?"

"No. I'll go home only after reaching you to your home." Your name please….?

"Kalpana…"

I looked at her. Our eyes met and the magnet of her sight drew my very being to its depth. I heard many songs being hummed in the deep of her eyes. We were walking together and I stopped an autorickshaw coming before us. All of us got into it and reached their house in Gagan Mahal Road. It was 8 P.M. Kalpana told me softly that the person waiting at the door was her mother Saradamma. Kalpana got down and lifted up her little sister lying in my arms. She told her mother, "See mummy, but for this gentleman, our Pratibha…" and described everything summarily and went into the house. Requesting me to relax on the sofa in the drawing room, Saradamma said to me gratefully,

"God is great, sir. I had asked them to come back at 6 P.M., but I began to feel anxious when they didn't turn up even after 8 P.M. Anyway you came as a god and discovered our Pratibha." By this time Kalpana brought some tea and biscuits and kept them on the teapoy. "See son," said Saradamma, "excuse me for calling you a son, please come here tomorrow for food...."

"I'm Mr. Sivaraj. I am studying for M.A. in Jammia Osmania. My room is in Barakatpura!" I finished my tea, had a glance at the sleeping Pratibha and took my leave after bowing to Saradamma.

"You shouldn't miss it tomorrow" said Kalpana affectionately. When I looked at Kalpana, my heart fluttered for a moment and silently longed for her.

From that day I used to spend my leisure hours in Kalpana's house, teaching her chess and gradually playing chess with her own life! Kalpana's mother Saradamma used to look after me with thc same motherly affection as with her daughter. In the beginning I used to visit them only once a week *i.e.* on Sunday. After a month or so I started having my dinner almost regularly with them out of affectionate obligation to Saradamma. Some of the family affairs that Saradamma related to me brought me closer to them : Her husband Mr. Vishawanath Chatterjee had left Calcutta and settled in Hyderabad as a Lecturer in English in Nizam College. He died of heart attack when he was still in his forties. They had only a meagre amount of Insurance and a few ornaments. Kalpana was fifteen then and Pratibha only four. With these two daughters she worked as a teacher in St. Patrick School for three years living in a small rented room.

At this time, Pratibha was afflicted with chronic typhoid. I visited the hospital day in and day out and attended to every detail. Saradamma's sense of gratitude had turned into affection towards me. Pratibha had developed a deep affection for me and used to call me Sivaraj Mama. Kalpana, like a jasmine that blooms silently and spreads its fragrance around, had infused my being with a new flavour. Saradamma had detected the attachment that was growing between Kalpana and myself and said, "Sivaraj, you have grown so intimate with us that I never feel that you are a stranger. That's why I would like to discuss something with you...."

"Please, tell me, madam."

"I'm worried only about one thing."

"Will you excuse me if I say something...."

"I have a distant relative of mine who wants to marry Kalpana. But, somehow, I don't consider him to be a good match for her. My daughter is very sensitive. One should be lucky to marry her."

"See madam, why not let me be that lucky man? Just one more year, I will complete my M.A. After that I will bring my father and finalize everything. Kalpana is like a flower. Her I will.... You should kindly agree to this."

Saradamma stood up silently and led me to the middle room and waved the wick lamp to the portrait of her late husband and gave it to me. While bowing to the portrait I touched Saradamma's feet instinctively. She lifted me up and caressed my head saying "Had he also seen you...."

"He is till alive in your eyes, madam."

Meanwhile Kalpana and Pratibha returned from the college and the school respectively. Pratibha burst out, 'Mama, Mama,' ran to me and hugged me affectionately. Saradamma called Kalpana and put the saffron mark on her forehead, "Kalpana, Sivaraj is really Pratibha's Mama from today. Just as he found Pratibha, he has found you also. I can understand your heart. Come on bow down to him." That day onwards Kalpana's childishness disappeared and she grew serious and like a candle lit in a corner, inspired all my activities with her words and behaviour. All of us used to go to the annual gathering of her college, or to our university function or to movies. One day with the pretext of seeing the University Botanical garden, Kalpana asked me, "Sivaraj, doesn't everything appear so cinematic?"

"Everything means?" I asked mischievously.

"Sometimes I fear"

I drew Kalpana to my side and said,

"You mean me."

She shut my mouth with her palm and said, "That's not the cause of my fear."

"Come on, tell me Kalpana."

"Had I not met you at all. What would have been my life? Where would you...Sivaraj?"

"Kalpana, there is no reason for you not to have me.... Don't think of imaginary fears. You are a very sentimental girl. You are a flower on a creeper meant for me, whereas I am a tree born to support it. Don't have even a remote idea of our separation. If that happens it means my death."

"And me? You are the earth of my life.... I have no other support except you." Tears trickled down her cheeks. I wiped her tears, and enheartened her by caressing her shivering hands and tidying her curls. The steadiness of her steps testified to her regain of confidence. Just within a few weeks after this event, there started the Rajakar Riot like a thunder. Just a few days after Nizam Shahi Farman came into power, the devoted nationalist and journalist Shobullakhan who regarded the Hindus and the Muslims as two eyes of the State was murdered. All the colleges and schools were closed down. Hence I returned to my village. The fierce communalism of Rajakars was rampant everywhere in the State. The entire civilian life was upset. Looting and raping were common. When the Indian army entered the Hyderabad State and hoisted the tricolour flag and the civilian life was restored to normalcy, I came to Hyderabad and stood before Kalpana's house in Gagan Mahal Road. I was shocked! Nobody knew where Saradamma had gone. I enquired all her friends and relatives. Some said that they might have gone back to Calcutta. Some others said they might have been victims of the Rajakars' Riot. I felt the earth under me was sinking, and the sky above me descend like a ceiling with a thud on my head. Kalpana, Pratibha, Saradamma! Kalpana, Kalpana. It is not possible to forget her in this life. I am still longing to meet her by some chance, even though ten years have elapsed now. She is rooted in my heart so deeply. Though so many years have gone by, her image is still green in my memory. I was breathing heavily in the midst of these fiery remembrances.

I heard the sound of somebody knocking on the door.

"Come in."

The bearer brought a tray with bread, butter and tea and kept them on the table. It was already seven o'clock. I hurriedly finished my tiffin and gave him the bill and mounted on my vehicle.

As the battering sound of the bike grew louder, the memories about Kalpana began to unwind themselves in my mind. As the bike was covering the distance, my restlessness was also increasing beyond control. The headlight of the bike was piercing the overwhelming darkness. The wind was blowing fiercely. The clouds were crowding in the sky as the memories about Kalpana were doing in my mind. As I came near Mehaboob Nagar, the motorbike began to jerk on the dark road and finally stopped. I got down the vehicle and checked up if there was some dirt in the petrol. But there was nothing wrong there. I mounted the motorbike again and kicked the pedal with all my force. But the vehicle didn't buz an inch. Meanwhile a few passers-by came and asked me, "What sir...does the vehicle refuse to move?"

"I don't know what's wrong with this. I checked up the petrol tank also. Every thing is O.K. there. What to do next?"

"Don't you worry sir, you just take it up another half a furlong and you will find a garage there in the corner," said one of them and went away. It started raining. I pushed my vehicle in the pouring rain up to the garage. As I came near it, the garage boy came up and led the vehicle to the shed and asked me to be seated on a bench.

"See, I have to reach Raichur tonight. If you could repair it...."

"The electricity has failed because of this wind and rain." The garage boy said and examined the vehicle with the help of a lantern. Meanwhile there came a person who not heeding me asked him, "Mehmood, what happened? Whose is this vehicle ?"

"Salam Saab. This gentleman sitting here...." "This is..." "Good evening. Don't know what's wrong with it. It happened so suddenly. I am Mr. Sivaraj... I was coming from Hyderabad... On the way to Raichur..."

"I remember to have seen you somewhere. Weren't you in Kachiguda...?"

"Exactly yes.... I did my Intermediate there...."

"Then you cannot recognize me, can you? I am Mohan...Mr. Sivaraj!"

"Ah, Mohan...you have changed so much.... Beside you have grown this beard also...."

"Already fifteen years have gone by. When I joined the Technical School at Secunderabad.... The rest of it later.... Come on. Your vehicle won't be ready tonight. You'll have to wait up to tomorrow morning.... You can stay here tonight. Come on let's go home...." His house stood on an ascent near the garage. Mohan went in, brought out a towel and a *lungi* and gave them to me. He said, "You dry up your head first. Come into my room and change your dress. Within ten minutes we covered the distance of fifteen years." "I may have to leave for Secunderabad any moment now, to attend to some car-bargain. There is still time, come on let us talk." Mohan told me many things summarily. As we were immersed in conversation, his wife entered the room and Mohan introduced her to me, "This is my wife Kalpana. Kalpana...this is Mr. Sivaraj.... I refer repeatedly to...my crony."

I felt as though I had been flung to the sky all of a sudden. The volcano about to erupt through Kalpana's eyes grew calm instantly. Hundreds of torches began to dazzle in my mind. This is...my...Kalpana...controlling my turbulence, I joined my palms to her and said, "Namaste." The tray in her hands began to shake and was about to fall down. Before that could happen, Mohan took it and kept it on the stool.

"Namaskar." Her voice sounded unfamiliar. Or was that suggestive?

"Kalpana, Sivaraj's vehicle had some trouble. This is what's meant by the unexpected. That this fellow should come to my garage after so many years!" "Very glad to meet you. He used tell me about you now and then. Please be seated. I'll come within a minute." While she was saying these words, the child crying from inside was heard. Kalpana stood up and went in.

"Is it your son?"

"No. Daughter. Her name is Sarada, her grandmother's."

"Her grandmother?"

"Sivaraj, that is a big story. That day, troubled by the Rajakars' Riot, these people got into my lorry in Hyderabad unexpectedly. Somehow we all escaped them and came here. Saradamma who had lost everything could not stand the sight of her youngest daughter being afflicted with typhoid. She died of heart attack. In the fit of the heart attack she tried to say something. But she couldn't speak; she had lost her power of speech. She just kept Kalpana's hands in mine. That's all. That was her last breath. Let it be. Why to bore you with all this? I'll come back within a few minutes. You please take some rest." After Mohan left the room I relaxed in the easy chair kept there in the corner. I felt as though my nerves were all splitting and my heart pounding. I felt as though my entire being was liquefying and sliding away from. Every moment I was being choked and sinking into an unknown abysm. I felt as though I was spinning in a whirlpool of emotions.

After a while, Mohan brought his little daughter and gave her to me. The five-year-old girl grew intimate with me within five minutes and started calling me, 'Mama, Mama' and began playing with me. "Did you see, how pretty is our Sarada ? She made you her Mama within no time," said Mohan. I picked up a small box from a large box. They were the same chessboard and coins that I had brought for them in the past. The King and the Queen were all together in the box. I picked them up and kept them in Sarada's hands and arranged the others on the chessboard. Thus I entertained the child. The Kings and Queens of the chess of my life were scattered in different places. One can bring together the scattered consorts in the chess. But can I...my Queen?

"Initially Kalpana had taught me this game. But later on I gave it up. Now I never play it. Sarada plays it now and then," said Mohan. Meanwhile Kalpana came, lifted Sarada in her arms and asked us to dinner.

While taking our food Mohan went on talking incessantly. But I remained silent. Once or twice at Mohan's suggestion Kalpana came and stood very near to me in order to serve *puri* to me. Kalpana appeared to have put on some flesh and looked better than before. Though the shocks of life had dimmed the fresh lustre of her eyes, they still exuded the calm and steady gleam of the moon devouring the storms and tempests. I had made little Sarada sit beside me. Somehow I hurried through my meal and got up. The old clock hung near the small dining table nearby struck ten. The horn of the car was heard outside. "Just a minute," said Mohan; "my friend from Secunderabad must have come...." He went out. I relaxed in the easy chair again. After cleaning the dining table, Kalpana came with little Sarada and asked her to hand over the *pan-bida* to Mama. I wanted to say something but I couldn't, somehow. I sighed and sighed. "Please take this *pan-bida*, Sir." Thinking that she might have remembered how I used to coax her to eat *pan-bida*, I asked her, "Where is that *pan-bida* and all? Mohan came in a hurry and said to Kalpana; "I must go to Secunderabad now. Sivaraj, I have to attend to a car-bargain. I'll return by tomorrow without fail. If I don't go now, that party will go to Calcutta. That was the agreement. I had asked them to send for me. They have come now. Please excuse me. Our boy is repairing your vehicle. You shall go only after I return tomorrow morning." Saying 'Tata' to everyone, Mohan kissed little Sarada and disappeared. I felt a choking sensation at having to experience this unexpected and embarrassing situation. The bed was prepared for me in the drawing room. The adjacent inner room was the bedroom for Mohan and Kalpana. With the child in her arms, Kalpana went to the front door and bolted it up. She came and told me, "You are very tired and drenched in the rain. Please take this rug. The rainwater leaks in here." She closed the window, went into her bedroom and shut the door. The zero bulbs that exuded the dim light in the corridor rendered the inner atmosphere unclear still. The rain poured as incessantly as the memories rushing from the womb of enveloping darkness. The lightning and thunders were interfering with the pouring rain. There was as if a competition between wind and rain, as result of which the window shutters were forced open and struck the walls. The irrevocable memories of my sweet life with Kalpana in the past rushed into my mind and interrogated my very existence. They pierced my breast and my entire body shook and sweated with fear. When the rushing wind slipped into my chest and whistled, the distant lightning winked at me like a ghost. I removed the rug given by Kalpana. I rubbed the sweat from my body and made a vain attempt of driving out the memories. I felt terribly hot and grew thirsty. In that dim darkness I stretched my hand for the water tumbler on the table. The tumbler slipped from my figures and fell down with a metallic ring. Awakened by this sound Kalpana came into my room and said, "My God, the window is still open."

"Let it be open, Kalpana. I am feeling very thirsty." Kalpana put on the light in the kitchen and fetched water for me. I quaffed it as though I was emptying all the memories into my gullet.

"Drn. Drn. Drn. Drn." The clock struck four.

"It's already four o'clock now. You didn't sleep properly." Kalpana was still standing. Though I wanted to ask her to be seated, words couldn't come out of my mouth.

"Sleep is a luxury for me," I said.

"Sivaraj?"

"Kalpana, Fate played such a strange game with us, didn't it?"

"Everything is the sport of Time," she stood near the stool.

"I have only one question to ask you."

"I myself am the only answer for that."

"It's not that. Are you happy?"

"Sivaraj, life has never given me a chance to think about happiness or sorrow. Nor had I the capacity to question the things that came my way. Hence I accepted life."

"Yes that's it. You accepted it. That's all."

"It's not merely that. That itself is life."

"Kalpana, no riddles please."

"Sivaraj, where's the riddle here? We come across so many things, whether it is natural, or inevitable or necessary; we come across so many kinds of persons. We compromise with them all in one way or the other. If we fail to do so, we see our life slides away from us. That's why I accepted life. And that itself, I think, is life, Nothing more to say, Sivaraj."

"Kalpana."

"I didn't learn these things in any school or college. Life... Life teaches everything. I never thought I would have the occasion to tell you these things after so many years. Anyhow I have narrated them to you. I am feeling relieved now." Meanwhile the cry of the child was heard inside. Kalpana hurried to the room. The pattering of the raindrops and the piercing wind had stopped. The silence in the room was intensified by the rhythmic tick tock of the clock. Kalpana was singing a lullaby to the child and putting her to sleep. Kalpana's words entered my ears and descended into each and every vein of my body. I felt sticky inside me and felt heavy. Experiencing a sinking and a floating sensation alternately I melted into the sound waves of Kalpana's lullaby.

The humid smell of the dim light exuding from the sticky

zero bulbs grew fragrant in the wind rushing from the window... I too was lulled.

I somehow felt released from some magical spell and lighter than flower and wind! All of a sudden Kalpana's cry hit my chest like a cricket ball which had missed its aim. "My God... Sarada...Sarada...?" Kalpana cried. I jumped up from my bed and rushed into her room. As she came out with the child in her arms and was about to collapse, I held her up tightly.

"Sivaraj, see there...a snake near the pillow."

"You come out first," I sent her out who was shivering all over. I searched in the room and picked up a rod with which I struck the snake, which was writhing restlessly in the corner. The snake was half-injured and recoiled back with a ferocious hiss. I struck it again and it fell flat with its tail flicking. The next moment it lay there dead like a rope and I lifted it up with the same rod and threw it into the gutter outside.

The darkness of the night was melting away as the silver light was creeping into the sky. When I went back to the door, Kalpana brought water for me and I washed my face and hand and feet. I took up the towel from Sarada's hands and rubbed my face and sat in the easy chair. Kalpana brought some tea for me. Her face was as serene as the morning sun. I sipped my tea staring at her and trying to decipher the feelings lurking out of her face. The jasmine sprouts were blown into the window and touched Kalpana's shoulders. Little Sarada, who stood beside me asked, "Mama, that flower," I lifted her in my arms, kissed her and stood her on the floor. I walked to the garage. The mechanic Mehmood said, "Salaam Saab, your vehicle is ready."

I thrust twenty rupees into his palm. "Our owner said this vehicle belonged to him. I don't want any money, sir" said he and returned the notes. I came back and saw Kalpana was sitting with her chin resting on her clasped hands. I said to her, "Sarada, I am going. See you." Kalpana said, "Why not wait until he comes? He may come any moment now. Had you not been here yesterday...."

"I did my part of duty. That's all.... Please tell Mohan.... I'll come some other time. My mother must be waiting for me since yesterday...."

"You must come...really?"

"I will, definitely. Otherwise, will Mohan keep quiet?"

"Please come without fail.... But...."

"Tell me, Kalpana."

"Not alone."

"O.K. is that all right? Sarada, Ta Ta!" I took the vehicle brought up to the door by Mehmood, mounted it and kicked the pedal. I changed the gear and started the motorbike. Drr. Drr. Drrrrrr.... I began to cover the distance. The speed of life stretched along the road was surpassing the speed of my vehicle.

□□□

5
BLOODBATH

KING DEVARAYA II was praised by one and all in Karnataka Kingdom to be a very wise man. His reputation had spread to the other kingdoms also. He had a son of his own who was extremely handsome and an expert in all the eighteen branches of learning. Prince Sivaraya — so he was called — used to spend most of his time in horse riding, hunting or swordplay with his companions. As he was extra-ordinarily handsome, he used to be stared at by girls with silent desire. The subjects of his kingdom used to imagine Sivaraya as the future king after his father and dream of happy days to come.

King Devaraya had a nephew also whom he had brought up as his own son ever since the latter had lost his father. Jayadeva — for so he was called — had totally forgotten his own late father and believed that King Devaraya was his father or even more than that. He was always treated on par with Prince Sivaraya. Both of them learnt their lessons in swordplay, horse riding and other martial arts from the same teacher. Sometimes King Devaraya used to treat Prince Jayadeva more affectionately than Prince Sivaraya. Prince Sivaraya used to feel jealous of his cousin and complain to his father secretly, "Father, do you think I am not your son? You always treat Jayadeva better than me. You never abuse him even when he commits blunders, whereas you punish me so severely even if I make the silliest mistakes. Why is that? Please tell me whether I am your son or not. If you don't like me, I'll bolt to the forest this very instant." Devaraya understood that his son was severely hurt by his fondness for Jayadeva. He smiled and walked near his son. He rested his palms on his son's shoulders, stared into his eyes and said, "My dear son, you are still young. You do not understand life yet. Your cousin Jayadeva is a forlorn who lost his parents in his childhood. He is after all my own brother's son. I, therefore, took up the moral responsibility of bringing him up until he can take care of himself. I show him special affection only because I want him not to feel the absence of his parents. With you I can be a little strict, because you are, after all, my son. You should not worry about these little things." He patted his son affectionately. Sivaraya understood the motive behind his father's behaviour with him and was convinced about it. The father told him further, "My son, please treat him as your own brother. Never be jealous of him." "All right, father," said Sivaraya and took his departure from the father's chamber.

Both Sivaraya and Jayadeva grew into handsome youths and lived like real brothers. One day they were riding their horses towards the forest for hunting. They overheard a few elderly gentlemen say, "Look, brothers should be like Sivaraya and Jayadeva. They are indeed ideals for our own children." Both the brothers looked at each other proudly and smiled. They were so happy to know that they had become models for others in their kingdom. Jayadeva who heard the public appreciation of his behaviour would thank his uncle King Devaraya for treating him with excellent care and affection. "He has never hurt me or denied anything to me," said he to himself. Similarly King Devaraya felt a sense of moral satisfaction to know that he had not discriminated between his son and nephew.

A couple of years went by quite peacefully and harmoniously like this. King Devaraya kept himself busy with his Sanskrit learning. The royal tutors used to come to his chamber and read out the texts loudly and explicate their significance patiently. The king had appointed twenty Ministers in order to facilitate the administration of the Kingdom. It was customary for a king to appoint only one Minister who could take care of the entire administration of the kingdom. But King Devaraya's appointment of several Ministers had created a controversy among the courtiers and laity. Many had laughed at the King's style of working and called him an impractical fool. But there were at least a few who admired his learning and idealism. King Devaraya had a working knowledge of astrology also.

One day one of his Ministers came to his palace and saluted him. The king asked him to be seated and enquired, "Dear Minister sir, what is the matter? Is everything all right in our Kingdom?" The Minister grew a little hesitant and said, "Everything is all right, Your Highness, except… something." He began to rub his palms. King Devaraya knit his brows and asked him, "What's that 'except something' sir? Your answer indeed puzzles me." Again the Minister sat at the edge of his seat rather nervously and mumbled, "I don't know how to express it, Your Highness. It is indeed a little delicate for me to convey it. One of our spies has brought the news today." Again the King's curiosity was aroused further. He sat up erect on his throne clasping the armrests firmly. He asked the Minister rather impatiently, "What's the matter sir? Please tell me. Why do you hide it from me?" The Minister cleared his throat and said, "It is a bit embarrassing for me to convey the news. Yet it is my duty to do so." King Devaraya was growing restless to hear the news. The Minister continued, "Your Highness, our spies have collected the shocking news that your nephew Jayadeva does not cherish affectionate feeling towards you in the heart of his heart, although he pretends to revere you outwardly. I, therefore, request Your Highness to be careful with him." The Minister remained silent because of fear. He did not know how the King would react to the news. King Devaraya contemplated about the news for a few seconds. The Minister sat watching him intently. Then the King relaxed into a smile and said, "Don't you worry about this news, sir. It must be the result of loose talk in the city. Jayadeva has trusted me as more than his father. He cannot have any ill-will towards me as I have never discriminated against him." The Minister was disarmed by the King's answer and did not know what to say further. He, therefore stood up and joined his palms in salutation to the King and said, "Your Highness, kindly forgive me for this news." King Devaraya leant against the back of his throne and assured, "Don't you worry about that sir. You have done your duty." Then the Minister walked out of the royal chamber silently.

A couple of months elapsed. King Devaraya immersed himself in his studies as usual. There was no disturbance whatever in the kingdom. The service in the temple was going on regularly and the brahmin priests used to be fed profusely. The King, therefore, steeped himself deeply in the study of religion and philosophy etc. His nephew was senior to his own son by about three years and lived in a separate palace away from his uncle's. Now Jayadeva had attained puberty and started ogling at girls around him curiously. King Devaraya's wife had suggestively conveyed this news to him who had taken it into his stride. He had said to his wife about his nephew, "If he cannot ogle at girls at this age, when do you think, he should?" The Queen had remained silent about it ever after. One morning King Devaraya was wading through a holy book in his chamber. Suddenly an attender bowed himself in and announced the arrival of a messenger from Jayadeva. The King allowed the messenger to be admitted. The messenger entered the chamber and bowed down to the King ceremoniously and said, " Your Highness, I have been sent by Prince Jayadeva. Since he is getting married today, he has requested you to send your son (Prince Sivaraya) and the Ministers to the wedding in his palace. He has requested Your Highness not to disappoint him in this regard." The messenger bowed once again to the King and took his departure. The King closed the holy book and deliberated inwardly, "The young Prince has lost his father and trusted me totally. Now it is my duty to treat him like my own son. Discriminating between my own son and him would be really a great sin. My conscience never allows that." He clapped twice and an attender rushed in instantly. He ordered him to fetch Prince Sivaraya. The attender bowed himself out of the chamber. After a few minutes Prince Sivaraya walked into the royal chamber with a smile and asked, "Why did you send for me, Father? What's the matter?" The

King answered, "There is nothing serious. Your cousin Prince Jayadeva has sent a message this morning that he is getting married today in his palace. He has requested me to send you along with our Ministers to the marriage feast." Hearing these words Prince Sivaraya grew a bit serious. For a moment he sat speechless. Then he made bold to say, "But, Father, he has been so jealous of me all these days that I don't feel like going there." King Devaraya bent a little forward and said in a confidential tone, "Look son, this jealousy and other petty feelings are all passing phases. One should not make much ado about them. You must forget these things on such happy occasions. When you get married, he also will have to attend it." Prince Sivaraya grew helpless by listening to the paternal advice. "All right, Father," said he, "I'll do as you wish." "Well, that's good, my son. That is the right spirit. You would take all our Ministeres also with you. That's the protocol," said King Devaraya. Prince Sivaraya agreed to oblige his father and left the chamber.

Devaraya thought inwardly that he could have the entire kingdom for himself if he could finish off his cousin and uncle in a surprise fashion. He, therefore, instructed his soldiers to hide themselves in the dining hall and attack the guests when they are at dinner table. The Commander in charge of the soldiers accordingly guided them as to how to accomplish everything systematically. But outside the palace big pandals were erected. The drum players and *shahnayi* players were playing a variety of tunes from the morning itself. The servants were busily moving about on the palace precincts. The citizens were slowly trickling into the palace compound.

Prince Sivaraya and the Ministers entered the marriage pandal. Their servants carried big baskets and boxes of clothes, gold and silver to be gifted to the bride and groom. The whole palace was humming with the talking of the crowd, punctuated by giggling and shouting. Prince Sivaraya and the Ministers were shown their seats near the central porch which was decorated with mango leaves, stripped silk and flowers. The bride and groom were conducted to the central porch where they went round the fire five times. The pot-bellied priest was giving them a chain of instructions. At last the groom tied the sacramental *tali* around the bride's neck by saying the Sanskrit mantra : *dharme cha arthe cha kame cha naticharami.* As the priest raised the pitch of his voice and chanted the last tag of mantra: *sumuhurte savadhana,* the crowed stood up and blessed the couple by sprinkling the sacramental *aksata* upon them. The drum and *shahnayis* outside the porch sounded loudly to match the jubilation inside. Prince Sivaraya's left eye was throbbing incessantly and he could not say why. Nonetheless he tried to ignore it as he was participating in a wedding ceremony. The royal servants were requesting the gathering in a loud voice to partake of the feast arranged in the large pandals. The people, accordingly, began to rush towards the dining halls. The marriage feast for the royal members was arranged in a separate hall of the palace. Prince Sivaraya and his Ministers were courteously conducted towards the dining hall by the royal hosts.

They walked into the corridor where they unbuckled their swords, daggers and hung them on the pegs there. They entered the large dining hall and sat on the wooden seats arranged in a row. They took off their turbans and jewel-studded caps. Then the servants brought silver plates and kept them before the visitors. Another group of servants began to serve sweet cakes and pickles etc. Prince Sivaraya looked around the hall, which was hung over with curtains at all the doors. He somehow felt that the servants who were serving the food were not as jubilant as they ought to be. Nevertheless when all the major dishes were served, the guests were requested to partake of the feast. Accordingly, they started tasting the delicacies. Meanwhile the main door through which they had entered was closed and bolted from outside. Still the guests did not take much notice of that as they were rapt in eating. As a few minutes went by, there was heard outside a sudden scramble. Prince Sivaraya was trying to guess as to what the matter might be. But lo! Before he could concretize his guess, there appeared a few soldiers with swords in hands and began to hack the guests who were eating the feast.

Few guests whose heads were severed mercilessly just sagged on the floor. Blood spattered around in the dining hall. The others who were panic-stricken by the unexpected attack stood up and tried to avoid the swords of the enemies. Prince Sivaraya who was also disarmed like his co-diners stood helplessly watching the situation. It did not take him long to realize that they had been systematically trapped. The enemies were hacking down the Ministers and other guests monstrously. He was shocked to see that his own cousin Jayadeva was leading the soldiers. Jayadeva's eagle eyes detected Prince Sivaraya and he instantly rushed towards the latter with his drawn sword. Prince Sivaraya who had no weapon in his hand did not know how to react. Nonetheless he picked up a plate and defended himself against Jayadeva who was striking at him with his sword. When Prince Sivaraya was holding the plate to ward off Jayadeva's sword, someone else stabbed him in the back which loosened his grip of the plate which fell down to the floor with a rattling sound. As Prince Sivaraya began to oscillate now, Jayadeva lost no time in dashing his sword into the former's belly. Prince Sivaraya yelled piteously, suffered a sudden blackout of consciousness. He sagged on the heap of other corpses. Life ebbed out of him slowly as his body lay there twitching and convulsing.

The laymen who were having their feast in the spacious pandal did not know what had happened to the Captains and Ministers in the dining hall of the palace.

Prince Jayadeva thought, "I have finished a majority of fellows. Now I must do away with that old fellow of an uncle also, so that I can be the monarch of this Kingdom." He, therefore, asked one of his confidants to dip a small dagger into deadly poison. The confidant, accordingly, brought an earthen pot of poison and dipped the blade of a dagger into it. Prince Jayadeva put the dagger in a golden bowl and asked his servants to take it along with him. He jumped and sat in the saddle and whipped the horse, which began to trot in a slow rhythm. The other horses of the servants followed suit.

King Devaraya reclined against the silken pillow beside one of his queens. She was smearing lime on areca leaves for her lord. "Sir, you have seen how your nephew got himself married. Should you not think of your own son's marriage at least now?" asked the Queen. "Don't you worry darling," replied the King, "we shall think of it very soon." He received the *pan* prepared by her and put it into his mouth and began to chew it slowly. He drew her to his side and hugged her tightly. A maidservant entered the chamber and announced the arrival of a messenger. The Queen stood away from the King in embarrassment. The King allowed the messenger to be let in. Within a few seconds the messenger bowed himself in and said "Your Highness, Prince Jayadeva has come to offer you a golden bowl as custom demands. He has requested Your Highness to accept it." The King felt pleased by the affectionate gesture shown by his nephew. He told the messenger, "Please ask him to wait in our *durbar* hall. I shall come there within a few seconds." The messenger bowed himself out. The King turned towards the Queen and said, "See how much affection my nephew has for me!" The Queen remained very silent. The King donned his royal gown and secured it with a belt. A small sword hung at his left side from the belt. He walked towards the *durbar* hall. As he entered it, Prince Jayadeva also entered there with a plate on which a golden bowl was placed. There were no guards around as it was a happy and private meeting. King Devaraya looked affectionately at his nephew but the latter had a studied smile on his lips. King Devaraya said, "O my son, please come." Prince Jayadeva said in a pretentious fashion, "I have come to offer this golden bowl to Your Highness." King Devaraya stood in a relaxed manner. Prince Jayadeva took up the golden bowl from the silver plate but before offering it to the King, he picked up the dagger hidden in the bowl and attacked the King. King Devaraya was flabbergasted by the unexpected and ungrateful act of his nephew. Nevertheless he grew alert and drew out his own sword and began to fend off. He yelled, " You scoundrel. Is this the gift you have come to give me?" He swished his sword with all his might and attacked his nephew. As Jayadeva tried to stab him, King Devaraya jumped and ducked and turned sideways and twisted. As the duel progressed, the anger in King Devaraya burst out suddenly. Fired by the release of all the latent energy in him, the King drew up his sword and struck it with full sway upon the enemy's neck. And lo! The head was severed from the trunk and thumped upon the floor bespattering blood all around. The trunk slumped on the floor in a pool of blood. King Devaraya was panting heavily. He said to himself, "I never knew this scoundrel had such intentions inside him. Had he had some power he would have definitely murdered me long back. I don't know what happened to my son who had gone to the wedding." He instantly rushed out to the horse-shed. He untethered a white horse and rode towards Jayadeva's palace.

He lashed his horse in order to reach the palace at the earliest. He entered the compound of the palace. The citizens were going in and out of the pandal. King Devaraya went straight to the dining hall inside the palace. He did not pay any attention to the salute of the guards there. He unbolted the door of the hall and lo he saw the disfigured cadavers of his ministers and captains in a chaotic fashion. Tears gushed out of his eyes incessantly. A wild fire began to burn inside him. He waded through the corpses to find out whether his darling son also was there. Lo! He saw the mangled body of Prince Sivaraya whose head lay beside it. As he saw it a conflagration swept through his entire body. He burst out, "My darling son, where did you go? What shall I tell your mother?" Tears gushed out of his eyes and momentarily blinded his vision. He caressed the cheeks of his son and cried like a child. He, then, mustered up his strength of soul and tore himself away from the dining hall, which had become a funeral hall as it were. He rode back to his palace and broke the news gently to his Queen who fell on the floor and set up a wail. All the womenfolk of the harem gathered around the Queen and began to cry and sob.

King Devaraya sent for the royal officers and ordered them to arrange the funeral of all the massacred captains, ministers and the prince. The officers accordingly made the funeral arrangements that very day. The next day the King sent for his Commander. After a few minutes the Commander bowed himself into he royal chamber and said, "Your Highness, may I know the order?" The King ordered him in a determined tone, "Commander sir, please see to it that all the fellows at Jayadeva's palace who were involved in this treachery are arrested and punished properly." The Commander said, "Your Highness, I shall attend to it forthwith." He bowed down again to the King and walked out from the chamber. Then the royal physician arrived there and began to bandage the wounds of the King.

6

The Circle of Vengeance

NAGAPPA WENT to the Bus Stand with a heavy wooden box, which belonged to some Tahasildar saheb of Naragund taluk. He was gasping for breath because of the heavy load on his head. As he went to the Bus Stand building, he asked the Tahasildar saheb to help him to unload the box from his head. The Tahasildar threw his umbrella to the ground and lifted the box and then together they lowered it down. Nagappa took the towel away from his head and wiped the sweat off his forehead and began to take long breaths. The Tahasildar saheb took out a rupee coin from the inside pocket of his black coat and gave it to Nagappa who took it and saluted to him and went away. Nagappa who was clad in the dusty blue uniform prescribed for the *hamals* straightened his limbs and stepped towards the Udupi canteen in the Bus-Stand building. He sat in a corner and ordered for a plate of potato-*bonda*. Nagappa was down in the face because he had lost all his day's earning in the game of cards the previous day. That was the reason why he had felt helpless that day. When he had gone to the house of Chandrasani for the night he had tried to forget his sorrow in the arms of the pretty prostitute. But after the rendezvous was over, Chandrasani had snatched away his watch when he told her that he would pay her the next night. His humiliation was unimaginable. He had come out of her house and had rushed straight to Parasuram's toddy shop, drank as much as he liked and forgot all the bitterness of the day. Parasuram who was kind hearted, offered the toddy on credit. Sometimes Nagappa's earning of Rs. 10 per day was sufficient to meet his day's expenditure. Because he had to spend for his tea, for his food, for his toddy, for his game of cards and for his women and for his *bidis.* Thus in the evening he used to become a pauper. Nagappa's stream of memories was disturbed when the waiter brought the plate of potato-*bonda* and a cup of water and kept them on the table. Nagappa who was monstrously hungry, devoured it within no time. He decided to change the house that night. He wanted to visit Bhimasani instead of Chandrasani whose rude behaviour he did not like. "She is a bitch," said he to himself and ordered a plate of *uppittu.* He finished it, drank his tea and came out of the canteen. He bought a bundle of Ganesh *bidi* and began to puff at it. Nagappa spent the entire day in carrying the loads from the Bus-Stand to the market and *vice versa.* That day he did not feel like joining the game of cards at the Temple of Sankaralinga. He did not know how to spend his evening. He, therefore, went to visit Bhimasani who received him cordially and satisfied the wild hunger of his body. Amply pleased by her amicable behaviour he paid her a rupee extra and came out. He decided not to drink that day. So he went to his room and slept there. Though he had put off the kerosene lamp and closed his eyes, he could not stop the rush of memories. He realized that he had spent his money and energy very recklessly and that man has no place in the society if he has no money. So Nagappa decided to become a 'man' by making money somehow or the other. He decided to get married and settle down in life. He did not know when he fell asleep.

He got up the next morning. He bathed hurriedly, went to the Temple of Sankaralinga, saw the early morning worship, paid his homage to the deity, came back to his room, donned his coarse cotton *dhoti* and Nehru-shirt. Nagappa went to the Bus-Stand and told his colleagues like Siddya, Ningayya and Hussain that he was leaving the town for good and was going to make his fortune in some village. The colleagues were touched by his words and encouraged him to go ahead. They took him to a hotel, offered him *sira, masala dosa* and tea and wished him well. Nagappa hugged them and bid farewell to them. With a small cotton bag in his hand he set on foot to Jagapur which was three miles from Naragund. As there was no bus route to the village, he had to go along the cart-track. Nearly two hours had elapsed when he reached Jagapur.

Jagapur was a notorious village in the entire taluk of Naragund. It was known for rowdyism, party conflicts and murders. That was the reason why the people of other villages used to be extremely afraid of the natives of Jagapur who were supposed to be potential murderers. Nagappa had heard all about the village and decided to make the best use of the golden opportunities there. Nagappa himself was known for his heroism at Naragund. He had the privilege of visiting the Police Station many a time. He realized that the atmosphere of the village was quite agreeable to his temperament. He became the leader of half a dozen rowdies and began to enjoy the prestige of his position. One of the distinctive features of Jagapur was a piece of land of nearly twenty acres, which was not accounted for in the village registers. There was no owner for that piece of land. According to the prevailing convention in the village the greatest rowdy would become the owner of that land and enjoy its dividends until he is murdered or defeated by another rowdy. Nagappa jumped at the opportunity. With the help of his half a dozen rowdies, he vanquished the present owner of the public piece of land and became the master of the same. He married a local girl called Parvatevva of a poor family and settled down in life. The notable factor about Nagappa was that though he was the unrivalled master of that piece of land, he had not maintained the agricultural paraphernalia like the oxen, bullock-cart and plough-shares etc. It was left for his disciple-rowdies to manage the same. Thus Nagappa had grown into the uncrowned king of the Kingdom of Jagapur. One more peculiarity of Nagappa's family was that he owned two cows. But he was not in the habit of tying them in the cattle-shed. He would let them free so that they could go into anybody's field and feed themselves bellyful. Nobody had the guts to question or to antagonize Nagappa. It was the question of life and death for the natives of Jagapur. That was why they would rather keep quiet than be the objects of Nagappa's hatred.

One day the two cows belonging to Nagappa's household went on feeding themselves in the fields of the villagers. At last they entered somebody's field and began to eat the green paddy of white jowar. The owner of the field who was sitting in the hut erected on the elevated scaffolding saw the crops being disfigured by the stray cows. He was irritated beyond measure. He gnashed his teeth and said, "These bloody cows!" He jumped out of the hut and leaving his wife there he ran to chase the cows with his whip. But the cows greedy of the green paddy went on running about the field and could not be driven out. The owner of the field grew more exasperated. He, therefore, ran back to his hut and brought the axe with a sharp edge. He walked towards the cows gently without making any noise and by ducking his head behind the jowar-stalks. Thus he slowly went behind one of the cows, raised his axe and brought it down heavily on it. The edge of the axe did not fall on the body of the cow but it separated the tail of the cow from the body. The blood spurted out and the axe was besmeared with it. Instantly the cow set up a pitiable howl and began to run away from the field. It was followed by its companion.

The cows came home, but one of them had lost her tail and the blood was oozing out of the wound. Nagappa's anger shot up to his brain and he began to boil with rage. He wanted to punish the villager who had dared to wound his cow. He summoned his companion-rowdies who came with axes and sickles in their hands. Nagappa went with his relatives around the village. He would go and stand before each house and shout, "Who has wounded my cow? Come out if you really are men." But none dared to come out. Thus he went from house to house and could not find anyone daring enough to face him. Bored by the lack of antagonism by the villagers, Nagappa returned home. But he had felt happy inwardly to know that nobody could be cross with him and that he had become the unrivalled hero of the village.

Adjacent to Nagappa's land of twenty acres, there was a piece of two acres belonging to Huchchappa. Nagappa had merged those two acres also into his own land. Embittered by the illegal encroachment of land, the poor farmer Huchchappa went to the lawyer called Dharmappa who was a native of Jagapur but who worked at the District Court of Dharwad. Lawyer Dharmappa was sitting with his other clients in the office-room of his house. Huchchappa saluted to him and narrated how Nagappa had encroached upon his land and all that. Lawyer Dharmappa was overjoyed to hear the case. For he was fed up with Nagappa's rowdyism in the village, but he could not accuse the latter because of his own professional preoccupation at Dharwad. But nonetheless he was waiting for some excuse or the other to involve him in some crime and teach him a lesson. He, therefore, cocked his ears and listened to all that Huchchappa had to say carefully. Huchchappa completed his words by saying, "You are like a god for the poor like me. Kindly save me from this danger, and get back my land for me." Lawyer Dharmappa was really touched by this imploration. "Don't you worry, Huchchappa, I will take care of him. Be patient and have faith in God and every thing will be all right." Huchchappa, overwhelmed with a sense of gratitude to the lawyer, prostrated before him and said, "I have sought your help. Drown me or save me. You are a god for me." Huchchappa was feeling confident now because of the promised help.

In the evening Lawyer Dharmappa put on his black coat and tie. Though the lawyer's suit was not necessary in the village, he was habituated to that. Huchchappa came at the appointed time. Together they went to Nagappa's house and knocked at the door and entered the room. Nagappa was drinking toddy with his followers and cracking ribald jokes. His eyes were reddish. Thus everybody there was fuddled with drinks. When Nagappa saw Huchchappa with the lawyer, he was a little puzzled. Everybody seemed to be frozen for a moment. Lawyer Dharmappa fixed his eyes on Nagappa and pointing his finger at him said, "Nagappa, you have encroached upon this poor fellow's land. That is illegal. You won't get any profit from the poor man's land. Don't harass the poor Huchchappa." As Nagappa listened to his words he felt as though somebody had hammered a peg into his ears. He grew wild with anger. He pointed his finger to the lawyer and shouted, "Don't tell me any thing, fool. Address yourself to my *chappals* at the door," and burst into a guffaw. Lawyer Dharmappa had never been insulted like this before. How could a famous lawyer like him be humiliated by an ordinary village *gunda* like Nagya? Lawyer Dharmappa shouted at the highest pitch of his voice, "You fool. Don't call me a lawyer if I did not take away that piece of land from you." Nagappa's wrath knew no bounds. Nobody in the village had ever dared to insult him like that. Nagappa shouted at the top of his voice, "Don't call me Nagappa if I did not hack you and sleep with your wife." Dharmappa's head began to reel with anger. He could not accept Nagya's challenge like a dumb sheep. He too, therefore, retorted, "Don't call me Dharmappa, if I did not hack you and sleep with your wife." Having sworn thus Dharmappa went back with Huchchappa. Huchchappa's heart was pounding like a machine and he did not know what turn the enmity was going to take.

The hatred between Nagappa and Dharmappa led to the formation of two parties in Jagapur. Both the parties began to dislike each other more and more actively and religiously. Each party began to conspire against the other. Both the parties had about forty members each. In course of time the people of Dharmappa's party murdered two of Nagappa's party-members on the banks of Hirehalla. The culprits were sent to jail but Lawyer Dharmappa had had them released by using his good offices and legal knowledge. Thus Lawyer Dharmappa had provided a matching rivalry for Nagappa. Dharmappa knew that the hatred renewed by the murder of the two disciples of Nagappa was going to spark off greater conflict. Therefore, he thought he should be careful about his own life. Immediately he went to Dharwad and bought a revolver. He began to keep the revolver with him throughout the day.

One day Dharmappa came to Navalagund where he saw a person belonging to Nagappa's gang. Dharmappa was seized with wrath. He followed the enemy in the market. The enemy caught sight of him and was staring at the lawyer contemptuously. Dharmappa did not like the devilish gaze of the enemy. He went away along the road leading to Nilavva's Tank and came back from the hillside road. He took out his revolver and shot at the enemy still loitering in the clothes market. The sound of the shot shocked the public and lo, the people gathered around the man whose chest was besmeared with blood and who had sagged to the earth. Dharmappa rushed back to his home at Dharwad. No sooner had Nagappa heard this news than he sued the lawyer to the court. The case was registered in the Court of Navalagund. But the shrewd Dharmappa bribed all the judges and lawyers who happened to be his friends and got himself free and escaped the legal punishment.

By this time, Kalinga, the son of the murdered man, had attained majority. A youth of hot blood as he was, he decided to avenge the murder of his father. He took an oath to murder the lawyer. Having had an inkling of this news, Dharmappa grew over-cautious. As days and months passed by, the members of Dharmappa's party went on murdering those of Nagappa's party. Thus Nagappa had to undergo a lot of humiliation as a result of his bad luck. Nagappa's wealth began to dwindle. Because of the maintenance of nearly forty members of his party, Nagappa's heavy purse went on growing thinner and thinner everyday. Nagappa closed all the three canteens of his ownership because of his inability to manage them. He was compelled to sell the entire herd of his sheep. Even then he had not enough money to maintain his followers. Now that he had lost his stature as a hero and been reduced to the level of an ordinary man, the members of his gang were losing their attraction for him. Slowly they began to forsake him and join Dharmappa's group one by one. Thus ultimately Nagappa was left with only four to five loyal servants. Dharmappa's party had grown bigger than Nagappa's now.

One day the members of Dharmappa's party wanted to materialize their gratitude to their master. They, therefore, came to him and made a clean breast of their intentions. They said they were solid in their intention to murder Nagappa. They narrated their plan to him, "Master, we have thought of a plan. We will succeed in our task if your kind self agree to it. Please listen. We will pretend to leave your party and join Nagappa's party and speak ill of you before him. Having thus taken him into our confidence we will one day bring him out of the village. You should wait with your revolver there near the bridge." They further narrated how the task should be accomplished very intelligently. Thus according to the pre-planned scheme, many of them joined Nagappa's party and went on pretending hatred for Dharmappa. Nagappa felt ecstatic at the turn of his good luck. Hardly had they spent three days when they brought Nagappa outside the village. Nagappa did not have the slightest doubt about the bonafides of his disciples. They had inserted only three cartridges in Nagappa's revolver and had secretly asked Dharmappa to escape them. When Nagappa came out of the village, he happened to see Dharmappa seated on the bridge. Lo, his hatred was instantly switched on. Nagappa held his revolver and shot at the lawyer. Dharmappa escaped the first bullet. Then Nagappa grew furious and shot the second bullet. Now Dharmappa escaped to the left side and escaped that also. Nagappa grew wilder still and aimed at the enemy and shot the third bullet. This time the bullet hit a hawthorne tree and the lawyer escaped once again. Nagappa lost all his zest and grew utterly helpless. He threw away his revolver and shouted at Dharmappa, "You fool, my reign in Jagapur has come to an end today," and started running away with his five loyal servants. In those days there was no regular government bus-service to Jagapur. Nagappa wanted to board a private taxi going towards Navalagund. But before he could do that, he was attacked by Dharmappa's followers. They dragged him from inside the taxi. Nagappa fell on his back on the earth and before he could get up, someone in the group dealt a heavy blow with a big axe. The axe fell on Nagappa's forehead and the bleeding skin turned down and fell on his eyes and blinded him. Nagappa's body sagged to the earth. Dharmappa's followers thought him to be dead and began to rush to their village. Hardly had they gone twenty steps away from Nagappa than they heard him groaning. They were angered beyond measure to know that he was not yet dead. They, therefore, returned with furious minds and hacked his throat and separated his head from the bust. Then as though to crown their murderous achievement, they hacked his phallus and stuffed it into the mouth of the disconnected head. After the accomplishment of the glorious task, the triumphant murderers went back to Jagapur. When they were busy burning the blood-stained garments of the murdered one in Dharmappa's house, the sound of knocking on the door was heard. Three police vans had come to Jagapur from Dharwad. Dharmappa could easily guess that they were none else but the policemen. Dharmappa did not open the door but told them that people were having their meals inside and he asked them to wait for a while. He arranged to feed the policemen also simultaneously in a neighbouring house. After everybody had finished his meal, the police constables adorned the hands of the culprits with shackles and took them to the Police Station at Dharwad. They were all accused of murdering Nagappa and a murder case was registered against them. They were all put behind the bars. But hardly had they spent two days in the lock-up than they were released because of Lawyer Dharmappa's influence and dynamism. Now Lawyer Dharmappa had incontrovertibly become the uncrowned king and unrivalled hero of Jagapur. The people began to fear him, revere him and love him simultaneously. Lawyer Dharmappa had a sense of relief and began to behave with a sense of abandon. He came to be endowed with the title of THE MURDERER OF THE ROWDY NAGAPPA.

Kalinga, who was aged twenty-five, was the son of a villager belonging to Nagappa's party. Kalinga had not forgotten how and why his father was shot dead by Lawyer Dharmappa at Navalagund. He was sharpening his dagger secretly. Once there was a fair of the temple of Lord Kalmeswara. The people of surrounding villages like Hunasikatti, Benakoppa and Kalakeri had flocked to the place. The Divine Car (*Teru*) was adorned with colourful pennants and mango leaves. Some touring shops were erected near the temple. There was a lot of hustle-bustle around there. All the men, women and children were rigged in their best garments. In the evening there was a play to be enacted by the Halageri Theatrical Company. The play started about eight o'clock at night. The stage pandal was erected across the road in front of the temple. People had sat on the road, on the platforms of the houses, on the roofs and on the trees. The play continued up to 2 o'cock at night. After the play was over, the villagers went home. As the weather was very stuffy that night many of them slept in the open air. Lawyer Dharmappa also planned to sleep outside the house on the platform. Dharmappa's wife somehow did not like it. Besides, her right eye was throbbing. She therefore implored him to sleep inside. But Dharmappa did not listen to her. He spread his blanket on the platform outside and relaxed there. Kalinga was waiting for the golden opportunity. Hardly had an hour passed when Kalinga came with an axe and hacked the sleeping Dharmappa. There was a big uproar in the village. The admirers of Dharmappa accorded a grand funeral to their beloved leader. The next day Kalinga was arrested and put behind the bars at Dharwad jail. He has been spending his days there ever since his imprisonment.

7
FELICITATION

I WAS sleeping in the bedroom after the feast of Sravan Monday. My wife and daughters were still having their meals in the kitchen. As I had finished, I was feeling heavy and began chewing *pan* and betel the sharp taste of which soothed my nerves. As I felt sleepy, I decided to postpone the reading of the famous book on anthropology by Dr. K. Iswaran and went to the bedroom and relaxed on the bed. I felt as though I was sinking in the water of peace. I was overwhelmed by that peaceful quietude. I do not remember how many hours had passed by the time when my wife came and bore her fingers into my flanks and turned me this side and that. I felt my peaceful harmony was torn to pieces. I could not help opening my eyes however unwillingly though it may be. My wife brought her face near mine and whispered, "See, there are some guests who have come to meet you." I was rather irritated by the arrival of the unwanted guests at an odd time. The extreme heat of the sun added to my irritation. I rushed to the bathroom, washed my face, donned the nehru-shirt, wound the lungi around my waist and came out to the front room. I said to them, "Good afternoon," out of formality. All the three of them stood up to suggest their respect for me. I asked them to be seated. Two of them were clad in *dhoti* and cotton shirts and one of them had worn trousers and a black coat. I could easily guess from the mustaches of the *dhoti*-clad gentlemen that they had come from some village. I asked them mechanically, "Where do you come from?" They seemed to be ecstatic of being talked to by me. Two of them enthusiastically said, "We have arrived from Channagiri, sir." "O, I see!" I said and grinned at them. They confirmed it by saying

"Yes sir, yes, sir." They seemed to be nervous and delighted at the same time. Meanwhile my practical self advised me to treat the guests with due respect and all that. I, therefore, got up, went into the kitchen and asked my wife, "Sasi, prepare some tea for the guests." I came back and joined the guests and began to gossip with them. We talked at random about the skyrocketing prices of sugar and cereals, the farmers' strikes, the false statements of ministers, the literature of the down-trodden (*dalits*) and protest (*bandaya*) etc. Meanwhile my wife called me from inside the kitchen. I went in and brought the tray (because our servant was away at the market) and asked them to help themselves. All the four of us sipped the tea and began to sweat heavily in the afternoon heat. The clock struck one and we turned our eyes at it and found it was 3.30 P.M. Now that all the formalities were completed, I took liberty to ask them as to why they had come to see me. I mechanically held the steel cup of aniseed for them to pick it up. They were staring at each other and hesitant to speak. At last the two gentlemen clad in *dhoti* beckoned to the man in black-coat to speak on their behalf. He, therefore, cleared his throat and said, "We are going to arrange a function in our town. We have, therefore, come to invite you for the same, Sir," and grinned. All the three began to gane at me expectantly. I began to deliberate the matter in my mind. Somehow I was not feeling up to it. But at the same time I did not want to keep them waiting for an answer. I, therefore, asked them as to the nature of the function they had proposed to arrange. The coat-clad person told me overenthusiastically that they wanted to arrange a grand literary function and surpass the neighbouring towns. I was amused by their intention. I said, "See, dear friends, if you desire to arrange a grand function, it would bc appropriate for you to invite the writers who have received many awards from the State and Central Governments. Why have you selected me of all the writers?" They seemed discouraged to hear my words. But one of the *dhoti*-clad men ventured to say, "No Sir, we do not intend to invite the writers of the far-off districts. We have decided to honour the writer of our own region by arranging a felicitation function. We have come all the way from our town to invite you. We have even advertised your name in the local papers. We hope, you won't disappoint us." He finished his words and joined his palms in supplication. My sense of irritation was slowly melting into sympathy. Because I was moved by his appeal. I had somehow decided not to go there alone. But before giving them my final decision, I tried to exercise another trick. I said, "In case you want to invite the writers of our region, why do you single me out? You may as well invite the other writers like the Nature-poet who resides at Kalyananagar or the exponent of Dalit literature who resides at Malamaddi? Before I finished the sentence I saw their faces were glowing with lustre. The coat-clad man instantly said, "We have already approached them, sir. They have agreed to come to our town. We request you also to accompany them." The moment I heard him refer to the other two guests, I began to feel some attraction for the function. I thought I could have nice time with them and decided to avail myself of the opportunity. But I did not want to betray my eagerness to go to their town. I said to them, "In that case, you will have two distinguished guests for your function. You can manage with those two. Why then do you want *me* there? I am not an active worker in the Dalit Movement. I am an old fashioned writer producing ordinary novels and stories. How do you justify my presence there?" For a moment they all remained silent. But the *dhoti*-clad person said, "We will be all the more happy to have you amidst us. Though you are not a member of the Dalit Movement or Progressive Literature, you are a senior writer. You have shown us your concern for the social evils in your novels. You have been a champion of the downtrodden without having the fascinating labels on your head. That is the reason why your novel was awarded the Great Russian Award. We deem ourselves really lucky to have you bless us, sir." I was surprised at the intellectual sharpness of the apparently simple-looking man. I had to revise my opinion about him and consequently began to respect him for his intelligence. I also felt elated secretly to hear myself being recognized and praised by the public. I thought that my novels had not failed to touch the hearts of the people. If the public has so much regard for me and my work, why should I ignore them? thought I. I cancelled my earlier decision and agreed to participate in their function wholeheartedly. At last I said, "All right, I shall come to your function." All the three of them were beaming with the joy of triumph. I asked them about the transportation-arrangement. They asked us *i.e.* all the three writers to go in a car and that they would pay the rent for the same. I stood up and joined my palms at them and they also did the same to me. We said goodbye to one another and they took their leave from me.

As I came to the kitchen to quaff some water, my wife shouted at me, "You agreed to go to the function, didn't you? You jump at the chance of being garlanded by these nobodies." I was irritated to hear these words because she could never understand my feelings, problems or difficulties. She had cursed me thousand times for being an impecunious writer good for nothing. She had repented in her youth of having married a fellow like me. She had cursed her father many a time for having not given her to either a Tahasildar, or a doctor or an engineer or even a clerk in some revenue department. Sasikala had compared my life with that of others and degraded me for not having had the normal amenities of life like an RCC building, a scooter or even an almirah at home. Whenever the neighbouring women asked her about our having a house in the town, she would ironically remark that her husband (that is me) would erect a building of unsold books etc. As I knew I could not do anything about it, I was reconciled to my lot. Instead of reacting to her words, I wanted to divert her attention to other details of domestic life. I reminded her of our plan to go to the market for some purchasing. She said she must buy an Ilkal sari, which she had liked most. I was happy to note that she did not refer to my literary function that evening any further.

I remembered the date of the function and spent the next day in preparing a sort of synopsis of what I was going to speak from the platform. I made up my mind to advise the youth of our country to open their eyes to the contemporary problems of life.

I wanted to enhearten them to protest against social injustice, to go in for love-marriage, widow-marriage, inter-caste marriage; to shun the dowry; to be revolutionary and progressive etc. That night I slept but could not get sound sleep at all. The thought of leaving the town early in the morning for that felicitation kept me awake throughout the night.

The next day, I woke up early in the morning around 5 o'clock. I hurried through my morning activities like brushing the teeth, attending to nature call, shaving and bathing etc. My wife prepared the parched rice and tea. I finished that within no time. I began to wait for the car, which was to bring the poet and the critic from Kalyananagar and Malamaddi respectively. Hardly had I spent five minutes, when the zooming sound of the car was heard outside. The driver began to honk the rubber horn. I got up hurriedly, gathered my papers and told my wife that I was going. Sasikala called me inside the kitchen and advised me not to strain myself at the function as I was suffering from weakness. I closed the door and stepped down towards the car. The poet and the critic inside the car welcomed me with their smiles, "We thought you won't come for this function. Isn't it a miracle to see you coming now?" I instantly answered, "How can I afford to miss the rare function? Can we ever hope to be felicitated like this every often?" The poet and the critic burst into guffaws of laughter. The driver Hasansab also smiled and started the car. The green colour of the car was very pleasant to look at. The fragrant fumes of joss sticks were circling inside the car. The whiffs of morning breeze were really invigorating to me. The foam leather seats were very comfortable. I wished I had a car like this. My dream of owning a car had never materialised though I had spent nearly thirty-five years in the profession of writing. As the car was running fast, I was lulled into sleep. But my sleep was disturbed when the poet with his typical feminine voice asked me as to what I was going to speak at the function. I told them briefly what I was going to say. I then asked the poet as to what he was going to speak. Nature poet as he was known, he said he was going to ask the budding poets of the town to understand Mother Nature and compose poetry about her. He said he would ask them to write poetry on trees, rivers, birds, beasts, and oxen etc. The next man to be tackled was the critic who was the leader of the Dalit Literature Movement. The critic lit his cigarette, inhaled a couple of puffs smilingly. The combination of the cigarette smell and the fragrance of joss sticks produced a strange smell inside the car. The smooth wheels of the car were churning the wind the wheezing sound of which was very inspiring to me at least. The leader of the Dalit Literature said that he was going to ask the young writers to write about the problems of the untouchables and of the exploited sections of the society etc. As all the three of us were rocked in the car rhythmically, we were lulled into sleep. I was thinking of the possible items at the function. They would, I thought, probably give us shawls, garlands of sandal chips, and idols of Bidariware in addition to the bananas and coconuts. They might also give us printed scroll of honour, I thought. I planned to hang the printed certificate in the front room itself and place the Bidari statue in the glass cupboard. My wife would really like the shawl and might give it away to our eldest daughter Daxayini, I thought. I did not know when I had fallen into sleep.

All the three of us woke up when the car jerked into a halt. My nose began to dilate at the attractive smell of the petrol. I enquired a passerby and learnt that we had come to a village called Belur. Our critic suggested that we should have some tea in the village canteen. As I was feeling thirsty I assented to it. We sat on the rickety wooden benches and began to sip our tea from the broken cups. Hasansab was pouring some water from the can into the cooling machine of the car. We ordered tea for him also. The Nature poet was staring at a cock treading a hen. The critic directed my attention at that and burst into laughter.

We sat in the car. The driver hurried through his tea and rushed back to the car and started it. The dark fields with the jowar stubs were rushing against us. The sun was growing hotter and hotter. Half an hour must have passed before we could descry the temple towers and the hill. The tarmac road had ended and the mud road had started. As the dust began to blow into the car, we shut the windows and coughed repeatedly. We were looking for the big and colourful pandal and the loudspeaker blaring the gramophone records. We asked our driver to take us towards the primary school building. As the car entered the compound, some *khadi*-clad persons came and saluted us by joining their palms. We got down and were led by the local people to one of the classrooms. The *khadi*-clad persons asked us to be seated on the green carpet. We relaxed against the pillows and began to wait for the hosts to welcome us. Meanwhile we asked the names of the two *khadi*-clad persons. They said they were Kallappa and Siddappa. The poet was dozing whereas the critic had lit his cigarette. I was feeling rather feverish and had slight pain in the belly. I asked Kallappa about the location of the function. He was rather disconcerted by my question. "Which function do you mean, sir?" I said, "I mean the Felicitation Function." Kallappa knit his brows and gaped at me for a moment. Then he answered, "I do not remember anything about that, Sir." We were puzzled by his answer. But we thought someone else would come to receive us. But meanwhile Siddappa brought three plates of mixture of puffed rice and *khara*. Though we did not like the stuff at all, we began to munch it for formality's sake. The puffed rice was too pungent to be eaten without water. The poet began to heave because of the sharp taste of it. The critic did not mind it at all. The canteen boy brought some tea the sight of which disgusted us. But since we wanted to have some liquid we had to drink it with great difficulty. The over boiled poisonous tea could not go down our gullets. We, somehow, succeeded through the ordeal. Again Kallappa and Siddappa disappeared for some time. We imagined that they had gone to bring the President of the Municipality, Mr. Goudar. Probably they have been arranging for our meals and speeches, we thought. The entire school building was looking deserted. The monkeys were jumping from the roof to the compound. I asked the poet to observe it. The mother monkey was jumping from wall to wall and tree to tree without any hesitation. It never cared for its young, which clung to it tightly.

It was 2 o'clock then. We were growing quite restless. The critic had exhausted a packet of cigarettes. The growing heat outside had affected us and so we remained silent. We lay on our carpet and began to count the beams of the ceiling mechanically. At last about 3 o'clock the sound of footsteps was heard and we cocked our ears and sat expectant. Somebody came and enquired us if we were the guests from Dharwad. We said, 'yes' and asked him as to where the President, Mr. Goudar was. He told us that President, Mr. Goudar was moving with an M.L.A. who had come to the town unexpectedly and that Mr. Goudar was busy attending to the M.L.A. He said, "Our President saheb has taken the MLA saheb to the Guest House, sir. He has, therefore, sent me here to ask you to go over to the Guest House." We were all disconcerted and felt deeply insulted, but we could not betray it so easily. The other two friends of mine beckoned to me to say something or the other to him. I said to him, "We do not come to your Guest House. We'll wait here. You ask your President to go there and come. We'll come to the function directly." He nodded his head and disappeared. We began to laugh at ourselves. The poet said that the school building looked deserted because the people had rushed to the Guest House. Nobody seemed to be bothered about the writers. Probably as a result of the hot-puffed-rice and the poisonous tea, I had developed a slight pain in the belly. I, therefore, was feeling uneasy. We were really puzzled by the behaviour of the people. The poet and the critic were getting upset and irritated. I was controlling them with hopeful ideas and wishful thoughts. Senior as I was to them, they could not help obliging me. We relaxed once again on the carpet. When we woke up, it was 5 o'clock. We were extremely depressed. Kallappa came once again and asked us if we wanted to have some more puffed-rice and tea. We thanked him profusely and requested him not to bother about that. We asked him if there was any possibility of the President of the Municipality coming over to us. He said that there was every likelihood of it. We were feeling hungry by that time. Half an hour elapsed again. There arrived Siddappa who, we thought, might bring the President. Siddappa did come and to our surprise told us that the President could not spare any time to come over to our school. "But what about the Felicitation Function?" I asked eagerly. Siddappa replied unhesitatingly, "The entire crowd has gathered there near the Guest House. The MLA is going to address the gathering there. They will felicitate you there itself. That is why they have asked me to bring you there." We were humiliated beyond measure by the answer. "All right," said I, "We will come there exactly at the time when the function begins. You may go now and come later." Siddappa went away without the slightest hesitation. The poet began to feel uneasy at having to speak before that huge crowd which had gathered to listen to the M.L.A. The critic did not feel upto speaking in the political function. We began to discuss among ourselves. None of us had ever had such a bitter experience in our life. We were never subjected to such a total indifference. We now came to the decision that we should not participate in the function at all. We had all lost our patience. Our faces were lustreless. I called out for our driver who came running and looked askance at us. He was puzzled a little by our serious faces. I ordered him, "Drive us back to Dharwad." We all got into the car, which began to zoom. We did not remember when we had fallen asleep. We woke up only when the car jerked into a halt near the Jubilee Circle. I remembered the payment of the driver. Since the driver could not get the promised amount from the President of the Municipality of Channagiri, we contributed Rs. 100/- each and gave it to the driver. He drove us to our respective homes. As I went and knocked at the door, Sasikala opened the door. She was puzzled to see my bare hands. Instantly she asked me, "Where is the garland?" I burst into a guffaw and asked her to feed me first, as I was monstrously hungry. After I finished my supper, I came to the bedroom and relaxed on the bed, my wife repeated the question, "Where is the garland?" I laughed again and told her that there was no felicitation at all and narrated every detail to her. But she could not believe me. She retorted "No, I can't believe that. Tell me which lady did you give the garland?" I could not control my laughter and continued to laugh incessantly. I said, "Do you expect me to think of a lady at the age of sixty?"

To which she instantly replied, "Why not? Does the sourness of tamarind ever decrease with the years?" It was impossible for me to convince her. That night she slept two yards away from me.

8

Pilgrimage to Kashi

WHEN GOVINDACHARYA finished his lunch and stood at the door, he noticed that the sun had reached the zenith. The whole front-yard was scorching with the hot sunlight. As usual the acharya ate the tiny bits of jaggery and drank a little more water. As he limped towards the platform built around the neem tree in the front yard, he felt his feet were burning. He lay on the platform, fanned himself and heaved a sigh of relief. The sandal mark on his bulging belly had dried up, but was damped here and there by the drops of perspiration. The acharya turned down and lay on his stomach. He could not tolerate the hot sun when he opened his eyes. Nor could he sleep when he closed his eyes.... His mind was full of thoughts...wretched thoughts... embarrassment and irritation. He tried to sleep well by putting aside all the crowding thoughts and fell into a nap. He was disturbed only by the hoarse voice of the postman. The acharya got up hurriedly and ran his eyes over the letters. He found that all the letters were addressed to his son and daughter-in-law Tulasi who came and stood there with curiosity. The acharya lay down once again. His anger was mounting gradually by degrees. By birth he had a contorted face. But when he was angry, neither his daughter-in-law nor her children would dare to go near him, let alone talk with him. It was so difficult.

When the suppressed thoughts burst out once again in his mind, the acharya began to fan himself quickly. Yet the whiff of wind could not make him comfortable, as it was only a mechanical act. His anger was directed at Srikanta living at the far off city of Hubli. "Should he not have any respect for his own father? Shouldn't he have some courtesy even to reply to my letter? He was all right before his marriage, but has changed a lot since then.... Under the influence of his coquettish wife, he seems to have forgotten every one of us. That way Srinath is a better boy...he respects me... though he does not talk much.... The third boy Gopi also is a fool. He doesn't have any concern for his father.... Whenever my legs ache...I have to call him and ask him to press them.... He keeps on wandering all the three times of the day...don't know...on what business! But I must arrange for his marriage also. I already know how much his wife would serve me.... This is the fate of people these days. Don't know if Srikanta's wife has passed only medical degree or if she has learnt some cooking also with it.... Wanted to go there for a few days...but no letter at all from that fool.... If only my wife were alive...this predicament would not have been there. I could have lived without any dependence upon these sons and daughters-in-law. My wife is a lucky one who left me to rot here in this hell and who resides in Heaven. One should not live long in old age, that too depending upon others.

Twelve years have elapsed since the eldest daughter-in-law Tulasi entered our house. She has been the mother of five children. She used to respect me, her father-in-law so much; but has changed a lot since the marriage of Srikanta.... Perhaps she expects me to be served by the second daughter-in-law. I am not so foolish as to put my morsel into my ears.... I can understand everything...and everybody's behaviour. Srinath who never used to argue with me argued so vehemently with me the other day.... Even that foolish Gopi belongs to their group.... He asks me to keep mum for everything.... What mistake did I make? I have spent all these years in observing purity and avoiding pollution.... How then should I eat the food cooked by Tulasi's mother? What has happened to Tulasi? Earlier she used to get up early, smear the god's shrine with cowdung, draw the tracery of *rangoli*, keep the tools of *puja* and prepare the consecrated food. She used to do all these things with such understanding and smilingly too. But now? She won't get up even up to eight o'clock.... Everything is done by that haired widow. Especially

I feel disgusted by that.... I said frankly...that nobody need attend to me and that I would attend to myself. Doesn't Srinath know that I cook my own food? Gopi also knows it.... Everybody is discreetly silent. If Bagu were alive? I would not have depended upon anyone.... I don't want a single *paise* from these sons as long as I have my ancestral land in my name.... Srinath is a professor and Srikanta is a doctor.... But what do I gain from them? Which son would sit patiently with me and discuss something with me? Which son would ever enquire after my well-being? Bagu made me a forlorn by her death...."

The heat of the sun began to decrease. The acharya's anger was also subsiding when his grandchildren returned from school. Instantly he shouted at them, "O Madhu, O Kitti. You must have touched the other boys in the school. Go and wash your hands and feet." Gopi, who returned home just then, snapped, "Why don't you keep quiet father?" The acharya's anger shot up to his pate. The abundance of his anger was let loose on Gopi. The acharya felt angry for not having the liberty even to advise his grandchildren. He, therefore, did not want to leave it at that. Tulasi was disgusted with the trouble caused regularly at her husband's return. She started thinking about consoling her husband.

Govindacharya threw the fan away into a corner and rubbed his chest and head with the wet *dhoti*. He began to mutter and pace up and down. He was ready to pick quarrel with somebody. He overheard Tulasi who stood inside the kitchen and invited him, 'Will you please come inside and have your tiffin which is ready?" The acharya felt confused. Will not acceptance of tiffin be tantamount to acceptance of defeat? thought he. But the flavour of the sweet *sira* flooded his nostrils. Unable to control his desire for eating, the acharya put on a fresh *dhoti* and sat on the wooden seat. As he began to gulp down the sweet *sira* mixed with ghee — which was delicate like jasmine — placed on the banana-leaf, he forgot his anger at his daughter-in-law. At the same time he thought as to why she should not take care of him like this everyday? When he was savouring the *sira* with childlike innocence, he was unable to understand the inner dilemma of the daughter-in-law who stood watching him.

The acharya leant against the trunk of the neem tree and spoke loudly to his friend Venkanna so that his words should be heard by his daughter-in-law also who was in the outer hall of the house. Venkanna was used to the acharya's habit of alternately scolding and praising his sons and daughters-in-law. But he had no courage to say 'yes' or 'no' to the acharya's words. Even today as soon as he heard the acharya say that he was going to Hubli, he advised him, "Please go there. Why do you wait here for his letter?"

When Govindacharya stood ready to go to Hubli, nobody dissuaded him, which puzzled him sadly. Anger and sorrow combined together and shook him deeply. He felt sad to know that everybody was bored with his presence. But he felt a little satisfaction to imagine his happy stay at his son's home at Hubli. There were only two persons *i.e.* son and daughter-in-law. He could get rare dishes of his choice prepared and savour them. "If I could be happy there, I need not return here. I should come here only for one reason, *i.e.* of having built my own house.... Otherwise who wants this trouble?"

When the acharya went to Hubli he was received with greater enthusiasm than he expected. The house was tidy and peaceful. Srikanta arranged for a cook called Narayana from Udupi side in order to make everything convenient for the father. The acharya beamed with joy to see that all the *puja* items — like *krishnanjana* box, *vibhuti*, and whetstone — were kept ready for him. The acharya had brought these things from his native place thinking that they might not be available here. But he was very happy with the arrangement made by his son and daughter-in-law and their humility. He, therefore, stayed there for eight days very comfortably. It was only for eight days that he spent his time peacefully. Then started the period of insoluble problems. Before Shalini could feel happy about the father-in-law's goodness, he started showing his true colour.

Shalini and Srikanta used to go to the hospital about eight o'clock in the morning and return home about one or two o'clock. They would have their lunch and relax for a while. They used to go to the office once again at four o'clock in the evening and return home about eight or nine o'clock. The acharya felt that the house was in his care all through the day. For the first two days, he felt happy about it. But after four or five days his dissatisfaction reached its climax. He thought, "Do they think that I am a dog to watch their house by eating the food cooked by that cook?" He complained that nobody cared for him.

Once Shalini took out the fruit juice from the refrigerator prepared *sherbet* and offered it to the acharya who forgot all about the purity and quaffed it. Likewise Shalini had shown him the place where the fruit juice was kept and asked him to drink it whenever they returned home late.

But today she did not understand why her father-in-law was in such a fierce mood when she returned home. Abuses gushed out of his mouth torrentially. "This house has been so unbrahmanical.... You have made it a Christian or a Muslim house. When I went to the fridge to take out the juice, I saw eggs kept in a row.... What pollution?.... What filth?".... I cannot see this filth with my eyes.... I will go away today itself...." Srikanta argued, "You don't eat eggs. Then leave it at that.... But why do you object to those who eat them?" "Shut up," thundered the acharya. Shalini shook with fear. When the acharya threw the eggs on the road, Srikanta tried to control his anger.

Govindacharya ordered Shalini to wear bangles on her wrists and questioned her as to why she did not worship the *tulasi* plant and why she did not light the perennial lamp in the *puja* room. He agreed to have his lunch only after Shalini confessed her mistakes and promised not to repeat them. When the acharya washed his fingers and walked out of the kitchen, he overhead Srikanta thundering at his wife, "I wanted to see if the father would fast today.... He does not understand his own mistake as long as we say 'yes' to all that he says. He thinks he is born only to advise others." The acharya felt deeply upset. He thought within himself, "What mistake did I do? I scolded my daughter-in-law only with a view to making her an ideal housewife...Oh. This fellow is a big doctor...who has no respect for his own father? Don't I have the authority even to advise my daughter-in-law? Should Srikanta not understand even this much? He allows his wife to sit on his own head. Did I ever give such liberty to my Bagu when she was alive? Oh, never."

Before two months elapsed, the acharya felt bored with that family, that city and the whole atmosphere. He began to worry inwardly, "My son is a doctor and my daughter-in-law also is a doctor. I came here thinking that I should spend my old age life here. Now already two months have gone by. Have they given me even a single injection? No. Then, some tonic? They think that their duty is over if they merely fed me. I made a mistake by leaving the rice of fine grains and clarified butter and coming here. These people are always busy with cinema, theatre and club. Does my son invite me at least once for such entertainments? My native place is far better than this Hubli. There I used to go for hearing the *purana* at least. Venkanna used to take me there...Gopi used to pester me to tell him stories. Time used to pass so quickly.... Poor girl Tulasi used to get up late in the morning perhaps because of indisposition. How can I understand the health problems of women?" Suddenly the acharya began to feel affectionate towards that daughter-in-law. Instantly he decided to leave the city and began to tie up the *Krishnanjana* box.

When Govindacharya stood ready to go, he felt disappointed to know that his son did not ask him to stay on for another four days — at least out of formality. Eager to know the reaction of the son and the daughter-in-law, he stood overhearing their conversation and felt deeply shocked. When Shalini sadly told her husband that her father-in-law was going away, Srikanta replied mockingly, "Let him go, why do you bother? Though we tried hard to keep him happy, he is not satisfied at all. He wants to have his own way.... What did he lack here? Milk, fruits and vegetables. If still he insists on going away let him go. There also, how long does the elder brother obey him out of fear? The elder brother's wife looks after him as if he is a child. Does he stay there happily? Even if you give him heavenly happiness, he is not satisfied and complains that it is hell itself." The acharya had no patience to overhear their words further. He contorted his face and began to pace up and down.... He swore to himself never to step into the fool's house.

He received a letter from his eldest son and learnt that the latter's wife had completed the seventh month of pregnancy. Before the acharya could leave Hubli, he was depressed by this news. A new problem had cropped up suddenly. Even if the daughter-in-law had to cook after seven months' pregnancy by putting on fresh garments, it would be tantamount to pollution. The acharya grew very anxious about it. He also felt that staying on at Hubli was like standing on a bed of thorns. At the same time he was eager to go away from Hubli. He did not know what to do. Every moment he felt that he was a forlorn. He felt anxious as though somebody was dismembering his body limb by limb.

Govindacharya had also heard reports about some people going to places of pilgrimage like Kashi, Mathura and Gaya by a special train. He, therefore, thought as to why he also should not go there. So far he had not bothered about such pilgrimages. He decided boldly to go there in order to be away from the wretched atmosphere of domestic life. But the problem about his food remained unsolved.

When the acharya informed his son Srikanta about his decision, the latter did not consent to it for fear that he might not adjust himself with other pilgrims or stand the strain of long journey on account of his old age. But the acharya grew adamant once again. Should he obey his son like a doll? He thought that these people were dissuading him not on account of his old age but were really worried about the train fare that they had to pay him. He, therefore, began to shout at them.

The ticket was reserved fifteen days in advance. As the special train was to start at Hubli Station, Srikanta, Tulasi, Gopi and the children had all gathered at the Railway Station to bid farewell to the acharya. They had observed the Satyanarayana Vow and prayed for his safe return. All his friends and relatives had come to the Station. The tins of dry fruits, dates, almonds, sugarcandy, boiled butter, parched rice, wheat flour, sweet balls and other eatables were packed perfectly in the acharya's trunk. Srikanta and Srinath had given him a rug, a sweater and a muffler lest he should suffer from cold. In addition, Srikanta had given him some medicines and explained how to take them. Until the train started, Tulasi and Shalini requested him to take care of his health and write letters. The acharya's mind was filled with dilemmas. "I am going to a far-off place.... That is why these people are happy, but pretending to be very polite," thought he and sat in the compartment in a ferocious mood. Though his sons and grandchildren bowed to his feet, he could not pay attention to that. Srinath and Srikanta requested him to write to them if he ran short of money on the way or if he found any difficulty in the special pilgrimage programme so that they could go and bring him back immediately. But the acharya's contorted face did not relax even then. He sat upright with pride in the compartment.

The train was moving. The acharya was trying to adjust himself to the atmosphere. Everything had been specially arranged for him so that he should not lack anything. There was no dearth at all for fruits. He had a purseful of money and a strong desire to eat. Nearly a month had elapsed after he had left his place, but he had never befriended any co-pilgrim in the compartment. He never participated in their chatting and laughing. He used to remain ever serious thereby showing off his riches.

The other pilgrims had converted the journey into an occasion for entertainment. They used to exchange information about their children, daughter-in-law, grandchildren and places... and become intimate friends as though for the past many years. The acharya found it rather strange that even the oldest pilgrim Nagesharaya would accost the taciturn ones and invite them for chitchatting. Though the pilgrims flocked to Nagesharaya like ants being drawn to sugar, the acharya never stirred out of his seat but sat tight, munching dry grapes and sugarcandy pieces. He used to listen to their gossip carefully and observe everybody minutely.

Govindacharya had begun to notice that the co-pilgrims lived like frogs in the well in the company of their kith and kin at their own houses, villages and farms. He never had a chance in his life to understand the life-styles of others. The pilgrimage to Kashi had made him understand the world around him like a newborn baby opening its eyes to observe the world around it. The acharya who carefully observed Nagesharaya's laughter, enthusiasm and merry talk felt disgusted with himself. He thought inwardly, "This old man is so carefree and joyous perhaps because he has got everything he desired in life." But he never went to the extent of befriending Nagesharaya. When he learnt that Tungamma had come on the pilgrimage out of the money collected from the income of her job of pounding rice into parched rice and that the widow Tippakka had come there with the help of money earned from the job of cooking at others' homes with the hope of attaining salvation, he really began to wonder at their sense of strong determination. In spite of having four sons who were big officers but yet did not give a single pie to their father, Ranganna had saved some money as a poor teacher for this pilgrimage. It was because of the acharya's acquaintance with Ranganna that he had been able to make the trip and compare his own life with that of others for a brief while. But yet he suffered from a sense of frustration.

Once Nagesharaya himself sat beside him and elicited some information from him about his family, children and others in order to make him relax his seriousness. But Nagesharaya was really surprised to learn that the acharya did not utter a single word of satisfaction though all happiness was available to him. After two days, Nagesharaya again drew the acharya into conversation, learnt about his health and happy life and remarked humorously, "Don't be angry, acharya.... Just a question....

Though God has granted you all this happiness, why do you remain morose like a man bearing the burden of a mountain?.... Please learn to laugh a bit." The acharya had stared at Nagesharaya fiercely as if he would swallow him. Did Govindacharya ever listen to others' advice? Never. He was habituated to speak out whatever he thought was right and expected others to assent to his opinion. Nagesharaya stood up and walked away from him.

Once again Nagesharaya drew the self-obsessed acharya with a contorted face into conversation and told him quite boldly, "See acharya, you have not laughed even once during these days and never relaxed your contorted face.... Shall I show it to you by holding a mirror?" Govindacharya thundered before Nagesharaya completed his sentence, "Why should I laugh? You say that I must laugh. What do I have to make me laugh? Sons....? Yes, I have a few sons...who have neither love nor concern, nor respect, nor even sympathy for me. Daughters-in-law....? They are also the same.... How can the daughters-in-law who are outsiders care for me when my own sons neglect me....?" Nagesharaya kept quiet and thought that he must have made a mistake in understanding the inner feelings of Govindacharya.

Everyone reached Kashi. Govindacharya felt uneasy by observing the enthusiasm and piety of the co-pilgrims. They felt proud and satisfied by the *darsan* of Lord Vishwanatha and the holy bath in the Ganga. But the acharya completed these formalities rather mechanically and sat leaning against the pillar of the temple. "Why are these people so happy? Perhaps they lacked money and could not have come here when they wanted to," thought the acharya. Nagesharaya saw the acharya seated alone and went past him. But the acharya himself accosted him and called him to his side, "What's the matter, *rayare*? Anyway the pilgrimage is coming to a close. You are lucky people who can spend your lives laughingly. God has granted you everything. That is the reason why you spend your time merrily. Now you return home and live happily. But what about me? I have got to go back to that hell of my sons, daughters-in-law and children...."

Nagesharaya replied with a laugh, "Where's the home for me, acharya? Forty years have elapsed since my wife died. Fifteen years have gone by since my son died in a railway accident near Mehboob Nagar. I have nothing left in my life."

"What!" Govindacharya exclaimed. Then Nagesharaya continued, "See, acharya...who doesn't want happiness? But can one get happiness if he goes in search of it? We have to generate happiness in ourselves. Happiness lies in being contented with whatever little we have. Happiness and sorrow are two states of our mind. Whatever we bring with our birth, we'll take it back with our death. But people remember how we live our life in between. Our happiness lies in what good we do to others. That is our fortune. If we harm others, that would be our sin, and our sorrow. We can attain peace of mind in feeling contented and satisfied with whatever little is given to us. What difference does it make whether we attain them in this mortal world or in Heaven? Both are the same."

Govindacharya was shocked by the new awareness awakened by Nagesharaya's explanation like a wounded snake and began to blink at him. Yes, Nagesharaya had attained everything by possessing nothing. But what about the acharya himself who possessed everything?

9

The Spider's Web

I HAD spent a lot of money on my election and succeeded in getting elected as an MLA. Later I was lucky enough to become a Minister on the strength of my caste and popular support. After assuming charge as the cabinet level Minister, I had to visit the different districts in Karnataka to streamline everything in the State Administration. I had decided to plug the loopholes in my department and bring law and order in the bureaucratic set-up. That day I had fixed the date of my visit to Dharwad and inspected the various offices of my department. My car zoomed along the road from Bangalore to Dharwad. I had to stay in the Circuit House on the elevated hill of Dharwad commanding a beautiful view of the surrounding landscape. My car was followed and preceded by the security officers' cars with flickering lamps on them. As I reached Dharwad via Hubli, the police constables and PSIs and the SP had grown alert and were following my car diligently. Later on I had to meet the members of my party and then participate in the public function in the Collector's Compound. As my car entered the Circuit House, the police officers saluted me with style and welcomed me with great respect and awe. The double room was decorated with new furniture, cushions and curtains. Everything was spic and span. A cup of hot steaming coffee was served to me as I relaxed on the decorated chair. The benzamin tree outside the Circuit House displayed a splurge of bright red blooms. From the western window of the room I could see the imposing clock tower of the Karnatak University building built in white granite rock. I remembered the great educationist, Dr. D.C. Pawate who struggled to build the Great University in Dharwad and named it as Karnatak University much against the will of the south Karnataka politicians. After my completion of morning ablutions, the cook brought me hot *idlis, masala dosa* and hot coffee for my breakfast. The officers appeared to have taken very keen interest in the inauguration programme and neglected their office work. I realized that they had taken so much trouble over the function only to reduce the time available for my inspection of their offices.

As I had become a Minister recently, I had a good reputation of being a man of discipline. People saw in me, a man who would not tolerate any official delay or corruption and the officers, therefore, were very apprehensive. I was secretly proud of my reputation.

A large gathering of people was there at Kadapa Maidan in the morning. I went there about 10.30 A.M. The police officers made way for my car. All the local politicians received me with joined palms and smile of recognition. Everything was kept ready and everybody was waiting for me to inaugurate the Mallikarjun Mansur Kalabhavan. I went straight to the main gate of the Kalabhavan and cut the ribbon and entered the corridor. The members of the Reception Committee led me to the large portrait of the late Pundit Mallikarjun Mansur fixed on the wall of the corridor. I put a large jasmine garland on the portrait and lit the two lamps beside it. The entire gathering of people clapped their hands in appreciation. Then I rushed to the Open Air Theatre to participate in the party meeting. We discussed with the party members how to retain a good name for us as well as for our party and how to win the hearts of voters to our side. By that time, I realized that I had very little time for the inspection of my departmental offices. As I was rushing through the inspection, a few people approached me and submitted a petition. I asked the Deputy Commissioner to look into their grievance, which was against the local Circle Inspector.

Then we returned to the Circuit House for lunch. When the lunch was served to me and other dignitaries, I found that the fried fish was very tasty. When I reached for the plate for another helping, someone hurried forward to serve me. "The fish is very good," I said, "where do you get it from?"

"The fish is from Karwar beach sir. I got it from there, because I know you like it," said the man.

"Oh, you got it from such a long distance?" I said and he smiled with a sense of satisfaction.

After the sumptuous lunch I chewed the delicious Kashmiri *pan-bida* with real gusto and belched with a sense of satisfaction. I moved to the lounge and sat chatting with the Deputy Commissioner. I asked him casually about the poor folk's complaint, "About whom are they complaining?"

The Deputy Commissioner looked at the man who served me the fish. The man sped out of the door. I understood the situation. The Deputy Commissioner said, "He is the local Circle Inspector. The hut-dwellers of Attikolla have complained against him for bribery."

The Muncipal President added, "They have complained to us also against him."

"Then it is a serious problem," I said, "we have to do something about it."

While chatting in the drawing room later, the Deputy Commissioner sat gazing at a spider's web at one corner of the ceiling.

In the evening I went in my car to the Collector's Compound to make my public speech to the local audience. Thousands of people had gathered in the large pandal. Loudspeakers were blaring. There was a big din. As I climbed the platform, the din subsided. There was pin-drop silence. The function began with a welcome song by some high school girls to the accompaniment of harmonium and tabla. The song was very serene and enthusing. Then the local MLA introduced me as a man of action and concern for poor people and justice. The flattery pleased me. I felt secretly elated. After his introduction, I stood up to speak. There was great silence of expectation everywhere in the audience. I began to speak in my clear and stentorian voice. I told them how we Indians should be proud of our country and our State and how we have to build a new nation and compete with other advanced nations of the world. This we could achieve only with hard and sincere work and by being free from corruption. The MLA had described me as a man of action and not of mere words. I, therefore, declared my resolve to put down corruption. I felt encouraged by the thunderous clapping in the audience and wanted to demonstrate my action-orientation. I, therefore, declared, "Today I have received a complaint against an officer about corruption. I learnt that there is some truth in it. I am, therefore, going to order the Deputy Commissioner to suspend that officer right now."

The dignitaries on the dais began to clap loudly. The audience also joined in the clapping. Before the applause could subside, someone at the back of the gathering collapsed and people surrounded him. My gunman rushed to the spot, returned and told me, "Sir, he is said to be one Mr. Durgadas, the Circle Inspector of this town. He is unconscious."

I felt deeply disturbed. I asked the Police Inspector sitting near me to take the man in his jeep to the hospital. Within half an hour of my return to the Circuit House, the Deputy Commissioner brought the news that the Circle Inspector had died before he could reach the hospital. The Municipal President remarked, "Who knows what diseases he had harbored?"

But I was deeply agitated. "His case is closed now. Why discuss it then?" said I and averted my face.

The visitors left the Circuit House one by one. At last, only the Deputy Commissioner and I remained in the room. I looked at him, but he was gazing at the spider's web. An insect was flying around it. It used to touch the strands of the web and fly away. But the spider waited patiently. How long can the game of death continue? At last the insect was trapped. The harder it struggled to extricate itself, the tighter grew the bond of the web. At last the insect's struggle ceased.

We looked at each other and I asked the Deputy Commissioner, "I am sorry — was Durgadas so very sensitive?"

"I know Sir. Poor fellow. He must have been shocked when he heard you declare his suspension. He must have felt forlorn. He probably wished to make the same request to you as he had to me," said the Deputy Commissioner.

"Tell me what his request was!"

"I do not know if I should talk about it. If we hide it, we will have to undergo Durgadas's condition. I do not say that Durgadas was a very honest man. Nor do I deny that we received a share. Everything is like a spider's web and everybody is sure to be trapped because of some attraction or inevitability."

I did not like his circumlocution. "Come to the point," I snapped.

Then the Deputy Commissioner cleared his throat and said in a gentle voice, "Six years ago, Durgadas was a Circle Inspector already and I was working as an Assistant Commissioner here. The then Deputy Commissioner used to be very enthusiastic about arranging grand dinners for visiting VIPs. He was himself a good eater. He used to arrange vegetarian and non-vegetarian food as well as drinks. The man who would arrange all that was Mr. Durgadas. Nobody bothered to consider how a low-salaried officer like Durgadas could meet the high expenditure of such parties. Nobody bothers about it even now. On rare occasions a high officer would ask for the bill and thank the hosts. Would the money offered by one or two officers suffice to meet the total expenditure?

"Durgadas was not a fool either. He thought that it would be a sign of incompetence if he were to spurn that work. He, therefore, found an easy way out. He knew there were a few huts on the government land near the Attikolla. Some huts were erected there with Municipal permission and some other without that. Thus, a slum came into existence on the Attikolla. Whenever the huts were ordered to be demolished, the hut-dwellers appealed to the leaders. How would the leaders allow the demolition? Durgadas knew that it was impossible for him to demolish them. But at the same time, he knew that he could extract some money from the hut-dwellers by threatening them of demolition. The money raised thus would be sufficient both for the arrangement of a couple of dinner parties during that month and for his own livelihood. Durgadas would repeat the trick the subsequent month also. The poor people's complaints against Durgadas were sent to the Government, but all of them were referred to the Deputy Commissioner, who was also implicated.

"Eventually, I was appointed to inquire into the matter. As usual, I sent a notice to him and asked for an explanation. His answer confounded me. He said it was true that he had extracted money from the hut-dwellers to arrange dinners for VIPs and added, 'Is there anything not known to you?' How could I answer that question?

"I suggested to the Deputy Commissioner to transfer the Circle Inspector to some other place. But he wanted to punish him. I suggested, 'You may transfer him to a place where there is no scope for such corruption. Why tarnish your image unnecessarily?' Luckily, he agreed and transferred Durgadas to some other place.

"But Durgadas was back here when I came here on transfer after six years. I was surprised to see him again. I came to know that there was nobody to look after the Circuit House satisfactorily. Some people advised the Deputy Commissioner to replace him with a better man. Hence Durgadas returned to this place again.

"I do not know whether Durgadas was happy or not this time. Now his family is not small unlike in the past. He has four children. His eldest daughter and son are studying in the high school. Besides, he has to maintain his elder brother also. He seemed to have been dragged into a whirlpool. In spite of all that, he would continue to squander many on feeding the officers. Besides, there were many who would encourage him. When I went to his home, his wife said tearfully that he had squandered the entire amount of festival advance of this month for the same purpose. I wonder if there is any beginning or end to this vicious circle."

I know I had not paid the bill for the food I had had here last time. Today, the fish that was offered by Durgadas was not yet digested. I felt very uneasy.

The Deputy Commissioner was staring at me. "We are all lovers of tradition, Sir, especially when it is convenient. We can see people like Durgadas in every department. But it is unfortunate that there are many leaders who deem it to be a sign of able administration to kill the serpent and feed it to the eagle. We should have thought about the evil consequence of this system long back. Excuse me Sir I had to tell you this only because you asked."

Much later, I lay in bed staring at the light overhead. Hospitality, obligation, festival advance, squandered money... complaint...a family of eight members. Durgadas would not have bothered about any of these. His sole intention was to please the higher officers.

What about me? Am I a man of principles?... I too have a wife and four children. Haven't I done so many illegal things for their sake? My inner voice asked me, "Can a man be like this?" My head began to reel...the light began to grow dim.... Did I kill him? I grew nervous and felt my heart with my palm. My heart had begun to pound incessantly. I rubbed my eyes, got up and walked a few steps. The wind flew against my head.... I asked myself if it was right for one in my position to be so sensitive.

My gunman announced that dinner was ready. I instantly remembered Durgadas. I said, "I am not hungry. Some fruit juice is enough." I paced up and down in the room. The attenders seated on the stairs disappeared into the darkness. Once again, I felt lonely. I wanted to forget the whole thing by rationalizing.

The breeze whipped me in the face. As its intensity increased, the curtains in the room began to flutter. The gunman came and said he had placed the fruit juice on the teapoy. I turned back slowly. I thought that probably, worries bother only those who worry and fear harasses only those who fear. I came back to the drawing room and sat on the sofa. The plastic cover on the glass of fruit juice was blown to the ground. I took up the glass to empty it, but I saw in it an insect of the size of a bean struggling and dying. My whole body shivered but I began to sweat. I kept the glass back on the teapoy and stared at the spider's web in the corner and the insect caught in it. I saw the dead insect floating in the fruit juice. "We can see people like Durgadas in every department, Sir." These words of the Deputy Commissioner pierced my heart again and again.

I got up from the sofa, tottered to the bed clutching my head in both hands and lay down. It was dawn when I woke up.

10

Basavanti

BASAVANTI WAS a young girl admired by every youngman of the village Nagarahalli secretly or publicly. It was because of her bewitching beauty that her husband Kalmesh had married her, though, of course, he was very poor and owned only two acres of land at Hunasikatti. But after the euphoria of early days of marriage had disappeared, it became simply impossible for her to rub along with her husband. She did not like the way he treated her. He would return home late in the night and that too fully drunk and beat her heavily or make love to her without any affection and fall into sleep snoring loudly. Even when she was right under the weight of his nakedness, she longed for the affectionate caresses of her early lover in the native village. That is the reason why one night she disappeared from her husband's home. Kalmesh was shocked a bit when he found that his wife had absconded somewhere without any intimation to him. He wanted to give the last trial to his luck and therefore, made a journey to Nagarahalli. He ordered his wife, "Return home with me immediately. Otherwise you need not step into my house ever in future." She replied blankly, "I'll not live with you. Our relation has come to an end," and walked briskly into the kitchen. Her mother requested her son-in-law to have his lunch. But Kalmesh, insulted by his wife's indifference said, "Food is not necessary for me," and journeyed back to his village Hunasikatti. He forgot all about Basavanti when he married another girl from a neighbouring village Jawoor.

Basavanti heaved a sigh of relief when she finally snapped her relationship with the beast of a husband. Her old lover, who had robbed her virginity in the jowar field before her marriage, had assured her that he would maintain her with all the care and affection. The house that she lived in was made of black mud and timber and had only two small rooms including the kitchen. Her father had died long back and now she had been living with her old mother and a sister of barely ten years. Though the entire village gossipped about her extra-marital affair, neither she nor her mother cared for it, simply because of dire poverty. "Would the wagging tongues ever feed us?" Thus did Basavanti try to console her mother who was sore about the ill reputation that was spreading around in the village. The young slip of a girl Mahadevi was blissfully ignorant about these problems and spent most of her time in playing with the neighbours' children.

Chinnappagouda was a tall and hefty man with a wife from a rich family and had two children. He had been a playboy ever since he had attained puberty. He had twenty-five acres of land, four bullocks and two cows. Two bonded laborers worked in his house around the clock. He lacked nothing in his life. A gallant by nature, he would be always on the look out for a pretty belle of the village for his entertainment. He heaved a sigh of relief when Basavanti acted according to his secret advice and returned to Nagarahalli after leaving her husband for good. "Though people may call you may concubine, you don't care for that at all. Secretly we'll be like married couple. I'll treat you not only equal to my wife, but even as better than her," he had whispered into her ears when he was still inside her in the dark room. He always felt a paradisal pleasure in her passionate company. So did she in his company and felt a new security.

Chinnappagouda never cared for the wagging tongues in the village. Everyday he went to Basavanti's house in the afternoon. As soon as he went in there and sat chatting with her, her mother would excuse herself and go to the Monastery and sit there watching the villagers or reciting the *Sivamantra.* Little Mahadevi would go out and play *chakka* or rope-dancing or mock-cooking with tiny utensils with her friends. Basavanti would enjoy staring at her lover's well-trimmed mustaches, silken turban, pleated *dhoti* and above all his wide chest and strong hips. Likewise, Chinnappagouda would sit gazing at her chiselled features, round face, black tresses, succulent breasts and inebriating bottoms. She would tell him all the stories and hearsay that she had heard or could remember and make him laugh. Similarly, he would narrate to her all the adventures of his younger days and keep her in good humour. "When I was a young boy of about sixteen," he said to her one day, "I had observed the purity mania of some widows. They never used to allow me to go near them or touch them. So one day I hit upon a mischievous plan. I took a bamboo of about six feet and burned its inside thereby making a good cylinder of it and carried it to the touring talkies to see a Kannada movie called *Bhakta Prahlada.* In the electric light I could make out where the widows had sat and I managed to squeeze my way through the gents and sat just behind the widows. The film was very good and people were responding to it with cheers and wails, as the occasion demanded. When an hour or so had gone by, I became alert about my mischievous plan. I adjusted the bamboo and placed it just behind those puritanical widows and made water in it very silently. I watched around me and was happy that nobody noticed me. When the film was about to come to an end, I got up and walked out of the talkies hurriedly leaving the bamboo there itself. I went to a nearby tree and stood behind it watching the fun. The gents came out first and walked slowly. Then a group of women came out cursing, "who's the widow's husband who has polluted us? Our saris are all soaked in urine. May his corpse be lifted. May he be roasted in hell eternally." They squeezed their urine soaked saris, stretched them to the wind and said to themselves, "Let's go home and have hot-water bath. Let's not come to this talkies ever again." I was laughing in a muffled voice behind the tree." Though Basavanti was listening to his narration with rapt attention, she could not hold back her laughter. She doubled up with many tiers of laughter. "What if you had been detected and beaten up by people?" asked she. "How could they detect it?" said he with a giggle. Then Basavanti would serve him with sweet-balls, puffed rice and tea. After chatting thus for an hour or two, Chinnappagouda would caress her, explore her sensuous nooks and curves until he had his fulfilment for the day. Then he would go back to his wife. Basavanti's mother would return home only after making sure that the daughter's paramour had left the place.

The love affair between Basavanti and Chinnappagouda graduated into a very intimate and almost illegal marriage. Basavanti's mother turned a deaf ear to all the gossip that was going on in the village. For, she had no other go except depend upon her daughter for two square meals per day, if nothing else. She had accepted the ignominy as part of her destiny. But the only thing that gave her some satisfaction was that her daughter was happy because of Chinnappagouda's economic support for her. She knew that Basavanti had now been able to own a golden necklace, bangles, ear-rings and bracelets because of Chinnappagouda's generosity. Basavanti grew richer and happier over a period of five years. She not only lived unmindful of the gossip of the village, but grew positively arrogant. Respectable women of the village began to hesitate having any friendship with her because of her illicit relationship with Chinnappagouda.

Basavanti's small house stood near the Maruti temple in the village. Her house had no regular bathroom. She, therefore, had erected four thatched walls of cotton-stalks beside her house and called it a bathroom. She, her mother and her younger sister used to take bath there in the morning. As there was no drainage system in the village, the stinking water began to flow out of her thatched bathroom and flowed across the road. The villagers who used to go to the temple in the morning to offer their prayers had to jump over the stinking water or sometimes slip down on the ground. With their bedraggled *dhotis*, they would walk back to their houses, cursing Basavanti all the while, "this shameless woman has no respect for Lord Maruti or for the people of this village. She has no sense to stop the flow of her bath water across the way to the holy temple. God will, one day, teach her a good lesson." The children in the lanes would simply laugh at the comic sight of the slush-smeared devotees. Although everybody cursed Basavanti, nobody had either the courage or willingness to approach her directly and ask her to control her bath water. They relied only upon Lord Maruti to redress the wrong done to the village by her.

Basavanti never attended any funeral in the village. She used to make occasional trips to Navalgund for marketing. She would go to Bangarasetty's shop where she had mortgaged a number of golden ornaments for some cash she needed for the urgencies of her life. It was in the same shop that she used to buy gold for the Goudasani Gangamma who had great trust in her honesty. Basavanti had a little problem of health. She used to suffer from frequent headaches. She would, therefore, request her lover for pills. Chinnappagouda would bring some pills from Hubli or Dharwad and offer them to her in his passionate privacy. Basavanti, thus, lived gloriously by the village standards. The womenfolk who went to the tank for fetching water would comment upon her, "Basavanti's eyes have gone to the top of her head now. She cannot see people in the village now even if they walk before her." But Basavanti was past caring for such comments. Half a dozen years went by like this in the enjoyment of their glorious love affair.

One day Basavanti's eyes grew dim all of a sudden. She just could not see anything around her. She had to grope in the dark as it were for her movements. Sometimes she would dash against a wall or trip over the threshold and fall on the floor thereby receiving minor injuries. She just could not understand what had come upon her. She began to pray to Lord Maruti in the nearby temple. For everything, she had to depend upon either her sister or mother. When Chinnappagouda came on his nocturnal visit, he was shocked out of his wits to know what had befallen his beloved. He assured her, "Don't you worry, darling. It might be a temporary problem. It may not last long." But Basavanti was not convinced or satisfied by his answer. That night he made love to her without any emotional attachment. Nor did she respond to him as she used to in the past. However, in the early morning he dressed up and wanted to go home. But before that he gave her a few ten rupee notes and asked her to go over to

Hubli and have her eyes checked up by a doctor. Then he walked slowly towards his home.

That morning Basavanti had her bath and breakfast of sweet-balls and parched rice. She walked to Sisvinhalli Railway Station along with her mother and a servant of Chinnappagouda. After waiting for an hour, they boarded the train and reached Hubli. From there they went to the Government Hospital by an auto-rickshaw. The servant made enquiry at the counter. At last they went to the E.N.T. department and waited there for another half an hour. When Basavanti's turn came, she entered the doctor's chamber with her mother's help. The doctor lit the torch and examined her eyes by stretching her eyelid wide. Then he made her stand before a scanning machine and scrutinized the graph, which appeared in bright green colour. Basavanti requested the doctor, "Father, please give back my eyesight by conducting operation if necessary." She joined her palms and saluted him. The doctor sat in his chair brooding for a few seconds. Then he said, "Your problem is not so easy as to be solved by me. You'll have to go to Bangalore for treatment. If you are willing to spend some money, I shall give a letter to a doctor at Bangalore." Basavanti was simply shocked out her wits by the doctor's words. For a moment she did not know what to say. The doctor was still waiting for her answer. At last she said, "All right, doctor, I'll go wherever you direct me to. All that I want is the return of my eyesight." Then the doctor took up his letter-head and wrote down a personal letter to his friend at Banglaore, kept it in a cover and handed it over to Basavanti. He said to her, "See, *amma*, this doctor is a very close friend of mine. He works in the Kempegouda Hospital at Bangalore. You hand this over to him. He will help you to get the necessary treatment." Basavanti gave the letter to her old mother, joined her palms in respect to the doctor and walked out of his chamber slowly, with the help of her younger sister. All of them had their lunch in the Renuka Hotel near the Rani Chennamma Circle. Then they returned to their village in a dust covered rattling bus.

It was nearing midnight when Chinnappagouda made his visit to Basavanti's house. As usual her mother and younger sister had gone to the Monastery yard to sleep. Chinnappagouda was eager to know the result of her visit to the doctor. He clasped her palms and asked, "What did the doctor say, dear? Has he given any medicine?" Even in the dim kerosene lamp, he was staring at her face askance. Basavanti nodded her head to the left and then to the right and said in a plaintive voice, "No." "But why? What did he say at least?" he asked her concernedly. "He said he can not cure me here. He has asked me to go to Bangalore. He has given me a letter and asked me to hand it over to a doctor at the Kempegouda Hospital." Chinnappagouda understood the gravity of the situation. For a few moments both of them remained silent. Somewhere a dog barked in the village. Chinnappagouda's heart began to beat fast. It took him quite a few minutes to calm down. "A trip to Bangalore means a lot of money. Besides I am a poor illiterate woman. I cannot go there alone, or even with my mother. I can do that only if you accompany me," said Basavanti in a weak voice. But Chinnappagouda said rather apologetically, "Dear, please try to know my difficulty also. I cannot stir out of the village because I have to attend to the farms. This is the sowing season. I must see that all the farms are sown at the right time." "Then how can I go there without a knowledgeable person?" asked Basavanti worriedly. "Don't you worry, darling. I shall give you enough money and send a loyal servant of mine, Siddappa. He is an intelligent youngman who will take you to Bangalore and bring you back safely," assured Chinnappagouda. "Then do as you please. What else can I do?" exclaimed Basavanti leaning against his broad chest. He, then, put off the oil-lamp and began to trace the rich deposits of her sensuous wealth.

Three days went by in waiting. Basavanti waited patiently for the money. Chinnappagouda rushed to the A.P.M.C. Office at Hubli to get his money that was long due to him for the cotton bales that he had supplied there. The fourth day, he returned to Nagarahalli. In the evening, he visited Basavanti as usual after dinner. He handed over the cash to her, "Take this money, dear. This will be enough for your trip to Bangalore and your treatment there. You don't worry. I am willing to squander money for your health." Basavanti took the wad of notes from him and kept it under the bed. She then caressed his cheeks with both her palms. Chinnappagouda drew her gently to his side and planted a few kisses upon her cheeks.

The next morning Basavanti went to Hubli along with her mother and servant Siddappa. Then they went to the Railway Station and boarded the Kittur Express at 9.00 P.M. They settled themselves confortably on their wooden seats. The train started with a screech and moved slowly. They dozed on their seats and therefore spread their mattresses on the berths and slept. The train gathered speed gradually of which they were not aware. However, after a lapse of nearly four hours, they were awakened by the sound of hawkers and the din of people in the Station at Davanagere. Siddappa ordered for three cups of coffee. All the three of them drank the coffee slowly. The train started once again. Basavanti's mother and Siddappa sat watching the profile of hills, tall coconut trees and thickets of small trees in the pale moonlight. But Basavanti could not see anything. Instead, she sat listening to Siddappa's description of the landscape and tried her best to visualise those things. Another five hours elapsed. At last the train jerked into a stop at the Bangalore Station. Dawn was breaking slowly in the eastern sky. They walked up to the busy Majestic Circle and searched for a modest lodge. Finally they found a Janata Lodge and rested in a double room for a couple of hours.

After completing the morning ablutions in the Lodge, they had their breakfast of *dosa* and tea and rushed to the Kempegouda Hospital in an auto-rickshaw. Then all the three of them walked to the Enquiry Counter. Siddappa asked about Doctor Somasekhar. The lady clad in white uniform gave him some directions. Then Siddappa led Basavanti and her mother to the chamber. He first saluted the doctor with joined palms and asked humbly, "Are you Doctor Somasekhar Saheb?" The doctor looked up at him through his glasses and said, "Yes, yes. What can I do for you?" Meanwhile he kept his stethoscope on the table. "Saheb, we have come all the way from Hubli. Dr. Patil has sent this letter to you," said Siddappa humbly and handed over the letter to him. Dr. Somasekhar took up the letter and glanced through it carefully. He, then, said, "I shall make all the arrangements for scanning. Please wait for half an hour. By the way who is the patient?" Siddappa pointed to Basavanti.

After an hour of waiting, Basavanti was led by Dr. Somasekhar into the scanning room. She was asked to lie down on the hard wooden board covered with rexine sheet. Four receivers were stuck on her forehead, temples and top of head. They were all connected by wires to the scanning machine. Dr. Somasekhar and other colleagues of his were all watching the graphs on the computer screen. After the scanning was over, Basavanti was asked to get up and go out. Siddappa led her slowly out of the scanning room. Dr. Somasekhar said, "The results of the scanning will be ready by the evening. You may go back to your lodge and rest in the meanwhile. You please come tomorrow morning about 11:00 o'clock." All the three of them went back to their lodge by an auto-rickshaw.

The next morning, they went to the Hospital and waited in the lounge. Dr. Somasekhar called them into his room. Basavanti was very eager to know what the doctor had to say. The doctor said, "See *amma*, you have to be operated on. Are you ready for that?" "I am ready, Saheb. That is why I have come all the way from my village," said Basavanti. "No, *amma,* don't be under the impression that your eyes are going to be operated on. Your case is very complicated," said the doctor. "Kindly tell me doctor saheb, what exactly is the problem with me?" requested Basavanti imploringly. Then the doctor said further, "See *amma,* you have lost your eyesight because of the formation of pus inside your skull. For that we'll have to open a fraction of the skull. You'll have to sign a bond. We'll not be responsible for any unforeseen event. The whole thing is a bit risky. You think twice before committing to any thing." Basavanti understood the gravity of the problem. Her mother and Siddappa also grew very serious. All the three went out of the chamber to a nearby corner and discussed the pros and cons of the operation. Siddappa said, "I feel, there is no guarantee of success in this operation. What shall we do now?" Basavanti's mother said with a lachrymose face, "No *appa,* I do not allow my daughter to die in this hospital right before my eyes. Let her live as long as she can in our village, though she may not regain her eyesight." "I also feel the same way," said Siddappa. Then Basavanti's mother asked Siddappa. "*Appa,* please go and tell the doctor that we would proceed to our village and consult our elders." Siddappa went to the doctor's chamber and returned after five minutes. Then they went back to their lodge, collected their bags and rushed to the Bus-Stand threading their way through the maddening crowd of Bangalore. Then they boarded the government bus bound for Hubli.

They reached Nagarahalli in the early morning. They were utterly tired because of their walk for three miles from Sisvinahalli. They took rest for a couple of hours. Then Siddappa walked to the tank with a pitcher. Chinnappagouda was sitting on the bank of the tank with his incarnadined mouth. He was surprised at the sight of Siddappa who had returned from Bangalore so soon. "*Le* Sidda, why did you return from Bangalore so quickly? What happened there?" Siddappa walked near Chinnappagouda, kept the pitcher on the earth and said in a pathetic tone, "Goudre, *amma* is very unlucky. Terrible misfortune has befallen her." Chinnappagouda knit his brows and asked him in an irritated manner, "Whatever has happened to her, tell me clearly, fellow." He waited patiently for the answer. Siddappa cleared his throat and narrated the whole story. Chinnappagouda's face grew pale gradually. Both of them remained speechless for a few minutes. Then Siddappa stepped down into the water and filled his pitcher and walked home. Chinnappagouda walked towards his jowar field where a number of daily wagers had gone ahead for weeding the grass. But Chinnappagouda was feeling restless and depressed by the news that he had heard from Siddappa. Time seemed to hang so heavily upon him. He didn't even relish his lunch in the afternoon. As soon as dusk fell on the earth, he rushed to Basavanti's house and enquired about her Bangalore trip. Basavanti told him that her mother would narrate everything to him. Accordingly Basavanti's mother narrated all the details of the case and the doctor's opinion. Basavanti was shedding tears silently. Chinnappagouda heaved a long sigh and said in a consolatory tone, "All right then. Let everything be as per God's wish." After dinner Basavanti's mother went to the Monastery along with her youngest daughter for sleeping there. Chinnappagouda hugged Basavanti and consoled her. He did not feel like indulging in his usual amours with her that night at least.

A month elapsed. Chinnappagouda started visiting her only twice a week instead of every night. Basavanti developed some doubt about her lover's bonafides though she could not articulate it to anybody. She noticed that she had grey hairs on her head and wrinkles on her skin. Some three months elapsed like this. Then Chinnappagouda started visiting her only once a fortnight. Basavanti began to feel more and more lonely and insecure. One day she asked him the cause. He replied, "What shall I do, dear? I have so much of work to attend to on the farms. I hardly get any time these days." Another three months elapsed when Chinnappagouda stopped his visits altogether. Basavanti waited and waited for him. But alas, he never came. Basavanti, therefore, fell to deep thinking about her fate, which had led her through the unexpected ups and downs of life. She had nobody to fall back upon except her helpless mother and immature sister. Neither brothers, nor maternal uncles nor any distant male relatives could come to her rescue at the moments of emergency in her life as they had not approved of her behaviour. She grew more and more inward and developed a sort of cynicism about life.

One day Basavanti was crying in a muffled voice. Her mother understood it and asked her, "Had you lived with your husband, would he have neglected you like this?" Unable to control her feeling, she also burst into tears. Thus both of them cried until they were exhausted. Basavanti had hardened herself inwardiy. The mother questioned her daughter, "What shall we do for our daily bread, my daughter? Shall I go for work in the *Goudasani's* fields?" Basavanti was angered a bit and interrogated, "Should I send an old woman like you for work? No, that shall never be." The mother tried to console her, "There is no other way, my daughter." Basavanti took a deep breath and said firmly, "Let him not come if he doesn't want to. I can live by myself as long as I can. I shall pledge my gold and live alone without him." The mother appreciated her daughter's courage inwardly.

The next day, Basavanti went to Navalgund with her mother and pledged her golden necklace and bangles and collected some money from the *saraf.* She did not have to sign any paper because of the mutual faith they had for several years. After returning from Navalgund, Basavanti decided to live on only one meal per day as a punishment for her illegal existence with her lover. She did not listen even to her mother's advice. Within three months she lost nearly half of her weight and began to look like a frightening skeleton. The mother was deeply worried about her daughter's declining health and cried before the neighbours who sympathized with her. But there was nobody to help them out. A few neighbours came to Basavanti's house and consoled her. But Basavanti did not show any diffidence. She told them, "I have accepted whatever has happened in my life and shall do so in future also." "Have your brothers come to see you, Basavanti?" asked one of the neighbours. Basavanti replied, "My brothers have severed their relation with me long back *i.e.* as soon as I left my husband. I don't think they would ever care to see me now." The neighbours heaved a deep sigh of sympathy and walked away to their homes. A week passed like this. Basavanti was waning day by day.

One day Basavanti refused to take her single meal also. The mother tried to force her gently to have at least one meal per day, but Basavanti said firmly in her weak voice, "I want to die as early as possible. I don't want to be a liability to any one." The mother sobbed in muffled voice and remained helpless. As hours went by, Basavanti grew weaker and weaker. After three days of total starvation, she breathed her last. The mother and sister fell on Basavanti's cooling body and screamed and wailed piteously. The neighbours who heard the mourning cries rushed to their house and joined the chorus of wailing and crying. "God, why did you not take me away first by sparing my daughter? Is there any mother unluckier than I?" wailed the mother. Then a few men came and bathed the dead body of Basavanti and sat it in a lotus posture against the wall and decorated it with *vibhuti* marks, flowers, and garlands and lit the joss sticks. Chinnappagouda who heard the news of his ex-beloved's death could not control his tears. He rushed to the spot and offered his last homage to her. He called his loyal servant Siddappa and gave him sufficient money to arrange the funeral rites properly. The members of the *bhajan* chorus sang about the ephemerality of life as described by the Sarif of Sisunal. Before the evening they took the dead body on a well-decked hearse and buried it according to the Lingayat rites and returned home silently.

After three days when the sepulchral gravity had thinned to a marked extent, three village women were walking towards the tank for water. They were carrying the empty pitchers on their heads. When they went past the late Basavanti's thatched house, they began to interpret her life in different ways. Kallavva said, "See friend, Basavanti went blind because she had let her bath water across the temple road." "No," said Mallavva, "that cannot be the reason. I feel that she suffered because she had abandoned her husband." "No, no, no," said Nilavva; "She had to die like that on account of the curse of Chinnappagouda's wife." "None of these might be the real cause of her suffering. It must be only because of her past *karma*," said Lingavva.

□□□

11

The Golden Servant

DURING THE Vijayanagara Empire there lived a chieftain called Biregouda in a village called Bada adjacent to Bankapura in the southern part of Dharwad district in Karnataka. Religious, truthful and heroic by nature, Biregouda was an ardent devotee of Lord Adikesava of the local temple. As an administrator he maintained perfect peace, law and order in his village. The natives of Bada were happy and led a fearless and peaceful life.

Biregouda had a devoted and understanding wife called Bachchamma who believed in hard work and respect for high values of life. Though Biregouda belonged to the shepherd community, he was respected by people of all communities in his administrative area. Though the couple had all the material comforts and sufficient wealth, they were secretly anxious about the lack of progeny for them. They, therefore, used to pray to their family deity, Lord Venkateswara of Tirupati.

One morning Bachchamma woke up in the early morning, sprinkled water on the threshold and put five marks of vermilion on it. Biregouda completed his bath and walked to the temple of Lord Adikesava. After offering his reverence to the deity, he returned home and sat in the kitchen. Bachchamma was patting the jowar *rottis* and baking them. She served the *rottis,* vegetable curry and curds to her husband. Biregouda savored the breakfast with real gusto. Then Bachchamma also completed her breakfast. Then both of them sat in the outer room of their house chewing edible leaf and betel. She remembered something and said, "See sir, yesterday I saw a dream in which Lord Venkateswara of Tirupati beckoned to me invitingly and then disappeared." "Is that so? My dear, I forgot to tell you. I too had a dream in the early morning today. I too saw Lord Venkateswara of Tirupati inviting me with his gestures." Bachchamma was really surprised and exclaimed, "Isn't it strange that both of us should have similar dreams?" "Yes, yes, that is really strange. Who knows when the Lord may cast his eyes on us?" said Biregouda. Bachchamma said, "I think the Lord of the Seven Hills has invited both of us to his abode to bless us. Why not we go there and have His *darsan*?" "Why not? That's a good idea. The pilgrimage to Tirupati will give us some peace of mind," said Biregouda. They decided to undertake a journey to Tirupati after a couple of days.

Bachchamma prepared some jowar *rottis,* dry chutney power, sweet balls and fried *kadabus* and packed them in a cloth-bag. On Monday, both Biregouda and Bachchamma completed the morning chores and bath. After having their breakfast, they set out on their journey towards Tirupati. They climbed the hills and dales, crossed the rivers and brooks and waded through the thick forests. On the way they watched the beauty of various birds, beasts, trees, creepers, sunrise and sunset and felt an aesthetic ecstasy. Thus they trudged their path continuously for about a whole month. Finally they reached the holy city of Tirupati situated on the undulated and sublime hills. Extremely tired of the journey, Biregouda and Bachchamma camped at the outskirts of Tirupati and relaxed for a few hours. The next morning they climbed the hill, walked to the imposing temple and had a *darsan* of Lord Venkateswara. Both of them felt an unprecedented peace and satisfaction in the vicinity of the lord. They observed many vows for a long period of forty-eight days and served the deity with deep devotion. After the completion of their vows, they had the last *darsan* of the deity and returned to their camp. That night Biregouda saw a dream, in which Lord Venkatapati approached him, gave him a fruit and asked him to share it with his wife. He ate the fruit according to the divine direction. Likewise Bachchamma also saw a dream in which she stood in front of the deity with joined palms and felt a mass of light rushed from the deity and entered her thereby electrifying her entire body. She felt an unprecedented ecstasy. She was suddenly awakened from the exciting dream. She was so happy that she narrated the contents of her dream to her husband. Both of them thanked the Lord of Seven Hills for blessing them. Then they started their return journey to Bada. On the way the couple visited many holy shrines at Mailara, Kuravatti, Devaragudda, Kadaramandalagi, Haveri, Kaginelli and Kunduru. Finally they reached Bada. Though they were extremely tired of the journey, they were beaming with an inexplicable sense of satisfaction. Everyday they meditated upon Lord Venkateswara and offered holy service to him in their abode.

Nearly a month and a half elapsed. Bachchamma noticed that she did not have her monthly period this time. Though inwardly she felt happy, she did not divulge the matter to Biregouda who was busy with his local administration. She wanted to confirm it before letting her husband know about it. She waited for another month very patiently. She was happy to notice that she did not have her monthly period for the second time also. Besides, she observed a slight bulge in her belly. Now she was so happy that she could not contain herself. She waited eagerly for Biregouda to come home from the village *chavadi.* Biregouda returned home at midday and jumped off his horse. He tethered the horse in the stable and entered the house. Bachchamma offered him cool water from the earthen pot. He washed his hands, face and feet and rubbed them clean with a towel. Then Bachchamma served him with the lunch of *holige,* ghee, vegetable curry, rice and curds. As Biregouda was monstrously hungry, he savored the delicacies with extraordinary gusto. Then both of them relaxed on the woolen mattress and chewed betel and leaf. "I have a surprise for you," said Bachchamma. "What's that?" asked Biregouda gently. "No, I am too shy to tell you," said she. "Don't be shy. Tell me what it is," persuaded Biregouda. Then Bachchamma took his right palm in her right palm and placed it upon the bulge of her belly. Then Biregouda understood that he was going to have a progeny in course of time. He burst out in ecstasy, "O Lord Venkateswara, you are really very great. You have listened to our prayers and granted our wishes." Then Biregouda kept his ear on Bachchamma's bulge of belly and listened. Bachchamma felt abashed and covered her face with her palms.

As days passed, Bachchamma began to vomit frequently. She also developed 'pregnancy desires' for a variety of eatables. Biregouda wanted to satisfy all her desires and got her whatever nut or fruit or leaf or herb she asked for. As the bulge of her belly grew more and more prominent, she could not walk about as quickly as in the past. She felt the smarts of pain as the baby within her womb kicked about. But she tolerated all that pain with the happy prospects of getting a progeny. As she completed nine months and nine days of pregnancy, she began to have labour pains. Biregouda quickly sent for a midwife. The midwife rushed to his house along with a few companions. Biregouda and his friends sat outside the house when the midwife and her companions were busy attending to Bachchamma's delivery inside. After an hour or so of waiting, Biregouda was thrilled to hear the shrill cry of a newborn baby. One of the women came out and announced, "You are lucky sir. You have got a son." Biregouda was extremely happy to learn the news and thanked Lord Venkateswara of Tirupati for having blessed him with a son at last. His dream was realized after a long and anxious waiting. That day happened to be the Thursday of Kartika bahula tadige of Anandanama Calendar year.

The couple was ecstatic about the birth of a son to them. Biregouda, therefore, offered special services to the local deity, Lord Adikesava and other deities in temples. He arranged for the lighting of countless wick lamps in the temple and distributed sugarcandy to all the people of the village. The people of the surrounding villages also jubilated over the birth of a son to their beloved chieftain Biregouda.

On the thirteenth day after the birth of the baby, Biregouda arranged for the cradling ceremony. Kith and kin, men and women, friends and neighbours gathered in his house in the evening. The *muttaides* sang beautiful songs in a chorus. The priest officiated over the ceremony. Then the *muttaides* passed the baby around the cradle for five times, and placed it in the cradle. They named him as Timmappa as he was born due to the grace of the Lord of Seven Hills at Tirupati. The women sang many more sangs before having their feast of *holige*, *kadabu*, rice and *sandige* etc.

Baby Timma happened to be a very smart and cute child and gradually grew into a very accomplished young man. Right from the days of his childhood, Timma had developed a special devotion to Divinity. He used to spend most of his time in visiting the local temples and singing devotional songs. He never missed the opportunity of listening to the religious discourses in his own village or in the neighbouring villages. He was excited by the examples of mythical figures like Rama, Krisna, Hanumanta, Bhisma, Dharmaraja and Arjuna etc. He developed a special liking for Sri Krisna.

As a boy, Timma used to watch the regular religious festivals conducted in the village. Every year the devotees of Bada used to bring the icon of Siddharaya on a palanquin from a village called Konanuru to Bada and settle it at some place of the village and conduct cultural activities like folk-singing, dancing and rituals. Timma used to watch the annual programme with great curiosity and attention and was deeply influenced by it.

Once a grand competition of drum playing was to be conducted in Bankapura. The drum-players of *Kuruba* communities from all the surrounding villages were expected to participate in the competition. Timma was excited by the very idea of the forthcoming event. He, therefore, asked Biregouda, "Father, please get me a drum. I wish to participate in the drum-playing competition." Biregouda was surprised by Timma's ambition. But he tried to dissuade him, "My dear son, you are still a boy. How can you compete with elders and that too experts in drum playing? It is better for you to watch them." But Timma insisted, "No, father. I must have a drum of my own. I will definitely participate in it." Biregouda understood the strong desire of his son. He did not want to discourage his only son who was the apple of his eye. He, therefore, ordered for a new drum and got it for his dear son. On the day scheduled for the competition, many shepherds from surrounding villages flocked to Bankapura. They wore half shirts and knee-length dhotis and carried the folded woolen blankets on their left shoulders. They carried large drums upon their chest hung from their necks. A large crowd had gathered on the open ground in Bankapura to watch the game. The drummers started playing upon the drums with sticks and palms thereby providing a deafening boom. The terrific sound produced from the drums of different sizes echoed in the village. Though a boy, Timma played his drum very dexterously and enthusiastically. He bent forward, thumped and rattled the drum. Then he clapped and struck the drum with his palms rhythmically. As he increased the tempo of the beats, he began to dance ecstatically. Biregouda, who watched his son's playing upon the drum so wonderfully, could not believe his own eyes. Bachchamma who stood in the crowd watching her son drumming shed silent tears of joy. All the villagers expressed their joy and wonder at Timma and exclaimed, "Look at the young boy who surpasses even the senior players in producing the precise beats so artistically!" They cheered him, "Vahva, Timma, Vahva, Vahva!" You are the pride of our village."

Biregouda, who knew the great potentialities of his son, thought of making proper arrangements for Timma's education. Instantly he thought of sending his son to Srinivasacarya, a great scholar of Bankapura. But a sudden doubt also arose in his mind. "Would the brahmin teacher agree to teach a boy of shepherd community?" doubted he. He consulted his wife Bachchamma about it. She counter-questioned him, "Why do you have such doubts beforehand? You first meet and consult the teacher. If he accepts our son, it is well and good. Otherwise we can think of an alternative plan." He tried to awaken her to the rigid caste system operative in the society of that time. He said, "You do not understand the subtlety of the problem. In our society, brahmins are known for their sense of superiority. They do not want to pollute themselves by any intercourse with sudras. That is the reason why I am a little hesitant to approach Srinivasacarya." Bachchamma said, "Of course, what you say is true. I can understand the problem. But there is nothing wrong in trying." Encouraged by his wife, Biregouda took Timma to Srinivasacarya's house. The acarya who saw Biregouda welcomed him, "Welcome to the Administrator, please be seated." Both of them sat on the mattress facing each other. Timma sat beside his father. After the exchange of amicabilities, Srinivasacarya came to the main point and asked him, "Dear Sir, what's the urgent matter that brings you to a poor teacher's home?" "Acarya Sir, you know my son Timma is very eager to be educated. I want to give him good education, which was denied to me by my fate. I, therefore, thought of you. Would it be possible for you to accept Timma as your student and tutor him?" Srinivasacarya beamed with a smile and said, "Administrator sir, why do you hesitate to ask this? I'll be only too glad to teach your son. I was even thinking of requesting you to send your son for tutoring. Nowadays it is so difficult to find deserving disciples. I shall carve your son into a beautiful statue." Biregouda was secretly overjoyed by the acarya's answer. He joined his palms in reverence and said, "I am very grateful to you, acarya sir. I hope and believe that you'll show the right path and direction to my son." Biregouda beckoned to Timma who bowed down to the acarya reverentially. Srinivasacarya said, "My dear Timma, you come tomorrow, and offer worship to Goddess Saraswati. Then we shall initiate you into learning." Biregouda and Timma bowed down to the acarya once again and took leave of him.

When Bachchamma learnt that Srinivasacarya had accepted her son as a student, she was extremely happy. The next morning Timma had his bath and walked to Srinivasacarya's house. He was received affectionately by the acarya and introduced to other students in his residential school. As per the guru's guidance, Timma offered worship to the icon of Goddess Sarada and distributed *prasada* to all the students. He bowed down to the feet of the acarya who blessed him to be a learned man. Then the acarya started the first lesson. He spread some sand upon the floor in the verandah and began to draw the Sanskrit and Kannada alphabets on it and asked the students to imitate it on the sand on other part of the floor. Timma observed everything avidly and began to copy it meticulously.

Timma attended school regularly and religiously. The acarya was extremely happy to observe that Timma was very quick in grasping the points taught by him. There was a remarkable brightness in Timma's eyes. As years went by, Timma began to absorb knowledge like a sponge. The acarya taught Timma and other students various branches of knowledge like poetry, drama, ethics, grammar, prosody and mythology including the *Ramayana*, the *Mahabharata* and the *Bhagavata*. When Timma reached the age of about twelve, he had achieved remarkable proficiency in Kannada and Sanskrit languages. The acarya was really surprised by the boy's precocity and immensely pleased by his rapid intellectual progress. He, therefore, used to call the boy "Timmarasa" affectionately. By that time Timma began to compose poetry in Kannada. The acarya was really flabbergasted by the precocity of the boy, his extraordinary power of grasping, logical mind and ethical discrimination. He, therefore, thought that his teaching had been more than fruitful. Like the acarya, Timma's parents were also extremely happy about his academic accomplishment.

After the completion of academic education, Timma was in need of administrative training. Biregouda, therefore, took him to a local teacher and asked him to train Timma in the martial arts. By now Timma had grown into a hefty and smart youngman. He began to attend daily classes and learn wrestling, swimming, archery, and horse riding and other martial arts. The teacher was really surprised at the rapid progress made by Timma in everything that he learnt. Timma thus developed a healthy body to complement his healthy mind and achieved a balance between the two. He matured day by day as the philosophical bent of his mind began to assert itself. He began to think deeply about the cause, the purpose, the nature and mystery of human life in general and tried to understand them as much as he could.

One day he sat under a mango tree outside the village and began to sing the *bhajans* of Lord Adikesava. His companions also sang by imitating him. Soon Timma closed his eyes and went on singing rapturously, oblivious of the world around him. His companions repeated his tunes. Lo! Suddenly there came a snake slithering from somewhere and held up its hood with a flourish. The companions who saw the snake with its raised hood stationed before them began to run for life. But Timma who was immersed in his ecstatic singing did not open his eyes until the *bhajan* was over. The snake swayed its hood before him for some time and then slithered away from there. Then the companions returned to the spot and awakened Timma from his trance by their noise. They asked him as to why he did not open his eyes and run away from the spot when there was a snake playing before him. Timma replied that he did not see any snake or thing as he was seeing the image of Lord Adikesava before his minds' eye. But his companions could not understand the meaning of his reply. They smiled at one another and returned home.

After a few days had gone by, Timma sat under a mango tree meditating on God. As the meditation reached its climax, he had a vision of Hanumanta, son of Vayu. He was really exhilarated by the spiritual experience. He returned home and persuaded Biregouda, "Father, please establish an icon of Hanumanta in the temple of Adikesava." Biregouda did not want to disappoint his only son. He, therefore, ordered for the moulding of a bell-metal icon of Hanumanta from a local blacksmith and saw to it that the icon was established ritually in the temple of Adikesava. Timma was very happy with his father for complying with his requests, and thought that the same task would continue in future. When Timma was developing cheerful dreams about his life in his thirteenth year, Biregouda fell ill most unexpectedly. Bachchamma and Timma took utmost care about Biregouda's health, by hiring the services of an *ayurvedic* doctor. But God had willed it otherwise. One day Biregouda breathed his last. All the villagers gathered at Biregouda's house, wailed and cried and arranged the funeral. Timma felt as though the glass palace in which he was living had been shattered to pieces. He hugged his mother and cried piteously. In-between his sobs he asked his mother, "Mother, will not father ever return? How shall we live without him? Who will help us in our life?" Although Bachchamma was herself disconsolate, she controlled her sorrow and tried to console him, "My dear son, your father left you and me as soon his tenure in mortal life was over. You are a young man now and should not be afraid of anything. You have to face life boldly. May the memory of your father embolden you to find your path in life. We have to depend upon God's grace, help and mercy." Timma tried to understand the deeper meaning of his mother's advice. His friends and other relations also tried to console him by their words of encouragement. But Timma missed his father conspicuously and suffered from a deep sense of loneliness.

After the death of Biregouda, Timma and his mother began to suffer from not only loneliness but also from a deep sense of emotional and financial insecurity. They heard rumours that Biregouda's arch-enemy Mallanayaka had rushed to the Emperor of Vijayanagara, carried tales against the late Biregouda and succeeded in getting the position of Administrator of seventy-eight villages. The people belonging to Mallanayaka's gang began to harass Bachchamma and Timma in many ways. At night, stones were pelted at Timma's house. Sometimes the rowdies were sent by Mallanayaka to pick quarrel with Timma and Bachchamma with some pretext or the other. One day somebody had bored a big hole in the roof of Timma's house thereby letting in all the rainwater. Bachchamma and Timma were deeply disturbed by the antipathy of men belonging to Mallanayaka. She, therefore, said to Timma, "My son I am feeling very lonely and insecure in this Bada. The rowdies of Mallanayaka may harm you any time out of jealousy and enmity.

Let us leave this village and go to our kith and kin at Kaginelli." Timma was convinced by his mother's argument. After a couple of days, they packed their belongings and went to Kaginelli in a bullock cart. Their stay with relatives in Kaginelli gave them a sense of security and satisfaction.

Kaginelli happened to be an important *paragana* during the Vijayanagara Empire. Situated in the rainy area of Kannada speakers, the village had an abundance of natural wealth and beauty. There were many temples and devotees in it. Kaginelli, therefore, provided a very congenial atmosphere for Timma to consolidate his spirituality. He used to visit the temple of Lord Hanumanta at Kadaramandalige, and the temple of Purasiddheswara at Haveri quite often. Sometimes he used to go to Bada also in disguise in order to render service to Lord Adikesava.

As a boy of eighteen, Timma started a night school at Kaginelli and trained the youngmen of the village to sing devotional songs and to act the roles of mythical heroes like Arjuna and others in the *Yaksagana* folk plays. He was himself an expert actor by now. He also used to arrange the performances of puppet plays. Thus Timma became well-known as a spiritually inclined youth, an actor, a musician, a poet and a scholar. But in spite of all these accomplishments, he had not neglected his routine duty of tending the sheep and goats.

One day Timma had his breakfast of *rotti*, *dhal* and curds. He took up a pickaxe and went to the field. He hitched up his *dhoti* between his thighs and began to dig the earth in order to root out the deep weeds. As he struck his pickaxe deep into the earth, the clods of earth were loosened and separated from the hard mass of earth. He perspired profusely as he worked hard. He struck the pickaxe into the hard earth with a thump. As he continued to strike his digging tool, suddenly he was surprised to hear a metallic sound instead of a thump. He struck for another eight or ten times and heard the thumping and metallic sounds alternately. Naturally he grew curious about the metallic sound and therefore loosened the earth there carefully. Lo, he was surprised to see half a dozen copper pitchers hidden in the earth. He lifted up the heavy pitchers from the depth of the earth and opened them. Lo, he was further surprised to see that the pitchers were filled with golden coins. By that time the midday sun had reached the zenith of the sky. Timma considered the wealth as a godsend and carried the heavy pitchers to his house one after the other. His mother Bachchamma was also surprised to see the golden coins in the pitchers. Timma did not want to hoard that wealth for his selfish purposes. Instead, he, like a truly detached person, spent it for ameliorative purposes like distribution of food to the poor, religious festivals, repair of dilapidated temples and holy service in the local temples. The people of Kaginelli who wondered at his non-possessive nature, considered him as a great donor and began to call him 'Kanakappa' or man of gold, and he grew more and more popular as days went by.

Mallanayaka, the arch-enemy of Kanakappa's late father heard about the popularity of the youngman through his friends and felt deep stings of jealousy. He even feared that Kanaka might become his rival in course of time. He, therefore, decided to murder Kanaka. He took a few of his followers from Bada to Kaginelli and surrounded Kanaka's house. Although Kanaka was well trained in the martial art, he never had a chance to exhibit the power of his brawn. When he heard the challenge by Mallanayaka and his gang, his righteous indignation being awakened, he rushed out of his house well armed and fought with them ferociously. But how could a single fighter face a number of enemies surrounding him? When one of Mallanayaka's gang struck Kanaka on the head from behind, Kanaka collapsed on the earth and lay unconscious. Mallanayaka and his gang took him for dead and ran away from there. By that time the friends and followers of Kanaka rushed to him, dressed his wounds and nursed him carefully. Consequently Kanaka recovered his consciousness, consoled his mother and friends. He broke into a reflective song about man's essential loneliness and need for the company of God. He took nearly three months to recover from pain. During this period he began to compose songs full of devotion to Lord Hari and preach the same to the villagers. This effort resulted in the composition of the famous poem called *Haribhakti Sara*.

Kanaka's reputation as a great devotee, poet, and disciplined man spread far and wide in the society and reached even the Emperor of Vijayanagara. He was, therefore, invited by Sri Krisnadevaraya to be appointed as the Administrator (Dandanayaka) of Bada and Bankapura. Mallanayaka who heard the news of Kanaka's appointment felt deeply jealous of his enemy but kept quiet because of his helplessness and fear of the Emperor. Kanaka's mother Bachchamma felt ecstatic about her son's turn of luck. As per the royal order, Kanaka sat in the *ambari* on an elephant and rode to Vijayanagara to participate in the Vijayadasami Festival.

Kanaka was thrilled by the sight of great temples of Virupaksa and Ganesa and other magnificent architectural buildings, palace and durbar. He was deeply impressed by the virtue and grandeur of Sri Krisnadevaraya. He stayed in Hampi for ten days and observed all the religious festivities with great attention. Kanaka saw a similarity between Lord Sri Krisna and Sri Krisnadevaraya. Suddenly an idea flashed across his mind, which inspired him to compose a poem called *Mohana Tarangini* in the near future. On the last day, Kanaka received the formal order of appointment as the Administrator of Bada and Bankapura, royal vests, a gem-studded sword and the title of 'Nayaka'. Kanaka Nayaka was thrilled beyond measure at the quirk of his fate. He had attained a high position without even struggling for it. He returned home with a sense of satisfaction.

As the administrator, Kanaka Nayaka dedicated himself to the developmental activities in Bada and Bankapura like the construction of reservoirs, canals, roads and repair of temples. By that time his mother had grown quite old and persuaded her son, "My dear son, now that you are financially well settled in life, it is high time for you to get married." Kanaka replied, "why this hurry for the marriage mother? Let's wait for some more time." Bachchamma reacted more strongly, "Don't you know my son, that I am getting old? Do you want me to slog forever? Should I not have the help of a daughter-in-law in the household work? Should I not play with my grandchildren before my death?" Now Kanaka Nayaka understood the serious import of his mother's words. He felt the urgency of his marriage and the importance of fulfilling his mother's wish. He said, "All right, mother, I understand the spirit of your words. Although personally I am not inclined to marriage, I shall get married mainly for your sake. Are you happy now at least?" Bachchamma brightened with hope and beamed with satisfaction. She got herself busy in looking for suitable brides and finally selected a bride from a famous family of Bankapura. Within a couple of months the wedding took place with great pomp and jubilation.

When the daughter-in-law was received into Kanaka Nayaka's house, Bachchamma endearingly named her as Laxmidevi. Kanaka Nayaka loved his wife deeply because of her virtue and courteous manners. He led a happy married life with her. Within a year after marriage, he was blessed with a son whom he named as Biranayaka after his grandfather. Thus Kanaka Nayaka was discharging his duties as an Administrator and as a householder in the external world. But deep inside him he was also maturing spiritually.

Kanaka Nayaka never knew that Lakkamma, daughter of Mallanayaka had decided to marry him. She had told her father, "Father, I don't want to marry anyone other than Kanaka Nayaka." But Mallanayaka had reacted very strongly against that, "Do you want to marry the son of my arch-enemy? Never. I shall never permit you to marry him. On the other hand, you may choose to marry any other young man of our community." But Lakkamma never wanted to marry any man other than Kanaka Nayaka as she had set her heart on him. Meanwhile she was shocked to learn that Kanaka Nayaka had married Laxmidevi, she therefore, decided to be a *sanyasini*.

One day Kanaka Nayaka was sitting in the temple yard. A

young lady with her head covered with the hem of her sari walked to him and fell prostrate at his feet. Kanaka Nayaka was really surprised by the salutation by a strange lady. But without betraying his sense of surprise, he asked her to get up. The young lady got up and stood before him. Kanaka Nayaka asked her, "Madam, may I know who you are and why you saluted me so ceremoniously?" The young lady looked at him passionately and said, "Sir, can you recognize me?" Kanaka Nayaka felt puzzled and said, "Madam, to be very frank, I cannot recognize you. Nor can I remember having ever seen you in the past." The young lady broke into a wan smile and said, "Dear sir, of course, you have never seen me as a young lady. That is why you could not recognize me. You had seen me when I was just a slip of a girl." "Is that so? I am sorry I could not remember that," said Kanaka Nayaka, and continued, "Now you tell me who you are, what your name is and what you want from me." The young lady cleared her throat and said, "I have come here all the way from my village exactly to answer your questions." Kanaka Nayaka waited in silence. She moved nearer to him and said, "Dear sir, I am Lakkamma, daughter of Mallanayaka." Kanaka Nayaka grew stiff at the mere mention of Mallanayaka. "Dear sir, don't be upset," said Lakkamma, "I know you hate my father and my father also hates you. But ever since I grew into a young lady, I have been loving and worshipping you in my heart. In fact I wanted to marry you in spite of my father's strong opposition. But God willed it otherwise. I learnt that you are married to Laxmidevi. I know that as an already married man you cannot marry me now. I had decided that I should not marry anyone other than you. Hence I have decided to lead the life of a *sanyasini* until my death. So far I have never had a chance to express my feelings to you. That is the reason why I have come to you secretly. Kindly bless me to lead a holy life." As she completed her sentences, tears gushed out of her eyes and trickled down her cheeks. Kanaka Nayaka was stunned by the revelation of her feelings and remained silent for a few moments. He quickly recovered his sense of surprise and said, "My dear Lakkamma, please pardon me for my ignorance. I never knew that you loved me so intensely and wanted to marry me. I wish you had married some other young man and lived happily. But you have taken a very stern decision to become a *sanyasini*. I really appreciate your extraordinary courage. May Lord Adikesava bless you to lead a holy life." Kanaka Nayaka lifted his palms and blessed her. Lakkamma once again bowed down to his feet, wet them with her tears, and walked back briskly and sobbing. Kanaka Nayaka sat on the stone slab until the figure of Lakkamma disappeared from his sight. While he appreciated her bold decision, he felt deeply agonized by her sacrifice of worldly pleasures at the prime of her youth. It took him many years to forget her plight.

As an administrator Kanaka Nayaka had to shoulder a great responsibility in planning and executing the welfare activities. He arranged for the construction of a barrage across the Dharma river and a canal from it to irrigate the land. Likewise he arranged for the regular car-festival and fair of Lord Sangameswara at the confluence of Dharma and Varada rivers and of Lord Narasimha at Kaginelli. Similarly he arranged for the construction of a Rest House (Vihara Griha) at Kaginelli and named the newly formed village around the Rest House as 'Dasanakoppa.' He made all arrangements for the livelihood of farmers there as also in the neighbouring villages like Kunduru, Niraligi, Chandapura, Maranabidu, Chennapura, Haveri, Kabburu, Aduru, Aluru, Uppuhunise, Sanguru, Kulenuru, Varadimelehalli and Naganuru. He arranged for the construction of the temple of Goddess Sakti at Kunduru.

One of the memorable features of his administration was the complete removal of thievery in his area. In addition to appointing nightguards in the villages, he himself used to patrol at night. He also arranged for the repair of many reservoirs in his area. The people enjoyed peace and happiness during his administration. What was really admirable about Kanaka Nayaka was that, in spite of his busy schedule of administration, he camped for a few days in Kaginelli and began to compose his famous devotional poem called *Mohana Tarangini*.

When Kanaka Nayaka was at the height of his power, some unexpected events happened in his life. One day when Kanaka Nayaka was supervising the repair of a reservoir, a servant rushed to him and broke the news that his wife Laxmidevi and his male child Biranayaka had died. Kanaka Nayaka felt as if a thunder had struck him. He whipped the horse which cantered towards his home. He was shocked to see the dead bodies of his wife and child. Soon friends and relatives gathered and began to arrange for the funeral of mother and child. Bachchamma was wailing piteously over the dead bodies of her daughter-in-law and grandchild. Kanaka Nayaka instantly realized the ephemerality of life. He completed the formality of the funeral rites and remained depressed for a few days. Bachchamma was more depressed than her son about the tragic deaths in the family. Kanaka Nayaka was undergoing a spiritual transformation at the deeper level of his heart. He felt the transitoriness of worldly life very acutely. After the lapse of a couple of months, Bachchamma tried to fortify his emotional make-up. She broached the subject gently, "My dear son, how long do you remain alone? Whatever was destined to happen did happen. You are still young and have many hopes and aspirations in life. You listen to me, you better marry another girl and be happy in life." Kanaka Nayaka listened to her silently and patiently and did not respond immediately. Bachchamma goaded, "My son, what do you say? Do as I tell you. How long do you brood about the past.?" Kanaka Nayaka did not want to hurt the tenderhearted mother. He, therefore, replied gently, "Mother, I understand your concern for me. But I am not at all willing for the second marriage. Enough of my attachment to this worldly life which is full of pain and agony, disappointment and disillusionment. Don't you bother your mind about my marriage. You be happy with things as they are." Bachchamma understood the serious import of her son's words and kept quiet.

Meanwhile Mallanayaka, the arch-enemy of Kanaka Nayaka, who had lost his power as well as daughter was deeply disgruntled and was sharpening his dagger secretly. At the same time several changes had been happening in the Vijayanagara

Empire. Emperor Sri Krisnadevaraya had died after twenty years of grand reign. The Empire had begun to decline gradually. Mallanayaka had carried tales to the next Emperor against Kanaka Nayaka. Consequently Kanaka Nayaka lost his position as Administrator of Bada and Bankapura. All these events shook him deeply and awakened his latent spirituality.

Once Kanaka Nayaka was walking at the foot of a hillock. Everything was hazy around him. Suddenly he saw a grand figure on the top of the hillock. He guessed that the figure was none other than Lord Tirumalesa. He seemed to hear the Lord ordering him to become His servant (dasa). Kanaka Nayaka was awakened from the dream. He was really excited by the dream. Within a few weeks he had many dreams of similar pattern. He, therefore, began to think along the lines suggested by the Lord of Seven Hills in his dreams.

Meanwhile, a big gang of ruffians from the neighbouring villages attacked the people of Kaginelli. Kanaka Nayaka had, therefore, to fight with the strangers to defend his own village Kaginelli. He and his companions held wooden staves and encountered the enemies. In that tussle and confusion, one of the ruffians stabbed Kanaka Nayaka and another struck him on the head. Kanaka Nayaka fainted and sagged down to the ground. His companions feared that he might not recover his consciousness. However, they carried him in a palanquin to Bada and nursed him carefully by dressing his wounds with medicinal herbs and leaves. Soon he recovered his consciousness, but took several days to recover from illness. One night he saw a dream in which his favourite god appeared and asked him, "Do you become my servant now at least?" Kanaka Nayaka replied that he would take a proper decision after the complete recovery of his health. Then Lord Tirumalesa mocked at him, "You are a blind fellow, though endowed with eyes, and a deaf one, though endowed with ears. Do you know who it is who came riding the horse and felled you to the ground?" Then Lord Tirumalesa showed him the form of a soldier riding a horse. Then Kanaka Nayaka confessed to his blindness, deafness and ignorance and expressed his repentance. Lord Tirumalesa seemed to caress his entire body as a result of which all his wounds healed and all his pride and worldly desires disappeared. His body seemed to be electrified by a new spiritual enthusiasm. He joined his palms in reverence to the gods and said, "Forgive me God. I shall become your servant as ordered by you." He was suddenly awakened from the dream, but he began to dance ecstatically. That was how Kanaka Nayaka was transformed into Kanakadasa, the golden servant of Lord Adikesava. As a happy coincidence, he received an official letter from the Emperor of Vijayanagara to relinquish his position as the Administrator of Bada and Bankapura. Kanakadasa did so happily and thought it to be a good riddance. He decided to dedicate himself to the service of God. He expressed his disillusionment with the worldly service in the following song :

> Enough of the worldly service, Rangayya,
> Enough of the service of human beings.
> I am indeed tired of this worldly service, Rangaraya,
> Let me now meditate upon Thy feet,
> O Master of the World...

Thus there was a great transformation in Kanakadasa's life. He discarded the Administrator's uniform and adopted a new type of garments. He clad himself in a *dhoti* up to his knees, a black woolen blanket upon his left shoulder, a turban on his head and a pair of thick *chappals* under his feet. He slung a mono-stringed instrument called *Ekadari* on his right shoulder, a basket from his left shoulder and held a pair of castanets in his left fingers. Having sought his mother's permission, he went to Kunduru, the confluence of Dharma and Varada rivers, Naganuru, Haveri and finally to Kaginelli. The people who saw him in his new garbs were surprised beyond measure and asked him as to what had happened to him. But he replied to them in plain words, "So far I served the human world as much as I could. Henceforth I shall be a servant of God and spend the rest of my life in the service of God." The people were disarmed by his answer and minded their own business. Then Kanakadasa wended his way towards Tirupati via Kadaramandalige and

Kuruvatti. After several days of journey he reached Tirupati in the evening. Though extremely tired, he ascended the mountain, entered the temple of Lord Tirumalesa and sat in front of the deity singing ecstatically until sleep overtook him.

Kanakadasa woke up in the morning and walked to a nearby garden where he had his bath. There he happened to meet a great devotee of Harijan caste called Rangadasa and asked him, "Dear sir, could you tell me how I should have myself initiated into *dasa*-hood?" He then told Rangadasa who he was and where he had come from and other personal details. Then Rangadasa explained to Kanakadasa, "Youngman, you can become a servant of God only by conquering the six enemies of man like lust anger, greed, avarice, pride, and envy and by feeling the presence of God in all things and beings of the world." Kanakadasa understood the serious meaning of his advice and bowed down to him. He said to Rangadasa, "Dear sir, I consider you to be my guru from today. Kindly bless me." Rangadasa waved his palms affectionately at Kanakadasa and blessed him, "May God bless you by His grace."

Kanakadasa, then, walked back to the temple, stood on one leg with joined palms in front of the deity and implored, "Lord Venkateswara, kindly make me your *dasa*." He entered into a trance of meditation and had a miraculous experience. Lord Venkateswara seemed to walk out of the *sanctum sanctorum*, place his palms on Kanakadasa's head and say, "Child, go back to Bada immediately, but keep on coming here occasionally." Kanakadasa had an unprecedented experience of being overwhelmed with divine light and felt a sudden horripilation. He sang the praise of the Lord passionately. Then he returned to Bada as per the divine order. After reaching Bada, he learnt that his mother was already dead. Deeply saddened by the death of the mother, he rushed to her grave and worshipped it with *bhel*-leaves and flowers and burst into a song,

> I was saved, O Lord, I was saved,
> At last my worldliness came to an end,
> I could now have the grace of
> Lord Padumanabha's lotus-feet.

and danced ecstatically. He felt as if the whole cosmos was his abode. He felt electrified by new enthusiasm. He seemed to hear Lord Adikesava ordering him to go to Kaginelli. He instantly dislodged the heavy icon of Lord Adikesava, carried it on his shoulder and wended his way towards Kaginelli.

When the news about Kanakadasa's transporting of the statue of Adikesava circulated in Bada and Bankapura villages, the people grew angry and wanted to protest against it. Kanakadasa had already reached Kunduru by then. The people rushed to the spot and tried to prevent him from taking away the holy statue. They shouted at him and threatened him in loud voices, "How could you take away our holy statue of Adikesava without our permission? asked one of them. "If you don't stop your misadventure, we'll have to kill you," said another. Others hurled many abuses at him. But Kanakadasa, being enraptured in his spiritual meditation, went ahead quite unmindful of the popular protest against him. Some people wondered at his capacity to carry the heavy statue without any strain on his part and attributed it to some supernatural power in him and feared and backed out. But some others wanted to bind him to a tree and take back the statue from him. Hardly had a man gripped the arm of Kanakadasa when another man shouted, "Lo, look there. Our Bada and Bankapura have caught fire and been burning." People turned round and looked at their villages. They were simply flabbergasted by what they saw. They attributed the calamity to Kanakadasa's miraculous powers and dreaded him more and more. They hectically rushed back to their villages to save their kith and kin, and salvage their property.

Meanwhile Kanakadasa had crossed the confluence of Dharma and Varada rivers. Some people came back to him to apologize and seek his pardon "O sire, kindly forgive us. We mistook you for an ordinary man. You are indeed a great man." Kanakadasa simply smiled at them and walked ahead. After crossing Haveri, he reached Kaginelli where he established the holy statue of Lord Adikesava. In course of time he got a temple built there, arranged for the regular service, car-festival and other religious programmes. From then onwards Adikesava came to be known as "Adikesava of Kaginelli." Everyday Kanakadasa gave religious discourses to the willing devotees. The platform on which he sat and gave the discourses came to be known as 'the platform of Kanakadasa's discourses,' Kanakdasa began to dedicate his entire life for religious composition, singing and preaching the path of salvation to one and all.

* * *

After settling down at Kaginelli, Kanakadasa's spiritual hunger grew more and more intense. He, therefore, began to reflect seriously about life and wanted to share his spiritual knowledge with kindred souls. He travelled from place to place, met the learned people and held discussions with them. In his earlier phase of life, he had already acquainted himself with the rudiments of religion from Tatacarya who was the first acarya of Tirupati temple and guru for Sri Krisnadevaraya. After becoming the Administrator of Bada and Bankapura, he had acquainted himself with H.H. Vyasatirtha Swami also. But now Kanakadasa wanted to have an advanced spiritual knowledge from the same guru. He, therefore, travelled to the confluence of Kapila and Kaveri rivers and went to the Sosale Monastery at Tiruma-Kudalu.

When Kanakadasa stood at the entrance of the monastery, the people did not admit him into the building, as he looked like a boor with his black woolen blanket, sling bag, *ekadari* and castanets. With a coarse turban on his head, matted hair, and beard and a knee length *dhoti*, he looked like an uncultured person to them. Kanakadasa told them, "Gentlemen, I have travelled a long distance and come here only to see His Holiness Vyasaraya Swamiji. Kindly allow me to see him." One of the orthodox brahmins of the monastery said to him, "Fellow, you will not be admitted into the sacred temple until we know the details of your caste, clan and whereabouts." Kanakadasa was surmised by the callousness of the orthodox brahmins. He replied to them, "Gentlemen, please know that my home is the whole cosmos; my master is Lord Narayana Himself and a foolish servant like me has no caste at all." But the brahmins of the monastery being strict adherents of *varnasrama* system refused to be convinced by his elevated answer. Then Kanakadasa tried to convince them with a more realistic answer

We are shepherds
And Birayya is our Lord
Who guards the herds
Of human-sheep...

When the brahmins heard his song, they burst into guffaws of laughter and ridiculed him, "Look at the foolish fellow singing his strange song!"

But Vyasaraya Swamiji who was busy with holy service inside the monastery had a telepathic experience of restlessness. He, therefore, came out of the monastery thereby surprising the office-bearers and disciples. Vyasaraya Swamiji looked at the disheveled figure of the visitor and instantly identified him as Kanakadasa. He conducted him into the monastery affectionately and consoled him, "My dear Kanaka, please don't be hurt by the crude treatment extended to you by my disciples and the staff of the monastery. Their practice of religion is at a lower, mechanical level and they haven't risen to its higher, dynamic level. I apologize to you on their behalf." Kanakadasa joined his palms in reverence and said to Vyasaraya Swamiji, "Your Holiness, I am not hurt at all by the behaviour of your people here, as I know the nature of our society. I have taken it in my stride. Your Holiness, I have come all the way from Kaginelli to seek spiritual knowledge of higher kind. I request you to be my spiritual guru and accept me as your disciple." Vyasaraya Swamiji was deeply touched by the sincere request of Kanakadasa. Deep affection welled up in his heart. He, therefore, said gladly, "My dear Kanaka, I really feel lucky to have a disciple like you. By teaching a disciple like you, I shall have real fulfilment as a guru. You attend my classes from tomorrow itself." Kanakadasa was more than grateful to his guru and took his leave after bowing down to him reverentially.

The disciples of Vyasaraya Swamiji began to whisper and murmur their complaints against Kanakadasa's low caste and beggarly appearance. They were deeply surprised by their guru's acceptance of a man from the shepherd community as his disciple. Vyasaraya Swamiji who noticed the uneasiness of his disciples called them and explained to them, "My dear disciples, I understand your dissatisfaction with Kanakadasa. But please don't underrate him on account of his lowly birth, which is rather accidental. In fact, he is an extraordinary man, a Maha Bhagavata, a great devotee of Lord Visnu, a Sanskrit scholar and a poet." Although temporarily silenced by the guru's explanation, the disciples who were orthodox by nature did not accept Kanakadasa as their classmate whole-heartedly. The only exceptional disciple who understood and respected Kanakadasa was Purandaradasa.

The next day Kanakadasa went to attend the guru's class. In order to avoid a sense of embarrassment to his guru, Kanakadasa volunteered to sit away from other disciples and listen to the lesson. "Holy sir," said he, "I shall sit in this corner and listen to your lecture." Vyasaraya Swamiji was really overwhelmed by Kanakadasa's sensitiveness and discrimination. He, therefore, blessed him whole-heartedly, "May you be a godly person." But the disciples did not like their guru's liberal attitude to Kanakadasa. They began to look at Kanakadasa with contempt. Vyasaraya Swamiji was deeply hurt by the airs and arrogance of his orthodox disciples. He wanted to convince them about Kanakadasa's greatness at appropriate times.

One day Vyasaraya Swamiji gave his lecture on the universality of divine spirit by quoting a few lines from the *Isa Upanisad*. All the disciples listened to the lecture attentively. As usual, Kanakadasa sat in a far away corner and listened to the lecture. After the completion of the lecture, Vyasaraya Swamiji gave a banana to each one of his disciples including Kanakadasa and said, "My dear disciples, you eat these bananas at a secret place where none can see you." The students took the bananas and went in different directions in search of some secret places.

The next day, before beginning the lecture, the Swamiji asked the disciples, "Dear disciples, can you tell me where you ate your fruits?" One of the disciples said proudly, "Sir, I went to the riverbank where there was nobody around. I ate my banana there." Another disciple said very confidently, "Sir I went behind a big rock and ate my banana." Yet another disciple replied, "Sir, I went to a nearby field and confirmed that there was nobody around there. Then I ate the banana quickly." Likewise, the other disciples described the secret places at which they ate their bananas. Vyasaraya Swamiji listened to their answers and smiled at their inanity. Then he called Kanakadasa and asked him, "My dear Kanaka, tell me where you ate your banana?" Kanakadasa took out the banana from the fold of his upper garment, give it back to the Swamiji and answered, "Holy Sir, ! did not eat the banana because I could not find any secret place which was not seen by the divine eye." Vyasaraya Swami was deeply satisfied by Kanakadasa's answer. When the other orthodox disciples heard his answer, they felt sorry for not giving the same answer at the right time though they knew it. Then Vyasaraya Swamiji declared to the orthodox disciples, "Dear disciples, are you convinced now at least that Kanakadasa is an embodiment of spiritual experience and not a mere scholar?" The disciples felt crest-fallen and walked away from there secretly envying Kanakadasa.

On another occasion, Vyasaraya Swamiji conducted another test. He came straight from the *puja* room to the classroom with some item hidden in his fist. The disciples stood up in respect for their guru. Then Vyasaraya Swamiji said to them, "Dear disciples, can you tell me what I am holding in my palm? I shall give the first *tirtha* to the one who answers correctly." There was total silence in the classroom. Then the disciples answered one by one. "Sir, you are holding a piece of jaggery in your palm," said one. "Sir, you are holding a flower in your palm," said the second one. "Sir, you are holding rice-grains in your palm," said the third one. The other disciples gave their answers according to their limited imagination. Finally came the turn of Kanakadasa who closed his eyes for a few seconds, sang a riddle-song of seventy-five lines and answered, "Holy sir, you are holding a '*vasudeva-saligrama*' in your palm." Then Vyasaraya Swamiji said, "Dear disciples, now I will open my palm. See what is there." Everybody was waiting anxiously to see what was hidden in the guru's palm. The Swamiji opened his palm and showed the '*Saligrama*' to everybody thereby proving the height of Kanakadasa's intuition. The other disciples bent their heads in shame and walked to their respective seats in the classroom. It was only Purandaradasa who admired Kanakadasa inwardly.

After an interval of a few months, Vyasaraya Swamiji conducted a very sophisticated test. After completing his regular class, he said to his disciples, "My dear disciples, you have studied all the spiritual sciences and become great scholars by now. Could you tell me who among you is capable of going to Vaikuntha?" The disciples looked at one another with a sense of embarrassment and remained silent. They could neither give the right answer nor confess to their ignorance. Then the Swamiji broke into a smile and asked Kanakadasa, "My dear Kanaka, could you answer this question?" Kanakadasa stood up, joined his palms in reverence and replied, "Holy sir, I may go if 'I' can go." On hearing this answer the other disciples grew furious and attributed it to his arrogance. But Vyasaraya Swamiji, who understood the spirit behind Kanakadasa's words, wanted to make it explicit to the ignorant disciples. He, therefore, said to Kanakadasa, "Kanaka, I could not understand the meaning of your words. Don't you think your answer smacks of arrogance?" Then Kanakadasa joined his palms in reverence and replied, "Holy sir, my intention was neither to show off my learning nor to insult anyone. What I meant by my words is that a man can go to Vaikuntha if he can overcome his 'ego.' I did not mean that I would go to Vaikuntha." Vyasaraya Swamiji was extremely happy with the answer. All the other disciples were disarmed and silenced by Kanakadasa's linguistic expertise and sophistry of explanation, but they felt deep pangs of jealousy, nonetheless.

Once Vyasaraya Swamiji completed the external worship of Sri Hari inside the monastery. Kanakadasa was sitting outside the monastery. After the completion of external worship, Vayasaraya Swamiji sat enraptured in a mental worship of Sri Hari. He mentally established the icon of the divine lord in the lotus of his heart and decked it with a gem-studded crest, earrings and other ornaments and offered flowers and incense etc. Then he wanted to put a garland around the neck of the icon, but found the crest to be too big to allow the garland. He was, therefore, worrying about how to solve the problem. Kanakadasa, who sat outside the monastery, had also enraptured himself in the mental worship thereby participating in his guru's mental worship. Kanakadasa suggested loudly, "Holy sir, why do you worry? You may first remove the crest, and put the garland and then place the crest on the head of the Lord." Vyasaraya Swamiji was surprised beyond measure by the mystical height attained by Kanakadasa. He came out of the monastery and said, "*Dasa* supreme, you are really a great soul. We deem ourselves lucky to have had you amidst us in this sacred complex. You have nothing to learn. You are a spiritual expert now. Mere learning, caste, or power will not help anyone for God-realization. We have blessed you wholeheartedly with spiritual wisdom." Vyasaraya Swamiji respected Kanakadasa by accepting him as an inner disciple. But the orthodox brahmin disciples felt deeply jealous of Kanakadasa and tried to treat him contemptuously. Once they kept some fishes in his basket and a pot of toddy in his sling bag secretly. Then they went to Vyasaraya Swamiji and carried tales against him. Vyasaraya Swamiji did not want to hurt Kanakadasa but on the contrary tried to prove his mystical height to the orthodox disciples. He, therefore, said jokingly, "Dear Kanaka, your classmates are eager to see what you have kept in your basket and bag. Could you show it to them?" Then Kanakadasa felt inside the basket and showed them a few lotuses. He then, dipped his hand into the sling bag and showed them a pot of honey. On seeing them, Vyasaraya Swamiji smiled with a sense of pride and satisfaction, whereas the orthodox disciples were deeply surprised and felt ashamed of themselves.

A few months went by in routine teaching and learning in the monastery. One day Vyasaraya Swamiji completed his lecture. All the disciples were about to leave the classroom. Vyasaraya Swamiji turned to Kanakadasa and asked him in a jocular way, "My dear Kanaka, can you show us God?" All the disciples including Kanakadasa laughed heartily at the guru's question. Then Kanakadasa replied in a lighter vein, "All right, holy sir. I shall show you God tomorrow at the time of *puja*." The orthodox disciples looked at one another conspiratorially and laughed.

The next morning a crowd of people gathered at the monastery at the time of the regular *puja* to see how Kanakadasa would show them God by his magical power. Everybody was eagerly waiting for the miraculous event. Suddenly a terrific dog with a lolling tongue came yelping from within the crowd and entered the monastery. Everybody was scared of the animal. They shooed it and beat it heavily with canes. The dog, therefore, ran away from there howling piteously. The people waited for long for the arrival of God and went away disappointed. The brahmins of the monastery were jubilant to know that Kanakadasa could not exhibit his miraculous power that day.

In the evening Vyasaraya Swamiji teased Kanakadasa, "Why, Kanaka, you did not show us God in the morning?" He turned to the other disciples and asked them, "My dear disciples, did you see God this morning?" "No sir, we did not see any God," replied a disciple. "How can a poor fellow called Kanaka show us God?" said another disciple. "It is sheer humbug," said yet another disciple. Vyasaraya Swamiji was waiting for Kanakadasa's reply. Then Kanakadasa replied in a very sophisticated way, "Holy sir, this morning God had come in the form of a dog, but these people did not recognize the spirit of God in it. God could be seen only by the inner *i.e.*, subtle eye and not by the external *i.e.* gross eyes." Vyasaraya Swamiji nodded his approval of Kanakadasa's explanation. But all the orthodox disciples felt abashed by it. Then Vyasaraya Swamiji said to him, "All right, Kanaka, these people failed to see God this morning. Could you show Him to them once again next time?" "In that case, I shall show God tomorrow at the time of *puja*," replied Kanakadasa.

Next morning people gathered again at the monastery at the time of *puja* eager to see God. Lo, there came a terrific cobra hissing menacingly and entered the monastery. All the people were scared and began to run for life. The whole monastery was empty of people, except Vyasaraya Swamiji and Kanakadasa. Vyasaraya Swamiji recognized the Lord Supreme in the form of the cobra, offered it milk and bid farewell to it. He was extremely pleased with Kanakadasa's mystic achievement. He said to him, "My dear Kanaka, I am very happy with your spiritual progress. I have taught you everything that I know. You have nothing more to learn from me. Now I advise you to go to the Narasimha Monastery at the confluence of Kapila and Kaveri rivers and achieve spiritual fulfilment through service to Lord Hari. I bless you whole-heartedly." Kanakadasa was overwhelmed with reverence for the guru and fell prostrate at his lotus-feet.

* * *

Kanakadasa went to the confluence of Kapila and Kaveri rivers and stayed at the Narasimha Monastery surrounded by natural beauty. He studied the Vedas and composed many devotional songs. One day, when he was sleeping, he dreamt a dream in which Lord Venkateswara of Tirupati invited him to attend the festival *i.e.* Kalyana Mahotsava on the tenth day of Vaisakha month. Kanakadasa was thrilled by the dream. He instantly woke up, completed his bath and morning *puja* and set about his journey to Tirupati. On the way he visited the holy shrines of Sriranga at Srirangapattana, Sivanasamudra and Sriranga and sang many devotional songs.

Kanakadasa had gone near Tirupati. He had to spend one more day in travelling to reach the holy place. Chinnappa, Chairman of the temple at Tirupati dreamt a dream in which Lord Venkateswara ordered him to receive Kanakadasa with honour as the latter was coming to attend the Kalyana Mahotsava. Chinnappa considered it as a divine order. Next morning, he took a number of people with musical instruments like drums, *nagaswaram* and cymbals, fruits and royal umbrellas to receive Kanakadasa and walked down the hill.

Kanakadasa left Govindarajapura, had his bath at Kapila tirtha and started ascending the hill. He looked like a beggarly devotee. Chinnappa and his company were trying to guess at the wonderful appearance that Kanakadasa might have. It went very difficult for them to identify Kanakadasa. Chinnappa saw a beggarly devotee and accosted him, "O Dasayya, do you know Kanakadasa by any chance?" Kanakadasa replied, "Yes, I know him. He is a beggar," and went ahead. Chinnappa sought further information, "O Ayya, let him be a beggar or somebody. But tell me where he is now." Kanakadasa replied, "How can I answer that? He is ahead of the following pilgrims and behind the preceding ones." Chinnappa and his company thought him to be a fool, ignored him and descended the hill. Meanwhile Kanakadasa ascended the hill and slept in a corridor of the temple by covering himself with his woolen blanket, unmindful of his hunger and thirst. He inwardly teased Lord Venkateswara for inviting him for the latter's wedding and neglecting him totally. At that time a stranger came there, offered him a grand feast and creamy milk. He then covered Kanakadasa with a striped cloth and asked him to sleep comfortably.

Meanwhile Chinnappa and his company went down to the foot of the hill and waited in vain for Kanakadasa up to evening. But they could not identify anyone as Kanakadasa. Deeply disappointed, they ascended the hill and returned to the temple. Then they happened to see a man covered with a striped cloth sleeping there in the corridor. They instantly shook and awakened him. Chinnappa asked him, "Gentleman, who are you? Where have you come from? Why are you sleeping here?" Then the stranger shook off the sleep from his eyes and said, "Dear brothers, I am a native of Kaginelli. I have journeyed from the confluence of Kapila and Kaveri. I am called Kanakadasa." On hearing the answer, Chinnappa felt deeply surprised and guilty. He stammered, "Excuse me, holy sir. We could not make out that you are Kanakadasa. In fact we went down the hill only to receive you, but we could not identify you. Kindly pardon me for my mistake." He fell prostrate on Kanakadasa's feet reverentially. He, then, conducted Kanakadasa to a good place and arranged for his stay there. Kanakadasa slept comfortably in the big room. The next morning he participated in the wedding ceremony of the Lord very enthusiastically and danced ecstatically.

Kanakadasa had regular *darsan* of Lord Venkateswara, thanks to Chinnappa. He composed a number of poems and sang them in the temple. Large crowds of devotees flocked to the temple to listen to his songs. Then Chinnappa showed Kanakadasa many places of pilgrimage like Kalahasti, Kanchi, Rameswara and Yadugiri. Kanakadasa composed many songs about Lord Cheluva Narayana of Yadugiri before returning to Tirupati.

Kanakadasa remained in Tirupati for a few years. Once during a festival, countless devotees were pulling the holy stone-car of Lord Venkateswara. The car trundled ahead for a little distance and stopped all of a sudden. People tried their best to push and prod the wheels of the stone-car but failed miserably. The stone-car refused to budge even an inch. Then Kanakadasa threaded his way through the crowd, stood in front of the stone-car and requested Lord Venkateswara not to be angry with these devotees. He sang a song of twenty-eight lines beginning with, "Come, O Treasure of Good Luck/Come O Ocean of Compassion." While singing this song, Kanakadasa pulled the rope of the stone-car and lo, the car began to trundle ahead. The people who watched the miraculous event, began to fall at his feet, praise him whole-heartedly and heap gifts of money, gold and silver before him. But Kanakadasa who was a detached soul did not pay heed to the gifts, but immersed himself in the mental *puja* of the Lord.

On another occasion, when people in Tirupati were asleep, they were awakened at midnight by a terrific sound of about hundred thunders piercing through the mountain range. The earth began to quake. People were flabbergasted and began to run about for life. But Kanakadasa got up from his bed, sat up with joined palms and sang a song beginning with "Why did you quake, mother./ At the midnight hour?/O Queen of the Master of the world." He completed the song and consoled the people around him. Then the earth stopped quaking.

* * *

After many years' stay at Tirupati, Kanakadasa remembered Lord Adikesava of Kaginelli. He, therefore, left Tirupati and returned to Kaginelli via Venkatagiri. The natives of Kaginelli were overjoyed to see him after a long interval of time and welcomed him with open arms. He participated in the car-festival of Lord Adikesava very enthusiastically. He had yet to visit a number of holy shrines. He, therefore, went to Kadaramandalagi and had the *darsan* of Lord Maruti. But unfortunately he was inflicted with stomach-pain there for three months. After recovering from the illness, he left Kadaramandalagi and visited Bada, Bankapura, Mundagoda, Yallapura and Ulavi. In Ulavi, he had the *darsan* of Lord Cennabasaveswara. He then, went to Gokarna where he had the *darsan* of Lord Mahabaleswara. Then he went to the Marikamba temple at Sirsi and advised people to stop the sacrifice of he-buffaloes. Then he went to the temple of Goddess Yallamma at Chandragutti and advised people to put an end to barbaric rituals like worship of petty gods, naked-service by females, and animal sacrifices. He succeeded in convincing the devotees of Goddess Yallamma of the futility of the conduct of barbaric rituals. He took up a drum and played upon it along with other drummers and sang the famous song, "Come on, and see / Our gods have come..." describing the entire history of Lord Visnu's ten incarnations in just fifty lines.

After leaving Chandragutti, Kanakadasa visited Banavasi (the famous kingdom of Kadambas) Muduru, Hanagallu,

Laxmeshwara and Gadag. In Gadag he camped at the temple of Lord Viranarayana and enjoyed listening to the regular recitation of *Bharata Kathamrita* composed by Naranappa a century and a half before Kanakadasa. Then he trudged his way to Pampaksetra (or Hampi) where he felt shocked and sad to see the degeneration of the capital city of once glorious Kingdom of Vijayanagara. He visited the temples of Vijaya Vitthala, Virupaksa, Uddana Virabhadra and Kodandarama and the Porch of Purandaradasa. He left Hampi with a heavy heart and toured to Swarnagiri where Narasappanayaka received him warmly and reverentially. Kanakadasa had a *darsan* of Lord Narasimha and sang the glory of Lord Visnu and his destruction of Hiranyakasyapa ecstatically thereby inspiring them immeasurably. Then he went straight to the house of a great Harijan devotee called Kanakamuni and rolled upon his feet reverentially. Kanakamuni exclaimed, "Dear sir, I deem myself very lucky to have your *darsan* and proximity." The company of the two kindred souls proved to the people around them that love of God transcends the barriers of caste, creed and the feelings of high and low. Kanakadasa stayed in Kanakagiri for many days and composed a hymn of 97 stanzas in *sangatya* metre entitled *Nrisimha Stava* glorifying Lord Narsimha.

* * *

Meanwhile Kanakadasa was very sad to hear the news of the demise of his reverend guru Sri Vyasaraya Swami and of his discerning friend and well-wisher Purandaradasa. He felt a deep vacuum in his soul for a few days and missed his guru and friend. He, then, went to Kaginelli and arranged for the regular service at the temple of Lord Adikesava. Then he toured to Nanjanagudu. While he was crossing a forest near Nanjanagudu, a few local people warned him, "Sir, you seem to be a stranger here. We would like to caution you at the right time. There is a terrific elephant in this forest, which has trampled many sojourners to death. We, therefore, advise you not to risk your life by entering the forest." Kanakadasa heard their words of warning with patience. But far from being scared by their warning, he entertained them by narrating the story of *Gajendra Moksa* in 53 stanzas.

By that time, the terrific elephant rushed there. People who saw it were so frightened by its intoxicated movement that they scattered away from there. But Kanakadasa stood there without any fear. The terrific elephant stood before him with its head bent. Then Kanạkadasa addressed it, "O king of elephants, why do you harass people? Please stop it. You are a devotee of Lord Hari." He caressed its back affectionately. Strangely, the elephant lifted Kanakadasa on its tusks. The onlookers who stood at a safe distance watching the strange event thought he was done for. But the elephant placed him on its back and walked in a dignified gait towards Nanjanagudu. People along the road bowed down to Kanakadasa reverentially. He dismounted from the back of the elephant at the main gate of the temple of Lord Nanjundeswara and blessed it, "Now you may attain liberation from mortal life by participating in the festivities of the Lord." The people were really surprised by the unexpected transformation of the terrific elephant into a tame one. They attributed it to Kanakadasa's miraculous powers. The devotees of the temple bathed the elephant affectionately, smeared its limbs with *vibhuti*, decked it with a colorful *zula* and took it in a procession round the temple.

Fascinated by the natural beauty of the region, Kanakadasa stayed in a hermitage near the bank of Kapila river and planned the plot-outline of *Nala-Caritre* that he had been contemplating to write. Then he went to Beluru to have a *darsan* of Lord Cennakesava. He stayed in a corner of the temple and composed the entire poem within a few months.

During Kanakadasa's stay at Beluru, his classmate and a great scholar Sri Vadiraja Tirtha, pontiff of Sode Monastery at Udupi visited the place and met him. Both the friends were very happy to meet each other after a long time and exchanged their happy memories. One day Lord Cennakesava appeared to Kanakadasa in the form of a child and exhibited childhood frolics. Instantly Kanakadasa's directed the attention of Sri

Vadiraja Tirtha to it and sang a song of five stanzas describing the childhood frolics of Sri Krisna. Sri Vadiraja Tirtha was deeply impressed by Kanakadasa's poetic talent and mystical height and therefore spent many days in his company. The religious discourses given by Kanakadasa in Cennakesava's temple were attended by large masses of devotees.

While in Beluru, Kanakadasa enjoyed the food consisting of *ragi* (millet) dough, *syavige* (vermicelli) and *rotti* (bread). The typical food of the area gave him an idea to compose his famous allegorical poem entitled *Ramadhanya Caritre* in 158 *bhamini satpadi* stanzas. In the same place, he composed some riddle-songs (*mundiges*) to tease and entertain the audience. He also advised people not to discriminate between high caste and low caste and not to follow the edicts of the Hoysala Emperor.

* * *

Kanakadasa, then, left Beluru and toured towards Udupi. On the way, he bathed in a brook near a village called Kiruvalli and completed his mental worship. Then he walked to somebody's house and begged for food. The owner came out of the house with fierceness and shouted at him, "O Dasayya, go ahead. I won't give alms to anyone." Far from getting angry with him, Kanakadasa prayed to Sri Hari, "O God, kindly grant him wisdom and generosity." He then, walked to the next house and begged there. Strangely, the owner of the house gave him enough food. Kanakadasa was neither angry with the former, nor elated with the latter. He partook of that food with a sense of equanimity and took rest in a mango grove outside the village.

The rich man who had disdained Kanakadasa by refusing to give him alms was twirling his mustaches with pride. Suddenly he felt giddiness and collapsed on the floor. The relatives were scared by the event and instantly brought a physician who examined his pulse-beats and opined that he was all right and had no disease. The rich man sat up, looked around in his house and found that the holy letters 'OM' were written all over the walls. He asked his relatives, "How did the holy letters 'Om' come to be written on the walls?" But his relatives could not see any holy letters on the walls. They replied, "Where are the holy letters of 'Om?' We cannot see any." They attributed his strange behaviour to some kind of madness. The cushioned seat on which he sat began to prick him like thorns. His palatial house looked like a thatched hut. The gold, silver, diamonds and precious stones in his house began to look like rusted iron, pebbles and shards. The children looked like Haridasas and his wife looked like a *sanyasini* clad in saffron robes. Finally he discovered by himself that all these peculiar changes in his house had happened due to the desdain that he had shown to Kanakadasa. He, therefore, sent some of his people with the instruction, "Go and search for Kanakadasa and bring him here." They went around in the village, searched for him everywhere and found him. They requested him with joined palms, "Reverend sir, kindly come to our house and cure our master of his madness." Kanakadasa replied dispassionately, "Your master is cured of his madness now that he has attained the knowledge of Reality." But the relatives of the richman requested Kanakadasa, "Holy sir, we implore you to come to our house and cure him." Accordingly Kanakadasa went to the richman's house. No sooner had the richman seen Kanakadasa than he fell prostrate on his feet and burst out, "O sir , you have lifted me from untruth to Truth. Kindly show me the path ahead." Then Kanakadasa talked to him in privacy and advised him to become a *Dasa* of God. The richman readily agreed to his suggestion. He distributed all his wealth to the poor people of the village and became a Haridasa along with his wife and children.

Then Kanakadasa left that village and entered the Sahyadri mountain range. He travelled from village to village. One day when he was resting under the shade of a jack fruit tree he was accosted by a gowda of the village, "Holy sir, you seem to have come from a far off place. I am the gowda of this village. I request you to partake of food in our house. Kindly bless us with your presence." Kanakadasa understood the ring of sincerity in the gowda's request and agreed to visit his house. He went to the gowda's house where he was offered an oil bath and treated to a grand feast. But Kanakadasa put aside many delicacies and partook of a simple meal of *ragi,* vermicelli, rice and curds. He blessed the gowda whole-heartedly for his hospitality and continued his journey.

After crossing Parasurama Ksetra, he reached Udupi and began to sing ecstatically about Srikrisna. He went to the front door of the temple of Lord Srikrisna and wanted to have a *darsan* of his beloved Lord. But his wish was not fulfilled. Mistaken by Kanakadasa's gawky and untidy appearance, the orthodox brahmins mocked at him and called him a "hack *dasayya*" and did not allow him to enter the temple. Nobody gave him alms also. Though hungry, he slept in a corner of the templeyard and dreamt a dream in which Lord Srikrisna appeared to him in the guise of a boy and teased him. Kanakadasa felt ecstatic by the dream vision and began to sing spontaneously. At that time Lord Srikrisna appeared to him in the guise of a cowherd and gave him a golden ornament and asked him to have his food. Kanakadasa felt puzzled for a moment and did not know what to do. Finally he relied upon God's grace, pawned the ornament with a *senubova* of Udupi, received ten coins and completed the formality of having his food. He, then returned to the templeyard and got enraptured in meditation and singing the *lila* and glory of Lord Srikrisna.

The Swamiji of the Monastery went to the temple to render the regular service to the Lord and was shocked to discover that an important ornament on the icon of Lord Srikrisna was missing. He could not even guess as to who must have stolen it. He even feared that he himself could be incriminated of thieving it. In order to forestall the possible incrimination or charge of irresponsibility, he forthwith sent a letter to H.H. Vadiraja Swamiji of Sode Monastery who came to Udupi via Peraduru within two days.

The next day a meeting was called in the big hall of the temple. All the devotees, priests and officers of the temple had gathered there. When the meeting began, H.H. Vadiraja Swamiji asked a couple of officers of the temple to identify Kanakadasa and bring him to the meeting place. Accordingly the officers of the temple searched for Kanakadasa around the temple and in the city. Finally they identified him and asked him, "Gentleman, our Swamiji has ordered you to come to the meeting at the temple. Please come there." Kanakadasa felt inwardly happy to hear their words and followed them. As he reached the big hall in the temple, he prostrated to H.H. Vadiraja Swamiji from a distance. The orthodox brahmins who saw the ordinary *dasayya* clad in rags began to comment upon the Swamiji mentally. Then suddenly H.H.Vadiraja Swamiji asked him, "O Kanakadasa, where is the Lord's ornament?" Now different people thought differently about Kanakadasa. Some thought him to be a thief. Some others wondered at the fact as to how an ordinary *dasa* could enter the *sanctum sanctorum,* which was heavily guarded. Yet some others marveled at his miraculous powers. Kanakadasa replied, "Your Holiness, I have pawned it with Vaikuntha *Senubova* as per the Lord's order." Now people began to laugh contemptuously and attributed motives to Kanakadasa. Then H.H. Vadiraja Swamiji asked the people to have patience and cross-questioned Kanakadasa. He replied, "Your Holiness, Lord Krisna appeared to me in the guise of a cowherd and gave me the ornament and ordered me to have my food. I, therefore, pawned it with the *senabova* for ten coins." Then H.H. Vadiraja Swamiji turned to the *senabova* and asked him, "Gentleman, what is your answer to this?" The *senabova* replied, "Your Holiness, it is true that Kanakadasa has pawned the ornament with me and took ten coins." The people who heard these words were surprised beyond measure. H.H. Vadiraja Swamiji took out ten coins from a pouch and gave them to the *senabova* and said, "Gentleman you take these ten coines and return the ornament." The *senabova* returned the golden ornament to H.H. Vadiraja Swamiji without any demur. Then the ornament was put again on the idol of Lord Krisna. Thus Kanakadasa wrought many a miracle at Udupi unconsciously. Although many people admired his mystic height and devotional fervor, they never treated him as equal to brahmins. But, however, they arranged to construct a separate porch near the chandrasala for his stay. It came to be called Kanaka's Porch (Kanaka Mantapa). Kanakadasa stayed in the Porch for many days and continued his devotional singing and meditation.

He, then, undertook a journey to different places connected with the life of Madhvacarya like Vadabhandeswara, Pajaka and Subramanya. Then he visited other holy shrines at Dharmasthala, Bhagamandala, Kolluru, Sirsi, Banavasi and historical places like Bilagi, Swadi, Ikkeri, Keladi, Hanagallu and finally reached Kaginelli.

* * *

He sat in front of the idol of Lord Adikesava at Kaginelli and sang the song of praise ecstatically. When he came into his senses, he saw an old woman standing before him with joined palms. As soon as he opened his eyes, she fell prostrate on his feet and requested him, "Swami, kindly save me." Kanakadasa asked her, "*Amma*, who are you and what do you want?" The old woman was deeply surprised and asked him, "Swami, how is it that you are not able to recognize me?" Kanakadasa replied gently, "*Amma*, you know, I am now an old man of about seventy-five to eighy. My eyesight has also grown dim now. I am really unable to recognize you." Then the old woman understood his difficulty and replied, "Swami, I am Lachumi, daughter of Mallanayaka of Bada." Then Kanakadasa remembered her and her father. There was a flash of recognition in his eyes. Lachumi narrated the whole story of her life in brief. "Swami, you know in my youth I wanted to marry you but could not do so due to my bad luck. At the same time I refused to marry another man selected by my father. Then I became a *sanyasini* and spent all my fifty years in meditation and holy worship of Adikesava. I wanted to wander about from one place of pilgrimage to another, but my being a woman came in the way. I, therefore, stuck to Kaginelli and spent my days in the meditation of Adikesava. Swami, I request you to give a direction to my life by your guidance." Kanakadasa listened to her story patiently and advised her dispassionately, "*Amma*, my advice to you is that you have total faith in Lord Adikesava, consider everything in the world as his *prasada* and keep doing your duty. You may also lead the life of a mendicant and take care of the temple in addition to having faith in Him." Then the old Lachumi joined her palms in reverence and said, "Swami, I shall do exactly as directed by you." Then she walked away from him.

Luchumi busied herself in the upkeep of the temple of Adikesava and regular service to the Lord. Kanakadasa spent a few days in Kaginelli receiving respect and food from the villagers regularly in return for his spiritual discourses. One day he dreamt a dream in which Srikrisna of Udupi appeared and invited him to his *paryaya* festival. The very next day Kanakadasa set about his journey towards Udupi.

* * *

Old age had its own effect on Kanakadasa's health. He did not have the earlier strength of youth. With his dimmed eyesight and weak limbs, it was rather difficult for him to make a quick journey. He, therefore, took his own time to reach Udupi. He stayed in the Kanaka Porch built for him earlier. But the orthodox brahmins drove him out of it. Kanakadasa never took it to heart, but considered even that insult as a blessing of the Lord and spent the night in a far away corner of the templeyard.

The next day, a grand *puja* programme was going on in full swing. Thousands of devotees had gathered in the sacred complex. Kanakadasa had an intense desire to watch the grand *puja* ceremony of the Lord. But the orthodox brahmins did not allow him at all into the front door of the temple. Without growing desperate he walked to the western *i.e.* backside of the temple, strummed the strings of his *ekadari* and sang a song of devotion to Srikrisna ecstatically. Lord Krisna seemed to have heard his intense prayer. Lo! There was a sudden crack in the western wall and a hole was created instantly. The idol of Lord

Krisna turned back and gave *darsan* to Kanakadasa. When Kanakadasa sighted the Lord, the glitter and shine of the Lord's ornaments dazzled his eyes. He stood there drinking in the sublime beauty of the Lord.

But the Swamiji who was offering the *puja* of flowers, incense and sandal etc., to the Lord was flabbergasted to notice that the idol had turned its face to the back side of the temple. He instantly alerted the officers of the temple and ordered them to examine what had really happened. Accordingly some people went round the temple, watched the hole in the back wall and marvelled at the miraculous event. One of them rushed back and reported to the Swamiji about how the idol of Lord Krisna was giving *darsan* to Kanakadasa who was singing with ecstatic rapture and shedding tears of joy. The Swamiji rushed to Kanakadasa and observed his rapture with a sense of awe. Inwardly, he felt ashamed of himself and of orthodox brahmins who had not allowed Kanakadasa to have the *darsan* of the Lord from the front door. After Kanakadasa came out of his trance, the Swamiji joined his palms in reverence and praised him, "Holy sir, you are really a great saint of our Land. We bow down to you. Kindly accept our deeply felt apologies." Then the devotees in large numbers fell prostrate on Kanakadasa's feet and expressed their reverence to him. The hole in the back wall of the temple came to be known as Kanaka's Peep-Hole or Kanaka's-Window. Then Kanakadasa returned to Kaginelli with a sense of spiritual fulfilment.

As a result of the long journey, Kanakadasa fell ill and remained bedridden for several days. He drank the juice of neem leaves for a couple of days and recovered his health gradually. He wished that the service of Lord Adikesava and the religious festivities connected with the temple should continue forever. One day a *palegar* of Kaginelli met Kanakadasa and asked him, "Holy sir, you are a great devotee of Lord Adikesava. You should see to it that the religious festivities of the temple are continued even after your death." Then Kanakadasa replied rather curtly, "Lord Adikesava will take care of Himself after my death.

Why do you worry about that?" The *palegar* felt a bit embarrassed by the answer, but yet continued to say, "Holy sir, I also feel concerned about the festivities of the temple even after your as well as my death." Then Kanakadasa counter-questioned him, "So what can you do about it?" The *palegar* said with a note of confidence, "Holy sir, I have a request to you. I volunteer to donate to the temple as much land as is covered by you by blowing a conch continuously without any break in the middle." Kanakadasa noticed the subtle egotism in the promise of the *palegar* and wanted to cure him of it. "All right sir, I shall do as desired by you," said Kanakadasa. He immediately took up a conch, walked ahead and stopped on the land belonging to Dasanakoppa village. A large crowd of people gathered there to watch the interesting scene. Kanakadasa started walking ahead and blowing the conch continuously. His cheeks were bloated with air. The booming sound of the conch echoed in the distant hills. The *palegar* and the villagers followed him curiously. Kanakadasa crossed two, three and four fields and there was no sign of his stopping the blowing. When the *palegar* observed it, he grew apprehensive. He instantly realized his folly committed out of egotistic pride. He, therefore, fell prostrate at the feet of Kanakadasa and apologized, "Holy sir, kindly forgive my foolishness and stop blowing the conch. I can donate as much land as is covered by you, and not as much as will be covered by you." Then Kanakadasa stopped blowing the conch as he noticed the *palegar's* realization of his own folly. The *palegar* wanted to retain his prestige by keeping the promise. He, therefore, donated all the land covered by Kanakadasa to the temple of Adikesava for the maintenance of the temple as well as for the conduct of religious festivities.

* * *

As Kanakadasa had grown old by now, he could not leave Kaginelli for other places of pilgrimage. He, therefore, got an idol of Lord Hanumanta and established it on the precincts of Adikesava temple. In his ecstatic dreams, he used to have communion with Lord Venkateswara of Tirupati and Lord Cennakesava of Beluru. He had elevated himself from the realization of *Saguna Brahma* to that of *Nirguna Brahma* where there was no schism between 'I' and 'Thou.'

After waking from the trance, Kanakadasa went to Kummuru for begging. Kummuru happened to be a village adjacent to Kaginelli. The people offered him porridge and buttermilk. After partaking of the simple meal he slept and did not wake up even after two hours of night. Then he was suddenly awakened. He opened his eyes and saw a column of dazzling light come near and enveloped him. Then it began to lead him. He followed it silently. The column of light slowly climbed the hilltop of Kummuru and stopped there. Kanakadasa also climbed the hilltop and stood there. Lo. What he saw there was an extraordinarily beautiful and holy idol of Lord Venkateswara of Tirupati. The promise made by the Lord in his dream had come true. He began to sing and dance ecstatically there and then itself. The people of Kummuru who heard the singing by Kanakadasa at that odd hour of night began to flock there. They were surprised and happy to see the idol of Venkateswara there on the top of the hill. The next morning they decorated the idol with flowers, erected a porch with festoons of flowers and leaves and offered holy bath and worship to it, which Kanakadasa named as 'Timmakesava.' In course of time, they built a temple for the deity. Kanakadasa spent his old days in the meditation of Lord Adikesava of Kaginelli and Lord Timmakesava of Kummuru.

* * *

One day Kanakadasa went to a tank to have his bath when he began to feel a strange kind of joy. He seemed to hear a faint voice, but he could not identify it. However, he completed his bath and then began to wash his clothes. He heard the voice once again, which said, "*Dasa* supreme, I shall also come with you." Kanakadasa began to look around for it. After a little careful hearing, he could make out the faint voice coming from beneath the washing slab of stone. He, therefore, lifted up the stone slab and found a beautiful idol of Cennakesava from Beluru smiling at and talking with him. He ecstatically carried it upon his shoulder and began to walk towards Kaginelli. The idol appeared to be as light as a flower. But when he went to Ingalagondi village near Kaginelli, the idol seemed to grow very heavy. Unable to carry it further, Kanakadasa established it on a hill in the village. The devotees of Ingalagondi built a temple there in course of time.

By now Kanakadasa was ninety-eight years old. He was a shriveled and weak old man. Once when Kanakadasa was sitting in the temple of Lord Adikesava, Lachumi, an old lady of eighty-five doddered up to him, fell prostrate on his feet and breathed her last. Kanakadasa appreciated her selfless service and arranged her funeral. In 1606, Kanakadasa left his mortal body and merged into the spirit of Lord Adikesava.

12

A Chronic Patient Became A Doctor

WHEN THE result of my M.A. was announced I was fairly happy that the long academic career had at last come to an end, although in the heart of my heart I was not really satisfied with the percentage which was much below my expectation and ability. What hurt me more was the fact that the duffers who knew nothing but parrot learning had scored higher marks than they deserved. But nobody was willing to believe me about this discrepancy in the result because that would embarrass and irritate at least those who were concerned with the issue in some way or the other. I, therefore, swallowed the academic insult and was trying to think of a job. When I had been to the department for the collection of my marks-card, I met Dr. Kallapur who noticed my low spirits and asked for the reason. I told him that I was not happy about my result. By the time I completed my sentence, tears had started to trickle down my cheeks without my knowing. He consoled me by revealing a secret and asked me to accept reality with a bold face. He said, "They have seen to it that you will not be a man. They have let you down very badly, and that too deliberately." Since he was my well-wisher I had full faith in him. Then he ordered tea for me. Until the tea was brought by the attender, Dr. Kallapur went on advising me as to how first class is not everything in life and that one should build up one's reputation on subsequent research work rather than depending upon a dubious first-class in M.A. etc. I felt relieved at last to some extent. I sipped my tea and left his chamber. On the way I happened to meet Dr. Desai whom I greeted. He asked me about the class that I had got in the examination. We were standing in the corridor. He asked me, "Hullow, Mr. Nandiswar, which class did you get in the exam?"

"Got high second-class sir" said I.

"That's good. You can easily get a job now," said Dr. Desai adjusting his spectacles upon his nose.

"But I am not happy about this result, sir. I had expected at least a first class. I have got first class throughout my career. It's only here that I am let down," said I with painful irritation.

"O, I see. I know you are a bright boy. You should have got a first class."

"........."

"Didn't I tell you to offer Linguistics as your optional paper? You could have easily got a first-class then," said he.

"But, Sir, I offered American Literature as my optional only because of my desire to go to America later," said I disturbedly.

"Don't be disheartened by this. Come on let us go to my chamber." He took me by the arm and led me to his cubicle. He lit his cigarette and puffed at it for a couple of times and said, "You know, Mr. Nandiswar, 'American Literature' is not as scoring as 'Linguistics' because the former has no objective type questions and no viva. Since it contains only essay type questions it is not very scoring. Why do you bother about a first class?"

"But it is a question of prestige, sir. I have never got less than a first class in my life except for this wretched M.A.," said I rather indignantly.

"I can understand your feeling Mr. Nandiswar, but a man's life is always more important than his degree."

"But it remains as a stigma in my life sir. I had never expected this kind of shock," said I worriedly.

"Take it easy, Mr. Nandiswar. Don't take it to heart." I excused myself and left his room. He was looking at me sympathetically.

When I came home, my mother and grandmother were very happy that I had got through the last examination and that I could get some kind of a job or the other. But I was not at all enthusiastic about it. I hurried through my meal and slept until evening. My mother rendered a special *puja* to the deities at home. In the evening my mother prepared hot *bhajis* and tea for all of us, because she know I was very fond of *bhajis*. I ate them, which were quite tasty. Then I went to the market and to Triveni Talkies. The movie started after the Indian Newsreel was over. The film was full of romance. The hero and the heroine were leaning, resting and rolling on each other. The stereotyped love song was repeating itself in the same old language. The audience in the dark were clapping, shouting, caterwauling, chuckling and giggling at the romance happening before them. But somehow I could not enjoy the film as enthusiastically as they did. I felt envious of the brainless rabble who could be so carefree. I got up in the middle of the show and came out. I walked home rather slowly through the market.

The next day I finished my breakfast and caught the University bus and went to the campus. I straightway went to Dr. Sudhakar's residence and pressed the call bell. The short professor who was in his white Nehru pyjama and shirt opened the door and asked me in. I handed over the cardboard box of sweets to him and bowed down to him in respect. He then inquired me about my result. I said, "I got a high second class, sir."

"Congratulations. You can try for a job now," he said.

"But I am not happy about my result sir. I had expected at least a first class. I have spent all my time, energy and scholarship money on studying and buying books. How can I get less than a first class?" I asked indignantly.

Dr. Sudhakar was taken aback by the direct question. His face grew pale and contracted for a while and he said, "You know examination is a game. Nobody can be sure about the results."

"But I had scored first class marks in all the tests and tutorials throughout the year. How can I get such a low grade only in the annual examination?" I asked him angrily and nervously. I knew I was talking to my Head of the Department.

"Yes, yes, that's very strange," he said rather embarrassedly.

"But you are the Chairman, you must knew everything. I just want to know what has happened in the exam," I asked.

Dr. Sudhakar lowered the pitch of his voice and said in a confidential tone, "You see, I am not supposed to tell you the official secret, but since you insist on this I will tell you. Keep it only to yourself. A Professor of your own community has let you down. He has been unusually strict in the evaluation. He said he has followed the Oxford standard."

I was consoled by the explanation though I was irritated far beyond proportion by the examiner's peculiar nature. I asked myself inwardly, "How could a Professor who has never studied at Oxford ever follow the Oxford method of evaluation?" I knew there was no answer to that question. I took an oath inwardly that I must prove my intelligence to the world by doing some research work of first class standard and take academic revenge upon the world.

I was appointed as a Lecturer in Basel Mission Junior College at Dharwad. My mother and grandmother were very happy that I could get a job immediately after my post-graduation. As I was an incurable bibliomaniac, I used to buy countless books in a local bookshop called Sahitya Mandir. Professor Nagaraj who happened to be the son-in-law of the owner of the bookshop used to sit in the shop in the evening and watch my purchasing of books. He knew my academic inclination and quest for knowledge. One evening when I went to the bookshop to buy some books, he was smoking his cigarette and watching the passersby. I greeted him and bought a couple of books. When I was about to leave the shop, Prof. Nagaraj asked me, "Mr. Nandiswar, where are you working now?" "Right now I am working in a local junior college, but I am also trying to get a job in Karnatak Arts college sir," said I. Then Prof. Nagaraj said, "Would you like to come to the Post-Graduate Centre at the City of Rocks as a Research Assistant?" "What are the duties of a Research Assistant, sir? In fact I am very keen on doing my Ph.D. I would also like to go abroad for higher studies, especially to Oxford." "If you join the Post Graduate Centre as Research Assistant, you have to help me in clerical work for an hour or two every day. Then you can do your Ph.D. After two years I shall help you to get a transfer to Dhawad. Then I shall send you abroad and make you an international figure." When I heard these words of my beloved teacher I was thrilled immeasurably. I hoped that I would realize all my secret dreams with the help of my beloved Professor.

I consulted my mother, grandmother, brother and guardian and decided to apply for the Research Assistant's post at the Post-Graduate Centre of the City of Rocks. When I received the appointment order from the Registrar, I was overjoyed. My relatives felt very happy about my appointment. I travelled in a bus from Dharwad to the City of Rocks and reported myself to duty as Research Assistant in English. My Professor and Chairman welcomed me very affectionately and introduced me to his colleagues who congratulated me. After a couple of days went by, I was assigned the clerical work of the department ranging from A to Z. Having lost my father very early in my life, I considered my Professor as a well-wisher and fatherly figure. I did not grudge doing any job to please him.

Once when Prof. Nagaraj had gone to Dharwad on leave, Mr. Reddy, who was one of my colleagues, told me, "Mr. Nandiswar, you are lucky to be appointed in the Post-Graduate Department." "I think our Professor liked having me here," said I innocently. Then Mr. Reddy, with a pock-marked face and a nasal tone smiled a mischievous smile and said, "Mr. Nandiswar, our Professor recommended you for this post because others refused to come here." "Is that so? I did not know the background. Could you tell me some details?" I requested him. Then Mr. Reddy told me the whole story in brief,

"Mr. Nandiswar, before recommending your case, Prof. Nagaraj tried to bring two others here. One was Miss Farida, the other was Miss Manjula. But both the girls refused to come away from their parents to this far-off place. He, then, recommended you for this post when none was willing to come here." I was awakened to the background of harsh reality but decided not to bother about it.

Mr. Sekhar who happened to be my teacher in the college had joined the Post-Graduate Centre as Lecturer a month before I joined. He was rather unhappy about the fact that I, his student, had joined service as his equal. I would easily sense that he was deeply jealous of me. I knew that he had no scholarship of any kind. His artificial pronunciation was his only property. He chummed up with Professor Nagaraj and began to collect intelligence about the colleagues and students in the department and convey it to the Professor. He also used to character-assassinate me and other colleagues and brainwash the students against us.

As I was very keen on my Ph.D., one day I met Professor Nagaraj in his chamber and said, 'Sir I want to register for my Ph.D. under your guidance." The Professor smiled a mischievous smile and asked me back, "Youngman, what is the topic on which you wish to work?" I said rather nervously, "Sir, I wish to work on Shakespeare's sonnets." Then the Professor lit his cigarette, puffed out the rings of smoke and questioned me, "What exactly do you want to discover in his sonnets?" Then I said humbly, "Sir, I am not very clear about what I may discover in them. But I would like to consider his sonnets as windows to his plays and highlight the thematic similarities between the two."

"But that may be ok for a big article and not sufficient for a thesis."

"Then which topic do you suggest sir?'

"You see, I cannot suggest ready made topics. You have to find out your own area of interest."

"But I want to do some work only on Shakespeare."

When the Professor heard this he wore a mischievous smile on his face and said, "Do you think you can do some original work on Shakespeare on whom the entire world has been working? Do you think it is a joke?"

"I know it is not a joke sir. But since I have a serious bent of mind, I want to do some work on Shakespeare, of course, with your help."

"But why do you want to cling to Shakespeare? You may find interest in other writers also. Why not read other authors for six months?"

I thought my Professor was my well-wisher and a father figure. I thought that his advice had a good intention behind it, which I would not probably understand right then. I, therefore, thought I would do well to obey my beloved teacher. I gave up the idea of registering for some more time.

For the next six months I spent most of my time reading a variety of authors like Christopher Fry, Edwin Muir, O'casy, Louis McNiece and a host of other writers.

After six months I met the Professor in his chamber and asked him if I could register now. He asked me how much I have read by now. I told him all about the authors I had read. He said, "That is not enough. But have you liked any of them keenly enough to be able to work upon them?"

"No sir, to be frank, I do not like to work upon them."

"In that case, you read for another six months."

"But I want to register as early as possible. Many of my classmates have already fixed their topics and registered for their Ph.Ds."

"Don't be in a hurry to register. Take it easy. Take your own time to do so."

My colleagues who heard about this situation were apparently sympathetic to me but secretly happy because of their jealousy towards me. Mr. Sekher told me later, "You are still young. You have still sufficient time to do your Ph.D. Take it easy. You have to enjoy life."

I was not satisfied with these false consolations by my Professor and the colleagues. I felt as though I was groping in the dark. Again I began to frequent the library and read different novelists, poets and dramatists. Slowly I started realizing the difficulty of choosing my author. The authors that I liked to work upon had already been exhausted by the western scholars, but the authors that I did not like were relatively still unexplored and could be worked upon. As my Professor did not suggest the exact author or topic, I consulted other senior teachers at Dharwad and Mysore who suggested some topics, which were not to my taste. By this time, Sekhar, one of my colleagues was awarded a foreign scholarship and went to England. My boss asked me to take a few more extra lectures for the post-graduate classes. Though unwilling to do so, I had to do it because the other colleagues of mine had agreed to do a little more extra teaching. Since a temporary Lecturer's vacancy was advertised at Dharwad campus, I applied for the same and attended the interview. The Selection Committee members asked me to be seated. The Vice Chancellor asked me, "Have you done any research?"

"I have been doing the preliminary work on Shakespeare," said I quite modestly.

"See, he has been working as a full time Research Assistant and he has not completed his Ph.D. work," the Head of the Department pointed out rather angrily.

"I could have completed my research work but my guide did not allow me to register, and most of my time was wasted as I was made to do the clerical work in the department," I said rather excitedly.

"........"

There was silence for a few seconds. All the members of the Selection Committee felt embarrassed by my frank answer. Then the Vice-Chancellor cleared his throat and said, "Mr. Nandiswar, this Lecturer's post is temporary. Why do you aspire for this? After the period expires, you will have to go back to the Research Assistant's post. That won't be good for you."

"But I don't mind that. The experience of a temporary Lectureship will help me have a permanent post later at least."

Then the Vice Chancellor looked at the Head of the Department and asked, "Do you have any more questions?"

"No," said the Head of the Department.

"You may go now," the Vice Chancellor asked me.

Then I came out of the Vice-Chancellor's chamber with a nonchalant mood.

The next day, I went to my guide's house. He was clad in his nightgown and smoking his pipe. He was quite indifferent in his reception to me. He asked me rather mechanically, "Please be seated. What's the matter?"

"When shall I register for my Ph.D. sir?" I asked a little seriously.

"Why are you in hurry to register? Are you confident that you can do some standard work to be accepted by the world?" he asked me in a mock-serious fashion, while puffing at his cigarette.

"How can I be confident at the very beginning? I would like to register at the earliest. I could not get even a temporary Lecturer's post because I did not have a Ph.D.," I said curtly.

He seemed to realize the gravity of my problem. He asked me to bring the registration form. I lost no time in obliging him. The very next day I went to his house, got his signature on the form, went to the campus, submitted the fee at the bank and took a receipt from the registration clerk. I heaved a sigh of relief to know that I was at last able to register with my guide after three years of waiting, — a time when my other classmates had submitted their theses and were relieved of their tension. Nevertheless I consoled myself on account of having registered on a very standard research topic which would earn for me an international reputation.

Then I began to spend more time in the library and started reading extensively. The more I read, the more confused I grew. One day, therefore, I went to the chamber of my guide and asked him as to how to make notes and whether I should take down the notes on white sheets or cards? Then my guide told me intermittently puffing at his cigarette, "How can I guide you in that? You have to decide about it yourself."

"No sir. Since I have to read very extensively I may get confused. That's why I asked you. Some people advised me to take notes on separate cards."

Then my guide lit a second cigarette from the butt of the first one, looked at me rather mischievously and said, "Why do you want to take down notes like that at all?"

I was a little puzzled and did not know how to react to his unexpected question. Nonetheless I made bold to say, "Then how to proceed with my research, sir?"

The guide then assumed a very dignified posture, his forefinger pressing lightly against his lower lip. He said, "I never took down notes in my career. You can make a mental note of all the points that are relevant to your topic. That's how a first class student should work."

His answer neither satisfied nor convinced me. But I could not dare contradict him. I was so puzzled that I instantly rushed to the canteen and had some hot *puris* and a cup of steaming coffee and began to think of an individual solution to the problem.

I began to read Shakespeare criticism in the University Library regularly. As soon as my lecture for the M.A. class was over, I used to have my light tiffin at the University café and then go to the second floor of the library, sit in a corner and wade through the books of criticism. Although I read quite widely I did not know which points to take down, as my own hypothesis was not very clear to me then. Sometimes I used to read pages together of a book but could not comprehend the exact argument contained in them. I was really puzzled about my own helplessness. Therefore, one day I went to my college teacher's home at Malamaddi. The Professor, Narayanachar came out after his morning worship was over. I was seated on the edge of the cane chair rather nervously. After exchanging formalities, I came directly to my problem, "Sir, I have a problem now. I want your advice on this."

The Professor adjusted his spectacles upon his nose and looked at me askance, and said, "Yes, what's that?"

"Sir, I have been reading a number of books for my research, but I do not know how to make notes. Sometimes I can't comprehend even the summary of the chapters that I read. Would you mind telling me how to get out of this?" I was holding the arms of the chair rather tightly and waiting for the guru's answer.

The Professor smiled and said gently, "Why, your guide must have told you how to proceed with your work? What has he advised you to do?"

I again smiled and said, "His suggestions are very peculiar sir. He has asked me to read all the critical works that are available on Shakespeare and make mental notes."

"Well that is an ideal suggestion. Why not follow it?" asked he leaning against the back of the chair.

"But sir, sometimes, to be frank, I cannot follow even the main argument of the British critics because of their difficult sentence-patterns. Then how to make notes from them?" By the time I completed my sentence, I realized that my voice had grown tremulous.

Then Professor Narayanachar crossed his left leg upon his right and said in a calm voice, "Young man, don't be discouraged. Don't think that this difficulty is special to you only. Every student must undergo this stage. Since most of us come from Kannada medium schools, we have to switch over to the English language, which is again used by the masterminds of Britain. Since we have to learn the foreign language only through the inanimate books, we have to struggle a lot with this language."

As I heard these words I grew more nervous and asked, "But how to make notes, if we cannot follow even the main ideas of these critics?"

"In that case, you do one thing. You just copy the entire paragraphs, which seem to be important to you though you may not understand them entirely. Don't think that copying is a waste of time. That will help you to concentrate. As you grow mentally, you will begin to understand the meaning of all the paragraphs slowly."

This seemed to be a more practical solution than the one suggested by my guide. I thanked my college teacher profusely and took leave of him. I felt relieved of a tension, which had built itself without my knowing. I climbed the hill of the Collector's Office and walked past the Training College. The long-jasmines and the lurid red roses of the Training College appeared more beautiful than they did usually. Then I went home and had my lunch. In the evening I bought half a dozen notebooks and from the very next day I began to make notes *i.e.* summarizing wherever possible and copying wherever difficulty arose from the critical works. All these days I was filled with a sense of satisfaction that what I was doing was not a waste of time. I worked like this for nearly six months. I had filled a dozen of notebooks with notes, but I could not begin the writing of a single chapter, as my synopsis was not yet ready.

For a couple of days I thought of a feasible synopsis but I could not arrive at one. I met a few friends of mine at the University and asked them about how they had managed to get their synopses. They told me that they had begun their work with the synopses given by their respective guides. I began to worry about why my guide had not given me my synopsis. One day I finished my breakfast walked past the Jubilee Circle and the Laxmi Talkies and reached my guide's house. He was in his white pyjamas and banyan. He held his cigarette between his forefinger and middle finger. The curls of smoke were rising slowly in the fashion of widening gyres. He asked me to be seated which I obeyed rather mechanically. He also sat on the cane chair and asked, "How are you? What's the matter, Mr. Nandiswar?"

I did not want to waste my time in mere formalities and therefore I said, "I am ok sir" and came straight to the problem, "Sir I don't know how to classify my notes and write the preliminary essay without having a synopsis. Please give me a synopsis."

"O, why do you bother about the synopsis?"

"But how can I concretize my ideas without a synopsis? How to organize my thoughts?"

"In that case you come tomorrow and collect your synopsis."

I took leave of him and returned home. Next day when I met him he had not yet prepared the synopsis. He smiled apologetically, took out a piece of white paper and began to scribble on it. I was watching him eagerly. When he finished it and handed it over to me I was rather taken aback and even nervous to know the extreme vagueness of it all. It referred to nothing but general issues like the human values, the concept of God, and man, life and death in world philosophy to be applied to Shakespeare's plays. I was really unnerved by the panorama of the scheme and did not know how to crystallize it. The scheme obviously appeared to be more philosophical than literary. I said, "Sir, this scheme sounds very general and difficult to concretize."

The Professor was rather exasperated at my remark and said, "You have to do such work only if at all you want to produce a standard thesis."

I became nervous at his words and did not know what to say. Still then I made bold to say, "Sir, the guides of my friends have given them concrete and workable plans. They are making fast progress in their fields. I request you to do something like that."

The Professor lent his elbows on the glass of the wide table, squinted his eyes and said to me, "Do you want me to follow the silly methods of other people? I am sorry I cannot do that."

I was really hurt by the curt way in which he spoke to me. Besides he did not seem to have any sympathy for me. I came out of his chamber and walked towards my room in the department. Mr. Swami, my colleague returned from his class and called me for tea. We went towards the canteen in the Men's Hostel. He asked me for the reason of my gloominess. I told him all about my guide's advice and asked him if I could leave this guide and seek some other guide in some other university. But he told me, "Please don't do that. If you cancel your registration with him, he will be furious and harass you in so many ways because, you know, he is so vindictive." There seemed to be a grain of truth in what he said. I just did not know what to do. We sipped our tea and returned to the department.

I spent another six months in reading the books voraciously and making notes. I would go to the University Library around 9 A.M. and return home about 7 P.M. Again after the evening work, I would sit down poring over the stodgy books of criticism, philosophy, psychology, and indology half of which I would not really understand. But my blind faith in the general growth of human intelligence kept me busy with my work. My mother would say about midnight, "It is past midnight now, my son. Stop reading now. You can read in the morning again."

Sometimes I would oblige her and sometimes I would not, because of my inward restlessness. Meanwhile, I learnt that two of my classmates had submitted their theses and were quite relieved of their tension. I grew envious of them and felt pity for myself. But again I suppressed my anger and anxiety. I began to buy the books concerning my research almost every month. One day my mother asked me, "My son, why do you waste so much money on books?"

"No, mummy, I need them for my research work."

"Do you have to read all these books?"

"Yes, mummy, and many more still."

"My God, how can your head be all right if you read so much?"

"I have got to, mummy, otherwise I will have to lag behind others in the competition."

"Why not get married and be happy, my son? Please relieve me of the household work and let me play with my grandson."

"Let us wait for another two years, mother. Once I complete my Ph.D., I will have no problems. I can settle down later on."

My mother was not really happy about my postponement of marriage, but she allowed me to follow my own plans, nonetheless. My younger brother had repeatedly told my mother that I had been wasting my money on books. He had also told her that there were many students who earned their Ph.D. without ever buying even half a dozen books. But mother who had a lot of faith in me kept quiet because she knew that I was not a fool to waste my time and money on worthless ventures.

Another six months elapsed. My table was cluttered with innumerable notebooks containing the brief and the lengthy quotations and paraphrases culled from the critical works. When I read them over and over again I felt confused and did not know how to organize them into separate chapters. Nonetheless I tried to write a preliminary essay which could be the first chapter of my thesis. It ran up to twenty pages. One day I felt eager to show it to my guide and get his suggestions. I, therefore, finished my breakfast quite early and caught the 9 A.M. bus to the University. The Professor had also luckily come to the department quite early. I said, "good morning sir" to him and sat on a chair nearest to him. As usual he lit his cigarette. I took out the essay from my Rexine bag and said, "Sir, I have written sort of a preliminary essay. Kindly go through it and see whether it is all right or not."

I handed over the stapled sheets of paper rather nervously and sat expecting his reactions. I was watching his face very curiously as he began to glance over the manuscript. He knit his brows, bit his lips and contorted his face. I grew more nervous to notice the change in his facial expression. After a couple of minutes he threw the article back towards me. The pages fluttered in the wind of the fan spinning above us. I arranged the papers properly and remained silent for a moment. Then the Professor said, "This is not the stuff I wanted, I say. This is mere trash. It is so schoolboyish. You have no judgement and no style."

I grew more nervous as I heard his words. My throat parched. I said, "This is the first attempt to write sir. Really speaking, I do not know the method of writing."

"I know, the Karnatak University has ruined you all. Besides, you north-Karnataka fellows do not have brains."

I did not know what to say. But to escape the sense of embarrassment of keeping quiet, I said, "Nobody has taught me these things at any stage of my life. But somebody or the other should teach me these things at some stage or the other, sir."

"Yes, yes, that is the tragedy of your life."

"Sir, I was not taught the research methodology any time in my life. Would you kindly teach me the same?"

"You see, I have no patience to teach that. You can learn it within half-on-hour if you read the MLA style sheet."

"I have read it sir, but somehow I could not grasp the ideas clearly. Things will be clear to me if you explain them."

"I am sorry I can't do all that."

"But my friends' guides have taught them these clues and steps, sir."

My Professor grew angry and said rather loudly, "You see, I am different from other guides. Don't expect me to do what the third-rate guides do."

"It's all right sir."

I gently excused myself and came out of his chamber. I felt I was in a pretty pass. Dr. Sitaram came to my table and we went to the hotel housed in the thatched cottage near the Social

Sciences Block. As we were sipping our over-boiled tea in the dirty and broken cups, I asked Dr. Sitaram about the research methodology. He said he could not explain all that to me, but instead, promised to give his MLA Style Sheet within a couple of days. I told him how my guide had refused to enlighten me on the research methodology. He said, "How can he enlighten you, when he himself is not a Ph.D. and has had no experience of this kind in his younger days?"

"Of course, that is also true. But he has done his research on an American poet which is published in America."

"You see, he has done it only after his fortieth year. Imagine the experience he must have had before doing that! There is no comparison between an experienced man like him and a young fellow like you."

"But how to learn the research methodology?"

"There is no other way than that of trial-and-error method."

We, then, returned to the department and dispersed.

Four months elapsed. The Head of the Department was away from City of Rocks for nearly a fortnight. The last date for the submission of examination forms was nearing. The students were supposed to give their applications to the senior most Lecturer in the department. Mr. Reddy who happened to be the seniormost Lecturer had been collecting them rather unwillingly. I did not associate myself with this work as I was tired of doing it for a number of years. Now the last date was over. All the applications were lying helter-skelter on Reddy's table. He did not bother about classifying them or correcting them or forwarding them to the Controller of Examinations. He tied them up with a piece of white string and kept them on the Professor's table. After three days the Professor returned from Dharwad and was exasperated to know that the examination forms were not at all forwarded. He seemed to have forgotten that he had assigned that work to Mr. Reddy. The Professor immediately sent for me. I knew I was in for trouble. I went to his chamber and sat on the chair. He said in angry but controlled tone, "Why have you not sent the examination-forms though the last date is over?"

"That is not my work sir. Prof. Reddy has kept them on your table without attending to them." The Professor was taken aback by the blank answer. He did not know what to say for a few seconds. He twacked once or twice. Then he continued, "But since you handle the clerical work of the department, you ought to have forwarded them."

"But I don't want to do the risky job of dealing with the examination forms. The seniormost man should do it. Besides, as I am not a clerk, I am not interested in clerical work. That takes away a lot of my time and comes in the way of my research," I said these words by deliberately controlling my mounting anger.

"I see."

I excused myself and came back to my chamber. Five minutes later I received a handwritten memo from the Professor. He then sent for Mr. Reddy who went to his chamber. I stayed in the department for an hour and returned to the city. I did not meet the Professor for my consultation about research until the end of the academic year.

When we reopened for the next year I was again burdened with the admission work. But I had to do it, however heavy it may be. My chamber was just adjacent to the Professor's. One day I had finished the listing up of the first lot of admission applications. I was relaxing. Miss Rosy, who had just passed her Previous M.A., came to me and asked me for her marks card. I searched for it in the big file and handed it over to her. She had cat-like eyes. She looked at me fixedly and wore a bewitching smile on her thin rosy lips. I could not resist engaging her in conversation. I asked her, "How did you spend the holidays?"

"I spent most of my days in Bombay, sir."

"What did you do there?"

"Just eating, wandering and sleeping, sir."

"How many films did you see?"

"Not many sir. Just a couple of them."

"Did you see the Malayalam film *Nellu*?"

"Yes sir. That is very beautiful. Did you like it sir?"

"Yes, I did. Immensely. By the way, would you mind giving me a list of important Malayalam writers?"

"I remember sir, but I had no time. I shall search for them and give you within a couple of days sir."

"All right, please do."

She wished me and walked away towards the corridor where her friends were waiting for her. I heard the giggling of girls from the corridor. I was again thinking of the second lot of admission-forms, which I had to tabulate. I took two carbon papers, inserted them between three large sheets of paper and began to write the names of the candidates with a carbon pencil. Yesavanta came and told me that the Professor wanted me to see him. I straightaway went to his chamber and sat on the chair. The Professor said, "I heard you were discussing something about Malayalam literature."

"Yes sir, Miss. Rosy had come for her marks card. I just asked her about some Malaylam writers."

"I see, you say you are doing your research work seriously. How is Malayalam literature connected with research, I say?"

I knew the Professor was furious. His face was contorted. I cleared my throat and said, "I was only asking her for a list of Malayalam writers. I did not discuss with her anything else."

"Do you want to be like me?" his tone was furious. "Don't talk with that girl any more."

"........."

I was so angry with the silly behaviour of the Professor that I left his chamber without even formally excusing myself. I rushed to the canteen in the hostel and had my tea alone. I decided to be frank and bold with him in case he should tackle me again on the same subject. Six months elapsed. For those six months I did not see him except for official work. At the end of the academic year I took a chapter to him for correction. It was the penultimate working day for that year. The Professor was already in the home going mood. He took the large notebook from me, opened it and glanced at a few pages. Then he said, "You see, I'm not in a mood to go through your chapter. Why not bring it at Dharwad? I'll be free to do it there."

"All right sir. In that case I shall do so sir." He handed the notebook back to me. I took it rather disappointed and excused myself from his chamber.

I packed my books, notes and other items and boarded the bus for Dharwad after the closure of the department. The very next day I finished my breakfast, took the notebook and walked towards the Professor's house in the hot sun. He welcomed me rather mechanically. He was smoking his hookah at home. I gave him the first draft and asked him to go through it and suggest corrections. He said he would return it to me within a week's time. I met him the next week and he asked me to see him the next week again. I went on seeing him almost every week until the end of three months vacation. When I saw him on the penultimate day of the summer vacation he said, "Mr. Nandiswar, I am sorry I could not see your chapter."

"But when will you see it sir?"

"Why not bring it to me at the City of Rocks itself? I will be free there as there will be no lectures for a fortnight. I'll give it to you within two days."

"As you please, sir."

He returned the draft to me. I was again disappointed to take it back. I walked home with a pale face. The next day I packed my books and notes again and travelled to the City of Rocks. On the opening day I could not disturb the Professor because of his journey-fatigue. The second day I took the draft to him. He took it, kept it on his table and asked me to see him after a week. I went on seeing him every week on Saturdays until the end of the academic year. I went on frequenting his chamber and house for four years but he never found the time to go through my essay.

By that time I was more than convinced that he was harassing me deliberately and systematically. I was so helpless that I did not know what to do. I could not eat or sleep well. I could not participate in the family festivals and feasts. I could not talk happily with my mother, grandmother and brother. I could not make friendship with girls although I very much longed to, because of my depression. I even thought of canceling my registration.

Shekar had returned and joined the department after completing his M.A. in Linguistics at Leeds University. One evening he called me to the hostel canteen. We had our tea and went for a stroll towards the Kusanur village. "How was your stay in England, sir?" I asked him casually. He said, "It was wonderful and enjoyable. There are ample opportunities for scholars. A hard working man like you must go abroad so that you may achieve something great." "Yes, yes I wish to go abroad one day. I must wait for a chance," said I. "I enjoyed life to the maximum there," said he with a smile. I said, "You must have enjoyed drinking and other things there." "Definitely I enjoyed my life there. I can never forget those happy moments," said Sekhar. I said, "It's good that you had a chance to go abroad." Then Sekhar lowered his voice said, "Mr. Nandiswar, I'll tell you an interesting experience." I cocked my ears and listened to him. Sekhar said, "When I stayed in the hostel at Leeds, there used to come a maidservant to clean my room with her vacuum cleaner. One day when I was lying on my bed, she cleaned my room and went away. After fifteen minutes she came again to my room and closed and bolted the door. She fell on me and began to kiss and hug me. It was a pleasant surprise for me. She stripped me and sucked my cock. I could not resist the temptation. Then I also stripped her and pounded her. Both of us came quickly. She gurgled with pleasure. Then she kissed me and opened the door and went away. From the next day onwards she began to come regularly to my room to have a pleasant fuck." I laughed and said, "So you have really enjoyed your stay at Leeds." Sekhar continued, "I had other experiences also. I had a classmate called Priya who had come there from Hyderabad. We used to drink together and have regular fucks in the hostel. Occasionally I used to enjoy some British girls also." I listened to him carefully and said, "So your stay abroad was as profitable as enjoyable." Sekhar leered mischievously and said, "You also try to go abroad as early as possible." I said, "Yes, yes, I have to wait for the right time." We noticed that it was growing dark everywhere. So we hurried to our hostel and began to prepare for the next day's lecture.

One Sunday morning I went in search of some acquaintance or the other. I was feeling terribly lonely in my room. I went to Dr. Kulli's house. He was reading a newspaper. He welcomed me and offered the daily. I glanced at the headlines. His five-year-old son brought a tray with two cups of tea and kept it on the teapoy. Dr. Kulli and I helped ourselves. Then we went on a stroll towards the Jevaragi road. On the way I said to him, "Prof. I would like to ask you an important question. You should give me a very frank and honest answer, will you?"

"Yes, I will. What is your question?"

"You know my problem with my Ph.D. guide. He is so peculiar, moody and incalculable that it is impossible to get along with him. He has not been paying any attention to my research. I have written two chapters which he has been unwilling to see for the last four years. So, I would like to cancel my registration with him. What is your suggestion?"

"Why do you cancel the registration? You may change your guide."

"But there is no other guide except him in our University. I'll have to approach other guides in other universities for this."

"I think it will go very difficult for you if you cancel your registration with him. In case you do that, he may harass you later and may see that you will never get a degree."

"How to solve the problem, then?"

"The only way out is to request and please him to help you."

"But I have exhausted all the means of pleasing him. I have slogged like an ass in doing the full time clerk's work for him. I have stopped talking to girls in the department lest he should be jealous of me. I spend all my time in reading and writing but he accuses me that I never study. Tell me, how to please him. It's easier to please God than him."

"I know the peculiarity of your Professor. It is very difficult to pull on with such fellows. But you have no future unless and until you get a Ph.D. You request him. That is the only way out."

We walked past the ceramic industry and went towards the overbridge. Then we sat on the bridge wall and watched the trains rumbling below it. It was already 12 o'clock when we returned upto the KSRTC bus depot and dispersed.

I had realized the futility of requesting my Professor and guide who was a hard-boiled sadist. Besides, bestowed as he was with brass ears, he used to enjoy listening to tales carried by malicious people and never bothered to verify them. My colleagues who were jealous of my industry and ambition feared that I may surpass them in the academic competition. They, therefore, thought of spoiling the relationship between me and my Professor so that my Ph.D. could be delayed inordinately. My anxiety about the delay in the progress of my Ph.D. provided ample joy and sadist satisfaction to my colleagues who did not have their Ph.Ds. at that time.

By now four years had gone by after my registration for Ph.D. By that time two of my classmates in other departments like Geography and Political Science had been awarded Ph.Ds. in their subjects. I knew that they were average in intelligence and wondered as to how they could manage to get their degrees within just four years. I felt envious of them and piteous of myself. That day I met my Professor in the department in the afternoon and told him, "Sir, two of my classmates in social sciences are awarded Ph.D. degrees. But I have not been able to make any progress." My Professor understood the tone of my words and said, "Don't you compare yourself with others. Youngman. In science and social sciences any fellow can get a hack-Ph.D. within three or four years. But it is very difficult to get a Ph.D. in English, especially on Shakespeare." But I humbly said, "But I must get my degree as early as possible sir. Otherwise, my own students might compete with me by using political pressure." "Don't you worry about a degree, youngman. Look at me, do I have a Ph.D.? I have become a Professor by virtue of the strength of my personality," said the Professor. But I added, "But sir, your days are gone. Nowadays we cannot get any promotion without a Ph.D. No strength of personality will help us." Our Professor was silenced for a few seconds. He did not know how to answer me. But he quickly managed to say, "Youngman. What I mean is that you will definitely get a Ph.D., but that should not be an end in itself. It should be a means to an end. Your thesis should be a real contribution to knowledge. The world should remember you forever. Don't be in a hurry to get your degree. You take your own time and turn out a solid piece of work." "That was exactly my original intention, sir. But such a stupendous task is not possible in the god-forsaken city where there is neither a good library nor an academic atmosphere," said I. "But you have to accept it as a challenge and get over the difficulty. Have you not heard the saying, 'Where there is will, there is a way?' Nothing is impossible for man," explained the Professor.

As I was an idealist by nature, I wanted to take up the challenge and carry it out successfully. I, therefore, began to read the plays of the great bard and criticism on them very diligently. Simultaneously I was reading Indian Philosophy in order to fertilize my mind and imagination. I used to study upto 12.00 or 1.00 o'clock at night. I never used to listen to radio or go to movies like my friends. Whereas I envied their freedom and insouciance, they called me a bookworm missing all the pleasures of life. One of my teachers had remarked that I was wasting my precious life in doing the thankless Ph.D. degree. I was indeed puzzled by his remark, which should not have come from an academician. But later reflection revealed the intent of his words. I thought that this teacher was himself a non-Ph.D.

who did not, therefore, have any respect for Ph.D. holders. He was a mere love-poet in Kannada who had come up in life through the nepotistic grace of the University authorities. I, therefore, ignored his remarks and stuck to my ambition of achieving something great in my academic life.

I studied the plays and criticism of Shakespeare for one year and made ample notes. My friends and roommates dubbed me as a bookworm, and made fun of me. My friends used to spend their time in eve teasing or cleverly seducing the college girls and narrate their adventures to me. I used to laugh at them and say to them, "Dear friends, although I am envious of your enjoyment of life, I cannot follow your path, because my ambition in life is quite different from yours." Another friend remarked, "You fellow cannot enjoy life as we do." All your time is wasted in reading and writing. Because of your serious look, you cannot attract girls to yourself. You have to talk to them nicely, flatter them. You must take them to hotels and lodges and then...." "Dear friends, I know I am a serious fellow and cannot go out of my way to flatter girls and do the other things suggested by you," said I rather mechanically. "I know you are a fool wasting your precious youth in reading your dry books," said another friend. By that time the clock chimed nine. I, therefore, excused myself and left the room to have my dinner at some hotel in the Station Bazaar.

I had managed to write a preliminary draft of my third chapter. I took it to my chairman's room and said, with a fearful heart, "Sir, I have written the third chapter of my thesis. Kindly go through it and suggest corrections." My Professor puffed at his cigarette and emitted small circlets of smoke out of his mouth. I watched the circlets growing into bigger circles until finally they lost their shape. "All right, Mr. Nandiswar," said the Professor, "you leave it with me for a couple of days and then see me." Then I excused myself out of his room and went back to my room to attend to the clerical work.

Meanwhile there had started a misunderstanding between my younger brother and myself. My mother, grandmother and younger brother used to stay at Dharwad whereas I used to stay in a room in the City of Rock. My younger brother was a research scholar at the University of Dharwad for two years. But when he was appointed as a Lecturer in a prestigious college, his attitude to the family had changed conspicuously. When I went to Dharwad on my monthly visit, I was shocked to learn from my mother and grandmother that my younger brother was deeply involved in an inter-caste love affair with a nurse quite senior to him. Being pressurized by my mother and grandmother, I had strongly opposed his love marriage on the grounds of family honour and social respectability. As a result he had become vindictive and wanted to take it out of me somehow or the other. After two days I learnt that he had gone to my Professor's house and carried tales against me and had succeeded in prejudicing his mind against me. When I met the Professor on the third day and wished him as usual, he did not respond with his smile, but remained rather stiff. I did not have the courage to talk with him further.

I used to meet my guide every week and ask him if he had gone through my first draft of the third chapter. Every week he used to promise me that he would go through it next week. About two years went by like this. I wrote another two chapters, but my guide never showed any interest in my academic progress. Instead, he began to burden me with more and more clerical work. My nasty colleagues had been carrying tales against me religiously and trying to spoil the relationship between my guide and myself.

Meanwhile my mother was pressurizing me to get married as she was getting old and desirous of playing with her grandchildren. She tried to convince me, "Your younger brother cannot get married unless you get married first. It is therefore high time for you to see some brides." But I said to her, "No mummy, I don't want to get married until I get my Ph.D. Please wait for some more years. Let my younger brother get married first, as he seems to be in a hurry." My mother did not force me any further. As the University reopened on the fourteenth

November, I went back to the City of Rocks and busied myself in the daily grind of clerical work, teaching and research.

One day I received a telegram from a friend of mine and rushed to Dharwad. When I reached home, my mother and grandmother told me in-between their sobs how my younger brother had got himself married to a nurse secretly in the Registrar's Office and how his wife had entered the house on the inauspicious New Moon night. I felt horrified as if the black Rahu had entered our life. I tried to convince my mother and grandmother and went back to the rocky city. About a year went by in tension and suspicion. My mother never got on well with her daughter-in-law who was a nurse by profession. My mother was deeply and variously insulted by my younger brother. She took it to heart, grew bed ridden and expired most unexpectedly at the age of forty-eight. I was heart broken and had the liability of looking after my grandmother. I had nobody to cook food for me or my grandmother. So I had to think seriously about getting married. My dream of getting married only after getting my Ph.D. was not realized. So under duress I made compromise with my ideal and got married and settled down to matrimonial life. I separated from my brother for good and considered him metaphorically 'dead' for me.

My guide had not cared to attend my wedding in spite of my invitation to him the previous day. Nor did my colleague Sekhar attend it, although I had personally invited him. All other friends and colleagues of mine attended my wedding and wished me well in life. But my guide had avoided it systematically. I felt deeply hurt by his indifference to his own student who had been serving him with utmost devotion. Six months after my marriage I met my guide and gave him another chapter, although he had not seen the earlier ones. As usual he kept them on his table for months together. Instead of giving me any concrete suggestion, he used to assign me more and more clerical work, occasionally issue memos to me thereby asking me to do more serious preparation for teaching. I used to be irritated by these memos, as I used to spend a lot of time in preparation for teaching and do the job very conscientiously. I began to understand that my guide was discouraging me deliberately and systematically. I introspected seriously and confirmed to myself inwardly that I was not a dull fellow as he made me feel and that he was snubbing me deliberately to cover up his own lethargy and indifference. I decided to bide my time patiently and wait for the favourable turn of luck. I felt that I was not at all a University Lecturer, but a fulltime clerk and therefore deeply repented of having joined the University service, that too in a god forsaken place. I had become a *sarana i.e.* a helpless man in the land of *saranas*.

One day I met my guide in the chamber and requested him, "Sir, this heavy clerical work of the department positively comes in the way of my research work. Besides, the post-graduate teaching takes away a lot of my time. You kindly spare me from the clerical work." My guide grew very serious and snubbed the butt-end of the cigarette on the ashtray. He was fuming with anger. He said in a low but firm voice, "See Mr. Nandiswar, you are basically appointed for clerical work. I am interested in you in so far as you are useful to the department. Your Ph.D. work is your private concern. You pursue your research work in your spare time." I was really taken aback by his callous answer. But still I mustered up my courage and requested him, "Sir, my batchmates have already got their Ph.Ds. and are likely to get their promotion. Compared to them, I think, I am lagging behind them." My guide listened to me patiently and said, "You don't bother about others who have got their hack-Ph.Ds. But you have chosen an ambitious topic. Therefore you have to sacrifice a lot for your degree." "But sir," said I humbly, "I cannot get any time for my personal research after doing the full time clerical work and post-graduate teaching." "I know all that," said my guide, "but you have to adjust your timing according to your requirements." "Kindly tell me sir, how to do that," said I. My guide lit another cigarette and said, "You see, Mr. Nandiswar, as soon as you go to your room in the evening, you should shut your door and start your reading from 7.00 o'clock in the evening and go on up to 1.00 o'clock at night," "I have been reading from 7.30 P.M. to 1.00 A.M. at night sir. But in our University library not even 10% of the books and journals required for my research are available," said I humbly. "But why do you need all those books and journals? You have to think seriously about your hypothesis and depend upon your own mental resourcefulness," replied the Professor. I was totally disarmed by the sheer impossibility of carrying out his advice. I knew quite well that although my thesis, or any thesis for that matter, depends upon the kernel of original thought or angle, it has to be corroborated with relevant data and documentation. Had my guide done his Ph.D. in his life, especially in young age, he would have understood the difficulties of Ph.D. work. But he had no experience. A non-Ph.D. as he was, he had very scant respect for other Ph.D. holders. He always prided himself on having an extra-ordinarily original mind and strength of personality. He, therefore, had no need for a label of a Ph.D. I realized the utter futility of arguing with him any further. Not that I could not argue with him, but I kept quiet because of my respect for him as my guide. I knew that further argument with him would only aggravate his anger. "All right sir, I shall try to do my best," said I and came out of his chamber.

As usual I used to study hard during nighttime up to 1:00 o'clock. In the morning I used to prepare for my lectures to post-graduate classes. During the office hours I used to be kept busy with the full time clerical work. As there was no connection between my research topic and my post-graduate teaching, there used to be no reinforcement between my preparation for research and the one for teaching. I used to find it very difficult to divide my time between the two. I had simply no time for enjoyment like watching movies or participating in picnics and tours or even the domestic festivals. I was missing life through my fingers.

One day I was returning from the hostel canteen to the department. On the way a crowd had gathered. Out of curiosity I went and stood near the crowd when I was flabbergasted by what I saw. Four hefty, swarthy and ruffian-students were inhumanly beating a sickly dark girl and pushing her from one side of the road to the other. No officer of the University had the courage to ask the ruffians to stop it. Everybody stood there as a mute witness. At that time a city bus came that way. The low caste ruffian-students brutally dragged the sickly girl by her legs and hoisted her into the bus. We stood there dumb with dismay. The next day we heard the news that the ruffians took the girl to the Government hostel and mass-raped her. After three days, the question of *gundaism* on the campus of the University was raised in the secretariat also. I cursed myself for having accepted employment in such a *gunda* University. All through the year there used to be one strike or the other on one pretext or the other.

That year, I was teaching W.B. Yeats's poetry to the previous M.A. students. Though I found Yeats's poetry very difficult, yet I took it as a challenge and prepared my notes very meticulously. Twice a week I used to teach Yeats and pack my lectures with a lot of valuable information and critical analysis. The students used to be cowed into silence by the wide range of information and enjoy my lectures. This continued for about two months. One day, after the departmental picnic to a nearby farm, my colleague Mr. Sekhar was in a jovial mood. He was in close touch with some hostel students through whom he used to collect intelligence about the performance and behaviour of other teachers of our department. When we bid goodbye to the students after the picnic was over, Mr. Sekhar and I were walking along the road from Station Bazaar to Super Market. He suddenly halted for a moment and said, "Mr. Nandiswar, I have a piece of news to you." I was a bit scared by his words as I knew he generally enjoyed teasing and scaring his colleagues by letting out some disturbing news gathered from his intimate connection with our Professor and Chairman. But without betraying my fear I asked him, "What's the news? Please tell me." He stared into my eyes and said, "I have learnt from our students that your lectures on Yeats are excellent. They are so full of admiration for you. They wonder at the fact that though you are the youngest teacher in the department, yet you know such a wide range of ideas." For a moment I did not believe him, as I was very familiar with his cunning nature. I, therefore, said, "Are you teasing me?" "No, young man," said he, "I am not teasing you. By God, I am telling you the truth. Our students are full of admiration for you." I also felt secretly happy that my hard work had not gone unnoticed. I said to Mr. Sekhar, "It is true that I have been working very hard on Yeats. I really deem myself lucky if my honest lectures are appreciated by our students." I was really very happy to know that Mr. Sekhar had talked with me without irony or malice for the first time in my professional life. I, therefore, took him to the Kamat Hotel in the Super Market and offered him good tiffin and tea. Then we said 'goodbye' to each other and dispersed.

Although Sekhar was a married man, he had regular love affairs with M.A. students. A girl called Pratima was madly in love with him. She used to write passionate love letters to him. She happened to be a daughter of a Government Officer from Bangalore. Sekhar used to move about with her privately and leak out entire question papers to her. He also used to brainwash her and prejudice her against all his colleagues. Although we knew about his Byronic behaviour, we did not have the courage to bring it to the notice of Professor Nagaraj. Sekhar used to supply intelligence about all of us to Professor Nagaraj; we kept quiet about his love affairs. Besides we had our own doubts about the Professor's believing in our complaints against Mr. Sekhar.

Next week I had my class for M.A. Previous. I had to cover a lot of portion. I, therefore, asked the students if they are free after the first period. They said they were free. I began my lecture at 11.00 o'clock and went on explaining the significance of symbols used by Yeats. I was not aware of the passage of time. The students listened to me with rapt attention and jotted down the points. I stopped my lecture only when my voice fell. I rushed out of the classroom with a parched throat. When I looked at my watch, it was nearing 2:00 o'clock. Dr. Sitaram who was one of my colleagues asked me, "Did you complete your marathon lecture?" "Yes, I took a special class in addition to my regular one," said I. Both of us went out of the department and walked towards the thatched hut where a canteen was run. We had some *mirchi* and tea. I was feeling relaxed for the day. While returning from the canteen, Dr. Sitaram lowered his voice and said, 'Do you know, our Professor stood near your classroom and eavesdropped part of your lecture?" I was a bit surprised to know that our Professor was doing so and did not know the reason for that. I said, "I do not know it." Then we returned to our chamber and sat attending to the soul killing clerical work.

Half an hour must have passed by the time when our attender Yasavanta came and said, "Professor saheb is calling you." I thought he must have sent for me for some urgent clerical work to be attended to. I, therefore, went to his chamber and asked him humbly, "May I know why you called me, sir?" "Please be seated," said he and lit his cigarette. I was eagerly waiting for his order. "What Mr. Nandiswar, did you have a special class today? You were speaking so loudly that your voice could be heard even in my chamber. You seem to have such powerful lungs." "I took a special class for W.B. Yeats's poetry as I had to cover a substantial portion, sir." After the class was over, I realized that I had exceeded nearly three hours." The Professor assumed a serious look on his face and said, 'What Mr. Nandiswar, you are a mere Research Assistant. Do you want to compete with me, your Professor by lecturing continuously for three hours?" I was totally disarmed by his unexpected complaint. My voice had already grown weak that day. Still I cleared my throat and answered humbly, "No sir. How can I compete you, my teacher? That was not my intention at all. I had to hold the special class only because I had to cover certain portion of the syllabus. That's all." The Professor's anger seemed lessened by the humility of tone in my answer. Yet I was inwardly shocked and embarrassed by his peculiar behaviour. I excused myself and walked out of his chamber. When I narrated the whole thing to Dr. Sitaram, he simply laughed at it and consoled me, "Dear Mr. Nandiswar, you please don't take the Professor's words to heart. We all know his nature." Then I caught the bus and returned to the city. That night I inwardly decided never to take special classes for M.A. students.

Two years elapsed in the routine teaching, research and clerical work. Our Professor called a departmental council meeting for the distribution of teaching work and the framing of the timetable. All the colleagues came and sat in their respective chairs. The Professor asked all of us about our preferences and choices of texts. Although I had been doing research on Shakespeare's Last Plays for the past eight years, I had never been given any of Shakespeare's plays for teaching. Unluckily for me, the entire paper on Shakespeare was removed from the M.A. syllabus as soon as I registered for my Ph.D. on Shakespeare. Hence I had to prepare separately for my teaching and for my research. There was no reinforcement between the two at all. I wanted to teach at least one play, especially one tragedy so that it could help my research work. My colleague Dr. Sitaram selected the easy Indian English texts as usual. The language teachers chose the grammar topics requiring no special preparation at all. When everybody's turn was over, our Professor turned to me and asked me, "Young man, which texts do you like to teach this year?" I cleared my throat and said quite humbly, 'Sir, if you allow me, I would like to teach *Hamlet* this year." Our Professor grew stiff and angry. He looked at the other colleagues and exclaimed, "Look at the arrogance of this youngman! He wants to teach *Hamlet*, which it is my privilege to teach!"

Everybody was scared by his angry words. My colleague, Mr. Sekhar was enjoying the scene because of his professional jealousy towards me. There was pin-drop silence for a few seconds which was embarrassing to everybody. Then I made bold to clarify further, "Sir, I don't say that I can teach *Hamlet* as efficiently as you. But teaching *Hamlet* will help my research on Shakespeare in general. If you think that I can't teach it, then you give me other texts." The Professor was disarmed by my humility and his anger seemed to subside. But nonetheless he said, "Youngman, I know you are very ambitious. One day you will end up teaching *Hamlet*. You are flying very high in the sky like a kite. I would like to pull you a bit when I can." I was totally disarmed by the frankness of his malice. This type of attitude I had never expected from my *guru*. Mr. Sekhar and Mr. Sitaram were smiling maliciously at each other. By that time the attender brought tea and biscuits for all of us. We had our tea and dispersed.

When I went to the department the next day, my colleagues were enjoying the joke of the previous day at my cost. Being a juniormost Lecturer in the department, I could not react strongly to my colleagues as almost all of them were jealous of my being the youngest University Lecturer. As usual I immersed myself in the routine clerical work of the department.

One Sunday evening I was going in a man-pulled rickshaw towards the Super Market area. Mr. Sekhar who came from the opposite direction in a man-pulled rickshaw, beckoned to me and halted my rickshaw. He asked me, "Mr. Nandiswar, do you mind joining me for a spree?" I said, "But I have no money for that today." "Don't you worry about the money. I shall play the bill. I am feeling very lonely today," said he. But I knew that in spite of his pretensions of friendliness, he was constantly carrying tales against me to the Professor and spoiling our relationship. I, therefore, refused to go with him. I said, "Sorry, I am going to the Super Market for some urgent work, I can't come." Mr. Sekhar felt insulted and went away.

Next day when I was returning from the University, I met a former student of ours, Mr. Virabhadrappa who was now promoted as a Police Head Constable. As usual he wished me with respect and invited me to the nearest canteen for a cup of tea. As we were sipping the tea, Mr. Virabhadrappa said, "Yesterday something interesting happened sir." "What's that?" I asked. "Yesterday I was walking along the Municipal Garden road sir. On the way I saw somebody lying unconscious on the gutter side. Because I am a policeman, I naturally rushed to the spot and to my surprise the unconscious person happened to be none other than our own teacher Prof. Sekhar." "Is that so? How come he had fallen unconscious there? Two hours before that he had met me and invited me for a boozing session," I said. "Then I examined him sir," said Mr. Virabhadrappa, "and found out that he was dead drunk and was not in a position to talk at all." "I see! What was the reason for him to get drunk to such an extent?" asked I. "Listen to me sir. I know that his family is at Dharwad. He stays alone in the hostel on the University campus. I called an auto-rickshaw, lifted Prof. Sekhar and sat him on the seat. Then I took him to the University hostel. It was nearly 9.00 o'clock at night by the time we reached the hostel. I shifted him from the rickshaw to his room and made him drink some tea and eat biscuits so that his intoxication might decrease. I watched him for an hour or so. Then he began to talk slowly." "This is really something unbelievable," said I and cocked my ears to listen to him further. "Listen to me sir," said Mr. Virabhadrappa, "When I asked him as to why he had drunk so much, he replied that he was deeply annoyed by the Professor." "How was he annoyed?" I asked him. "It seems," said Mr.Virabhadrappa, "he had given some twenty pages draft of the first chapter of his thesis on Arthur Miller. He had written it after doing hard work for six months or so. Then the Professor had glanced through the draft and commented that the whole thing was schoolboyish and trashy. Prof. Sekhar who had returned from England after getting his M.A. in Linguistics felt deeply insulted and diffident. He, therefore, tore up the written pages of the chapter, burnt them angrily and decided never to do his Ph.D. under the Professor. Because of his terrible frustration, he came to the city and drank heavily to forget his sense of humiliation. While doddering back from the bar to the bus stop near the Super Market, he fell unconscious on the gutter side." I was really surprised by the strangeness of the event, as I knew Mr. Sekhar always hobnobbed with the Professor and carried tales against all the colleagues of the department. He enjoyed a special intimacy with the Professor. We, therefore, thought that the Professor might help him to complete his Ph.D. earlier than any of us could do.

"See, Mr. Virabhadrappa, our Professor is a very peculiar man in the world. Even if Aristotle were to come and stand before him, he would insult him by calling him a brainless fellow. Prof. Sekhar was under the impression that the Professor ill treats and insults only me and not him. He used to enjoy at my cost. Now he has tasted the strange nature of the Professor to whom he supplied regular intelligence about the departmental life." Virabhadrappa burst into a hearty laugh, and said, "It is difficult to understand the Professor. Similarly Prof. Sekhar's trick has recoiled upon himself." By that time a big crowd was gathering in the canteen. We, therefore, got up and walked away.

Another three years rolled by in regular clerical work, teaching and research. By that time our post-graduate centre had been converted into an independent University by the State Government. We were given ninety days time to exercise our option for return to the main campus at Dharwad. I was the first man to apply to the Chancellor for my transfer to Dharwad. Immediately other eight persons including our Professor and Mr. Sekhar also applied for transfer to Dharwad. Thus totally there were nine persons who were genuinely interested in transfer and were eager to get out of the God-forsaken City of Rocks described by the Urdu poet as Rose Garden. Sixty days had already gone by when the new Vice-Chancellor joined the University. As there were no Senate, Academic Council or Syndicate in the young University, the Vice-Chancellor was given by the Chancellor full power of all the three absent bodies to take independent decision. One day the new Vice-Chancellor called a special meeting of the teaching and non-teaching staff of the University in the big hall. We all attended the function. The hall was packed to capacity. Our Professor was absent on the weekend as usual. The Deputy Registrar welcomed the new Vice-Chancellor and the Finance Officer garlanded him. Then two seniormost Professors of Kannada and Chemistry Departments spoke about the dreams of teachers and non-teachers about the new University. They hoped that one day the new University would become an institution of international reputation. All the members of the audience clapped very enthusiastically. Finally the new Vice-Chancellor stood up with a wan smile on his swarthy face and thanked all the staff of the University for welcoming him. The audience again clapped loudly. But he continued his speech with a negative note. The audience grew pale with disappointment. The main points of his speech were very disheartening. He said, "Ladies and Gentlemen, I request you not to have great dreams about this young University. All of you know that the UGC will not give any grants to this University for three years. Until then we have to manage with the meager grant to be received from the State Government. We don't have sufficient money even to pay your regular salaries. We cannot carry on any developmental activities for many years to come. Anyway, the Chancellor has given you ninety days time to apply for transfer to the parent University at Dharwad. Those who are interested in transfers may apply and return to the parent University." He had thrown a big wet blanket on the enthusiasm of the audience. After the vote of thanks, the function came to an end. The teachers were so disappointed that they began to think of applying for transfers. Within the last thirty days, there were another twenty-five applications for transfer.

After the expiry of the ninety days' time, we were eagerly waiting for the Inter-University Board meeting at the Chancellor's office to take place. We were all dreaming of returning to our native city, Dharwad. After about a week's time the first list of transfers was announced. According to these rumours only those who had given money to the authorities in the Chancellor's Office or used high level influence were transferred. About Mr. Sekhar it was whispered that he was transferred because of the high influence used by his father on the Chancellor. His father happened to be a national level musician who requested the Chancellor to help his son to get a transfer. The Chancellor was touched deeply by the old man's request and instantly asked his secretary to issue the transfer order. As for the other transferred teachers, there was a rumour that they had warmed the palms of concerned authorities in the Chancellor's Office.

Those of us who were not transferred felt deeply disappointed. The University officers consoled us by saying that we have to wait for the second list of transfers. Our Professor was also deeply disappointed by not getting his transfer. But in spite of our disappointment, we were very happy to get rid of the canker of the department, Mr. Sekhar. All the colleagues in the department had nicknamed him as "Sakuni" having a very bad influence on our Professor who was well-known for his brass ears.

When I went to the department on the reopening day after the summer vacation, Mr. Reddy was in charge of the department in the absence of the Professor. Mr. Reddy ordered for tea. The attender went out of the chamber to fetch tea. "What about Mr. Sekhar? When is he going to be relieved from here?" I asked. Mr. Reddy said, "He got himself relieved from this department two days ago." "How lucky is he! We don't know when we'll receive our transfer orders," said I. Mr. Reddy said, "Mr. Sekhar is very lucky. His father used high influence with the Chancellor and got him transferred." "Yes, yes," said I, "in a way, his departure is a good riddance for the department here. Our Professor will be helpless without a telltale like Sekhar around him." Mr. Reddy articulated his pent-up anger and said, "It is good that the scoundrel Mr. Sekhar left the department. The department will have more peace in the absence of that Sakuni figure." Both of us laughed heartily and went back to our routine work.

A new Government hand, an IAS officer had joined as the Registrar of the new University. He began to apply the rules of the University very strictly. He asked the Deputy Registrar of the academic section to study all the Ph.D. files and see if they were in line with the regular rules of the University. Consequently all the Ph.D. registrations which had crossed the limit of six years had to be either cancelled or renewed legally. My guide had never bothered about the time limit of my Ph.D. as he was primarily interested in extracting asinine clerical work from me. I was really fed up with the guide. I had mentally decided to give up my Ph.D. under his guidance if the worst came to the worst and seek a new academic route with some other guide. One day, I received a letter from the Registrar of the University asking me for the renewal of my registration failing which it would be cancelled. I felt really disturbed. I worried if I was fated at all to get my Ph.D. in my life. My colleagues who pretended to be my well-wishers, felt happy about my anxiety and began to talk among themselves in hushed voices. I was literally in tears and did not know what to do. I took the Registrar's letter to my guide and showed it to him. He lit his cigarette and puffed at it. He glanced at the letter. I said to him, "The office wants to cancel my registration as it has exceeded the limit of six years. It is actually eight years now after registration. Either you get my registration renewed without any fees or I shall have to give up my Ph.D." I sat with a downcast face. The guide seemed to be touched by my helpless condition as much as irritated by the bureaucratic letter. In all the eleven years, the University had never taken such a drastic step. My guide took a deep breath and said, "Don't you worry, Mr. Nandiswar, I shall fight with the Registrar and get your registration renewed without any fees." I said, "Please do whatever you wish to do, sir. I don't know just what to do." I came out of his chamber with a dispirited heart. In a way, I was a little happy also to know that although my guide never cared for my academic progress, he had now to answer the office.

After a week's time, my guide attended the Ph.D. Registration Committee meeting at the Registrar's office presided over by the Vice Chancellor. I attended to my regular clerical work and teaching in the department. In the afternoon I went to the thatched canteen to have my snacks and tea. Some clerks from the Registrar's office had come there for tea. They wished me and told me, "What Prof. Nandiswar. Today there was a big quarrel between the Registrar and your guide in the office." The other clerks laughed heartily and said, "Yes, yes, it was wonderful to watch the grand quarrel between two big personalities." In-between the dialogues, we were sipping our tea. I asked one of the clerks, "Can you give me some highlights of the quarrel?" He replied, "Your Professor accused the Registrar that he does not know enough English. Then the Registrar said that he is an IAS officer and knows better English than the Professor. Then your Professor hit back that he knew only clerical English and not standard literary English." I was listening to the report with rapt attention. My Professor had been well-known on the University campus as a very tough and egoistic person. Normally no officer dared to cross him. But the new IAS officer had tantalized him for the first time. Then another clerk said, "The Registrar asked your Professor as to how many Ph.Ds. he had produced in his thirty three years service. Your Professor felt exasperated beyond measure and replied that he did not believe in producing trashy, unprintable Ph.Ds." We sipped our tea. I was inwardly glad that somebody at last had heckled my Professor and alerted him about his academic duties. "Tell me then what happened?" I asked the clerk. He said that he only overheard the quarrel and did not stay long there to listen to the whole session. The other clerk remarked, ''These quarrels are good, in a way. There is an evidence of new life coming on the campus." Then we paid our bills and walked away from the canteen to the department.

The next day I went to the department and took my class for M.A. Final students. Then I attended to the clerical work. I took the office latters to the Head of the Department for his signature. He signed them promptly. When I was about to return to my chamber, the Professor said quite proudly, "Mr. Nandiswar, yesterday I fought with the office and got your Ph.D. term extended. You don't have to pay any penal fees for that." "Thank you sir," I said. "You can submit your thesis within two years," said he further. "My final chapter is ready sir. But you have not seen the earlier chapters yet," said I deliberately. "You write your chapter. Then we shall sit together and discus them," said he. "All right, sir," said I and came out of his chamber. I was a bit happy inwardly to notice that finally he had become serious about my Ph.D. at least under the official pressure if not out of any concern for me.

About six months passed in routine clerical work, teaching and research. In the month of December, our Professor received a letter from the Governor's office. He told us in the tea meeting that he was appointed as the Chancellor's nominee for the selection committee for the appointment of teachers at Bangalore University. Meanwhile a young lady Kamaksi who had returned from Canada after her divorce from her first husband had joined our department as a temporary lecturer. As she never had any teaching experience in the past, she used to feel very diffident about teaching the difficult authors to M.A. students. One day she told me that she was a receptionist in an advertising firm in Canada. That was perhaps the reason why she used to bob her hair, and prink herself with lip-stick and collyrium. She used to speak good convent English, although she had no wide reading. Our Professor had a special liking for her.

For one whole week, our Professor was away on other duty. We all knew that he had gone to Mangalore University for the selection of teaching posts. In our regular tea meetings, Ms Kamaksi used to wonder at the moodiness, childlikeness and the suspicious nature of our Professor when details of his nature were described by our colleagues. But she used to be grateful to him for helping her with temporary appointment.

The Professor returned to the department after a week's time of O.O.D. He looked very fresh and healthy. All the colleagues gathered in his chamber for our regular tea meeting. After the usual amicabilities were over, The Professor said with a superior air, "You knew, I went to Mangalore University as the Chancellor's nominee. I made the right kind of selection." "Who were the candidates and whom did you appoint, sir?" asked Dr. Sitaram. The Professor replied, "We appointed a lady called Bimala as selection grade Reader. And a man called Ramaswami as Reader under Merit Promotion scheme." Then I asked the Professor out of sheer curiosity, "What is the doctoral topic of

Prof. Bimala, sir?" "No, no, Ms. Bimala doesn't have a Ph.D., but she has a brilliant mind," said the Professor. "But Dr. Ramaswami is a Ph.D. from Cambridge, sir. Then how can he be placed under Merit Promotion scheme which has a lower salary scale and status?" The Professor puffed his cheeks for a moment and sat erect. He lit a cigarette and blew a couple of rings of smoke. He said, "I know all that. But I have no respect for Ph.Ds. Anyway, Dr. Ramaswami has been in the department and eligible for Merit Promotion. But this lady has no previous service in the department. She has just returned from America and is without a job." My colleagues and I were rather puzzled by his argument. I could not control my righteous anger and said, "In that case, you could have appointed that lady as a lecturer and placed Dr. Ramaswami as Selection Grade Reader sir." The Professor smiled mischievously and said, "Actually that lady had applied only for a lecturer's post. She had not applied for a Reader's post at all. But I fought for her vehemently. I pleaded that she should be appointed as Selection Grade Reader because she has a brilliant mind. Besides, her father and I were jail mates in 1942. So I had to help his daughter." I felt deeply upset by his argument. I asked him, "Then what about Dr. Ramaswami with a Cambridge Ph.D. sir? Don't you think he deserves it better?" The Professor replied, "Well, he had had his days at Cambridge in the past. Now he must make some sacrifice." By that time the attender brought tea for all of us. We sipped our tea and dispersed. While I was going to the library with Dr. Sitaram, we met Dr. Krisnamurthy on the way and told him what our Professor had done in the selection of teachers. Dr. Krishnamurthy who was humorous by nature cracked a joke instantly, "Your Professor must have appointed a lady with a brilliant mind in a brilliant body." All the three of us doubled up with laughter. Dr. Sitaram remarked, "Our Professor suffers from an inferiority complex because he himself has no Ph.D. Therefore he upholds the non Ph.Ds. and disdains the Ph.D. holders with a vengeance." "Yes, yes. That is very true. But what to do ? Such people have power in their hands and decide the fate of others," said Dr. Krisnamurthy.

The next year, there was an acute demand for two lecturers in the department caused by the vacancies created by the departure of two lecturers to other Universities. Dr. Reddy had left the department as he was appointed as Reader in some other University. But the University authorities could not make immediate appointments because of the procedural delay caused by bureaucratic rules. Hence the Vice-Chancellor had permitted our Chairman to recommend one or two guest lecturers. So one day, our Chairman called a meeting of the departmental council and asked for our opinion. I suggested the name of Prof. Hiremath who had retired from the college service in the city. Our Chairman knew that Prof. Hiremath was a senior person with many books to his credit. He, therefore, agreed to recommend Prof. Hiremath. When the demand for another guest lecturer came up, my colleagues suggested a few names. But the Chairman turned them down with some pretext or the other and wanted to recommend a young lady lecturer in a local junior college. He said her name was Urmila who hailed from Bangalore. All the colleagues in the department had heard about her good looks and coquetry. But nobody could dare cross the Chairman in this regard. The Professor said, "You see, the presence of a lady in the department electrifies the atmosphere and makes men more decent and cultured." We, the colleagues smiled meaningfully at one another and kept quiet. We dispersed after having our regular tea in the department.

The next week, Miss Urmila reported herself to duty as a guest lecturer. She had a tall and slim figure and very fair complexion. She wore her cosmetics very conspicuously. Her lips were painted with rose coloured lipstick, her eyes lined with dark collyrium and her cheeks were smeared with rose colour. She had bobbed her hair. On the whole, she was a very lively and talkative lady of about 30 years age who befriended people almost instantaneously. The students also liked her because she happened to be a new guest lecturer. Our old colleague Ms. Kamaksi chummed up with Miss Urmila and soon they began to hobnob with each other. Miss Urmila used to come to the department about 2.00 P.M. to teach the M.A. classes after attending to her regular duty in the local junior college in the morning. Every day our Professor used to stand at the window at 1.30 P.M. and wait for her arrival like a passionate young lover. The colleagues who had noticed this habit of the Professor used to whisper among themselves and keep quiet.

As days went by, Miss Urmila and Ms. Kamaksi became close friends. As expected, Ms. Kamaksi used to learn more and more details of Miss Urmila's family background and life style. Miss Urmila was quite frank with other men colleagues also. But the details about Urmila's life collected by Ms. Kamaksi were more interesting and authentic than the ones that the men colleagues could gather from their conversations with Miss Urmila.

As for me, I was worried about the completion of my Ph.D. as early as possible and get rid of the decade-long mental tension. Our Professor who used to be depressed for the past three years because of his domestic problems, grew now more cheerful. We all knew that his daughter who was studying in a medical college of Hubli had been abandoned by her lover after two years of illegal living together. Now he used to spend most of his time with Miss Urmila in the department in the afternoon. She was more or less of his daughter's age.

By now I had completed the entire draft of my thesis in an amorphous way. I wanted my guide's help in giving it a pedagogical shape and finish. During the past ten years, he had not looked into a single page. I was not lucky enough to have timely and periodical help and guidance from him. One day I met him in the department and requested him, "Sir, would you mind glancing through my first draft of the thesis? If you suggest corrections and alterations, I can get them typed neatly. All the chapters are ready now." The Professor could not come out with any pretext this time, as he had exhausted all of them on me. "Shall I bring the first chapter tomorrow?" I asked. Now he could not dodge me at all, as he had been insulted by the University authorities in this case. He said, "Mr. Nandiswar, I cannot read your draft in the department because of the disturbance here. You better come to my room in the Guest House on Sunday afternoon. We shall discuss and correct your thesis over the beer." I was inwardly very glad that he had finally agreed to look into my draft, although I knew I had to spend a lot of money on his costly beer. "Yes, sir, I shall come to your room on Sunday afternoon. Of course, I shall bring some beer and snacks also with me," said I gladly and took leave of him.

The next Sunday I bought three bottles of beer, and a few snacks and put them in a shoulder bag and caught the 10.15 A.M. bus at the City Bus Stand near the Station Bazaar. The bus followed the serpentine path showing us half the city, picking up passengers all through the way. When the bus reached the University campus, it was 11.00 o'clock. As it was a Sunday, the whole campus looked deserted. I got off the bus and carried the heavy bag of beer bottles towards the University Guest House situated on a hillock. My guide stayed in a room in the Guest House. I climbed the steps of the hillock and walked towards the room of my guide expectantly. But when I reached his room, I was rather disappointed to see that it was locked. I wanted to inquire somebody in the opposite room. But I found that that room was also locked. There was nobody around there to make enquiry. So I carried the heavy bag gently lest the clinking of bottles in the bag should attract the attention of people unduly. At last I went to the counter of the Guest House and asked an attender about where my guide must have gone. The Khaki-clad attender replied gently, "Nagaraj saheb has gone to Sedum in the morning in somebody's car." Then I asked him further, "Do you know when he may return? He had asked me to come and meet him by 11.00 A.M." "I don't know when exactly he may return. But if he has told you to wait, you may be seated on the sofa there in the lounge sir," replied the attender.

"All right," said I and carried my bag to the lounge and sat on the sofa there. The whole Guest House looked deserted because of Sunday. I sat watching the trees and birds through the window. After half an hour's waiting I felt bored. I, therefore, walked out of the Guest House towards the old Biradeva temple. The village men and women were occasionally coming to and going away from the temple. The sun was growing hotter and hotter as he had reached the zenith now. Then I walked back to the lounge of the Guest House and learnt that the Professor had not returned. I felt deeply disappointed. I repented of having registered under such a moody and non-cooperative guide. I cursed my cruel fate. I waited for another half an hour. But the Professor did not come. Then I realized that it was too late for our reading session. I thought, even if the Professor returned at 1 o'clock, he would have his lunch and rest for the afternoon and may not be able to start reading my draft until the evening. Besides I was also feeling hungry and needed rest in the afternoon. But I did not know where to keep the beer bottles. I did not want to take them back as they were meant for my guide. I could not leave them with the attender in the Guest House because he may not be a reliable person. Then I suddenly remembered that my Professor's close friend Dr. Siddappa stayed in the University Quarters beyond the hillock of the Guest House. I, therefore, thought of keeping the beer bottles in his house. I slowly climbed down the hillock carefully by threading my way through the tall grass and thorny bushes and watching out for snakes. I managed to climb down the steep and slipping hillock and walked towards the University Quarters. I spotted Dr. Siddappa's house and pressed the button. As the call bell sounded Dr. Siddappa opened the door and welcomed me affectionately, "Please come in Mr. Nandiswar." He asked me to be seated. I was sweating heavily as I had climbed down the hillock in the hot sun. He switched on the ceiling fan. Then Dr. Siddappa sat in front of me and asked me, "What's the matter? How is your Ph.D. work progressing?" I cleared my throat and said, "Sir, ten years after registration, my guide has agreed to have the first look at my first draft of thesis. He had asked me to come to the Guest House about 11.00 o'clock. I, therefore, came there at 11.00 o'clock and waited until now. It is already 1.00 o'clock now. You know sir, my guide does not read my script without the holy *tirtha* to go with it. I, therefore, brought some beer bottles and snacks for him, but he has not returned to the Guest House even now. I did not know where to keep these beer bottles. I have, therefore, brought them here. Please keep them in your house and give them to our Professor after his return." Dr. Siddappa commented, "Your Professor is a brilliant man, but is very lazy by nature and unwilling to help anybody. But there is no way out except wait on his mood and mercy. I know you are a very honest researcher. God will definitely help you." I knew Dr. Siddappa was a well-wisher of mine. Several times he had said to me, "If I had a student like you working under me in my department, I would have placed you on my head and danced." I said, "You know sir, I have served him for the past twelve years more than like his own children. But he has not cared to look into my draft up till now." In spite of my self-control tears trickled down my cheeks. I wiped them with my handkerchief. Dr. Siddappa who was heavily built, walked up to me, patted me on the back and tried to console me, "Take it easy, young man. God will definitely help you. Your hard work will not go a waste. I shall talk to your Professor to help you to get your degree." I listened to him silently. I excused myself and took leave of him. I caught the 1.30 bus and came back to the city.

The next day when I met the Professor at the department after my class, he said, "Mr. Nandiswar, I am sorry I made you wait for me. I had to go to some town unexpectedly." "It's all right sir, I waited for four hours and went back. By the way, did you get the bottles I had left at Professor Siddappa's house?" I asked. "Thank you very much for that. I shall use them for two days," said he. I was secretly happy to know that he was apologetic about his absence on the promised day. I thought it augured well for me at least the next Sunday. Meanwhile I was busy with teaching and research. Next Saturday I met him during the recess hour and asked him, "Sir, shall I come tomorrow for discussing the thesis?" "Yes, yes. You may come tomorrow about 4.00 o'clock in the evening. We shall read and discuss your chapters until 7.00 o'clock. Then we can have our beer," said he. I was quite happy to learn that he was at last ready to cast his eyes on my first draft for the first time in about ten years' time.

The next day happened to be a Sunday. In the morning, I read some authors for teaching and made notes. After my lunch and siesta, I got up and went to the Station Bazaar. I saw some college teachers, who happened to be my friends, were going to movies or clubs for entertainment. I felt deeply envious of them, as I could not enjoy life like them. I was fated to slog and suffer in life. Then I bought three bottles of beer in the Rolex Bar. I carried them in a shoulder bag. Then I bought some packets of *ghati*, chips, and a few *samosas,* and kept them in the bag. I rushed to the City Bus Stand and caught the University bus. The bus took about fifty minutes to reach the University. There were only about ten passengers in the bus. When it reached the University campus about 4.00 o'clock, the campus looked deserted. The students and staff of the University were waiting for the bus to go to the city for marketing and seeing movies. I climbed the steps of the hillock and walked into the Guest House. I went straight to the Professor's room and greeted him. He welcomed me and asked me to be seated. I asked him where I should keep the beer bottles. As he had no fridge in his room, he asked me to keep them in the bucket with cool water. Then he ordered for two cups of tea for us. The servant of the Guest House brought the tea. We sipped our tea and started reading the first chapter of my thesis. I was very nervous and eagerly waiting for his comments. As he went on reading the lines of the typescript, he pointed out the minor grammatical and stylistic inaccuracies and scolded me. I humbly replied that I would correct them. I was eager to know if I had made any error of logic or judgement in the first chapter dealing with the epic vision of the major poets of the world. To my satisfaction, I found that he did not find fault with the argument in the first chapter. He added a few words here and there and deleted a few words here and there. After three hours of solid work, he gave me a green signal to make a fair copy of the first chapter by carrying out his instructions.

But now it had grown dark everywhere. It was about 7.00 o'clock. I felt happy that at least one chapter had been approved by my guide nearly six years after I had written it. Then I kept the snacks like *ghati,* chips and *samosas* on the tray. I brought all the three bottles of beer and kept them on the floor. I opened a bottle and poured some beer into a glass and said, "Please, have your beer sir." We started crunching the chips leisurely. "What about you? You did not pour any beer to your glass?" He asked. Then I said humbly, "I do not want to have any beer sir. You please have it." Suddenly the Professor's face grew into a scowl. He said with controlled anger, "Then sorry, Mr. Nandiswar, I will not take any beer from any body if the offerer also does not drink it." I felt nervous that I was spoiling the game. I wanted to make it up as early as possible. I, therefore, said apologetically, "In that case I shall have only one beer sir. You may have two." Then we sipped our beer leisurely and munched the *ghatis* and chips. As minutes went by, I felt my whole body was growing cooler and calmer with the effect of beer. About 8.00 o'clock, I thanked the Professor, excused myself and rushed to the bus stop. After waiting for ten minutes, I caught the bus and returned to the city with a sense of satisfaction.

The next Sunday, the same ritual was repeated. The Professor had read and approved the second chapter. For about ten Sundays the ritual was continued. At last when the entire first draft was approved by the guide, I heaved a temporary sigh of relief. For the first time in my life I began to eat and sleep well. About twelve years had elapsed since I had started rubbing with my tough guide. I took about three month's time to get the hand written manuscript transformed into a rough typescript. Again I waited on the guide's mercy and convenience and had another half a dozen reading sessions with the libation of beer and snacks. He did not see the typescript as attentively as he had seen the first draft. He glanced through it hurriedly, skipped many pages and asked me to check the mistakes by myself. In the second and the third chapters there were a few repetitions and I wanted to see if the guide noticed them. But he did not seem to notice them. Since he was an internationally reputed scholar, I thought that everything in the typescript was all right, as he had not pointed out any repetitions. In the last reading session he said, "Now the thesis is complete in all respects. You can get it typed in six copies and bound beautifully and submit." I felt quite enthused to have won the war. I sipped my beer with him. I thanked him profusely and took leave of him.

The next week I went to Dharwad for the summer vacation. On Monday I went to the typist's home and gave him the entire manuscript and requested him to type it neatly as early as he could. "Don't you worry sir," said he, "I shall do as early as I can." I thanked him in advance and returned home with a lightened heart. For the first time in my life, after fourteen years of teaching service, I felt a bit free from the academic tension. I began to eat well and spend some time with my wife and child. My grandmother was happy to notice that I was relatively more cheerful in my domestic life now.

Every week, I used to collect the typed chapter and take them to my guide who had also come to Dharwad for his vacation. After four weeks, I had submitted all the chapters of the thesis to him so that he could have a final glance at them to make it complete in all respects. He asked me to see him after a week's time. I returned home and began to read some writers of my choice for sheer pleasure of reading. Now there was no pressure on my mind to read only the authors connected with my thesis. One evening, when I was sitting with my grandmother and chatting with her, she advised me, "My dear boy, now that you have got rid of your academic tension, you start living cheerfully. You eat and sleep well and play with your child. After all life is meant to be enjoyed." I agreed with my grandmother's advice and promised her not to neglect my domestic pleasures henceforth.

Although my guide had promised to glance through the typescript, he could not keep up his promise. Every week I used to see him at his home and return rather disappointed. When I met him for the fourth time on the fourth week of April, he was busy talking with his relatives. I asked him politely, "Have you glanced through the typescript sir? My typist is waiting for the green signal. I wish to complete the whole process during the vacation." The Professor lit his cigarette and emitted the curls of smoke out of his mouth. The children and the relatives were talking and giggling loudly in the inner hall. Then the Professor went into his room and came out with the typescript and gave it to me. I was eagerly waiting for his answer. He said, "See, Mr. Nandiswar, I have not been able to see your typescript at all. You better see it once again, correct the mistakes and give it for final typing." I was deeply disappointed by his lack of concern for me, in spite of all the service that I had rendered to him for more than a decade. But at the same time, I was happy that he had at least permitted me to give it for final typing. "All right, sir. I shall do accordingly." I collected the typescript, thanked him formally and walked home with mixed feelings. I thought if I could correct my own mistakes of style and judgement, why do I need a guide at all? Moreover, how do I know that I have made mistakes unless my guide points them out? I could have shown my thesis to some other senior man and even paid some fee for the editorial service. But alas, there was nobody available in Dharwad. I knew that such service was available in some cities and that theses were even ghost written by senior scholars for a substantial fee. Unfortunately no such amenities were available in my native place.

The next day I decided to leave everything to the will of God and gave the entire material to the typist and asked him to complete the final typing within three or four weeks. I kept myself busy with light reading during the month of May. After a month, the whole thesis was neatly typed and beautifully bound. It ran into six hundred fifty-eight pages. The bulky size of the thesis was very impressive. I felt proud of myself for having done such a work in spite of all the odds of my life. By that time, the summer vacation was over.

I left Dharwad for the City of Rocks to be present in the department on the reopening day. My Professor had travelled separately by train to the City of Rocks. On the reopening day, all the colleagues gathered in the department for the common tea. When everybody was sipping his tea, my Professor said proudly to the colleagues, "See, gentlemen, our youngman is submitting his thesis today. He has written an excellent thesis on the best dramatist of England." My colleagues saw my bulky thesis and seemed to be impressed by it.

All of them congratulated me for completing a challenging task. I thanked them mechanically and kept quiet. In the heart of my heart, I knew that my Professor had not paid sufficient attention to my thesis like chapterization, structure and texture of writing. But I would not express it either. My sole intention was to get rid of the burden as early as I could. I, therefore, took the signature of my guide on all the four copies of the thesis and on the covering letter. The clerk of the department entered the letter number and date in the dispatch register. Then the attender carried the four copies of the bulky thesis on his shoulders and walked with me to the office of the Controller of Examinations. I submitted the four copies at the inward section of the Examination Office and took an acknowledgement and heaved a sigh of relief. Then I took the attender to the canteen-hut and offered him hot *mirchi* and tea.

I busied myself in the routine of teaching and light reading. Every fortnight or so I used to visit the Examination Section to check up if my papers were moving from table to table. The office took nearly six months to contact an Indian and a foreign referee. I felt happy to notice that things were moving smoothly. I, therefore, kept quiet for about three months. Meanwhile the Controller of Examinations who had come from Bangalore University as a lent hand left the University of the City of Rocks. The teaching and the non-teaching staff arranged a farewell party to him. Then a Principal of a local College was appointed as the

Controller of Examinations. I met him in his office after he joined the office and congratulated him on his appointment to a responsible post. One day I went to the Examination Section and enquired if my thesis was dispatched to the Indian and foreign referees. The clerk concerned told me that he had not received the Vice-Chancellor's approval yet, and that he was waiting for it. I visited the section almost every week for three months and was surprised to learn that the letter had not come at all from the Vice-Chancellor's office. I was deeply disconcerted about the inordinate and irrational delay in the matter. I, therefore, wanted to verify the dispatch number and date of the document in the Vice-Chancellor's office. I met the P.A. to the Vice Chancellor and requested him to verify the details. He and I together searched for the letter very meticulously for two hours. Finally we discovered that there was no entry at all about my paper. The P.A. to the Vice-Chancellor told me that perhaps the Ph.D. file was missing. I was deeply shocked by this inference. I instantly rushed to the Office Superintendent of the Examination Section and explained the whole thing to him. He was very sympathetic to me as he happened to be from my own native place. He understood my anxiety and told me, "Professor, obviously, your file is missing. Somebody must have done some deliberate mischief." I grew pale with anger and helplessness. I asked him, "Why should this happen only in my case? I have not antagonized anyone in my life. People should have nothing against me." The Office Superintendent tried to console me, "Don't you worry, Professor. When the earlier Controller of Examinations left our University for Bangalore University, he must have misplaced it somewhere. Or someone else must have hidden the file somewhere. You please don't worry. Even if the original file is missing, we shall build up a duplicate file and streamline every thing." I joined my palms to the Office Superintendent and requested him, "Please do your best and show me a way out of this." I walked back to my department and explained all the bureaucratic chaos to my Professor. He was also surprised by the Kafkaesque mystery of the Examination section.

He tried to enhearten me by asking me to collect all the duplicate letters connected with my thesis.

Within two days I hectically searched all the duplicate papers and gave them to the Office Superintendent. He said, "Now, don't you worry, Professor. I shall build up your case in the quickest possible way. You eat and sleep well today and don't have any tension." I joined my palms to him and took leave of him.

I frequented the Examination Section for about three weeks almost regularly and saw to it that the letters of invitation were dispatched to an Indian and a foreign referee. Then again I waited for nearly two months to learn that both of them had luckily accepted the University's invitation to act as adjudicators of my thesis. I heaved a sigh of relief temporarily and immersed myself in the routine of teaching and reading and writing critical articles on Indian writers who were not as taxing as Shakespeare.

Another six-month elapsed. Meanwhile two reminders were sent by the University to the two examiners. At last after eight months, when I went to the Examination Section, I learnt that the Indian referee from Vallabh Vidyanagar had sent his report recommending the award of Ph.D. degree to me. I asked the Office Superintendent to show me the report. Initially he hesitated to do so as the matter was confidential. But after my persuasive request, he agreed to show it to me secretly so that I could have a hurried glance at it. When the entire staff of the Examination Section left the office for their lunch during the recess hour, he opened the file and showed me the letter of recommendation from the Indian examiner. I had a quick glance at the letter and grasped the contents. Although I was happy to know that he had recommended the award of Ph.D. degree for my thesis, I was not happy to note his careless and left-handed compliments. From his remarks I could easily make out that he had not read all the chapters of the thesis, but had glanced at only a few chapters. Besides, he was not a Shakespeare scholar himself. He had missed many finer aspects of my analysis and comments. I was inwardly angry with my guide for recommending the name of a man not deeply steeped in Shakespeareana. His views appeared to be random and indifferent. Anyway, I thanked the Office Superintendent profusely and walked out of the Examination Section. I told all these details to my guide who consoled me by saying that the examiner was not a Shakespeare scholar but happened to be a friend of his, whom he had met at Delhi about fifteen years ago, but who had a very beautiful wife. I was really nonplussed by his answer and kept quiet.

I was secretly worrying about the foreign examiner's opinions. I had heard from the academic people that the British examiners were very rigid, conservative and uncompromising in their views about academic standards. They were said to be sticklers for academic excellence. By contrast, the American examiners were said to be more liberal and humanistic in their approach to the third world scholars. But unfortunately my thesis had to be sent to a British examiner as the topic of my thesis happened to be Shakespeare. Not merely that! It had been sent to a world famous Shakespeare scholar heading the Shakespeare Institute at Birmingham University in England. In spite of the lurking fear in my mind, I felt proud of being examined by an international scholar in the field. Anyway, I left everything to the Almighty God and began to pursue my teaching, reading and writing.

In the month of August, I went to Dharwad and spent three days with my wife, child and grandmother. On the fourth day when I wanted to book my ticket for the City of Rocks, my wife began to create a hell of a problem for me, "I shall come to that city along with my child." I tried to reason with her, "If you come with me, who will take care of the grandmother who is too old to take care of herself?" My wife began to shout at me and use the worst possible abuses. She twisted my fingers and pinched my hands and shouted at me, "You idiot, have I married you only to be away from you for years together?" I tried to convince her, "No no, not like that. You please understand the contingencies of our life. Grandmother cannot walk properly, she suffers from rheumatism. Nor can she cook as her eyesight is very dim. I, therefore, request you to be here to take care of her. Later we shall go on a tour by making some arrangement for her." My wife tweaked my forearm tortuously and shouted again, "You scoundrel, did you marry me only to look after your old hag? I should not have married an impecunious teacher like you. Had I married an engineer or a doctor, I could have led a royal life. Fie upon you, brainless pauper." Her harsh words hurt me so deeply that I recalled the whole saga of my suffering right from my childhood. My wife was simply unable to imagine the intensity of it. Tears gushed out of my eyes involuntarily. I began to sob uncontrollably. When my wife saw me, she again taunted and hurt me, "Do you, a man cry like a coward?" I simply had no answer for her callous question.

The next day, I requested a few neighbours to take care my grandmother in our absence, and took my wife and child to the City of Rocks. My wife seemed to be quite happy in travelling in the bus with me, but I was inwardly worried about my grandmother whom we had left alone in the big house at Dharwad. We reached the City of Rocks in the early morning. All through the night I had not slept properly. In spite of sleepiness, I had to go to the University by 10 o'clock bus. I was secretly hoping that the foreign examiner would have sent his report. As I went to the Professor's chamber and greeted him, we exchanged amicabilities. Then he said gently, "The foreign examiner has sent his report." When I heard these words, my heart began to flutter with excitement. "Has he recommended the award of the degree, sir?" I asked anxiously. The Professor's face grew grim. He said, "No, he has not recommended the award of the degree. He has asked you to revise it." When I heard this, I felt as if my whole being was disintegrating. I was about to faint, but I controlled myself with a strong will. I said in a weak voice, "I would have been happy if he had rejected it. In that case it would have been sent to another examiner. But this revision means we have to send the thesis again to him and that too to his satisfaction." My ten years struggle has been a wash in the water." I was literally on the verge of tears. The Professor tried to console me, "Don't you worry. It means another six month's work." "But sir, having spent ten solid years for the thesis, I am really sick of it now. How can I work on it once again?" queried I. "Take it easy, young man. I am sorry that such a thing has happened. But face it boldly." I stood up and silently walked out of his chamber. I knew that this would not have happened if he had not been careless and indifferent about his guidance. I was deeply disturbed. I boarded the 4 o'clock bus. Though my friends talked with me, I was not in a mood to talk jovially with them.

As I came to my room, my wife asked me why I was so pale today. I told her about the foreign examiner's report and how I had to spend another six months in revising my thesis. She cursed my guide and my bad luck. She asked me to give up the research work and live my life as I have a permanent job. But I told her, "But I can never hope to be a Reader without having a Ph.D. It is a question of my academic survival." She ignited the kerosene stove and began to prepare tea in the room. I lay on the bed to relax. My four-year-old son fell upon me and began to rub his face against mine. I was feeling deeply restless. I tried to mollify him and sit beside me. But he continued to play with me by rubbing his face against mine, without caring for my threats. Tension was mounting in my mind. I was so irritated that I began to beat him with all the force that I was capable of. Frightened by my reckless thrashing, my little son began to cry and ran away from me. I sipped my tea and lay on the bed relaxing. I felt deeply sorry for my innocent son who could not understand my tension. He joined his mother's company outside the small room and spent his evening playing with the neighbouring children. I felt so sorry for my son that I wanted to mollify him. I, therefore, went out at night, brought some cakes and gave them to him. I was happy only when I saw a smile on his face. Though I had been staying in a small room as a forced bachelor, my wife had come with my son to stay with me for about a fortnight's time. She used to cook in the small room on the kerosene stove. But the owner of the house thought that we were leading a family life in a small room by cooking in it. He thought that we were going to stay there permanently. One morning he called me out and asked me to vacate the room by the end of the month. I told him that my wife and child would be returning to Dharwad after a fortnight's time and that he need not worry about the rent. But he said curtly, "No, no, we need the room for my daughter who is studying engineering. You better search for a room elsewhere." I was deeply hurt by his curt answer. "All right sir, I shall search for a room elsewhere within a week's time." When I told this to my wife, she was furious and began to pressurize me to search for a small house elsewhere in the city. Accordingly I searched for a small house in the city which was near the City Bus Stand and shifted the luggage there from the small room.

After shifting to the small house, we took a couple of days to adjust ourselves to the new atmosphere. The small house belonged to the father of a past lady student of mine. After a few days, my wife began to feel bored with the life in the small house as she could not befriend the neighbouring women a majority of whom happened to be illiterate, puritanical and egoistic brahmins. She wanted educated and liberal ladies as her friends. But that was not possible in a traditional brahmanical lane. I simply did not know how to solve the problem of my wife. Besides, my attention was directed to the revision of my thesis. Then she said she felt bored with the life in the City of Rocks and wished to return to Dharwad. I was secretly happy to note that with the return of my wife to Dharwad, my grandmother would have a caretaker for her. I, therefore, travelled in the bus along with my wife and little son and reached Dharwad the next morning. I was happy to see that my grandmother was happy to see all of us back at home. After spending three days with my family, I returned to the City of Rocks to spend my lonely days in the small house.

I used to meet my guide every Saturday evening over a couple of beer bottles and seek his guidance in revising my thesis. I deleted two small chapters, which were repetitious according to the foreign examiner. Then I provided some explanatory details about the technical terms of Indian aesthetics, which the foreign examiner had failed to understand due to his ignorance of Oriental thought. I was really impressed by his intellectual honesty, which was conspicuously missing in the Indian examiner. I was also proud of myself to know that the foreign examiner had praised the positive aspects of my thesis. He had said that on the whole the thesis was well thought out, well organized and written in a high standard style and shown his special appreciation of my analysis of the theatrical aspects of Shakespeare's last plays.

One day I met Dr. Siddappa, the Chairman of the Department of Mathematics casually in his room. He welcomed me affectionately, ordered tea for me and tried to sympathize with me. "Don't you worry, Mr. Nandiswar, you revise your thesis and resubmit it. Don't take it to heart. I know how hard you have worked for it," said he. I replied, "Of course, I am revising it sir. But my guide should not have ignored me so much, especially when I trusted him totally and served him like a lackey for the past thirteen years." He consoled me, "I really pity you for your bad luck. Your Professor is a very lazy man and does not care for anybody. Besides, he never worked for a Ph.D. in his life and therefore, does not have the knowledge of research methodology. He has confessed it before me." I said, "No sir, there is no doubt at all that he is a brilliant man and I don't question his capacity. My only complaint is that he has been supremely indifferent to me and has no concern for my future career. Had I had my Ph.D. some eight years ago, I would have become a Reader long back and perhaps gone abroad also." Dr. Siddappa said, "Yes, yes. What you say is correct. I feel really sorry for you for your bad luck. Your Professor is of course, my close friend, but he is a very peculiar man. He thinks that if he helps you to get your Ph.D. early, you will be out of his control. He, therefore, wants to prolong it as long as he can." I knew Dr. Siddappa had confirmed all my secret doubts about my Professor. I thanked him and returned to my department.

One day I telephoned the typist at the Government printing press and asked him to come to my house urgently in the evening. After I returned home I waited for him. He came about 7.00 P.M. and knocked at my door. I recognized his voice and opened the door. He greeted me amicably and sat in the chair. "Why sir, you have shifted from a small room to a small house. Have you brought your family?" asked he. "No, no. I have taken this small house so that my family may come and stay for a few days now and then," replied I. "Yes, sir, I understand. How much money you have to spend on this? What a sheer waste!" exclaimed he. "What to do ! this is my bad luck," said I. Then he asked me, "why did you call me sir? Do you have an article to be typed?" asked he. "No, no, you have to type my thesis," said I. He was rather surprised and asked me, "Why sir, you had submitted your thesis. Have you written another thesis?" "No friend. This is my bad luck. What to do? The foreign examiner has asked me to revise my thesis. You know I have to work under the worst guide under the sun. He did not guide me properly and did not see my chapters carefully and completely, although I served him like a slave for thirteen years." The typist was all sympathy for me. He said, "Sir, I have typed more than a hundred theses by now, and not a single thesis has been rejected or revised. Yours is the first such case that I have heard in my typing career. Your guide seems to be the worst fellow in the University. Why should the whoreson accept any Ph.D. student if he is not interested in guiding?" I was happy to note that he was giving expression to my own latent anger. I said, "I am the only Ph.D. student slogging under him for the last thirteen years. I don't know when I'll be released from his clutches." The typist sympathized with me once again and consoled me, "Don't you worry sir. We all know that you have worked very hard for more than a decade to deserve two Ph.Ds. God is great. He will definitely help you." Then I gave him the whole bundle of revised script. He kept it carefully in his bag. Then I took him to the nearby Kamat Hotel and offered him some snacks and tea. He wished me and took leave of me.

After fifteen days of continuous typing and correction the revised version of the thesis was ready. It had been reduced from 650 pages to 450 pages. Both the typist and myself went to the local binder and ordered him to prepare four xerox copies of the same and bind. Three days later we went to the binder and collected the four neatly bound copies and returned home. I gave the typing charges of thousand rupees to the typist and thanked him profusely.

The next day I carried the four copies to the department and showed them to my guide. He was quite satisfied with the contents and get up of the thesis. He wrote a detailed note about how two chapters were eliminated and how certain concepts of Sanskrit aesthetics were clarified and elaborated for the information of the foreign examiner. The handwritten script was typed again by the clerk of the department. Finally a covering letter was added to the explanatory note. After entering the details of the case in the dispatch register of the department, I asked the attender to carry a copy of the thesis to the Examination Section. He obliged me willingly. I met the Office Superintendent and requested him to expedite the dispatch of the thesis to the foreign examiner at Birmingham. He readily agreed to oblige me. I heaved a sigh of relief for the time being. I decided inwardly that I would rather go without a Ph.D. than revise it once again.

Now that a big burden was off my mind, I decided to pay attention to my domestic life, which I neglected for years together. I thought of searching for an engineer to prepare a plan for a house and the possibilities of getting a house building loan. Some four months went by in expectation. I did not know how the foreign examiner would respond this time. However, I requested the Office Superintendent of the Examination Section to send a telegram to the foreign examiner. He did so immediately. Within a week's time a reply telegram was received from Birmingham that the work was under way. We waited for another fortnight.

One day I finished my M.A. Final class and walked towards the canteen-hut. On the way I happened to see the Office Superintendent who congratulated me with a smile. "What's the matter? Why this congratulation?" I queried. He replied, "The foreign examiner has recommended the award of Ph.D. degree for your thesis." I felt ecstatic about the result. I said, "At last God has opened his eyes upon me." The Office Superintendent tried to cheer me, "God is great. Your hard work will never go a waste. You will be rewarded for it sooner or later. But you should have a lot of patience." I said, "As you know sir, I have had the patience of a Christian ass." I requested him to expedite the process of fixing the Viva at the earliest possible time. He promised me to do his best.

I returned to the department and told the news to my Professor who was happy to hear it. He felt his prestige as a guide was saved. We ordered for some tea and drank it with a sense of satisfaction. After a week's time, the Examination Section wrote to the Indian examiner at Vallabh Vidyanagar to give a convenient date for Viva and began to wait for his answer. There was no reply from him for two months. I was getting scared because within another three months my Professor was going to retire. I thought I must get the degree before his retirement. Hence, some ten telegrams were sent to the Indian examiner every second day. From the delay in his response, I could make out that the Indian examiner was a thoroughly callous and indifferent person. In my imagination, I visualized him as an elder brother of my own supremely indifferent guide.

After a week's time, my own guide urged the Examination Section to send a reply-paid telegram every two days. The Office Superintendent arranged for that also. We did not know if the examiner at Vallabh Vidyanagar had a residential or office phone. Another twenty days went by in sending the reply-paid telegrams every second day. Finally at the end of the month, my guide received a reply letter from him. I thought my problem was solved. But alas, it was not solved so easily. The examiner of Vallabh Vidyanagar had written also to the Examination

Section that he was not able to travel by train the long distance from his place to our University at the City of Rocks but that he could come up to Bombay and asked me, the candidate and my guide to come to Bombay on a particular date *i.e.* 30-3-1986. My guide was not enthusiastic to go to Bombay. Perhaps he wanted to harass me as long as he could. I simply did not know what to do. The viva was compulsory according to our University rules. Besides, the University was about to be closed for the summer vacation from 1st April. I was deeply worried about my academic fate.

The Vice-Chancellor who was a Professor of Literature knew my plight and the sadistic nature of my guide. One day I went to the library to see some latest journals. There I met the VC's secretary accidentally and wished him. He wished me back and called me to his room. He told me the summary of the conversation between the VC and my guide that he had overheard the previous day. My guide was reluctant to go to Bombay for viva and was planning to postpone it further. But the VC had forced him to go to Bombay and conduct the viva before the end of the vacation. It seems the VC had also requested my guide to earn a good name by helping at least one Ph.D. student in his lifetime. My guide was said to have felt deeply embarrassed by the VC's advice. I thanked the VC's secretary and returned to my department.

The Examination Section had confirmed the date of the viva on 30-3-1986 in the English Department of Bombay University, Bombay and authorized my guide to go to Bombay along with me and bring the viva report. The Finance Section had sanctioned the first class T.A. and D.A. to my guide as well as to the examiner from Vallabh Vidyanagar. As for my expenses, I had to bear them out of my own pocket.

My guide called me and ordered me to reserve two berths for him and me in the Madras-Bombay Express on 29-3-1986. He was ready to 'rough it out' for me. But I was secretly worried about my financial problem. I had no money at that time. But I could not neglect it either. I, therefore, rushed to a close friend of mine who took me to a local Finance Corporation and helped me to get a loan of Rs. 3000/-. I thanked the friend and the Manager of the Finance Corporation, and returned to my small house.

In the evening, I rushed to the Railway Station and reserved two berths from the City of Rocks to Bombay. I was happy that things were concretizing in my favour. The next day when I went to the department, I told the Professor that I had reserved two berths to Bombay. He asked me to keep the tickets with me safely.

On the 29th March, my Professor asked me in the department to come to the Railway Station in the evening and wait for him there. In the evening I took my suitcase and rushed to the Railway Station and waited there. Within ten minutes the Professor came to the Station with a suitcase in his hand and accompanied by his beloved, Urmila of 30 years. She jokingly asked me if I could take her also to Bombay. I said 'yes,' but she refused to come.

The Madras-Bombay Express roared and thundered into the Station exactly at 7.55 P.M. The Professor and I entered our reservation compartment and sat on our seats. The vivacious Urmila waved farewell to us. Within five minutes, the train screeched and started moving slowly out of the Station. Then it gathered speed. It halted at Solapur, Miraj, Pune at regular intervals and reached Bombay by 6.00 A.M. There was a big crowd in the Victoria Terminus. The Professor and I carried our suitcases and threaded our way through the crowd, climbed the stairs and entered the waiting room. There was a big queue for the bathrooms and lavatories. However with great difficulty, we completed our morning ablutions and changed our dress. Then we kept our suitcases in the cloakroom and walked out of the Victoria Terminus. On the way we entered a small hotel and had our breakfast of bun and potato bhaji and hot tea. The Professor smoked his cigarettes in a chain fashion. It was 10.00 A.M. by then. I observed the magnificent buildings, wide roads and colorful girls with great admiration. Then we hired an auto-rickshaw and went to the English Department of Bombay University. It was already 10.45 A.M. Although my Professor had written to the Chairman of English Department of Bombay University well in advance to spare a room for my viva examination, the Chairman had not come there at all. We inquired the clerk of the English Department about the working time of the department when all the teachers are available. He replied that Bombay being a big city, everyone is hard pressed for time and that many teachers do not meet one another for weeks together as they come to the department at the scheduled time of their lecture and go away immediately after. We learnt that they are not present in the department from 11.00 A.M. to 4.00 P.M. as we do in our Universities.

My Professor and I sat near the main gate of the Bombay University waiting for the examiner from Vallabh Vidyanagar. He was expected at 11.00 A.M. We went on staring at all the staff entering the gate and trying to identify the examiner. My Professor told me that he had seen the examiner about fifteen years ago and hoped to recognize him. We waited and waited and lost our patience. The examiner did not turn up even after 11.30 A.M. I began to have a secret doubt if he would come at all. If he did not come, what would happen to my viva voce exam? I began to worry. My Professor also began to have some doubt about the arrival of the examiner. He therefore said to me, "Mr. Nandiswar, in case the examiner does not turn up to Bombay, I shall return to the City of Rocks tonight by train. But I shall give you a letter. You take the letter and go to Vallabh Vidyanagar by some train, show this letter and get his report." When I heard this suggestion from my Professor, I was deeply shocked for a variety of reasons. Firstly I did not have sufficient money for the unexpected extension of journey from Bombay to Vallabh Vidyanagar. Secondly, I thought it was not proper for me to go alone to the examiner without my guide. Thirdly, what if the examiner was out of station when I went there. I simply did not know what to do. I prayed to God secretly to solve my problem somehow or the other. I told my Professor, "Sir, we shall wait for another hour or two here. If he doesn't turn up here, I shall go to Vallabh Vidyanagar." Both of us sat on the bench near the gate staring at every man who looked like a member of staff. People were entering the University building continuously. Among them was a short burly man with chubby cheeks and clad in a blue suit. My Professor stood up and rushed to him and asked him, "Hope you are Dr. Dev. Hope you recognize me?" Dr. Dev said, "Hullow Prof. Nagaraj, how are you?" Both of them shook hands with each other. My Professor introduced me to the examiner who shook hands with me amicably. Then he said, "I am so sorry, Prof. Nagaraj, for having made you two to come to Bombay. I could not make the trip to your far off City of Rocks." My Professor said, "It's all right. Any way we have come all the way to Bombay for the viva. We are glad that you have kept your promise." Then the examiner, my Professor and I walked to the English department and inquired the clerk if the Chairman of his Department had come. The clerk replied in the negative. Then my Professor asked him if there was a big room available for conducting my viva. The clerk said that there was no room free at that time.

All of us felt irritated and disconcerted by the clerk's answer. Then the examiner suggested to my Professor that we might go to a good hotel and conduct our viva there. It was agreeable to all of us. Then we walked out of the University building. The examiner introduced us to his younger brother who was an engineer in Bombay. He drove us all in his Ambassador car to a posh hotel. We climbed the stairs and entered an air-conditioned room and occupied our seats on the cushioned sofas. The engineer sat watching our viva. The examiner asked me some questions about my thesis. I answered him clearly and satisfactorily. In the course of our examination, he asked me something about Shakespeare's critics. I replied that the German, the French and the Japanese critics on Shakespeare are more original than the British critics who are very pragmatic. But the examiner opined that the British critics were more concrete in their opinions whereas the Germans were very vague and abstract. Although I did not subscribe to his opinion, I said 'yes' to satisfy him. The viva voce went on for about half an hour or so. Then the examiner wrote out his report on his letterhead, signed below it and put his seal on it. He congratulated me by addressing me as a Dr. His younger brother and engineer congratulated me very jovially and whole-heartedly. I felt a great relief from tension. Then the engineer ordered for *samosas,* cakes and nescafe. All the four of us savored the items leisurely and with a sense of satisfaction. The waiter came and kept the bill on a plastic plate with aniseed. I took out a hundred-rupee note and tried to keep it on the plate. But the jovial engineer said, "No, no. Dr. Nandiswar, you should not pay the bill. Let it be my pleasure to celebrate your doctorate." He forced me to take back my money and gave the bill and heavy tips to the waiter. Our Professor took the signature of the examiner on the T.A. and D.A. bill and told him that the amount would be sent to his address by our University. Then the examiner said, "I must hurry to Ahmedabad now for some urgent work." Then all of us stood up and walked out of the hotel. My Professor and I said 'good-by' to the examiner and the engineer when they sat in their car and started it.

Both my Professor and I were happy that a big academic headache of fourteen years was over at last. We walked leisurely along the colonnades of Bombay window-shopping. A number of smuggled goods were on sale under the columns of large buildings. We could not resist the temptation. My Professor bought a big leather purse and I bought a folding umbrella. As we walked ahead, we saw a cozy bar and restaurant near the Victoria Terminus. I gently asked the Professor, "Sir, shall we have our lunch here?" He easily assented to it. We entered it and sat on the comfortable seats. The Professor lit his 555 cigarette and began to puff out the curls of smoke. The waiter came and kept the menu on the table. I ordered two Kingfisher cold beers. The waiter brought two bottles and poured the frothing beer into our glasses. We tinkled our glasses and cheered each other and sipped the tasty beer. Slowly the beer began to have its effect on my Professor. He seemed to have felt guilty about his deliberate negligence of my Ph.D. He said voluntarily, Mr. Nandiswar, you should have earned your Ph.D. a few years ago." I did not want to anger him at the happy moment of my life. I said gently, "Though I worked very hard, I could not get my Ph.D. at the right time. My fate is very cruel to me. My own brother betrayed me and my treacherous colleagues back-bited me." My Professor knew his own weakness for listening to tell-tales indiscriminately. My words touched him deeply. He sipped his beer and said, "Life is very cruel. Such things happen in our life. But don't you take it to heart. You have got your Ph.D. degree, though a bit late." I wanted to bring to his notice my academic losses. I said, "I missed many chances of promotion and foreign fellowships, sir." He sipped his beer again and said, "Don't you worry. You forget the past. You apply for the Reader's post and I shall help you to become a Reader." But I said, 'But I don't want to stay in the City of Rocks, sir. I want to go back to my native town Dharwad, but unfortunately there is no vacancy in the Karnatak University. I, therefore, want to go to Kuvempu University at Shimoga." The Professor had emptied his first bottle of beer and therefore I ordered the second bottle for him. He sipped another mouthful of beer, lit another cigarette and said, "In that case, you apply for the Reader's post at Kuvempu University. Although I may not be on the Selection Committee, I shall see that you are selected as Reader. You may head the Department and build it up properly." I thanked him formally for his promise, although I did not believe in the effect of his promise. Then we ordered some *nons* and ghee rice and finished our lunch. I paid the bill gladly. Then we walked slowly towards the Victoria Station.

We sat on the plastic chairs of the Victoria Terminus watching the hustle and bustle of travellers. The Professor lit his cigarette and emitted many rings of smoke. He asked me, "Do the people in our University cast aspersions on Urmila?" This question came to me most unexpectedly. I knew how he, a man bordering on sixty had taken a fancy to the thirty-year old coquette called Urmila and how people used to gossip about their love affair. But I could not dare speak the truth lest he should harass me further academically. I, therefore, told him a white lie, "No sir, nobody in our University casts aspersions on her." As the evening advanced, the Victoria Station became more and more crowded and there was a big din. The rumble of trains, the hullabaloo of travellers and the regular announcements and advertisements on the TV had converted the Station into a veritable hell of cacophony.

By 7.00 P.M. we had some snacks and coffee in the open canteen of V.T. We boarded the train *i.e.* Bombay-Madras Express by 8.00 P.M. and sat on our reserved seats. I slept well all through the night. We reached the City of Rocks on Sunday morning. We had our coffee once again. I called an auto-rickshaw, made the Professor sit in it, and gave the fare to the driver and asked him to leave the Professor at the University campus. Then I took a cycle-rickshaw and reached my small house. As it happened to be the Holi Festival Day, children and young people were throwing colour on one another. I lit a cigarette to celebrate my final relief from academic tension.

The next day I went to the University by bus and walked to the department. Three of my colleagues came to me, congratulated me by addressing me as Doctor. But my senior colleague Dr. Swami did not show the courtesy to congratulate me at all, perhaps because he thought me to be a rival for him in the future promotion. Whenever the colleagues in the other departments came to congratulate me by calling me a Doctor, I used to ask them to call me a belated Doctor. I described myself as a chronic patient who had succeeded in becoming a belated Doctor. I took my class for M.A. Final in a jovial mood.

In the afternoon, Urmila, the guest lecturer and beloved of my Professor stormed into my room and congratulated me profusely and chatted with me very jovially. In the course of conversation she told me that she was disowned by her parents on account of her liberal behaviour and that she was not destined to get married to anyone as Mars was in an adverse place in her horoscope and that she would became a widow soon after her marriage. I really felt deep sympathy for her who looked so vivacious in her outward behaviour. Then she reminded me, "Now that you have earned your Ph.D. degree, that too on a difficult topic on Shakespeare, you must give us a grand party." I could not refuse to throw a party when she was insisting on it. I promised her that I would arrange it the next evening. Then she went away to her class for lecturing. After an hour or so, I walked to the Professor's chamber and told him that I was arranging a wet party to him on the next evening. I asked him. "Sir, how many bottles of beer shall I bring tomorrow? Shall I bring four or six?" The Professor wore a mischievous smile on his lips and asked me back, "How many bottles of beer can you afford to bring?" I thought for a few seconds, calculated the amount mentally and said, "Sir, I can afford to bring up to eight bottles, in addition to snacks." Then he said, "In that case, you may bring a carton (*i.e.* dozen) of bottles. I shall pay for the remaining four bottles." I knew my Professor's extraordinary weakness for beer. I also knew that he never took any hot drinks. I promised him that I would bring a carton of Kingfisher bottles the next day. Then I returned to my small house.

Next morning Kallappa the attender of the department came to my small house. I took him to the nearby Rolex Bar, bought a carton of Kingfisher beer and asked him to take the box to the Professor's room in the Guest House. I gave him some tips, which he received gladly. He carried the box on his shoulder and walked to the City Bus Stand. I returned to my small house, finished my bath, and went to a hotel for lunch. Then I boarded the bus and went to the University. I carried a bag full of different snacks for the evening party.

I took a class for M.A. Previous students on Bertrand Russell. Then I went to the Library to consult some latest journals and back numbers. Many of the Library staff congratulated me on getting my doctorate from the toughest guide on the campus. Then I walked back to the Department and wrote a letter to my wife at Dharwad. By 4.00 P.M. all the colleagues left the Department. The Professor also slowly walked back to his room in the Guest House. The attender Kallappa was closing the windows and locking the classrooms. I took my bag of snacks and walked towards the Guest House.

Students and staff were waiting for the city buses with anxiety. As soon as a bus came, they would rush madly into it because of the uncertainty of the arrival of the next bus. I walked slowly towards the hillock on which stood the Guest House. Then I climbed the stairs slowly. When I reached the Guest House I stood still for a moment and looked at the campus, which sloped westwards. The evening sun was covered by rosy clouds. I carried the bag of snacks to the Professor's room and gently knocked at the door. The Professor opened the door and welcomed me affectionately. I was surprised to see the women's clothes like brassieres, blouses and petticoats being hung on the bars of the two cots. It was really embarrassing for me to see them. I also had heard about how the Vice-Chancellor was furious about the Professor's living together with a beloved who was of his daughter's age. I sat on a chair and kept the bag of snacks on the teapoy. Then Urmila came out of the antechamber. We greeted each other. "Shall we start it sir?" asked I. The Professor nodded his assent. I brought the glasses and two bottles of beer from the antechamber and kept them on the teapoy. Without my asking, the Professor said, "Miss Urmila has come here to wash her clothes, as there is acute water scarcity in the city." I did not know how to react to it. But I managed to say, "Yes sir, there is acute scarcity of water in the city." Then I poured the frothing beer into two glasses. Then Urmila sat with us and asked me, "Pour a glass of beer for me also." I was a little surprised by her request for beer. I, therefore, asked her, "You had told me that you never took any drinks." She broke into a mischievous smile and said, "Yes, yes, I had told you like that. But I take beer some times, especially in such company." I was silenced by her honest answer and poured some beer into her glass also. All the three of us said 'cheers' and sipped the frothing chill beer. I felt a smoothing coolness in my gullet and stomach slowly. We chatted about a number of things. I remembered how Urmila had once confessed to me that she wanted to commit suicide because of her inauspicious horoscope. In the course of our drunken conversation, when she referred to her personal problems, I felt a deep pity for her and told her, "Miss Urmila, whatever may your problem be, you please don't think of suicide." The Professor seemed to have been shocked by my remark. He turned to her and asked her, "Younglady, why do you contemplate suicide? "You never told me this?" Urmila grew pale in the face and sat silently with a bent face for a few seconds. Then I volunteered to explain her difficulty to the Professor. "Sir, she told me that Mars is in adverse position in her horoscope and hence her marriage will not be a happy one." The Professor was greatly surprised, "Oh, this is news to me!" He then turned towards her and said, "Younglady, why did you not tell me this earlier? You don't believe in the horoscope and all that. Were I a youngman of twenty-five or so I would have married you no matter how inauspicious your horoscope is." Urmila sat blinking and silent. A couple of tears trickled down from her eyes. She soon wiped them. I cursed myself for spoiling the jolly atmosphere of the party. In-between our sipping of beer, we used to crunch some chips, *ghatis* and groundnut. Urmila suddenly got up and said, "I have prepared some hot *paddus*. I shall get them." She went into the antechamber and brought the aromatic *paddus* and kept them on the teapoy for us. We ate them with real gusto. I realized that Urmila was a culinary expert which was one of the reasons why she had caught the fancy of our Professor. As the two bottles were empty, I brought another two bottles from the antechamber and poured the beer to all the three glasses. Miss Urmila sipped the beer without any hesitation. We chatted on a variety of topics in our intoxicated relaxation. As I saw the clock on the wall and noticed that it was nearing 9.00 P.M., I thanked the Professor and Miss Urmila, excused myself and rushed out of his room. I hurriedly climbed down the steps of the hillock and boarded the city-bus in great haste.

The next day many of my friends and colleagues in the other departments who came to know about my doctorate after a chronic suffering for more than a decade, came to my department and congratulated me. They knew that all the formalities of the examination were over, and that the formal announcement would take a couple of days. In the evening I was walking in the Station Bazar when Dr. Purohit met me unexpectedly and congratulated me on my earning a doctorate. I said, "I am happy that I got my Ph.D. at last, but so unhappy to get it so late. In your science departments one may get a Ph.D. within three years. But I had to struggle for fourteen years." Dr. Purohit tried to console and enhearten me, "We know that your Ph.D. is inordinately delayed. But we admire your extraordinary courage and perseverance in dealing with the most egoistic man on the campus. It is as if you entered the cave, held dialogues with a tiger and came out safe." "In a way what you say is true. I had asinine patience for fourteen years. Nearly half of my career is wasted for a mere Ph.D. and I missed many chances of promotion and foreign fellowship," said I with a note of disappointment. Then Dr. Purohit consoled me, "We know all about your suffering. After all life is more important than career. You better start enjoying life now. Forget about the past." Then Dr. Purohit walked away towards the Railway Station.

Then I went to the Maratha Mandal Library and glanced through the newspapers. Somebody nudged me. When I turned to my right, I saw Dr. Shivaraj smiling at me. His spects sparkled in the tube lights of the Library. "Come on, let's go out," said he. We together walked out of the Library and sat in a small canteen. Dr. Shivaraj congratulated me on my earning a Ph.D. and said, "At last your fourteen year exile is over." But I said, "But sir, my exile is worse than Rama's. You know why? Rama's exile of fourteen years was a very short period of time compared to his life span of thousand years. Besides Rama lived in the forest along with his wife and brother. But fourteen years exile in a life span of seventy is indeed a very big chunk. Besides, I had to live away from my wife and child for all these years." Dr. Shivaraj burst into a hearty guffaw and said, "Youngman, I know you have suffered a lot. Now at least, you forget the past and make the best of your life." We sipped our coffee and walked out of the canteen.

In the evening as I was strolling in the Station Bazar near Patel Chowk, Dr. Siddayya met me. Both of us had our coffee in a self-service hotel and walked to the Railway Station. Travellers were rushing in and out of the Udyan Express. The hawkers and tea-vendors were shouting at the top of their voices. As the train screeched out of the Station, the big din subsided gradually. Dr. Siddayya and I crossed the rail tracks and climbed the second platform. We saw many retired and old men sitting on the benches and chatting in their weak voices. We walked to a vacant bench and sat on it. Dr. Siddayya congratulated me on my earning the doctorate. I thanked him formally. Although Dr. Siddayya was about fourteen years senior to me, he was very kind and free with me. He was an ardent believer in Vedanta philosophy. I told him, "Dear Professor, do you know at what cost I had to earn my Ph.D.? My Professor brought me to this backward University in this City of Rocks with the promise of helping me to get a transfer to the Karnatak University of Dharwad. But in fact, he worked against my transfer simply because he could not get his transfer. He had promised to send me abroad. But he had no foreign contacts at all. And he wasted my precious fourteen years for a simple degree of Ph.D. He was systematically cruel and cunning with me. I never knew that my guru could be so inimical to me though pretending to the contrary." Dr. Siddayya listened to my sad tale very patiently and began to console me in Vandatic terms. He said, "My dear friend, I know what a great egoist and sadist your Professor is, because he happened to be my teacher also twenty-five years ago. He has never helped anyone positively in his life although he talks eloquently about life and literature. I know you are the first and last Ph.D. student who worked under him. But according to Vedanta as paraphrased by Saint Nijaguna, your Professor is not your real enemy, but your own fate. You must have committed some sin in your past life. You have to pay the price for that in the present life. Your sadistic and terribly egoistic Professor is only a penal agent of your past *karma.*" As I was a believer in *karma,* I easily agreed with him and said, "Yes, yes, what you say is perfectly true. I blame my Professor, my jealous colleagues, the backward University and the City of Rocks only because of my anger and frustration. What I should really blame is my bad *karma* in the past life. Otherwise the events of my life look absurd and defy any convincing explanation." By that time the Madras-Bombay Express rumbled into the Station. Travellers began to rush in and out of the compartments. We watched them with curiosity. As soon as it left the Station, we got up and walked out of the Station. We parted after greeting each other.

The University was closed for the summer vacation on thirty-first of March. I, therefore, returned to my hometown Dharwad the very next day. After a week's time a friend of mine sent me a couple of copies of the notification of the award of Ph.D. to me. I felt quite relieved at last. I mailed a copy of the notification to *The Hindu* daily and wanted to see if the editor would care to publish it. I spent the vacation in real relaxation and domestic happiness. Meanwhile I learned that the summer vacation had been extended from fifteenth June to thirtieth June. It was really a blessing in disguise for me, because it enabled me to spend an additional fortnight with my granny, wife and little son.

When I reached the City of Rocks and went to the Department, on the first of July, I was surprised to learn that my Professor had retired on the previous day, *i.e.* 30th June. I heard rumours from my colleagues in other departments that the Vice Chancellor was so angry with our Professor for his staying together with his beloved in the Guest House that he had deliberately extended the vacation upto 30th June so that the Professor could not get extension of service on technical grounds. I thought it was my duty to see and pay my respects to him. I, therefore, walked upto the Guest House on the hillock and greeted him. He seemed to be furious and helpless at the same time. I talked amicably with him and took leave of him. While I was climbing down the steps of the hillock, a clerk greeted me and whispered to me that the Resident Engineer had issued a notice to our Professor to vacate the University Guest House within twenty-four hours. I really felt pity for my beloved Professor.

After two days I learnt from my friends that the Professor had shifted his luggage from the University Guest House to a rented house in the City of Rocks. It was rumoured that he, a man of sixty was living with his beloved coquette of thirty. I did not know how to react to the surprising news.

When I went to Dharwad for my monthly visits to my home, I went to the Professor's house and met his wife. When I asked her if the Professor had come back, she replied tearfully that he had let her as well as all other members of the family down by abandoning them for good. She replied in-between her sobs that he had gone after that coquette from Kerala. I felt deeply sorry for the Professor's wife and tried in vain to console her.

After spending three days with my granny, wife and little son, I left Dharwad unwillingly and returned to the City of Rocks. A very surprising news was awaiting me. As I boarded the city bus in the Station Bazar, a friend sitting adjacent to me said that our Professor had married the coquette from Kerala by exchanging garlands in Dattatreya temple at Ghanagapura, a holy shrine famous for exorcism of ghosts from the haunted persons. I remained silent with anger and embarrassment.

Now that I had earned my Ph.D. with great difficulty, I had been banking upon it for a rise in my profession. I knew I had suffered a lot on account of three reasons. Firstly I had chosen a very difficult and challenging topic on a world famous dramatist removed from me in space by about six thousand miles, and in time by about four hundred years and in culture to a great extent. Secondly the place of my research happened to be a City of Rocks, a god-forsaken place where there was neither a good library nor scholarly ambience. Thirdly, I had to work under the most difficult, egoistic, indifferent and lazy guide who suffered from a non Ph.D. complex and who had brass ears and therefore listened to all sort of tales against me by my jealous colleagues. Since I had braved though all these hindrances, I hoped that my suffering would be compensated for by at least a belated promotion.

The University of the City of Rocks advertised the Reader's post in a local newspaper, through which I glanced in the public library in the evening. I was quite thrilled by the advertisement of the Reader's post as I thought that I deserved it.

The next day I rushed to the University Office and bought a set of eight application forms. I spent nearly a week's time in filling up the complicated forms, getting the Xerox copies of all the relevant documents, testimonials, lists of publication etc. I spent a lot of money on this. After a week, I took the bundle of application forms to the new Chairman, Dr. Sitaram and got them forwarded to the Registrar. I thought secretly that I was the only candidate who really deserved the Reader's post, as I had earned my Ph.D. and had many publications in national and international journals.

Some six months had elapsed after the advertisement of teaching posts in the local newspaper. By that time we heard the rumour that the Professor had left the City of Rocks for Bangalore along with his new and second wife. It was said that he had used all his resourcefulness to get her transferred from the Government Junior College of the City of Rocks to the one in Channapattana but that they were staying together in Banglaore.

I was waiting for the interview for the Reader's post in the University of City of Rocks. The DPAR clerk told me confidentially that there were only three applications for the Reader's post including mine, and that the two other applicants were about six to seven years junior to me and had neither Ph.D. nor publications as they were only college teachers. Then I thought that I being the seniormost candidate with fifteen years of postgraduate teaching, a Ph.D. on Shakespeare and five critical works and twenty-five research articles, was sure to get the

Reader's post. I also heard the rumour that one of the applicants who was about seven years junior to me happened to be the daughter of a central Minister and that they were wielding very powerful political influence over the Vice Chancellor of the University.

When I was returning from the office, I met a Professor friend of mine from the Mathematics Department who had some access to the official secrets of the University. We discussed the forthcoming interview and tried to visualize our future. I told him that according to the UGC norms, I must get the Reader's post. The Professor of Mathematics who was my well-wisher said gently, "I know your highest merit. But our Universities never follow the UGC norms honestly. They always follow practical and opportunistic methods. You know our Vice-Chancellors happen to be puppets in the hands of politicians. Their sole intention is to please the Ministers, MLAs and MPs and never to maintain academic excellence." I agreed with him totally as he had spoken the harsh truth. We went to the nearby hut-canteen and sipped the over boiled tea.

On the day of the interview, I carried my suitcase filled with my fat Ph.D. thesis, five critical books, twenty-five articles, forty reviews and other academic documents, to the University and waited in the hall adjacent to the Vice-Chancellor's chamber. The other two applicants also had come and sat there. One of them was a youngman of about thirty from a degree college from Chitradurga. The other was the daughter of a central Minister who had neither a Ph.D. nor any publications. She was short, lean and dark and very unimpressive to look at. Although she was called Chandrika, she was as dark as the New Moon Night. When I looked at those two candidates, I secretly felt confident that I was sure to be selected. As the Selection Committee members walked into the Vice-Chancellor's chamber, my heart began to palpitate with tension. The PA to the Vice-Chancellor was rushing in and out of the chamber. The phones were ringing again and again. Then I saw the P.A. rushing into the Vice-Chancellor's chamber and tell him that the central Minister was calling him on phone. The Vice-Chancellor left his chamber, went into the inner chamber. I suspected that something fishy was happening. After five minutes the Vice-Chancellor returned to his office chamber. The attender took a tray of teacups into the office chamber. All the three of us sat there blinking at one another. My heart had begun to pound incessantly. After another ten minutes, the bell rang. The attender in the white uniform called out my name. I carried my suitcase into the Vice Chancellor's chamber and greeted all the members of the Selection Committee. I sat in my chair, opened the suitcase and displayed all my books, my fat Ph.D. thesis, bundle of research articles and reviews on the table before me. The Selection Committee members picked up the thesis, books, articles and reviews and glanced through them. The Vice-Chancellor beckoned to them to start interviewing. One of the members with drooping mustaches from Bombay looked at the list of my publications and said, "Your bio-data is very impressive. Why have you done so much research?" I was really embarrassed by the latter part of his question. But I managed to reply, "That is because I believe in achieving something in my life." Then I answered his other specific questions about Indian English writers. Then the second member from Viskhapattanam asked me, "What's the topic of your research?" I replied, "I have worked on Shakespeare's Last Plays." Then he asked me, "Why did you choose such a difficult topic?" I replied, "Because he is a substantial writer, though very difficult." Then he asked me specific questions on Shakespeare's plays which I answered properly. He said, "I am very happy with your answers." Then the third member from Varanasi asked me something on Commonwealth Literature, especially about Chinua Achebe and Wole Soyinka. He nodded his approval of my answers. Then the Vice Chancellor asked me, "You may go now." I hurriedly gathered all my publications, stuffed them into the suitcase and carried it out of the VC's Chamber. I left the hall, walked to the lounge and sat there with a sense of relief. I realized that my interview had lasted for half an hour.

The attender called out the second applicant. The young lecturer from Chitradurga, spic and span in his safari suit went into the VC's chamber barehanded. I looked at my watch. He returned from the VC's chamber within ten minutes with a pale face. When the attender in the white uniform called out for the third and last applicant, the sickly and swarthy daughter of the Minister walked into the VC's chamber. I looked at the needles of my watch. She returned from the chamber within five minutes with a lot of perspiration on her face. She walked out of the administrative building without looking at anyone. I returned to my small house and relaxed. Throughout the evening and night I dreamt of being selected as a Reader in English because of my high qualifications.

The next day I went to the department and engaged my class for M.A. Final. When I returned to my chamber and lit a cigarette, Dr. Sitaram came to me and said, "Come, let's go and have some tea." I got up and walked with him to the hut-canteen. We sipped our tea silently and lit our cigarettes. Then Dr. Sitaram said, "Come on, let's go and sit under the shade of a tree for a few minutes." I walked with him to a nearby mango tree. I deliberately did not ask him about the result of the interview held on the previous day. Dr. Sitaram saw a buxom girl near the hut canteen and joked in his usual uninhibited manner, "How I wish I could fuck her." I answered him, "I know your wish remains only a wish and never becomes a reality." He burst into a guffaw and replied, "What else can we do except talk about it?" Then both us of remained silent for a couple of minutes, which was a little embarrassing. Then Dr. Sitaram broke the silence, "Mr. Nandiswar, I have some unpleasant news for you. But don't take it to heart." I said, "What's the unpleasant news? Let me know it." Dr. Sitaram lowered his voice and said, "Yesterday you did very well in the interview but I am very sorry to tell you that you lost the chance."

I was puzzled by his answer and even thought that he was joking with me as usual. I cleared my throat and asked him, "Do you say that I am not selected as a Reader?" Dr. Sitaram said gently, "Unfortunately, not selected." My heart began to palpitate with a sense of shock. "Then who is selected?" He replied, "That dark daughter of the Minister has been selected." I was shocked out of my wits. I asked him in consternation, "But she has neither a Ph.D. nor publications. How can she be selected?" Dr. Sitaram patted on my back and tried to console me, "Cool down, please cool down. In fact I tried to defend your case as other members had placed you at the top of the list." "Then, how was she selected?" I asked with agony in my voice. He explained, "You see, the Vice Chancellor is also very helpless. He has been heavily pressurized by the central Minister. Even the President of India has sent a letter to him to select her. Besides high influence she has other advantages also like being a lady and that too belonging to scheduled caste. What more do you need?" "What if I go to the High Court?" He replied, "Nothing will happen even if you go to the High Court, because the Court will uphold the opinion of the Selection Committee." I was really angry and burst out, "What if the Selection Committee itself is over led by the politicians and ministers?" Dr. Sitaram replied, "There is no way out from the vicious circle." I was deeply disturbed by the absurd drama called the interview. I experienced and learnt that the idealistic UGC rules were made a farce by the opportunistic practice of the University authorities. Then we got up and walked back to the department.

In the evening I was strolling along the Station Bazar when I happened to meet Dr. Kudari who sympathized with me, "I am very sorry to learn that you missed the Reader's post in spite of having a Ph.D. It is really absurd that a junior fellow without a Ph.D. or publications has been selected simply because she is the daughter of a Minister." We walked upto the nearby canteen and sipped our tea. I said, "Dear friend, the University did not give me the Reader's post in the past on the ground that I had no Ph.D. But now when I have a Ph.D. they have avoided me by selecting a college lecturer without Ph.D. as a Reader because she belongs to the reservation category and happens to be the daughter of a Minister."

Dr. Kudari said, "Dear Dr. Nandiswar, nowadays Indian Universities have become the playground for politicians. All the UGC norms are either thrown to wind or adopted for vested interests." Then I said, "If such anomalies happened in appointments and promotions in the highest institute of learning like a University, how can you expect academic excellence? How can a meritorious man work hard or cheerfully when he is suppressed or ignored by the University?" Dr. Kudari supported me whole-heartedly. "Yes, yes, what you say is perfectly true. That is the reason why brilliant Indians want to leave India and settle in foreign countries where they are recognized and respected." Then I said to him, "Dear friend, I wasted my fourteen years for a Ph.D. by neglecting my family life. What is the reward for my hard work? Losing the Readership to a junior duffer? Today I have decided to stop doing all my research and take less and less interest in teaching also. I have severed my emotional attachment with the University." Dr. Kudari advised me not to be depressed and took leave of me. Then I walked back to my small house in a depressed mood, slumped on the chair and brooded over the futility of academic achievement in India.